"*The Black Tower* weaves history and fiction together in the trademark style—
linguistic brio, a slick
propelled Bayard's w
Bayard is a fearlessly c
____ both pl

"Delicious. [Bayard] im
more than two centuri
dauphin. A-"

"Louis Bayard repairs t
makes brilliant applicati
run researcher, Bayard t
ose affectations."

"Bayard doesn't revisit th
with a great deal of styl
his ability to recast the p
Dark, surprising, and Ba
torical thriller."

"In the world of historical
into intelligent thrillers."

"Louis Bayard finds fiction
writer of historical thriller
and nineteenth-century wri
of Monte Cristo."

"A tale that has as much ene
ward."

"A compelling and sympathet
stellar third historical. Baya
writers today can match the a ____ ..... devising an intelligent thriller with
heart."
                                          —*Publishers Weekly* (starred review)

"Having previously channeled Dickens and Poe, historical novelist Bayard throws
down the gauntlet to Dumas in another high-energy melodrama. The novel's
witty succession of trapdoor endings, culminating in 'the quietest of abdications,' keeps surprising us. Who says they don't write 'em like this anymore?
Long may Bayard reign."   —*Kirkus Reviews* (starred review)

"In his fast-moving tale, Bayard deftly places details to make history come alive."
—*Rocky Mountain News*

"In addition to the many fine, quirky character portraits and the visceral depiction of a chaotic France still reeling under the regime change, Bayard offers a rip-roaring plot full of smart and funny turns."
—*Booklist* (starred review)

"Readers be grateful, *The Black Tower* breathes life into the world's first police detective, Vidocq, an overdue ... the gripping and nuanced story races through the parlor rooms and back alleys of Paris, Louis Bayard shows why he is at the forefront of literary historical fiction today."
—Matthew Pearl, author of *The Dante Club* and *The Poe Shadow*

"A fascinating detective story about one of the world's most compelling mysteries. Bayard's scholarly and beautiful heart-stopping prose always keeps before us the possibility of an improbability—what mystery is all about."
—*Louisville Courier-Journal*

PRAISE FOR

The Pale Blue Eye

"Louis Bayard, who adroitly pulled off the stunt of dramatizing Tiny Tim's adult life in *Mr. Timothy*, turns from Charles Dickens to Poe with debonair wit. . . . He maintains a convincing nineteenth-century tone, though the sleuth seems appealingly modern, keeping the quirky Poe on track. . . . Ingenious . . . with a rich knowledge of Poe's life and work."
—*Entertainment Weekly*

"Another literary tour de force. . . . At novel's end, the reader may want to start again from the beginning."
—*Kirkus Reviews* (starred review)

"[A] tour de force. . . . An intense and gripping novel. This beautifully crafted thriller stands head and shoulders above other recent efforts to fictionalize Poe."
—*Publishers Weekly* (starred review)

"Shockingly clever and devoutly unsentimental. . . . Reads like a lost classic. Bayard reinvigorates historical fiction, rendering the nineteenth century as if he'd witnessed it firsthand."
—*New York Times Book Review*

"It is to Bayard's huge credit that he carries off not only the cold and miserable locale with an atmospheric darkness worthy of his illustrious subject, but also that Poe himself walks and talks so convincingly throughout the pages of this novel."
—*Washington Post*

"Seamlessly blends Poe into an engrossing whodunit worthy of its inspiration. "
—*USA Today*

"Bayard's ending brilliantly upends the entire novel. Doubt Bayard's plotting abilities? Quoth the reviewer: 'Nevermore.'" —*Christian Science Monitor*

"Bayard has produced a nuanced, wonderfully written tale, one worthy of the old master himself." —*Baltimore Sun*

"What makes this more than a well-crafted thriller . . . is Bayard's gift for language. He finds a voice that's old-fashioned but not stilted. And he paints incredibly vivid pictures." —*Atlanta Journal-Constitution*

"An uncanny and original portrait of the famous writer. Captures the imagination with exquisite details and a compelling, disquieting story." —*Denver Rocky Mountain News*

"Full of delightfully unexpected twists that continue to the very last pages of the novel." —*Denver Post*

"Brilliantly plotted and completely absorbing, ending with the kind of shock that few novelists are able to deliver." —*The Sunday Times* (London)

"Exquisitely rendered character study, imaginatively gothic, compelling." —*Miami Herald*

"A moody, cunning mystery. . . . Bayard ingeniously weaves in motifs from Poe's work . . . to thrilling effect." —*The Observer* (London)

"Bayard has captured the elegant writing style of the period without compromising his mastery of pace and tension. This is crime fiction of the highest order." —*Historical Novels Review*

"Poe, an exacting critic . . . would have been impressed by Bayard's intelligence and fluidity as a writer." —*Oregonian*

"A superb, lyrically written yarn. The style is so deft and delicious and the plot so Poe-haunted that it drives the narrative to its unexpected and shocking conclusion." —*Providence Journal*

"Well-wrought and suspenseful." —*Buffalo News*

"Louis Bayard is a writer of remarkable gifts: for language, for imagination, for that mysterious admixture of audacity and craftsmanship that signals a major talent in the making." —Joyce Carol Oates

"With echoes of Conan Doyle and Poe himself, Louis Bayard has written a first-rate thriller with language that sparkles on the page. Bayard's Poe is just what we want to imagine of Poe as a young man: wonderful, strange, and a little creepy. He's the perfect partner for our narrator, and their chemistry is as electric as the harrowing story they're wrapped up in." —Dustin Thomason, coauthor of *The Rule of Four*

"In *The Pale Blue Eye*, Louis Bayard pays a stunning and fitting tribute to Edgar Allan Poe—not only in his crafting of a twisty, gothic mystery that would have delighted the master himself, but in his use of a young Poe as a character. A gorgeous, melancholic tale from a fearless writer. I can't wait to see what Bayard does next." —Laura Lippman, author of *To the Power of Three*

"Finely executed prose. . . . An exquisitely rendered character study, imaginatively gothic, compelling." —*Memphis Commercial Appeal*

PRAISE FOR

Mr. Timothy

"Inventive and amusing." —*New York Times Book Review*

"With its linguistic razzle-dazzle, *Mr. Timothy* is a mock-Victorian tour de force: a shilling shocker that touches the heart and makes it race." —*Wall Street Journal*

"What a terrific book." —*Detroit Free Press*

"This mix of thriller and literature is as rich as a Christmas cake. . . . A spirited adventure." —*Atlanta Journal-Constitution*

"This 'Christmas Carol' for the new millennium is highly recommended. If you have not had your fill of ghost-ridden heroes, needy orphans, and foggy nights in cobblestone streets, this sequel—with its breakneck plot, colorful characters, and the reappearance of Scrooge and the Cratchits—will fill the bill." —*Library Journal*

"Clever . . . sly . . . wonderful." —*Washington Post*

"There isn't one throwaway sentence in this fabulous Victorian mystery. . . . A subtle character examination and a page-turning plot, one truly engaging book." —*Entertainment Weekly* (Editor's Choice)

"Richly and sensually written." —*The Spectator* (London)

"*Mr. Timothy* provides some poignant moments, making the always-valid point that families can be formed wherever there is trust, generosity, teamwork, and a little Christmas magic." —*San Francisco Chronicle*

"Like Dickens, Bayard exposes the poverty and casual exploitation of children in that most self-serious of eras, and if he's a bit more explicit, well, this is the twenty-first century, after all. . . . A clever premise and smartly detailed prose." —*Kirkus Reviews*

"Inventive. . . . Bayard drenches the reader in the underbelly of 1860s London and, in true Dickensian fashion, makes us care passionately about the fates of his characters. . . . A first-rate entertainment." —*Booklist*

"Divinely crafted novel. . . . It is impossible to avoid being caught up in caring about the story." —*Denver Post*

ALSO BY LOUIS BAYARD

The Pale Blue Eye

Mr. Timothy

Fool's Errand

Endangered Species

THE
BLACK
TOWER

Louis Bayard

HARPER ◐ PERENNIAL

NEW YORK • LONDON • TORONTO • SYDNEY • NEW DELHI • AUCKLAND

In memory of my dad

A hardcover edition of this book was published in 2008 by William Morrow, an imprint of HarperCollins Publishers.

P.S.™ is a trademark of HarperCollins Publishers.

FIRST HARPER PERENNIAL EDITION PUBLISHED 2009.

Designed by Laura Kaeppel

The Library of Congress has catalogued the hardcover edition as follows:

Bayard, Louis.
   The black tower : a novel / Louis Bayard.—1st ed.
      p. cm.
   ISBN 978-0-06-117350-9
   1. Vidocq, Eugène François, 1775–1857—Fiction. 2. Detectives—France—Fiction. 3. France—History—19th century—Fiction. 4. France—Kings and rulers—Fiction. I. Title.

PS3552.A85864O77 2008
813'.54—dc22   2008005059

ISBN 978-0-06-117351-6(pbk.)

09   10   11   12   13   OV/RRD   10   9   8   7   6   5   4   3   2   1

To endure is the first thing that a child ought to learn,
and that which he will have the most need to know.

—Jean-Jacques Rousseau

France: Before and After the Revolution

❧

1770   Marie-Antoinette, daughter of Empress Maria Theresa, marries the French dauphin, Louis-Auguste.

1774   Louis-Auguste, upon the death of his grandfather, becomes Louis XVI.

1778   Marie-Antoinette gives birth to her first child, Marie-Thérèse-Charlotte.

1785   Marie-Antoinette gives birth to her second son, Louis-Charles.

1789   A mob destroys the Bastille, triggering the outbreak of the French Revolution. Parisian marketwomen march on Versailles and force the royal family to live under guard in the Tuileries palace in Paris.

1790   The royal family attempts to flee France. They are stopped near the French border and returned to Paris.

1792   Revolutionaries imprison the royal family in the Temple.

1793   *January*   King Louis XVI is executed.

        July   Louis-Charles is separated from his family.

        October   Marie-Antoinette is executed.

1795   Louis-Charles' death is announced. Body is buried in un-marked grave in cemetery of Sainte-Marguerite.

1799   Napoleon installs himself as First Consul.

1804   Napoleon crowns himself Emperor.

1815   Napoleon's defeat at Waterloo culminates in his exile at St. Helena. Louis XVIII (younger brother of Louis XVI) is now permanently installed as King of France.

1821   Napoleon dies.

1824   Louis XVIII dies. His younger brother, the Comte d'Artois, becomes Charles X.

1830   July Revolution forces Charles X to abdicate. Charles' cousin, Louis-Philippe, Duc d'Orléans, is proclaimed king.

The Bourbons

MARIE-ANTOINETTE
(1755–1792)

LOUIS XVI
(1754–1792)

LOUIS-XAVIER-STANISLAS
(1755–1824)
Comte de Provence, later Louis XVIII

CHARLES-PHILIPPE
(1757–1836)
Comte d'Artois, later Charles X

MARIE-THÉRÈSE-CHARLOTTE
(1778–1851)
later Duchesse d'Angoulême

LOUIS-ANTOINE
(1775–1844)
Duc d'Angoulême

LOUIS-JOSEPH
(1781–1789)

CHARLES-FERDINAND
(1778–1820)
Duc de Berry

LOUIS-CHARLES
(1785–1795)
later Louis XVII

SOPHIE-HÉLÈNE-BÉATRIX
(1786–1787)

PART I

Saint-Cloud

13 Thermidor Year II

1st meeting with Prisoner: shortly after 1 A.M. Prisoner alone in cell.
Dinner had not been eaten. Nor breakfast.

Stench <u>extreme</u>, cd be detected thru grating. Must speak to Barras
re conditions. Piles of excrement <u>everywhere</u>. Urine, sweat, mold,
rotted skin. Surfeit of rats. Maggots, cockroaches, lice.

Prisoner discovered in cot, approx. size of cradle. (For reasons unknown, Prisoner refuses to sleep in bed.) Ankle protruding at unnatural angle. Knees & wrists <u>extremely</u> swollen, blue & yellow.

Prisoner wears only scraps of filthy cloth, ragged trousers. No longer
bothers to dress or undress. Ribs clearly visible thru skin. Arms &
legs entirely fretted w. sores, purulent. Body covered, head to toe, w.
vermin. Bugs & lice to be found in every fold of sheet, blanket.

Prisoner started when door was opened. Turned head slightly twd
us, made no other move. Eyes opened a fraction when I lowered
candle to face, immediately closed again. Light acutely painful. Appears Prisoner has not been exposed to light of any kind in at least 6
mos, may be considered functionally blind.

No initial reply from Prisoner when I bade him gd morning. Did not
respond to questions. Faint exhalation detected thru lips (coated in

yeast). Lge black spider crawling up neck. Rat was found chewing Prisoner's hair, extricated w. difficulty. This occasioned Prisoner's first words, which were to thank me.

I asked Prisoner to stand. Prisoner declined. After repeated requests, he attempted to rise but wanted strength. W. assistance, he was able to take 2 steps—extrmly painful, by all appearances. Prisoner collapsed as soon as I removed my arm. (Guard, who was present thruout interview, declined to assist me in raising him up.)

Having returned Prisoner to cot, I promised to return next day A.M. to begin treatment. Upon hearing this, Prisoner, in barely audible voice, begged me not to bother. Prisoner observed it was his fondest wish to die. As soon as God would allow.

Must speak to Genl Barras re <u>cleaning cell</u>, obtaining more light for Prisoner. Knee most pressing medical concern. Prisoner wd benefit fm bath, exercise—contact with family, friends, <u>anyone</u>. Must speak to Must also

What have we done

CHAPTER 1

The Beggar at the Corner

I'M A MAN of a certain age—old enough to have been every kind of fool—and I find to my surprise that the only counsel I have to pass on is this: Never let your name be found in a dead man's trousers.

NAME, YES. MINE is Hector Carpentier. These days, *Professor* Carpentier, of the École de Médecine. My specialty is venereology, which is a reliable source of amusement for my students. "Come with us," they say. "Carpentier's going to tell all about the second stage of syphilis. You'll never screw again."

I live on the Rue du Helder, with an orange tabby named Baptiste. My parents are dead, I have no brother or sister and haven't yet been blessed with children. In short, I'm the only family I've got, and at certain intervals of calm, my mind drifts toward those people, not strictly related, who took on all the trappings, all the meaning of family—for a time, anyway. If you were to pin me down, for instance, I'd have to say

I recall the lads I went to medical school with better than I recall my own father. And Mother . . . well, she's present enough after all these years, but from some angles, she's not quite as *real* as Charles. Who was perhaps not real at all but who was, for a time, like family.

I THINK ABOUT him every time I see a penta. One glance is all it takes, and I'm standing once more in the Luxembourg Gardens, somewhere in May. I'm watching a pretty girl pass (the angle of her parasol, yes, the butter brightness of her gloves), and Charles is brooding over flowers. He is always brooding over flowers. This time, though, he actually plucks one and holds it up to me: an Egyptian star cluster.

Five arms, hence its name. Smaller than a whisper. Imagine a starfish dragged from the ocean bottom and . . . never mind, I can't do it justice. And, really, it's not so remarkable, but sitting there in the cup of his hand, it lays some claim on me, and so does everything else: the Scottish terrier snoring on a bench; the swan cleaning its rump feathers in the fountain; the moss-blackened statue of Leonidas. I am the measure of those things and they of me, and we are all—sufficient, I suppose.

Of course, nothing about our situation has shifted. We are still marked men, he and I. But at this moment, I can imagine a sliver of grace—the possibility, I mean, that we might be marked for other things. And all because of this silly flower, which on any other day, I would have stepped on like so much carpet.

HE'S BEEN ON my mind of late, because just last week, I received a letter from the Duchesse d'Angoulême. (She is staying at Count Coronini's estate in Slovenia.) The envelope was girt round with stamps, and the letter, written in her usual shy hand, was mostly an essay on rain, sealed off by prayers. I found it comforting. Word has it that the Duchess is penning her memoirs, but I don't believe it. No woman has clutched her own life more closely to her bosom. She'll hold it there, I expect, until the coroner assures her she's dead.

Which may be a long time coming. God's funny that way. The more his servants pine for his presence—and make no mistake, the Duchess does—the longer he keeps them shackled to the old mortal coil. No, it's the blasphemers he's aching to get his hands on. Take Monsieur Robespierre. At the very height of the Terror, Robespierre decided that the name "God" had too much of an ancien régime color to it. In his capacity as head of the Committee of Public Safety, he declared that God would henceforward be known as the Supreme Being. There was some kind of festival, I believe, to celebrate God's promotion. A parade, maybe. I was only two.

A few months later, with half his jaw shot off, groaning toward the scaffold, was Robespierre already composing apologies? We'll never know. There was no time for memoirs.

ME, I HAVE acres of time, but if I were to write up my life, I don't think I could start with the usual genuflections—all those ancestors in halberds, I mean, the midwives catching you in their calloused mitts. No, I'd have to start with Vidocq. And maybe end with him, too.

A strange admission, I know, given that I spent no more than a few weeks in his company. Fifteen years have passed with virtually no word from him. Why, then, should I bother revisiting the terrible business that brought us together?

Not from any hope of being believed. If anything, I write so that *I* may believe. Did it really happen? In quite that way? Nothing to do but set everything down, as exactly as I can, and see what stares back at me.

AND HOW EASILY the time slips away, after all. I need but shut my eyes, and two decades vanish in a breath, and I am standing once more in . . .

The year 1818. Which, according to official records, is the twenty-third year in the reign of King Louis XVIII. For all but three of those years, however, his majesty has been reigning somewhere else entirely—*hiding*, an unkind soul might say, while a certain Corsican made a footstool of Europe. None of that matters now. The Corsican has been locked away (again); the Bourbons are back; the fighting is done; the future is cloudless.

This curious interregnum in French history goes by the name of "the Restoration," the implication being that, after senseless experiments with democracy and empire, the French people have been restored to their senses and have invited the Bourbons back to the Tuileries. The old unpleasantness is never alluded to. We have all seen enough politics to last us a lifetime, and we know now: to take a hard line is to take a hard fall.

I know it, too—although I am young when this story begins, so young I scarcely recognize myself. Four years shy of thirty: thin and pink and inclined to catch cold. My father has been dead for some eighteen months. He left me and Mother the house I grew up in, as well as some undeveloped land in the Chaussée d'Antin, which I have already lost through bad speculations. To be specific, I was the chief investor in a pretty, bony dancer named Eulalie. She had dark eyes and a stealthy sort of smile, it seemed to climb round from the back of her head, and a way of softly clicking her wrists in and out of joint which never lost its charm.

I've heard it said that dinners and plays and carriages and gloves cost nothing in Paris. This is certainly true if you're not the one paying for them. And Eulalie, in the time I knew her, never paid for a blessed thing—it was part of her allure—and when, under duress, she admitted that she owed two thousand francs to the dressmaker and another thirteen hundred to the upholsterer and, oh, God knows what else, it was the most natural thing in the world to sell my father's land and walk about in muddy bluchers and a single black suit.

I learned after a time that the money was going to a law clerk named Cornu, who had been keeping company with Eulalie through five years and two children.

Scenes always disgusted her, so we never had one. She left me a cellar of memories, which is where I spend most of these early days of the Restoration. Rummaging. My mother and I reside in the Latin Quarter, and to make up for the lost assets, we've begun to take in lodgers—students, mostly, from the university. Mother, in her tulle cap, presides over the dinner table; I fix leaks. Squeaks, too, if I can. (The joists are a bit rotten on the third floor.) In my spare time, I haunt the university's laboratories, where Dr. Duméril, an old friend of my family, suffers me to carry out experiments, the nature of which no one is quite clear on. I tell people I am halfway through a monograph, but in fact, I've been halfway through this monograph for about two years. The only part I've finished, really, is the title: "The Therapeutic Efficacies of Animal Magnetism in Conjunction with Divers Orientalist Practices of Ancient. . . ."

Oh, I won't go on. I once rattled off the whole thing to my mother, and her face assumed a look of such bottomless misery that I resolved never to speak of it again—and nearly resolved to drop the project altogether. If I'd been braver, I would have.

Why did I mention the monograph? Oh! Because I am coming home from the laboratory on the morning in question. No, that's not quite right. I am coming home from Le Père Bonvin.

It's Monday. March the twenty-third. Spring, to be exact, although word is late getting to Paris. About a week ago, a front of green-gray drizzle-ice settled in like a malevolent houseguest. The old distinctions between air and water no longer hold. Everywhere you hear splashing—your own, the man behind you, the woman ahead—and everywhere a roiling liquid darkness, as if we're all frogs in a sunken kingdom.

Umbrellas are useless. You clap your hat on as firmly as it will go and pull up your lapels and carry on. Even if you have nowhere to go . . . go!

Yes, that describes me pretty well as I turn into the Rue Neuve-Sainte-Geneviève: grimly resolved and going no place in particular. Except home. The street is empty, except for Bardou, who lifts his head a bit by way of greeting. Bardou is my chief coordinate, for he keeps his corner vigil no matter what the conditions. Long ago, they say, he lost his arm in a paper mill, and though he works now and then as a church beadle, he always comes back to his station by the old condemned well, and whenever I pass, I try to drop a coin or two his way (more copper of late than silver), and he shows his appreciation by tipping his head an inch to the side. It's our ritual, obscurely comforting in its outlines.

But on this day of March the twenty-third, this ritual will be violated in a rather shocking way. By Bardou himself, who commits the singular offense of *looking* at me. Angling his face toward mine and *fastening* on with a real intent.

Is he chiding me for my stinginess? That's my first thought, I admit, but as I make my way down the street to my house, another possibility strikes me, and this is more shocking than being stared at. The possibility, I mean, that this is not Bardou.

I'm laughing even as I look back. *Not Bardou.* The same crooked, huddled form. The tattered hat and the leather shreds of boot, always threatening to come apart but never quite managing. And the stump, for God's sake! Twitching like a divining rod. *Not Bardou?*

He vanishes from my thoughts the moment I enter the house. The student lodgers have gone to their lectures; Mother has taken Charlotte, the maid, to buy curtains at the Palais-Royal; I am alone. Precious minutes lie before me, waiting to be squandered. I kick off my boots and incline on the horsehair settee, the one that no one is supposed to sit on, and I read Talma's notices in the latest issue of the *Minerve Française* (which I had to lift from Le Père Bonvin because we can't afford to subscribe) and I . . . I was going to say reflect, but *dozing* seems to cover it. When the knocking comes, I feel as if I'm being dragged from a canyon.

Never mind. I drape the newspaper over my face. *Charlotte will get it.*

Ah, but Charlotte's not home. No one's at home but me, and the knocking is coming louder and faster. I can ignore it, I've done that before, it's an aptitude of mine, but the rapping grows only more urgent, and in my dazzled state, I begin to wonder if it might not harbor a *code*, which will never be explained until I answer the door, and I have no time to ask if I want it explained, I'm running into the foyer and pulling back the bolt and throwing open the door. . . .

And there stands Bardou. His head bowed, his voice choked.

"A thousand pardons, Monsieur."

It's the most shocking thing he's done yet. *Standing*. For the first time in my memory . . . and maybe the last. His bent frame inscribes slow circles in the air. A second more, he'll give way altogether.

"Some bread," he gasps, steadying himself against the lintel. "If you . . ."

I should make this clear. There is not an ounce of charity in me at this moment, only a prickling of terror. I don't want him to die on our parquet floor. Because, even if I manage to spirit the body away, Mother will *smell* him, seeping into her wax, and it will be one more item on the scroll of offenses, and this scroll is no piece of paper, it is something endless and coiling and half fluid, it is the pink tongue of a great serpent, flicking at my neck as I dash toward Charlotte's pantry. . . .

He mustn't die on our floor. He mustn't die on our floor.

There's no bread, but there's . . . something that *resembles* bread . . . a macaroon! A week old, perhaps. Perfect.

Back I trundle with my stale sweet, a thin smile penciled on my face, and there, on the front stoop . . .

No one.

From behind, I hear a clearing of throat. It is Bardou. Transposed by some strange agency to our dining room. Leaning against our buffet.

"I've. . . ."

The words die in my throat as he grabs the macaroon and downs it in two bites.

"Ugh," he says, flinging the wrapper away. "Lizard shit."

And then he lowers himself into the very settee I've just vacated. (The one that no one is supposed to sit on.)

And again the words—the bourgeois reproaches—won't come clear, for I am just now remarking the change in Bardou's voice, which is shaking off years with each passing second.

And this is nothing next to the alteration in Bardou himself. He is coming undone. The ribbons tumble from his empty sleeve, and his lone arm scurries into the hollow of his breast, and in mere seconds, another arm has miraculously appeared where there was only stump.

Like a hydra, I think, staring in wonder. *Growing new appendages*.

"See here, my good fellow, I don't know what you're up to. . . ."

He pays me no mind, he's too busy dragging his hands across his face—and taking Bardou's face right with it.

And why stop there? Why not yank the white hair straight off his head, like a bird molting in a single stark second?

There he stands, the brazen nestling. Hair: a damp sward of chestnut. Mouth: wryly puckered. Grayish blue eyes presiding over a voluptuous nose. And, most troubling of all, the faintest trace of a scar on his upper right lip.

"You should—you should be aware," I stammer. "There's a guardhouse. Not two blocks away."

The stranger smiles into the handkerchief that is even now smeared with the remains of Bardou, and in a suave and strange voice, he says: "Four."

"Pardon?"

"*Four* blocks," he insists, with a priest's patience. "Corner of Cholets and Saint-Hubert. We can go there right now if you like."

And then comes the most remarkable transformation of all. He straightens. No. That doesn't begin to describe it. He *grows*. As though he's suddenly discovered another five inches of spinal column and is unfurling it to a previously unguessed length. Before my eyes, the tiny old cripple from the street corner has become a strapping man of five and six. Square and proud and blunt, built along geological lines, with thick strata of muscle bleeding into outcroppings of fat—and the fat somehow bleeding back into muscle, so that he remains an indissoluble unit, a thing of bestial power, shaking you down to your larynx.

"I must ask you to leave this house right now," I say. "You have— you have presumed far enough on my charity. . . ."

There may be a tremor in my voice, but I wouldn't know. I can only hear the stranger's dry muttering undertone:

"Call that a macaroon . . . paving stone, more like it . . . what does he think he's . . ." And then rising to his own declamation: "Christ, don't you have something to wash it down with?"

His eyes light on a bottle of half-drunk wine on the buffet. Wrenching the cork free, he grabs a glass from the china cabinet, holds it skeptically to the light (eczema spots of dirt appear from nowhere, as though he's called them into being), and then decants the wine with great care into the glass, running his truffle nose round the rim.

"Better," he says, after a couple of sips. "Beaune, is it? That's not half bad."

And me, I'm . . . looking for weapons. Amazing how few come to hand. A couple of butter knives. A candlestick. Maybe Charlotte left the corkscrew in the drawer? How long would it take to find? How long to . . .

But every last calculation ceases the moment he says:

"Please, Dr. Carpentier. Have a seat."

CHAPTER 2

Death of a Potato

JUST LIKE THAT, he's disarmed me. And for one excellent reason: He has called me *Doctor.*

In these early days of the Restoration, no one thinks me worthy of that title, least of all me. And so, even as I lower myself into one of the dining chairs, I am *rising* toward that *Doctor.* Striving, yes, to be worthy.

"Well now," I say. "You know *my* name, and I have not yet had the honor of—of being introduced."

"No, it's true," he concedes.

He's on the prowl now—sniffing, inspecting—compromising everything he touches. The rectangular fruitwood table with its matted surface. The clouded, chipped carafes. The scorch marks on the ivory lampshade. Everything, under his touch, gives off a puff of meanness.

"Aha!" he cries, running his finger down a stack of blue-bordered plates. "Made in Tournai, weren't they? Don't look so ashamed, Doctor. There's nothing like convict labor to keep the porcelain cheap."

"Monsieur. I believe I have already begged the honor of knowing your name."

His merry eyes rest on me for a second. "You have, indeed, and I do apologize. Perhaps you know of a man called . . ."

And here his fingers form a bud round his mouth, and the name flowers forth, like a shower of pollen.

"Vidocq."

He waits, with great confidence, for the dawning in my eyes.

"You mean—oh, he's that *policeman* sort of fellow, isn't he?"

His smile dips down, his eyes shrink. "*Policeman* sort of fellow. And Napoleon is just a soldier sort of fellow. Voltaire told a good joke. Honestly, Doctor, if you can't get things in their right scale, I despair of you."

"No, I don't—I mean he locks up thieves, doesn't he? He gets written up in the papers."

A grandiloquent shrug. "The papers write what they like. If you want to know about Vidocq, ask the scoundrels who tremble at his name. They'll write you whole tomes, Doctor."

"But what has Vidocq to do with anything?"

"Vidocq is me."

It has the air of afterthought the way he says it. As though, having breathed the name into the air, he need lay only the gentlest claim on it. And this is more declarative than if he'd shouted the news to the chandeliers.

"Well, that's all very well," I say, folding my arms across my chest. "But do you have any papers?"

"Listen to him now! Papers! Please, Doctor-eating-off-your-convict-made-china, tell me why I need papers."

"Why, you come in here. . . ." I'm amazed to find my anger rising in direct proportion to his. "You *barge* in here, Monsieur Whoever You Are, with your little tricks and your *faux* stump, and you say, '*Voilà!* Vidocq!' and expect me to believe it. Why should I? How can I be sure you're who you say you are?"

He mulls it over. And then, with some regret, informs me:

"You can't."

It is a good lesson to get out of the way. Eugène François Vidocq, if so he is, will not be held to the same empirical standards as the rest of the world. Take him at face value or go to hell.

"Very well," I say. "If you're this Vidocq fellow, tell me where Bardou is."

"Having a lovely week, I assure you, with the Bernadine sisters. Tending to their melons. I think you won't find him eager to return to his street corner, Doctor."

"But why would you go to such lengths in the first place? Taking his place on the corner, dressing like him, *looking*—"

"Well, now." The stranger leans into the table. "If a hunter is tracking prey, Doctor, he must take care not to be seen."

"But who is the prey?"

"Why, you."

And in that moment, I twitch my head to the side, and there, in front of the settee, lie my empty boots and my half-read newspaper.

"And why should you have any call to hunt me?" I ask.

Except I already know.

Eulalie.

With distressing speed, the writ scrolls out in my head. Eulalie and her law clerk . . . fencing stolen plate . . . captured by the gendarmes . . . *we'll let you off this time if you give up your mastermind* . . . and who better to give up than poor little Hector? Won't he do anything for Eulalie—*still*? Won't he go to La Force for her?

And back from my shriveled clod of heart comes the answer: *yes.*

"It's absurd," I say. "I've done—what could I have—"

"Now now," he says, working the crick out of his neck. "If there's interrogating to do, you really should leave it to me. That's what they pay me for, you know. Let me see. . . ." He gulps down another draft of wine, swipes his arm across his lips. "You could start by telling me what a certain Monsieur Chrétien Leblanc wanted with you."

"I don't know anyone named Leblanc."

He smiles softly. "You're quite sure about that, Doctor?"

"As sure as I can be, yes."

"Well then, it's a very funny business. Because I'm here to tell you that Monsieur Leblanc knows *you*."

Fumbling once more in his shirtfront cache, he draws out—not another arm, no—a piece of butcher's paper. Flecked with wax, stiff with grease. And from this corrupted surface, the words leap up: hot, black.

DR. HECTOR CARPENTIER
No. 18, Rue Neuve-Sainte-Geneviève

He's behind me now, the terrible stranger, watching me read, wreathing my neck with his breath. The air grows confused with wine.

"That is your address, is it not, Doctor?"

"Of course."

"And that is your name?"

"Yes."

"And I believe you have the honor of being the only Dr. Carpentier in all of Paris. Don't think I didn't check," he adds, cuffing me gently on the ear. "Damnit, though, I'm still hungry as the devil. Anything else to eat? That *fucking* macaroon . . ."

A moment later, I hear him rustling in the pantry, arraigning each article as he finds it. "Chestnuts have seen better days. . . . Pear preserves? I think *not*. . . . Cheese looks all right, except . . . well, *that's* a scary purple, you don't see *that* particular . . ."

"This is ridiculous!" I call after him. "I've never received a Monsieur Leblanc here! I'm not—"

Not even a practicing physician . . .

But pride cuts me short. Or else it's the sight of the stranger, re-emerging with a potato in his mouth. A *raw* potato, crammed like an apple into a trussed pig.

"Well, Doctor." He grinds out a hunk of its hard flesh, mashes it into submission. "We're certainly—in agreement on—on one point. You couldn't have—received Monsieur . . ."

"Leblanc."

"*Leblanc*," he echoes, through whirling pellets of tuber. "For the simple reason . . . he never made it here."

"Well, then, why are you bothering me? Why don't you question *him*?"

Another hunk of potato. Another round of gnashing.

"Because he's . . . mpxxcchsik. . . ."

That's how it comes out, I'm afraid. He puts up a single finger—*Wait, please*—but it's a good long minute before his larynx breaks free.

"Because he's *dead*."

The taste of the raw potato must finally breach his senses, for all of a sudden, it comes sluicing out in a fast brown stream—right into the waiting carafe.

"Thought it was a bit riper," he mutters.

And my first thought is, yes: Mother. Must clean up the mess before Mother gets here. I'm already reaching for the carafe when he intercepts me.

"Three blocks from here." (His sausage fingers curled round the carafe handle.) "That's where the unfortunate Monsieur Leblanc died. Not too far from the Université where you spend so much of your days."

He pushes the carafe away, takes one long step toward me.

"Monsieur Leblanc was killed on the way to seeing you, Doctor, and I'm counting on you to tell me why." He brushes a pebble of damp potato from my coat. "If it's a question of which confessor you'd prefer, I should tell you I'm a much easier touch than God. At the very worst, you'll get a few years of state-supported education in a cell of your choice. Think of it as an exercise in character building. *Come* now, tell Vidocq all about it. Before"—and here he gives me the most knowing of smiles—"before Mama Carpentier comes home and gets her little white feathers ruffled."

He steps back and contemplates me for a moment. Then, wheeling round, he upends the wine bottle. A single crimson drop touches down on the dining table's surface.

"Oops, we're out! Be a good man and fetch us another, would you?"

CHAPTER 3

The Chamber of the Dead

IT'S THE WAY of the human conscience, I suppose. A man suggests you're guilty of something, and the more you say you're not, the more it sounds like you are. The voice rings of tin, the heart rattles like a fistful of beans, and every *no* sounds like a *yes*, until you can actually feel this *yes*, inching onto the parapet of your lip . . . when your interlocutor grabs the bottle of Burgundy—the one you fetched for him not half an hour ago—and peers into its jungle green interior and, in a voice tinctured with resignation, announces:

"Out again."

Then he waggles his finger at the glass of wine sitting unmolested before you. The one you haven't had the stomach to drink (thanks to him).

"Are you—do you—"

And, seeing you shrug, he hoists it straight to his mouth. A long leak of satiated breath and then a belch, fruiting the air. He looks down at himself. He sees, as if for the first time, Bardou's rags. He draws out a watch.

"Time to go."

For *both* of you to go, that's what he means. He is moderately surprised to find you remaining in your chair.

"I need to show you something," he says.

And still you don't move, and rather than explaining himself further, he lifts his voice into a gently mocking register.

"Maybe you need to leave a note first? In case she worries?"

And here's the damnable part of it. You *were* going to leave a note. And all you can do now is squeeze yourself into your boots and stare at the newspaper still lying on the floor and think (you can't help it): *This is all that will be left of me.*

Your legacy: a half-read journal, a half-finished monograph. But you can't do more than pause because he's already swung the front door open and stepped out on the stoop with the air of a man surveying his estates. He's waiting for you.

"Coming," you mutter. "Coming, damn you."

LATER TODAY, I WILL reflect on the curious fact that he came alone. No other officers, no squad of gendarmes to subdue me. Not even a weapon, as far as I can tell. He'd watched me long enough to know: I could be handled.

And was he wrong? Here I am, climbing without a second thought into the carriage waiting round the corner. Waiting, benumbed, as he barks the address to the driver above.

"Quai du Marché!"

He pulls the curtains over the windows and yanks up his sleeves— only to remember he doesn't have sleeves, only Bardou's damp rags, which cling to him now in the form of an apology.

The cab must recently have carried a wedding party, for there's a scrap of lace caught in the door and a scattering of hothouse orange blossoms and the snapped-off handle of a Japanese fan. And overlaying everything a ripening scent, like something that would waft from a tannery. *His* smell, I suddenly realize.

"Where are we going?" I ask.

"Paying a little call at the morgue, that's all." He smiles faintly, shakes his head. "You still don't believe me, Doctor."

"No, I—"

"You don't think I'm *him*, do you? Not another word, damn you! Here!"

Into my lap drops a round pasteboard card, wedged between two pieces of glass. On one side: the arms of France and the words SUR-VEILLANCE ET VIGILANCE. On the other: a single surname, VIDOCQ, in triumphally raised gold letters.

"Signed by the prefect himself," he says dryly. "If that eases your mind, Dr. May-I-see-your-papers."

It doesn't, how could it? It only gives me leave, finally, to call him by that name. And still I hesitate.

Vidocq. Say it, for Christ's sake. *Eugène François Vidocq.* Come at it in pieces, if you must, syllable by syllable. *Vee. Dohk. Vee. Dohk* . . .

EVEN IN THESE early days of the Restoration, it is a famous name. It comes, you might say, with its own exclamation point. Terror of thieves! Scourge of crime! Bonaparte of the *barrières*!

Only a couple of years past forty, and yet he already drags behind him a full complement of legends. There are people, for instance, who swear they were at Denoyes' cabaret the night he raided it. They remember him staring down a dance floor of knife-wielding thugs and, in a voice that resonated as far as the Bastille, ordering them to quit the premises. One man demurred and lost a finger. The rest obeyed without a murmur. (Vidocq chalked white crosses on the worst offenders as they passed so that the policemen waiting outside would know which to arrest.)

And what about the time he tracked down a thief, knowing only the color of the man's curtains? Or when he waded right into a Tuileries reception and plucked a confidence man in the act of bowing to the King? Or captured the fearsome giant Sablin in Saint-Cloud while Sablin's wife lay in the throes of labor? (Vidocq had enough time left over to catch the baby and to serve as godfather.)

One night, they say, he insinuated himself into a group of assassins stationed outside his very own door. Sat with them all night, they say, waiting for that accursed Vidocq to show up, then joined them in their despondent trek home—where, naturally, he'd stationed a tribe of gendarmes. (His reward was a tumble in the sheets with the ringleader's mistress.)

Legend has it that if you give Vidocq two or three of the details surrounding a given crime, he will give you back the man who did it—before you've had time to blink. More than that, he'll describe the man for you, give you his most recent address, name all his known conspirators, tell you his favorite cheese. So compendious is his memory that a full half of Paris imagines him to be omniscient and wonders if his powers weren't given him by Satan.

And yet he is doing God's work, is he not? To hear the papers tell it, Vidocq, in the space of a few years, has sent hundreds of malefactors to prison. The ones that remain abroad cross themselves at the sound of his name. If a robbery falls apart at the last minute, it's Vidocq's doing. If a credulous old widow manages, against all odds, to keep her jewels, blame it on that scoundrel Vidocq. If an innocent man lives to see another morrow, who's behind it? The accursed Vidocq, that's who.

All it takes some nights is a shift in the wind's direction, a creak on the stair, and the name flies like an oath from their throats.

Vidocq. Vidocq is abroad.

AND NOW THIS same Vidocq is pounding on the roof of our cab, as if to gouge out a straighter path for his words.

"Driver! A little faster, will you? Oh, and don't forget to stop at Mabriole's bakery. I want to show this bastard what a macaroon tastes like."

Folding his arms across the swell of his belly, he regards me with a look of naked skepticism.

"You're not a fainter, are you?"

"No, of course not."

"Well, that's a relief. You look like one."

I'VE ALWAYS THOUGHT of the morgue as the fullest realization of democracy. Anyone can enter: man, woman, child; dead, alive. You don't even have to give your name. When Vidocq and I arrive a little after two, I catch only the faintest glimmer of a concierge. I'm already moving, like everyone else, toward the glassed-in chamber that opens off the main hall.

Through the panes, three biers slope toward us like grain chutes. On each bier, a body. To be kept here another twenty-four hours and then, if no one claims it, shipped straight to the medical schools, ten francs a cadaver. And so hundreds of still-living souls crowd round this window every day to keep their friends and relations off the dissecting table—or else to enjoy the spectacle of someone else's death. I've seen more English tourists in the morgue than in the Louvre.

"Come," says Vidocq.

He takes me by the elbow, draws me down a corridor. We pass into a room with yellow calico curtains and a horsehair settee and . . . and, most troubling of all, a pianoforte. I reach for middle C. It pings back, in perfect tune.

"What do you want?" Vidocq grumbles. "The morgue keeper's family has to pass the time, don't they?"

We enter a room with no flowers, no pianos. No furniture, not even a window. Only a black marble slab, draped in white cambric, and two candles, blazing in sconces.

Vidocq grabs one of the candles, walks to the head of the table, and peels back the sheet to reveal the slumbering head beneath.

"I don't believe you two have met," he says, in a voice dry as shavings. "Dr. Carpentier? Monsieur Chrétien Leblanc."

CHAPTER 4

The Missing Fingernails

IT'S VIDOCQ'S LITTLE coup de théâtre, of course, and it depends for its effect on shock, which is the one response I can't provide.

To a medical student, after all, a body is a body. The only surprise in this case is to find Chrétien Leblanc's body still here. Under normal circumstances, he would have been borne straight to Vaugirard or Clamart or, if money were wanting, the potters' field at Père-Lachaise. It's clear enough Vidocq wants me to have this private audience, and nothing more can happen until I do, and so at last I do ply myself against this *face*, oily with candlelight. The bush of hair inside his Roman nostrils and the chin cleft, deep enough to hold a thumb, and the threads of blood worrying his sealed eyelids. The scalp has shrunk back to reveal a grubby stripe of gray beneath Leblanc's blackened locks, but the whiskers are still neatly combed, the brows trimmed, and his pores breathe out the sweet-sharp scent of pomade.

"Maybe fifty-five, fifty-six," says Vidocq. "We can't be sure." He's standing so close behind me that his chin actually tickles my shoulder as he talks. "Ring any bells, does he, Doctor?"

"I don't know him."

"You're sure?"

"Absolutely."

Vidocq grunts. Laces his hands behind his head and tips himself back against the wall.

"He didn't leave any family. Took us two days just to find someone who could identify him. Thank God for creditors, Doctor! A shoemaker on the Rue Dauphine came round to swear a complaint. Said some bastard named Leblanc had stiffed him on a pair of boots and skipped town. 'Skipped town?' I said. 'Gone to a better world, more like it.' Well, wasn't the shoemaker fit to be tied? He took one look at that body and said, 'Damn your soul! Where am I supposed to get my seven livres now?' "

Vidocq chuckles. "I'd have been happy, naturally, to pay him out of Leblanc's private funds, but the wallet was long gone when we found him. The clothes, too. Leave a body lying around long enough, every last article goes. Even the gold crowns. No," he says, his voice trailing down. "I'm afraid the only personal effects left on Monsieur Leblanc were his drawers."

He leans over the cadaver. "There there," he murmurs, and in a gesture startling and soft, he runs his hands through the strands of perfumed hair. "You can imagine, Doctor," he says, looking up. "I come across a few corpses in my line of work, Doctor. Robberies gone bad, usually. Sometimes a victim protests too much. Or the thief's a bit of an amateur. Something goes wrong, he can't cut the purse free, he panics. Or the victim *knows* the thief and has to be——" He looks up at me. "It's quick, usually. And clean. *This* was less quick and less clean."

He pulls the rest of the sheet off. He says:

"What do you see?"

No, this is what he says: "What do you see, *Doctor*?"

"Well, now." Maybe you can hear it: my new baritone. "Judging from the *joints,* rigor mortis has largely dissipated. Muscle proteins have begun to decompose. Which would indicate he's been dead at least thirty-six hours. No, I'm sorry, make that forty-two."

"Why forty-two?" he asks.

"I don't believe you've met," I answer, extending my hand toward him.

Sitting on the tip of my finger is a fly. Robed in emerald, drowsy-still.

"*Lucilia sericata,*" I say. "The greenbottle, to you and me. Usually the first insect to arrive—thirty-eight hours at the earliest. This one looks like he's had a few more hours to feast."

And as if on cue come the answering buzzes of other flies, gathering at the same table. One of them even lands on the bridge of Vidocq's nose. He pushes his lower lip out and sweeps the fly away on a current of air.

"Forty-two hours," he murmurs. "That means . . . dead before nightfall . . . well, how do you . . ."

And suddenly: the first whisperings of piano from the next room. Scales, executed with light precision. It could be anybody, but my mind seizes for some reason on the image of a young girl. Ringleted and pin-afored—the apple of the morgue keeper's eye.

"No signs of head trauma," I say. "The fatal blow must have come—*here*—just beneath the left rib cage. A longish sort of thrust, perhaps from a—a—"

"A *poignard,* I'm guessing. Or a dirk."

"Now this is curious." My fingers step across Leblanc's hairless torso. "See these lacerations? No more than an inch in diameter. By my count, there are a good half dozen on the chest alone."

"Four more on the back," says Vidocq.

"Fairly shallow. No more than half an inch, as far as I can tell. You might have done as much with a dinner knife." I frown, run my index finger across the scapula and back to the neck. "I could almost . . ."

"Yes?"

"Assuming he didn't inflict these himself . . ."

"Yes?"

"I might almost believe they *wanted* him to bleed. Before they killed him."

Taking the candle from the sconce, I move the light across him in rippling pools.

"Is this how the body was found?" I ask.

"Not exactly. We had to clean it up a bit. There was a goodly amount of dried blood, especially around the fingers."

"The fingers?"

"Mm. The right hand. Couldn't even see it at first for all the damned blood. Look for yourself, Doctor."

He watches as I raise Leblanc's fingers to the light. The piano has fallen silent now, and the only sound is the buzzing of the flies and a distant trickle. And the windings of an étude.

"The fingernails," I say at last. "Three of them are missing."

"Not just missing," Vidocq answers, smiling grimly. "Pried loose."

He drops a small buckram bag on the marble table. Three ragged patches of cuticle scatter into the light.

"We found them when we went back to the scene. I'm sure Monsieur Leblanc was loath to part with them."

One of them is resting in my palm now. Hard. Like a flake of amber.

"Oh, the memories," says Vidocq. "I once saw Bobbefoi do that to one of his pals in the *bagne*. With a saddler's awl. You never heard such screaming. Bobbefoi figured the fellow for being a police spy, but he got the wrong man. Lamentably." He strokes Leblanc's brow. "There there, old bear. We're almost done."

"The knife wounds," I say. "The fingernails . . ."

And in this moment, the music from the adjoining room seems to twine with my own thoughts, drawing them into their natural key.

"They *tortured* him, didn't they? Before they killed him."

Vidocq shrugs, takes a couple steps away.

"Torture's a simple business, Doctor. You either want your man to hurt or you want him to *give*."

"But what would Leblanc have to give?"

"A name, maybe. The name of the very fellow he was going to see."

And with that, the remains of Chrétien Leblanc's fingernails are obscured by the piece of paper that Vidocq showed me less than an hour ago. How different it looks to me now.

DR. HECTOR CARPENTIER
No. 18, Rue Neuve-Sainte-Geneviève

The great Vidocq is yawning now. No need to suppress it. He lets it pop his jaw open and swell his neck column and flush his lungs out.

"Don't think I mentioned," he says at last. "We found the paper in a tiny leather pouch. He'd tied it round his waist and tucked it in his drawers, if you can believe it. You could have searched him all you like, you would've been hard-pressed to find it. Not unless you had him on a slab in the Paris morgue."

His fingers lock round one another and pulse in tiny motions.

"Leblanc lived on the Rue de Charenton, we know that much. A good long walk from your neighborhood, Doctor. My guess is he was being followed from the moment he left his apartment."

"Then why didn't they—"

"Oh yes, I had the same question. Why didn't they just follow him straight to your house? *Tell* us, old cod." He runs a finger round the dead man's ear. "Why *didn't* they? Did you catch them on your tail? Maybe you threw them off the scent, is that it? Went in circles, took a wrong turn or two. Maybe you even tried to save yourself by making for the nearest station house." He blows into the dead man's ear: two gentle puffs. "But they didn't let you, did they? Poor old salmon."

The étude keeps coming, like a river. And as I drag up horns of my own hair, it seems to me I am knocking the music off balance. Just to give myself company.

"If Leblanc was coming to see me . . ."

"Yes."

"And he didn't want—whoever it was to know . . ."

"Yes."

"Then why didn't he just commit my address to memory? Why go to the trouble of keeping it on his person?"

He smiles down at Leblanc's bare white abdomen. "I think he had in mind—well, I almost blush to say it, Doctor—someone like me. If the very worst happened, he wanted to put the information where I'd be sure to find it." He coos into Leblanc's fleshy ear. "And who better than Vidocq, eh? Who better?"

I'm sitting down before I realize there's a chair waiting to catch me.

"Leblanc was protecting me," I say softly.

"Oh, it's all guesswork, of course, but I look at *this*. . . ." His hand describes the length of Leblanc's body. "I look at *that*. . . ." His index finger glances down on the scrap of paper. "I say to myself, 'Leblanc did everything but cram that piece of paper up his ass.' And all I can think is he wanted to keep them from doing to you what—what they did to *him*."

I have only a very dim sense of Vidocq now, weaving round me in the darkness—until his hand lands with a light explosion on my shoulder.

"And a fine job he did, eh, Doctor? Here you are. Still in the flower of your youth, more or less." He plucks a thread of something from my coat. "How does it feel, I wonder? To have your life saved by a man you've never met?"

I will say this: There's no judgment in his voice. I think he just wants to know.

"Old turtle," he says, bending over Leblanc's face. "I am honored by your trust. Leave it to *us* to finish the job, will you?"

ONLY LATER, ONLY much later will I register that shift from singular to plural, *I* to *us*. It will dawn on me that this was the moment it turned, although it could well be there *was* no single moment—nothing that could be called back. Much as I might have wished to.

"Go to sleep now," whispers Vidocq.

He pulls the sheet back over M. Chrétien Leblanc. Setting the candle back on the sconce, he pauses one last moment—not in prayer, exactly, but in some kind of suspended thought. Then he stalks out of the room, stopping only to cast the reproach that I am half expecting.

"Maybe you'd rather stick around with the maggots?"

I never do see her, the piano player of my imagination. But by way of compensation, her sonata comes after me: a spring tide of notes, catching me as I pass into the main hall. I will never again be able to hear Mozart without thinking of greenbottle flies.

CHAPTER 5

An Astounding Reemergence

VIDOCQ'S MOVING AHEAD from the moment we step out of doors—and with such a bounding gait that I have to jog just to catch up. He scatters plumes of rainwater and mud as he goes, and there I am, following, *ever* following, mincing round the puddles he's fording, shielding my hat from the horse droppings that are anointing him.

"Excuse me . . . Monsieur Vidocq?"

"What is it now?"

"I was wondering if perhaps I might go home now."

He looks at me in a state of unvarnished amazement.

"And why would you do that?"

"Well, it occurs to me there's—I imagine there's no further *use* for me now."

His jaw swings gently open.

"Insomuch as . . ." I tender him a propitiatory smile. "I mean, given that I can't make a—a *positive* identification of the unfortunate Monsieur Leblanc, I can't see what more I can do for you."

He lowers his head until it's level with mine—until I can actually feel his breath scalding my cheeks.

"Listen to me, you little prick! A man's been murdered, and *you* know something about it. The more pieces we find, the more something might jog that timid little memory of yours, and I want to be there when something finally pops out, because I don't think you're quite so idiotic as you look."

His face is wrinkled with disgust as he wrenches himself away from me.

"Monsieur Can-I-Go-Home-Now. You'll go home when I fucking tell you!"

And with that, he turns his back on me and charges down the street—*daring* me not to follow. It is then that the question, the obvious question, startles my lips apart.

"Where are we going?"

But the hope of receiving an answer is negated by the sound of my own voice: bleating and braying, cracking me *open*, as it were, to reveal the small green quivering heart-fruit beneath. I resolve never again to ask him where we're going. And I never do.

TRUTH BE TOLD, we don't seem to be going anywhere. The drizzle has stopped for the time being, and a dandelion glimmer has plumped out the drifts of cloud. It's a fine time for a walk.

And what a pair of strollers we make. Me in my black trousers, shiny at the knees, and the black coat vented at the elbows. Vidocq, striding like a deposed king in Bardou's sodden rags. After some time, he pauses at a street corner to realign the leather scraps that pass for boots, and in his best honey-and-cloves voice, he says:

"I hope I haven't distressed you unduly, Doctor."

"Why should I be distressed?"

"Oh, some men don't like being thrown off their schedule."

I tell him I don't really have a schedule. To speak of. He shakes his head.

"Doctor, may I submit that that's horseshit? I've spent no more than a day following you, and I've already got you dead to rights. École de Médecine in the morning, nine-thirty to eleven. Followed by Le Père Bonvin, where you buy your single cup of coffee, followed by a sugar-and-water. You sneak your little newspaper into your coat. (They don't chain down the papers at Bonvin's, do they?) You go straight home. A little catnap, some afternoon puttering. Dinner with Maman and her boarders. A walk just before bed, with a pinch of tobacco in the left cheek. You walk around the block and no farther. You go to sleep, repeat next morning. Do I have it about right?"

So many ways to protest. I could tell him that, some mornings, I stay at the École all the way to noon. That I treat myself now and then to a chocolate at the Café des Mille Colonnes. That I only take tobacco at night if Charlotte's cooking doesn't agree with me.

But these are all just different ways of admitting he's right. So I remain silent, which is in itself a confession.

"Yes, you're a man of regular habits, Doctor, considering you've no—"

Job, he means to say. Life. Something stops him from finishing.

"Yes indeed," he says, nodding slow. "I could set my watch by you."

And then, perhaps because this strikes him as too close to an assertion of faith, he adds: "It's the same with all criminals."

We cross the Pont St.-Michel, we trot up the Rue des Arcis, a right on Neuve-St.-Méderic . . . and almost at once the streets begin funneling down. Which is to say the old Paris closes round. The roar of the boulevards gives way to the clatter of paving stones. The streets wind and dart, turn their backs on you, stop you dead. Sewers split open before you like unsutured wounds, and houses built centuries ago totter forward in raiments of black.

No great plan at work, here in the Marais, but there is a kind of unnatural order. As sure as the sun rises and sets, the late-winter rain will leave brackish tides pooling against the corner posts, and this water will merge with the slops toiling downward through blackened gutters to produce that peculiar mud, so Parisian in its odor and provenance. If you kick in your boots too hard, you'll actually taste some, flying into your mouth like a retracted insult. You'll smell it, too, and *feel* it with every step: a squelch beneath the stone and a slight release, as though the city is giving way beneath you.

Where are we going?

Not even two in the afternoon, and there's a candle in every window, and the light seems to partake of the same medium as the air and the ground and the water, so that even when your eyes are open, you have the strangest feeling that they're closed.

Never mind, my companion knows the way. He takes his bearings not from celestial but from human bodies. Washerwomen, wheelwrights. A ragpicker with a basket and hook. Beldams, in groups of four, gossiping on doorsteps. Vidocq knows where they'll be before he's even seen them. Already calling out to them, isn't he, with the swagger of a stagecoach driver pulling into the courtyard of an inn.

"Good afternoon, ladies! Saying our rosaries, are we? . . . Hey, Gervaise, you pile of shit! You still owe me thirty sous on that cock of yours. Never mind, just keep a place for me at next Sunday's fight, will you? And bring a bird with some heart in him! . . . Ah, is that the sun I see or Mademoiselle Sophie? Why, you're *better* than the sun, it's true. . . ."

Even his gait changes as he approaches them. The right foot drags slightly behind him, like an embarrassed child, and the left foot skates through the drifts of mud, and his *hands,* those great bear claws, tease the air.

"Oho, it's Tambour! Haven't seen you since you went to the *bagne.* But what are these phials you're foisting on the public? Herbal panaceas? Why, Tambour, I had no idea you were such a philanthropist— hey now, do any of these potions give a fellow bigger balls? My friend here might want some. . . ."

They all stand stock-still as he approaches, with the frozen half-smiles of guests at a Tuileries garden party. It comes as a surprise when we turn onto the Rue des Blancs-Manteaux to find a man not just standing but coming *toward* us, with a turnip sack over his shoulder.

"Chief," he says, in the mildest of tones.

"Allard."

They stand there, staring over each other's shoulders, making scraps of small talk, lofting an oath or two at the weather. And then Allard, without altering his cadence, murmurs:

"He's inside."

"How long?"

"Since eleven."

Vidocq cuts his eyes north. "Woman, too?"

"Whole family."

"Give."

Allard swings the turnip bag off his shoulder. Before I can protest, Vidocq stuffs it into my arms.

"Don't jiggle it, Doctor, if you'd be so kind."

Motioning me to follow, he stops in front of a poulterer's window, where he makes a show of interest in a Norman goose. Then, without a word, he draws me inside the adjoining building. The door closes after us, he puts a finger to his lips, he points . . . *up*.

But who would have guessed *up* would mean five floors? With a heavy bundle in your arms? By the time we reach the top, I'm rubbing my shiny forehead on the turnip bag, and Vidocq's belly is swelling to twice its normal stoutness—all the more so because he's trying to still the sound of his own breathing. A minute passes, the belly contracts . . . Vidocq puts his knuckles to the door and raps, lightly, three times.

"Who is it?"

"Friends."

From inside, a scatter and a scuffle. Moments later, the door opens on a young woman—maybe not young at all—skinny as a limpet with a cat-nose and vole-eyes.

"Ah!" cries Vidocq. "La belle Jeanne-Victoire!"

"Monsieur Eugène," she says, even as glass.

"I'm looking for Poulain, my sweet."

"Not at home, to be sure."

"Ahhh." His eyes execute a quick sweep of the room. "Then we'll just wait for him, if you don't mind."

She pauses to consider, but he's already stepped around her, and the only thing left to consider is *me:* hat in hand, smiling with reflexive courtesy, clutching that mysterious package to my breast.

"I don't believe you've met," Vidocq calls back.

It is a strange feature of Parisian apartments: The closer they get to Heaven, the more hellish they become. A ground-floor apartment will, often as not, come with a nice fireplace, a rosewood dresser, Utrecht velvet on the armchairs, even a garden. By the time you get to the garret, you can feel the cold bleeding through the plaster cracks, you can *hear* the worms eating into the boards.

And yet people do live in the high-ceilinged pen that Jeanne-Victoire calls home. No doubt they freeze in the winter, but why bother with a fireplace when the drafts would kill any fire? Why bother with curtains when there's no light? Or wallpaper when your walls ooze a putrid tar? Even the floor has been stripped down to its foundations, and as for furniture, there's a pair of straw pallets, crawling with dust mites, and a table listing on three legs. Everything else is a melee of rags and old shoes and broken boards and broken bowls.

And a single baby.

I don't see it at first. I'm just trying to find a place where I can, in good conscience, *stand,* and this means nudging away some old stockings and a birdcage, and it's in the act of relocating a kettle that I see, lying atop a chafing dish, something soft and purple-cheeked and still.

So very still I'm already reaching toward it—looking for a pulse point—and then I see the eyelids shudder and the hands feint in my direction.

It holds my eye, this baby. And it never makes a sound.

"In blooming health, I see," says Vidocq, peering over my shoulder. "I congratulate you, Jeanne-Victoire. Your third, isn't it?"

No embarrassment in her eyes, either.

"The first with Arnaud," she says.

"Ah, yes. You *would* need to start over again with Arnaud, wouldn't you? A whole new accounting system for Arnaud."

"Monsieur does not look so blooming himself. Police work must not be paying as well."

He grabs a fistful of Bardou's dirty blouse and grins like spring. "Austerity measures! Vidocq lives to serve!"

He opens his arms wide. As though he were about to embrace her and everything in the room. Squeeze the life out of it.

"You wouldn't have a pipe, would you?" he asks.

She shakes her head.

"My mistake. I could have sworn I smelled one."

"Arnaud keeps one around, of course. For when he's here."

"Of course." Then, as if the thought has just occurred to him: "Do you mind if I look at his? I'm in the market for a new one."

"Ah, what a pity, Monsieur. I can't remember where he—"

"Never mind!" he cries, reaching into a broken water pitcher and pulling out a length of briar pipe. He smiles as he waggles it between his fingers. He flares his nostrils. "Mm, still smoldering. Now that's what I call good tobacco."

Her chin is tucked all the way down to her collarbone, as though she's getting ready to charge. But all she says is:

"Arnaud will be so sorry to have missed you, Monsieur."

"Not half as sorry as . . ."

His eyes widen. Putting down the pipe, he steps round an overturned washbasin and pauses behind an old sheet-iron furnace, angled against the wall. Then, with a look of faint regret, he tips the furnace over.

The door swings open, and out tumbles a man. The sort of man who could fit inside a furnace: small and wiry and jointy, with scabbed elbows and gray skin and eyelids squeezed so close together that even astonishment can't drag them apart.

Vidocq gazes down at him with a dotard's grin. "Ah, Poulain. What a stroke of luck! Say, you wouldn't mind having a drink with us, would you?" He crooks his thumb toward me. "Me and my pal here? We've come to toast the new baby. You're not too busy? Well, come on, then."

CHAPTER 6

The Incident of the Hobnailed Boot

THERE IS NOTHING so sad, I've always thought, as wineshops in the middle of the afternoon. Or the women who run them. I submit to you the Widow Maltaise. A nest of white hair, uncertain in its provenance, woven into a large blue kerchief. A calico dress and a calico *face,* cottony with years. One eye droops low; the other draws itself imperiously high. The voice comes straight up from her feet, like coal from a seam.

"It's Vidocq again. Death of my trade."

He wraps his arms round her. "Ooh, I'll make it worth your while. Don't think I won't."

She fans us in the direction of a table. Minutes later: a carafe of blush, three pewter plates, and the remains of someone's veal, fringed with tooth marks. And, of course, her disapproval, settling over us in strands.

"Has to come here," she mutters. "Can't do his business at Pontmercy's. Always darkening my door . . ."

"Well, now, Poulain!" Vidocq cinches his arm round the man's tiny shoulder-ridges. "It's been too long, my friend! And how pale you are. Put some *wine* in the system, there's a good fellow."

A billiard table sits lost in shadows, one of the cues still cocked against the baize. On the bar there's a trough of snuff, lacquered over with spit. In the corner a cat, fumed in liver, nibbling on a rat bone.

"Wine's not bad," mumbles Vidocq. "Veal's a bit tough." From his mouth, he draws out a fragment of bone. "Maltaise must be leaving bits of herself in it. Now then, Poulain, I don't suppose you're familiar with a gentleman named Chrétien Leblanc."

"Should I be?"

"No, it's just—sorry, got something stuck in my—seems Monsieur Leblanc met a *final* sort of end last Sunday. No, don't look like that, I'm not saying *you* had anything to do with it. Things *happen* in Paris, I know that. Doctor, you finished with your wine? You're sure?"

He drinks this one at a more deliberate pace. And with about a third still left, he does something unexpected: lowers the glass beneath the plane of the table and, when he's sure Poulain isn't looking, tips the rest of the wine onto the floor.

"Here's my problem, Poulain. I've got this friend—Pomme Rouge, you know him? Over on the Rue de la Juiverie? Well, it seems yesterday morning Pomme Rouge was asked to fence a watch. Oh, I'm sorry, *purchase*. Not a very expensive watch, but then the watch's owner was not well off. He did have the wherewithal, though, to engrave his monogram on the case. *CXL*. Chrétien Xavier Leblanc."

Vidocq inclines his head, as though he were still sounding it in his mind's chamber.

"Well, you can imagine my shock when I hear that this owner of dead men's watches goes by the name of Poulain, alias Coubert, alias Lamotte. Yes, my friend, all *your* names. Popping up, as they will do. Why, it was enough to make me wonder if you had some—some *accidental* connection to the deeply unfortunate Monsieur Leblanc.

"And wasn't I relieved to learn you were already spoken for that evening? Oh, yes, I asked around. Two extremely reliable gentlemen placed you at Mère Bariole's on Sunday evening, from six onward. It *was* Bariole's, wasn't it, Poulain?"

The smaller man stretches out his legs, contemplates his feet.

"Well, now," Vidocq continues, "you can guess what an ass I felt like. Even *thinking* you were—well, I won't say it. But then my good friend here—oh, I'm sorry, have you met Dr. Carpentier? I know, he looks twelve, but believe me, he's one of the most feared men in Paris. His testimony *alone* has sent more than a dozen men to the gallows. They call him God's Third Eye, don't they, Doctor? No, don't blush, it's true. Well, Dr. Carpentier tells me that Monsieur Leblanc, the *ill-starred* Monsieur Leblanc, was likely killed—when was it, Doctor?— oh, that's right, early Sunday afternoon."

He pauses, as if the intelligence is still filtering through. Then, speaking in tones of deep abashment:

"And, Christ Almighty, didn't I feel even sillier! All this time, I was checking your whereabouts for Sunday evening, and it turns out the whole business went down in daylight." He raps himself on the head. "Knock knock! I say, Vidocq, is anybody home?" Chuckling, he slides his chair closer. "And the worst thing about it, my friend, is now there's no one to account for you. From, oh, let's say noon to three-thirty." He strokes the end of his nose, smiles crookedly. "But maybe you can do that for us."

I will later learn this from Vidocq: A man either confesses on the spot or after great resistance. There are two paths only, and Poulain takes the second.

"I was with Jeanne-Victoire," he says.

"Naturally."

"She'll back me up."

"Of course."

"I was napping, Monsieur. A man like me needs his rest."

"Working *nights* as you do." And as if to demonstrate his allegiance, Vidocq lets out a hippopotamus yawn. "Doctor," he says, rubbing his eyes, "do you still have that bag with you?"

What a surprise to find it coiled round my ankle.

"Just set it on the table, would you?" drawls Vidocq.

He grabs a hunk of snuff from the common fund and takes a stroll across the Widow Maltaise's creaking floorboards.

"Now it's an interesting thing," he says, circling back to us. "On the day in question, there was a fair amount of rain. Which, I don't need to tell you, leaves a bit of mud, eh?" He stares at Poulain, as if waiting for reassurance. "*Oceans* of mud. Now when I first made the acquaintance of the unfortunate Monsieur Leblanc, I noticed something rather curious. Not three feet from his person. Would you like to know what it was?"

"If you like."

"A footprint."

He takes another draw of snuff.

"Well, you know what they say about me, Poulain, I never forget a face. Or a footprint. *Yours* in particular. I checked my little file, just to be sure. *Poulain, Arnaud. Size: bantam. Footprint: also bantam. Right boot bears telltale mark, crescent-shaped, from where hobnails have come out.*"

Poulain folds his arms across his bird chest.

"Boots lose their nails," he says.

"They do."

"Footprints get washed away."

"They *do*. Yes, this one *would* have been washed away if I hadn't scooped it up. Every last bit of it. Why, a few hours in my office, it was hard as plaster."

Tickling his arm into the turnip bag, Vidocq draws out a square of black clay, rimmed with straw . . . stamped with a single boot, like the fossil of an ancient fish.

"Now," he says, all air and light. "If you'd be so good as to take your boot off."

In the end, Poulain is like the ruffians at Denoyes'. When commanded, he obeys. He can't see any other road.

"Ah, you see," says Vidocq, placing the boot in the clay impress. "Fits like a corset. And look, see there? The crescent—the exact shape. Yes, my friend, I believe we have a match."

Not a trace of smugness in him, I will give him that. He has the air of a church artisan admiring someone else's transept.

"The boot never lies, my friend. But then it never needs to. Put it back on, there's a good fellow. No, wait. Allow me to tie."

In a single swift motion, he laces Poulain's boot to the chair leg.

"No offense, my friend. It's just a little precaution we take. But you're still looking a bit pale. Hey, Mama Maltaise! Another carafe for my friend here!"

How slowly he pours this time around. As if the wine were the accretion of a single thought.

"Poulain," he says, pushing the glass gently toward him, "you're many things—believe me, I know *all* the things you are—but not a killer. Not yet."

Cupping his hand under Poulain's chin, he leans into him, eyes blazing.

"Tell us how it went," he whispers. "And maybe old Vidocq can find something in his bag of mercy, eh?"

From somewhere in the dark recesses, I hear the Widow Maltaise's cat, luxuriously bathing its paws.

"I was lucky," says Poulain. "That's all."

"How do you mean?"

"I mean I just happened to be there. Minding my own business, if you must know. Helping myself to a muffin cart."

"Your own, of course."

Poulain's eyes squeeze even tighter. "I believe it was left behind by someone."

"Go on."

"And then I heard some noises, all right? In the alley off Rue des Maçons."

"What sort of noises?"

"Oh, it was—I don't know—shit-being-knocked-about noises. I thought I'd have a look, in case there was action."

"And that's where you first saw Leblanc."

After careful consideration, he gives a nod.

"What was he doing?" Vidocq asks.

"Getting his stuffing taken out."

"He wasn't yelling? Or calling out? Most men would have, I think."

"He'd have liked to, I'm sure. They had a gag in his mouth."

"*They*," Vidocq says. "More than one."

"Two."

"Recognize them?"

"I should say not," says Poulain. "You won't find me consorting with amateurs."

"What makes you think they were?"

"Fuck's sake, they went through his pockets, but they didn't take any money! Just a blessed envelope. I mean, why cut down the tree if you're not going to shake the branches?"

"Tell us what happened next."

I'm not sure I can convey the thing Poulain's lips do. A twisting, a deformation—we'll call it a smile.

"I yelled for the police," he says.

Eyes shining, Vidocq pats the smaller man's hand.

"Having already made sure there *weren't* any police."

"'Course."

"And it worked? Your little ruse?"

"Bastards tore off like hares. Blood still on their paws. Didn't even stop to take the man's shoes. That's why I say they weren't professionals."

Vidocq stares at the cue still lying on the billiard table. "So the two men are gone," he says. "The coast is clear. Down comes Poulain."

"I was only going to stay a minute. See what I could find on him."

"And you took a watch. A wallet, maybe."

Poulain shrugs.

"His clothes, too?" asks Vidocq.

"Wasn't time."

"Ha! Someone horning in, eh?"

"No," he says. "Nothing like that."

And for the first time, something seems to trouble the flat canvas of Poulain's face. With the faintest shudder, he leans toward Vidocq and whispers:

"Bastard went and grabbed me."

"*Who* grabbed you?"

"Why, the dead one. Who else?"

CHAPTER 7

From Beyond the Grave

CAREFULLY, VIDOCQ POURS himself another glass. And this time—I'm watching—he drinks the whole glass. With a voice as level as an altar, he says:

"To me, that would imply your dead man was not so very dead."

"A couple yards short," Poulain allows.

"He grabbed you where? Round the ankle?"

"Both ankles, I think. Wouldn't have guessed he had the strength in him."

"Mm."

"Damned inconveniencing."

"Yes."

"And him babbling the whole time."

Vidocq pours himself another glass. And this one he doesn't drink. Just sets it on the table.

"Babbling? I thought he was gagged."

"I took the gag off, didn't I? See if he had any gold in his mouth."

"And what exactly was he babbling?"

"Christ, I don't know. Something about . . ." Poulain's eyes spring open. "*He's here*. He said somebody or other was *here*. Said it over and over, like a fucking parrot."

The silence, the essential silence of the wineshop pours round us once more. This, I realize, is when you've given Vidocq the most. When you shut him up completely.

"He didn't tell you *who* was here, did he?"

"No. And I wasn't about to stick around and get a name, thank you very much."

Vidocq nods. He nods again, at half the speed.

"Very well, Poulain, you have this *body* hanging off you. What next?"

"Well, what else? Pry him loose and take off."

"Ah."

"You think I want him getting a read on me? Saint Peter chucks 'em back sometimes, doesn't he? He turns *this* one back, it's La Force for me."

Vidocq looks up at the ceiling, as though any minute a body might come crashing through the timbers.

"The money," he says. "From the wallet and the watch. What'd you spend it on?"

"Ran through it at Mère Bariole's. Me and Agnès had ourselves some sport."

And then an unexpected thought draws his voice into a new, a wondering register: "I should've bought me some new boots."

"Nothing for the baby?" asks Vidocq.

"Why?"

Vidocq opens his mouth to answer, but the Widow Maltaise is glaring down at him now, lambent with rage.

"Finish your business, Vidocq. Or I call the police."

There it is: the strange mystique that surrounds him. He is considered *apart* from everything—even the Prefecture that nominally employs him. The law is one thing, Vidocq another.

He pats her arm. He clucks in her ear.

"Just a few more minutes, my sweet. Oh, and the veal was an astonishment to the senses, did I mention?"

By now, Poulain has had time to work out a new tone. He's the beggar at the gates of Saint-Sulpice.

"See here, Monsieur," he says. "I've been straight with you, haven't I? Answered everything you asked? Seems to me I shouldn't get any time for this."

And Vidocq, he is now the designated representative of Saint-Sulpice, sad in his duty.

"Oh, I see your point, Poulain, I do. But there is the little matter of you stealing. From a nearly dead man. And confound it, you've had such a busy career, I'm not sure Monsieur Henry can look the other way this time." He pours the thief one last glass. "I'll certainly speak to him, if you like. Tell him what a help you were."

Poulain stares into his glass, unskeining the path of his future. And having followed it as far as he can, he scratches his chin and rubs his scalp and looks up, dark-eyed, hard-mouthed.

"Can I keep my pipe?"

"Of *course,* my friend, of course. And I'll tell you what, on Sundays, I'll send over Agnès. Or else Lise. *She's* good for cheering a fellow up, isn't she? And you know what else? I'll look in on Jeanne-Victoire when I can. And the baby."

"You can have 'em," growls Poulain. "That slut's more than a man can bear."

Something stirs now behind Vidocq's eyes as he stares the thief down.

"She always spoke highly of you, Arnaud."

WHO CAN SAY why, at this moment, I should feel obliged to speak—for the first time since coming here?

"The baby," I say. "Tell me the baby's name."

Scowling, Poulain spits it out like a seed.

"Arnaudine."

The sight of our faces carves the scowl deeper.

"It was *her* idea. She couldn't give me a boy, so she figured 'Arnaudine' was next best. She's soft that way, if you must know. I always say it'll be the death of her."

"Very wise," says Vidocq.

He pushes back his glass and staggers out of his chair—and, before anyone can draw another breath, tips Poulain's chair over.

The thief, bound at the ankle, meets the floor with every last bone in his body. A stifled cry, a tremor of doubt. Vidocq stands over him, serene.

"Skulls are soft, too, aren't they, Poulain? You'd be amazed."

And then, stepping over the thief's supine figure, he graces me with a smile.

"That's enough for today, Doctor."

CHAPTER 8

A Spy Unmasked

IT'S NEARLY SIX in the evening when Vidocq brings me home. He has borrowed from Allard an overcoat with a triple cape. From a secondhand clothes dealer, he has acquired (without in any obvious way paying for it) a hat, broken near the band. He has run some spit through his hair.

What better signal that we are returning to civilization? To my own, my native clime, though I no longer recognize it so well. I turn the corner of the Rue Neuve-Sainte-Geneviève, I pass the old condemned well where Bardou used to sit, I hear the rhythmic grunts of Monsieur Tripot's pigs, running loose in the gutters. I stand on the front step of my very own home, and still I can't help thinking I've taken a wrong turn.

But then the door is swung open by Charlotte, parched and freckled, and there can no longer be any doubt.

"He's home!" she calls back down the hall. "Madame Carpentier, he's home!"

Mother is hanging back by the drawing room doors: a shivery black spectacle in her tulle cap and woolen petticoat. The skirt has been refashioned from an old dress. The slippers have long pulled away from her feet, they seem bound to her now only by habit. Her hands form a funnel round her mouth. She says:

"Oh."

"Monsieur Hector." Charlotte is charging toward me. "Are you—"

"He is quite unharmed, ladies," answers Vidocq, stepping out from behind. "As you can see."

I will never be certain which part of him Mother fastens onto first. The shabby hat? The tufts of spit-slicked hair or the bullying breast? I tend to think it's the confounding bulk of him—the *hole* he makes in his surroundings.

"I was about to send for the police," she says in a thin voice.

"But there was no need, Madame! The police have already sent for your Hector." Vidocq takes the back of my neck in a loose, proprietary grip. "This very afternoon, your son has demonstrated exceptional mettle in an inquiry of unspeakable urgency."

"Inquiry?"

"He would be only too glad to tell you, I'm sure, but he has been sworn to secrecy. By the Prefect himself."

"By the—"

"Oh, he's got a brilliant mind, your son. All of Paris seems to chant his praise! Just the other evening, you know, I was passing an hour or two in the library of the Duchesse de Duras, and she said to me—perhaps you know the Duchess, Madame?—she pulled me by the sleeve, and in that charmingly raspy voice of hers, she said, *'You must introduce me to the marvelous Dr. Carpentier!'*"

It is those last two words that change the tenor of the conversation. For Mother is even less accustomed to hearing me called Doctor than I am. Her mouth shrinks into a black line.

Vidocq pauses to puzzle out his offense. "A thousand pardons, Madame. I neglected to introduce myself. I am Vidocq."

It's quite something, the bow he tenders her. Not the gently top-pling head of your average Parisian gentleman but something explo-sive and battle-bred. (I will later learn he was a sergeant-major.) It all but finishes off poor Charlotte, who is rubbing her ears in wonder.

"This is your daughter, Madame?" asks Vidocq.

"Our maid," says Mother, in a voice stiff as whalebone.

"Ah, I see loveliness is a prerequisite of living *chez* Carpentier." His lips graze the knuckles of the young woman's hand. "What pretty fin-gers. Like precious corals strewn across a beach."

Charlotte's face, I should say, is always a kind of mottled coral, from bending over fires and clambering up stairs. At this moment, though, something violet bleeds up through the strata of skin. Mother, no fool herself, steps forward and, in the tone used by elderly marquises with dustmen, thanks Vidocq for bringing her son home to her.

"Why, think nothing of it!" he cackles. "It was my dearest—"

"Good day, Monsieur."

He's still there when the door closes on him—scratching his ribs, twisting his mouth.

"So nice to make your acquaintance," I hear him say from the other side.

There is nothing shining in Mother's face, but there seldom is. I can recall her laughing only four times in my life. (Four times more than my father.) Hers is a face for storing time in. Even her limestone-colored eyes, which must once have been beautiful, seem layered with years in some precise and biologically determinable way, like a shelf of sedimentary rock.

"We had no idea where you were," she says.

"I know."

"You might have left a note."

"I am very sorry, Mother."

"As if I don't have enough to do without wondering if you're dead or dying or I don't know what. As if I don't . . ."

She seizes a shawl from the nearest hook, and her voice, when it comes back, is low and snappish, like something prodded out of its corner.

"Well, take your coat off, for goodness' sake. Naturally, your boots are filthy. Never mind, there's no time to brush them. Our guests are seated for dinner."

FROM THE MOMENT we first had to take in boarders, Mother persisted in calling them *guests*. Behind this affectation, I've always believed, lies a thin dry vein of hope. Guests *leave*, don't they?

Whereas the three young men crowded round our dining table give every evidence of staying. Forever, possibly. In the beginning, Mother had vowed never to take students because she had heard they eat too much bread. But in the Latin Quarter, you don't get much choice in the matter. Students are as numerous as the stars, as ineradicable as rats.

These three arrived in a pack of their own: stout comrades from the École de Droit. They immediately took the liberty of calling my mother Mama, a name she loathes but feels obliged to answer to. *Their* names are unimportant. (I'll forget them, anyway, as soon as I'm gone.) Let us call them by their defining traits, beginning at the bottom of the power chain with Lapin. Rabbity face, rabbity soul. Next, Rosbif, named for his favorite meat (too expensive to be served here) and for the way he dines on the flesh of others. Finish with Nankeen, named for the elephant-leg nankeen trousers he sports in the summer, with stirrups of rust-colored braid. The son of a Rouen magistrate, Nankeen is the wealthiest of our boarders, which means that, for 1,500 francs a year, he gets to sleep in my father's old bedroom (with whomever he has brought back with him that evening). Also, he gets to take his coffee in the courtyard, beneath the lindens.

Tonight, the three students are engaged in the preprandial ritual of baiting Mother's fourth tenant: a retired professor of botany, fully eight decades along. The students call him Father Time. This is not an honorific. Father Time wears a ragged necktie and polishes his shoes with egg yolk. For the last year, he has been selling off his orchid volumes, one by one, to pay the rent and even so is two months behind. Mother might have evicted him long ago, but he is an old friend of the family, although neither he nor my mother ever speaks of days past.

"Father Time!" shouts Rosbif. "You've got something in your beard, old boy."

"What'd you—I didn't quite—"

In addition to his other infirmities, Father Time is nearly deaf. He used to bring an ear trumpet to the table, but the students took to tossing croutons into it.

"There!" cries Rosbif. "I've got it! Why, I do believe it's a grub. Imagine, gentlemen, a whole colony of fauna living in Father Time's beard."

"Call the exterminator," says Lapin.

"No, too hasty, my friend! We must call in France's greatest scientists. There are species here entirely unknown to man."

"Charlotte," says Mother, gently unfolding her napkin. "The pears look delicious."

This is her way of changing a subject. It is also her way of cloaking her own economies, for she is most lavish in praising what has cost her the least. The pears, for instance, cost two liards apiece. The potatoes were bought (slightly rotten) for ten sous. The mutton she personally haggled down to a franc and fifty centimes. She will praise them in that order.

"Thank you, Madame."

Charlotte's voice is barely audible as she circuits the table. How distracted she is! She must still be feeling Vidocq's lips on her hand. I watch her wandering out of the room, only to wander right back in. I watch her pour cream into Lapin's wineglass. And when she tries to take my plate before I've even started eating, I finally have to tap her on the wrist.

She gives me a private grin, and I give her one back. Because I don't know what she's about to do.

"Monsieur Hector," she announces, "has had quite the adventure today."

One by one, the three students tilt up their faces, set their knives down. The room grows still.

Mother moves swiftly.

"Hector has been hounded for an entire afternoon," she says, "by a perfectly dreadful man. Who smells of spirits and bear grease and I can't even say what all else."

A few more seconds pass as the students decide whether this resolves the question or merely suspends it. They are just reaching for their knives again when Charlotte's stage whisper stops them in midmotion.

"Vidocq."

I see the makings of a smile on Rosbif's wine-tinctured lips.

"Not the scoundrel!" he cries.

"Why, he's not!" Charlotte swats the back of his head with her apron. "He's the terror of criminals everywhere, he's—he's the reason we can sleep with our throats bare."

"Oh, that's good! He's the last man in the world I'd trust with my throat."

"The very last," agrees Lapin.

"My dearest Charlotte, has no one ever told you? Your precious Vidocq is nothing more than a petty criminal."

"It's a lie."

"May God strike me down if it is. Why, I tell you he's been a cherished guest at some of France's finest penal institutions."

An irked look wells out of Mother's eyes. "That can't be," she says. "He's some sort of police creature, isn't he?"

"*Creature*," says Nankeen, adjusting the spectacles on his Greek nose. "How well you put it, Mama Carpentier. It's the usual story, I'm afraid. A blackguard chafes at prison confinement and volunteers his services as police spy, a profession which demands only effrontery and a complete want of conscience. Small wonder Vidocq should prove so well suited to it."

"I'll tell you what I heard," says Rosbif, chiming in. "Before he was done, he peached out every last one of his friends, just to curry favor with his new masters."

"Peached out," repeats Mother, squinting. "I don't know what that means."

"It means *betrayed*, Mama Carpentier."

And then—from nowhere, it seems—a low smoky voice slides across the table.

"Last I heard, betraying criminals was a good thing."

We turn and find Father Time mouthing into his plate. Unaware, maybe, that anything slipped out.

In a quiet voice, Nankeen asks:

"What was that?"

"Nothing."

"I'm sorry, I thought I heard you speak."

"It was nothing."

"Are you quite sure?"

"Yes."

Behind the screen of her napkin, Mother is whispering.

"Hector, is all this true?"

"I've no idea," I mutter.

With a peal of triumph, I would almost call it joy, she cries:

"I knew there was something not right! Didn't I, Charlotte?"

"And now," says Nankeen, "this saintly Vidocq has clawed his way to the top of the police hierarchy. And if one required any more proof of how really cunning he is, one need only remark on the startling development that has been bruited in all the papers. This Vidocq, if you can believe it, has founded a brigade of plainclothes police. It is known as the Brigade de Sûreté, and it is composed entirely of thieves, deserters, and scoundrels—the human offal who have ever been his closest companions." He smiles into his lace cuff. "One can't help but admire the diabolical brazenness of the man. With the full consent of the Comte Anglès and Monsieur Henry, he has succeeded in blurring every last boundary between good and evil. It's impossible anymore to tell the law enforcers from the law breakers."

"From what I hear," says Lapin, "he splits the crooks' take with them. And when they won't pay up, he pitches them in jail."

"Oh, Vidocq is simply exemplary of his kind," answers Nankeen. "Scientific studies have quite conclusively demonstrated that the criminal mind is incapable of being rehabilitated. You may dress up a rogue, you may give him a job. Drag him to mass, drive him down the Champs-Élysées. He will always revert to his old ways." A note of tragedy floats into the monotone. "It's incontrovertible, I'm afraid."

"Hector," says Mother, once again whispering behind her napkin, *"if you ever allow that man in our house again, I don't know what."*

"But he wasn't . . ."

I'm about to say he wasn't in the house. And then I'm stopped by the memory of him—*here*—bestriding this very chair. Swearing and glugging wine and spitting out macaroons and half-eaten potatoes. Just the thought of it tickles my lips apart. I think I may even be on the verge of laughter when I hear Nankeen's voice, ever so faintly curdling.

"Monsieur Hector. You haven't yet told us what this Vidocq fellow wanted with you."

I clear my throat. I clear it again.

"I'm afraid I'm not at liberty."

He doesn't pursue the matter. He doesn't need to. Rosbif and Lapin gladly take up the chase.

"Not at liberty, he says!"

"Come now, Monsieur Hector!"

"Must we drag it out of you?"

"The royal family needs a new physician, is that it?"

"Ha! Everyone knows the king's gout is getting worse."

"I'm sure once King Louis has had a dose of—I'm sorry, Monsieur Hector, what's that business you're looking into? It always escapes me."

I explain that my research would likely be of no interest to them. In a voice of soft astonishment, Nankeen cries:

"Now why do you say that? Don't you know you're the talk of the École? Why, my intern friends inform me that Monsieur Hector, when at last he bursts the trammels of his laboratory, will *astonish* the world with his findings." Puzzlement creases his brow as he turns to Rosbif. "They *do* say that, don't they?"

"Oh, yes. Great things are expected of Monsieur Hector."

"And aren't we fortunate to have gotten him at the ground level? We must be sure to record all our impressions for the sake of future biographers."

It's not that I lack for defenders. There is Charlotte, for example, who has been standing all the while in the doorway, glowing like a coal.

"For your information," she declares, "Monsieur Hector was praised just the other evening. By a very important personage."

"And who would that be?" asks Nankeen, his eyes ghoulishly glittering.

Too late to stop her. She squares her shoulders, charges.

"The Duchesse de Duras!"

In the face of such laughter, the chandelier over the table actually rattles. The air wrinkles round, and the curtains dance in tune. I sit in the heart of the noise, where, if one can attain the right level of abstraction, everything becomes quite still. Tonight, however, I glance up and, to my surprise, find Father Time looking back. A second or two, no more, but there flashes between us—well, call it a shared condition.

"Hector," says Mother. "I don't know where that horrible man took you, but you smell like a sewer or worse."

Stunned, I raise my cuff to my nose, and the aroma of Vidocq comes coiling through my sinuses. That strange, *animate* scent.

He's marked me, I think, sinking back into my chair.

And in the same instant comes the overtone of Leblanc's dying breath.

He's here.

IT'S A LITTLE after nine o'clock, and I'm taking my evening walk. The same walk I take every night, as Vidocq has pointed out, at the same time. Around the block and no farther.

Tonight, it's true, I briefly consider changing the pattern. When I come down the steps, I could decide to turn left instead of right. I could take the Rue des Postes south to the Rue de l'Arbalète. Or take the Vieille Estrapade de Fourcy toward the Panthéon. If I were really feeling bold, I could walk east all the way to the Jardin du Roi. Cross the river into the Faubourg-Saint-Antoine! Why not?

In the end, I do what I always do.

I smell like myself now.

There's a moon: a half-nibbled peach. Patches of pocked sky, too, where the clouds have yawned clear. For the first time in weeks, it seems, the higher architecture is declaring itself, and as the plaster housefronts and the piles of garbage rear up on every side, I'm visited with that old feeling of walking through an alpine pass.

And then, as if I had personally commissioned them, the day's events etch themselves across the canvas. I see the baby on the chafing dish. The widow Maltaise in her blue kerchief, and Poulain, flopped in the sawdust, his boot still tied to his chair. And Mozart and greenbottle flies and the veined blue marble of Chrétien Leblanc. One by one, they file past. Like things that happened to a living man.

16 THERMIDOR YEAR II

Have met consid difficulty in getting Prisoner's cell cleaned. Tower guards say lingering too long in pestilential air wd be fatal. Refuse to go inside, assist in any way. (One confided in me that they are afraid of being branded royalist sympathizers.)

Have relayed my concerns to Barras. This A.M., spoke with officials of the Commune. Informed them that Prisoner's health—survival—depends on hygienic surroundings. No amt of physic can overcome contagion. V. insistent on this point. Was told to await Commune's decision.

17 THERMIDOR

Word has come. Commune has authorized 2 men to undertake cleaning of Prisoner's room. Men are to be duly appointed reps of French people, discreet, politically pure, etc.

22 THERMIDOR

8 A.M.: appointed cleaners arrived w. buckets, mops, lge quantities of soap. Soon realized they wd need more.

Dust, dirt, excrement everywhere. Mattresses damp all the way thru; atmosphere fetid—poisonous. Work lasted 1 full day—extremely arduous—required freq rest intervals, occasional vomiting. Both men at var times bitten by rats, fleas, spiders. Everything is alive in this room, said one. Companion was heard to say he'd seen cleaner sewers.

Prisoner remained in cell thruout. No movement observed until section of shutter removed fm window—first time in 6 mos—upon which he turned twd light. Stood for some moments w. sun on face, eyes half closed. When asked if light was painful, Prisoner answered in affirmative. But declined to remove himself.

23 THERMIDOR

Commissaries have at last agreed to bath for Prisoner. I sent cook's assistant, young Caron, for tepid water, bathed him myself. Sent for Mother Mathieu (mngr of Père Lefèvre's tavern) to cut & comb hair. Hair full of scurf, reached to shoulders, had not been washed in many mos. Exceptionally tender—combing v. painful for him. Mother Mathieu able to clip Prisoner's toenails & fingernails, which were length of claws, consistency of horn.

Garments (entirely infested) removed & burned, replaced w. entirely new linen suit, including pantaloons, waistcoat, jacket.

At end of day, undertook 1st complete examination of Prisoner. Genrl condition v. shocking. Head droops. Lips discolored, cheeks hollow, v. pale w. greenish tinge. Limbs extremely wasted, disproportionately long in comparison to torso. Stomach enlarged. Suffers fm acute diarrhea. Extremely sensitive to noise. Averse to speaking.

Body rife w. ulcers, yellow & blue, most pronounced on neck, wrists, knees. Have attempted to lance & dress but this occasioned grt pain in him. Will endeavor to do more in days to follow.

Most pressing concern: knee. Swollen to twice normal size. Color unhealthy. Prisoner unable to walk w/o extreme pain.

Prognosis: v. poor. Am preparing full medical report for Barras. Hopeful that, w. aggressive course of intervention, Prisoner's condition can be arrested. New environment wd be v. helpful. Have taken liberty of removing surplus bed fm room of Prisoner's sister so he may sleep in greater comfort.

Was forced to reprimand 1 of Temple guards, who, upon entering Prisoner's room, shouted, Back in your corner, Capet. Explained that, from now on, Prisoner was to be called Monsieur. Guard remonstrated, said there are no more "monsieurs," we are all "citizens" now, etc. I was insistent on point, citing authority invested in me by Barras.

Upon hearing my request, Prisoner observed that "Monsieur" was too distressing to him, begged not to be called by that title. When asked which he wd prefer, Prisoner said he wd answer only to "Wolf Cub." When it was pointed out that Prisoner was not animal but boy, Prisoner was seen to smile, for first time. Appeared to pity me greatly.

He asked then how old he was? Nine, I said. Yes, that's right, he said.

Will make it a point, in future entries, to refer to Prisoner as Charles.

CHAPTER 9

A Journey to Luxembourg

FOUR DAYS HAVE passed since last I saw Vidocq, but still I feel him. Every time I take my walk around the block or stroll over to the Rue d'École de Médecine or sneak a newspaper out of Le Père Bonvin, it's *his* voice, insinuating in my ear. . . .

I could set my watch by you.

And then on Friday morning, something knocks me out of my accustomed orbit. A letter. On lilac stationery with flaking gilt edges and a coat of arms indifferently embossed at the top—paper so brittle I don't trust myself to hold it.

Dr. Carpentier—

Recent events surrounding the late M. Leblanc compel me to write. I wonder if I might entreat you to call upon me tomorrow morning at ten o'clock. You may find me in my apartment at No. 17, Rue Férou.

Failing any further communication from you, I shall await the
pleasure of your company. Your discretion is earnestly requested.

Baronne de Préval

The name seems as brittle as the paper. A baroness!

My first thought is that Nankeen and the other boarders are having me on. My second thought—and it's the thought I've been having from the moment Vidocq came into my life—*You've got the wrong man.*

More than that, the wrong class. The closest I've ever come to aristocrats is Sunday afternoons on the Champs-Élysées. Now that the Bourbons are back, it's the best kind of sport, sauntering through the elms while the coupés sweep past. Horses with rosettes in their ears, drivers in wigs and cravats, and through the windows, snatches of powdered skin, a Chinese ivory handle, an uncinching mouth-bud. The notion that one of these women might stop the carriage and usher me in with her superbly enervated arm seems as likely as the King asking me to cure his gout.

In short, there are reasons to doubt this promotion. Look first at the man who brought me the message. Not the usual liveried footman but a common porter, older than Mont Blanc, snarling at the few sous of gratuity I drop in his palm.

Next, look at the address. The Rue Férou, a quiet little spoke off the wheel of the Luxembourg Gardens, far removed from the thrum of court life. What business does a baroness have living there?

All afternoon, all evening, I limn the many reasons for declining the invitation. By the next morning, I've accepted. I even know why. It's the last thing Vidocq would expect of me.

PARIS IS FOGBOUND this morning. The smokes of last night's fires, woven with sewer fumes and the evaporations of three weeks' rain, lie in sepia drifts on the mansards, in the gutters, along the trees and

wagons and vendor booths. Thickly scalloped and all the same moving—*renewing*—as if the city itself had been caught in the very act of
breathing.

The only discernible parts of no. 17, Rue Férou, are a façade
of rough yellow-daubed stone . . . three small windows with blinds
drowsily lowered . . . and a wrought-iron knocker carved in the shape
of a winking satyr. The knocker won't move, so I have to pound on the
door, which is answered by an old concierge, dressed in black merino
and grinning like a procuress.

"Dr. Carpentier, yes! She's expecting you."

Taking a candle, she leads me up two flights of stairs—an act for
which her body is deeply unqualified. She has to *haul* it forward, dragging each leg like a valise.

"You were able to find the way? Oof. Mornings like these, I can
barely see my own nose. Grrm. The Baroness will be so glad to see
you. I'm always telling her, you know, invite some *young* people for a
change. Fwoof. Much better than those old goats in their—kroomp—
blue stockings and their dirty vests. Always *mooning*, aren't they? The
old days. Pwiff. I say what's done is done, bring on the next. I've always been that way. Ploonf."

She stops at last before a door of besmirched oak. A knock and then
a bearlike roar.

"Madame la Baronne! Your visitor is here!"

Then, by some prearranged ritual, she turns the handle, opens the
door three hairs wide, and backs slowly away, her gasping chest bent
parallel to the floor.

I see worn red tiles under a threadbare carpet. An old round table, a
low sideboard topped by a hanging mirror. A bench, unanchored. And
a short-backed armchair, the type of grim, cured artifact that might
have been lifted from a Breton widow's cottage.

A magnificent woman is sitting there.

No, let me be clearer. A magnificent woman *was* sitting there. She
was wearing peach blossoms in her hair and a gown of loose lawn to

accentuate her glorious bosom, and she had doeskin gloves of a paradisiacal whiteness.

But that was thirty years ago. Today, the white has sickened into yellow; the lawn has given way to a black damask dress, no longer fashionable; the fichu has been mended so many times there is almost nothing left to mend.

And that once-handsome, that still-handsome face has hardened into something unyielding and curatorial, like the tablet of a lost civilization.

"Dr. Carpentier." A lightly tickled contralto. "How good of you to come."

She rises from her peasant's chair and offers me her gloved hand. Not knowing what to do, I close it round. With a hint of charity, she draws herself free.

"You must excuse me," she says. "You are not quite the man I was expecting."

I am going to ask what she *was* expecting, but I'm stopped by the thing I missed on my first canvassing: the spectacle of her eyes. One brown, one blue—*borrowed*, I would almost conceive, from two different women.

"Would you care for some tea, Doctor?"

She serves it herself in porcelain that, I am relieved to see, was not made by convicts. She tells me . . . well, I'm not conscious of much more than the music of her voice. I'm dimly aware of the concussion of spoons . . . a settee, a sisal rug . . . and finally a natural history cabinet, empty except for a few seashells and a line of red morocco bindings.

"Ah, you are coveting my library," she says in an ironical tone. "Those are the memoirs of my late husband, the Baron. He was ambassador to Berlin under Louis the Sixteenth."

Not knowing how to answer this, I say nothing, and this proves to be the very signal she was waiting for. Setting her teacup down, she folds her hands in her lap and, with a conscientious and abiding air, as if she were showing visitors round a house, begins to speak. And all the facts that should have been elicited after days, even weeks of small talk and trust building come tumbling out now in a helpless profusion.

"We lost everything, of course, during the Revolution. The Jacobins nationalized our lands, *that* much we were expecting, but then most of my jewels were lost on the way to Warsaw, and the Baron made rather a hash of the money we had left. He made a rather poor émigré, given how accustomed he was to travel. *Voluntary* exile was one thing, he used to say, involuntary quite another. He chafed, poor thing. Always intriguing to come back *here*, where he was least wanted."

She picks up her cup, rests it briefly on her underlip.

"Intrigues, I am sad to say, cost money. At least *his* always did."

With a rush of undercoats, she rises. Opens the cabinet with a scant pressure of hand, strokes the morocco bindings.

"This is what's left of his estate. A life in ten volumes. To the end, he was persuaded that someone would publish it." She takes the leftmost volume in her hand, holds it out to me. "*This* one might be to your taste, Doctor. It follows the Baron from his nativity in Toulon to his brief and, if I may say, unexceptional term as *intendant* of the Limousin." She rubs the spine with her knuckles. "I find it is the only volume I can bear to read myself. The others fall a little too near to home. Why, good morning, puss-puss!"

I feel it before I see it: a friction against my trouser leg. Then an unstable spectrum of black and white and orange, bounding into the Baroness's open arms.

"Is puss-puss just waking up? What a sleepy puss it is! It's the fog, isn't it? Yes, puss-puss loves the fog, doesn't he? Come see, can you *see*?"

In the shadows of the sconce light, they become, briefly, a unitary organism: limbs coiled toward a common purpose, murmurs twining with mewls.

"I'm afraid I must pose an indelicate question," she says.

It's some time before I realize she is talking to me. Her voice hasn't quite come back to its human register.

"If you like," I stammer.

"Were you followed?"

"No."

Such a ring of conviction in my voice, and the truth is I have no clue. I'm still getting used to the idea that I'm worth following.

"It is my turn to be indelicate, Madame la Baronne."

"By all means."

"What possible connection could you have to Monsieur Leblanc?"

With manifest regret, she sets down the cat, and in that moment, I have—for the first time—the full dint of her attention. I fairly blanch before it. The smile alone, whetted against a million drawing rooms and antechambers.

"Doctor, I find myself longing uncharacteristically for exercise. Would you do me the honor of escorting me?"

THE FOG HAS begun to lift from the Luxembourg Gardens, but everything above our heads is still shrouded. The statuary. The fountains. The palace itself, where the Chamber of Peers—dried-up remnants of old monarchies and empires—make the rattling sounds of coffined men. Even the canopies of the plane trees have been sheared away, leaving only the trunks, damp and scarred, lining our path like battle trophies.

For someone who takes little exercise, the Baroness has a rapid step. I have to quicken my own to keep pace with her. Before long, though, our feet are moving together in a companionable rhythm—I could almost believe we've been meeting like this for generations, wearing out a trough in the gravel.

"You're still a young man," she says at last. "Twenty-five, perhaps?"

"Twenty-six."

She nods, abstractedly.

"It was nearly that many years ago I met Chrétien Leblanc. A summer afternoon in the Stare Miosto in Warsaw. I was dining out of doors—a bowl of *krupnik*, I remember—and I looked up, and there he was, in his blue stockings and this rather faded frock coat. He was *watching* my soup, the way a cat watches a rabbit. In spite of myself, I was touched."

Her gloved hand exerts a barely perceptible pressure on my left arm.

"Leblanc was an émigré, too, in his own way. Lacking the curse of a title, he had weathered it out longer than most of us, but he, too, was obliged to leave Paris before long. In a hurry. He was wearing that look we all had at first, as though someone had dragged us into one of Montgolfier's balloons and tumbled us out before we'd quite landed. He was still finding his balance when I met him." She steps carefully round a puddle. "We fell into conversation. I liked his manners, and by the time he had finished my *krupnik* for me, I had formally engaged him."

Even through the fog, I can see where we are walking: along the parapet of the Pépinière, near the Rue de l'Ouest. I can hear the uproar of sparrows and woodpeckers and linnets.

"My husband left behind a great financial ruin," says the Baroness. "I was correspondingly obliged to dismiss our servants. Leblanc was good enough to stay on for some time, and when he could no longer afford to, he continued to visit me at regular intervals, simply to see how I was faring. I rather think he kept me alive."

A tiny grunt as she slackens her pace.

"It was Leblanc who persuaded me to come back to Paris with the Bourbons. 'Bonaparte is gone,' he assured me. 'You may be happy once more.' He overestimated me, I'm afraid. But I did consent, if only to please him. My one condition was that he find me a place as far as possible from my old life."

With a gesture as eloquently foreshortened as any by Mademoiselle Mars, she sketches her present environs.

"Here I am," she says.

"I am sorry for your trials, Baroness."

"You needn't be, Doctor. Many have endured far worse. And there is something to be said, after all these years, for simply being alive. At any rate, you cannot have come here to lavish pity on an old fossil like me."

"I still don't know why I've come, Madame."

Keeping her left foot still, she executes a slow pivot with the right—training her eyes in every direction.

"A week ago Wednesday," she says, "Leblanc came to me in a most agitated condition. He told me he had come into possession of a particular object, and in order to authenticate it, he required someone—shall we say someone of a certain *estate*. However fallen."

"What was this object?"

Whether she hears me or not, I can't say, for she quickly tacks on.

"Having satisfied himself that the object in question was authentic, Leblanc told me he required someone else to make a further identification. Toward that end, he set about locating a Dr. Carpentier in the Rue Neuve-Sainte-Geneviève."

"He never reached me."

Her slippered foot sketches a circle round a shorn-off robin's wing.

"I thought as much," she says.

She looks at me now, her blue and brown eyes gleaming with their opposed intelligences.

"Doctor, I am by no means an exemplary woman. I have wished evil on many people in life, but I would gladly call up every last flame of hell if I could be certain that Leblanc's killers were on the pyre."

"May I ask, Madame, how you learned of Monsieur Leblanc's death?"

She looks at me a while longer. Gives her lower lip a soft bite.

"Leblanc had a habit of visiting me every Monday morning, precisely at ten. He was regular as the dew that way. Monday last, he failed to show. Indeed, he sent no word of any kind. It was most unlike him. Having failed to find him at his lodgings, I did what any Parisian might do. I took myself straight to the morgue. There I gave the concierge a very close description of Leblanc and, at the cost of a few sous, was led to the"—she stops—"to the gentleman in question. Doctor," she says, "would you mind if we sat?"

There is a bench not ten feet off. With my handkerchief—my only handkerchief—I wipe it dry for her. She nods her thanks and drops onto the bench by scarcely visible degrees, her spine never once unbending. She sets her parasol alongside her. She examines her gloves. She says:

"Doctor, I wonder if you quite know where you're treading."

"No," I answer. "I never do. You may see from the condition of my boots."

She resists the temptation to look down, but something unexpectedly warm brews from those strange irises.

"It would be pleasant to trust you," she says.

"I don't yet know what I'm to be trusted with."

And that's the last thing either of us says for some five minutes. A curious thing happens, though. As we sit there, the fog begins to pull apart, like an emulsion dissolving into its constituents, and I realize, with a small shudder, that we are sharing this park with other human beings.

But what is there to dread about *these* specimens? A grisette, slumped halfway off a bench. A convent-school girl and her grandfather, sharing cheese and brown bread. A pair of law students. In normal weather, I would scarcely have remarked on any of them. This morning, there is something miraculous about their very ordinariness.

I say:

"He's here."

The Baroness's face turns an inch toward mine.

"Those were Leblanc's last words," I tell her. "He was announcing someone's arrival. Whose?"

And rather than meet my eye, she stares at a space just to our west.

On the other side of the path, three yards down, sits an old soldier, crouched over the *Quotidienne*. He wears a Louis XV uniform, with a pair of crossed swords on the back and, hanging from his neck, the Cross of Saint-Louis. He's the kind of relic you regularly find in places like these, keeping warm with memories, exchanging insolent glances with Napoleonic officers, sporting a large white ribbon in his button-hole to show he's on the right side of history.

Of all our newfound neighbors, he is the one who attracts the least notice. Why, then, is the Baroness stiffening at the sight of him? Pricked by chivalry, I am about to suggest we change our seats, when I am stopped by the Baroness's voice, calling across the gravel walk.

"Monsieur Vidocq, would you care to join us? You'll be able to hear much better."

CHAPTER 10

The Double Eagle

STARTLED, THE OLD soldier glares out at us from the caves of his eye sockets. In the next moment, his papyrus skin is rent by a grin, familiar in all its essentials, and I know the Baroness has struck true.

The surprise is that Vidocq himself doesn't seem to care. Springing up on a young man's feet, he bows low and, in a voice of pickled suavity, says, "My apologies, Madame. I was reluctant to force myself on you."

"Ah, but I have read a great deal of you in the local press, and I have never been given to understand that *shyness* is one of your faults, Monsieur."

"Perhaps not," he says, bowing still lower. "But in the face of such extraordinary powers of discernment, I do find myself at a loss for words."

"Madame," I interject. "Would you excuse us?"

I draw Vidocq aside; I lean into his ear. Rage is rising up inside me, but all that comes out is a muffled splutter.

"How—how did—?"

"How did I know you were making *private* inquiries?" he growls. "About police business? If you must know, it cost me twenty seconds and ten sous. Madame la Baronne will either have to hire more discreet porters, or *you* will have to become a better tipper."

It's one of his gifts, I suppose. In the act of being caught, he manages to catch you.

"So you're telling me I may not even venture out of doors without consulting you."

"Of course you may," he hisses back. "If you'd like to meet the same fate as Leblanc."

"Messieurs," interjects the Baroness. "If you insist on communicating sotto voce, we might as well adjourn to my lodgings." A light pinking in her cheek as she ponders the implications. "In my younger days, I should have balked at bringing *two* gentlemen home. I'm now at the age when it might actually enhance my reputation."

WE'RE WIPING THE fog's remnants from our skin—it feels like the oil from a drake's feathers—and Vidocq has gently kicked the Baroness's cat out of his way, and the Baroness is humming something as she sets down her faded silk parasol, and I'm met once again by the feeling that I've been meeting her in this way for many years, gathering in the same room with the old round table and the Breton peasant's chair. The way the Baroness slips into her bedroom, for instance . . . isn't that the kind of casual disappearance one can effect only with longtime friends? And please note her uncluttered gait as she sweeps back into the room, as though she were setting up a game of whist.

Except that she's carrying not a card table but a cross-legged stool in blue satin. And the illusion of domesticity ends in that moment, for this article, so elegant and uncompromising, no longer fits with our surroundings.

Even the Baroness doesn't know quite what to do with it. She makes as if to set it on the ground, then reconsiders and gathers it in her lap, hugging it toward her like a spaniel.

"Monsieur Vidocq," she says, "it has taken me at least an hour to trust Dr. Carpentier. Is there anything you can tell me that would, in your case, accelerate the process?"

Vidocq—from pride, maybe—has kept his makeup on all this time, and some of those assumed years cling to him even now as he strolls toward the Baroness's sideboard.

"Madame, I could say I'm honest as linen, and how should I expect you to believe it? I will say only this. I consider every crime in Paris to be a crime against *me*. A personal affront, yes! And it is only when that crime is avenged that I consider my own honor to be restored."

He stands there, studying the image of his altered face in the looking glass.

"As a young man," he continues, "I spent more than my share of time in prisons. The very worst, Madame, I can assure you. I was punished a thousand times over for a single passing indiscretion. The only thing that kept me from surrendering to despair, finally, was the belief—no, the *certitude*—that I was not like the wretches around me. As much as I deserved to be free, I knew there were men who deserved to be where I was. I had *tasted* their character. I knew that society could survive only so long as they remained apart from it. That belief has been my salvation—then and now."

An actor at the Odéon might have fitted out such a speech with all manner of curlicues and italics, hurled it straight to "the gods," but Vidocq utters it in a single pacific register and then locks his gaze onto the Baroness's as if she were the only audience he ever coveted.

"Madame," he says. "You are wise to husband your trust. With me, you may invest it freely. And before this day is out, you will have your return."

And still she hesitates. Though the mask of her face does begin to slacken.

"I believe you mentioned an object," he murmurs.

Getting no response, his voice grows even softer.

"An object that Monsieur Leblanc asked you to identify."

She nods, briefly.

"Would you happen to know where he found it, Madame?"

She draws a long breath, which she releases in staccato segments.

"He never told me," she says at last. "His correspondent preferred to remain anonymous."

"So he had no idea who this correspondent was."

"Apparently not."

"And did Leblanc take this object with him?"

"No."

It's amazing to watch him now, those big feet treading as lightly as a cuckolder's.

"What did he do with it, then?"

"He asked me to hold it in safekeeping. Until such time as he could retrieve it himself." She makes a grave study of her cuticles. "Leblanc was ever an optimist."

"You have the object, then?" asks Vidocq.

"Yes."

Restraining himself is almost too much labor now. It cinches his lips, tortures his syntax.

"Might we prevail upon your goodness to favor ourselves with it?"

She looks down then and, like someone roused from a drunken slumber, discovers the blue satin stool in her lap. Her hand traces the length of one leg until it meets an obstruction: a kind of gleaming garter, indissoluble from the stool, or so you might think, until the Baroness's chalk fingers loosen it with a quick flurry.

Vidocq lays it out on the table, even as I grab a candle from the nearest sconce. There, against the grains of mahogany, lies a hoop of gold, worried and notched, spotted with tarnish.

"Small," I hear myself say. "Too small for a bracelet."

"Too large for a ring," adds Vidocq. "An *adult's* ring, that is."

He draws it closer to the candle flame. A smile flickers across his lips.

"For a *baby*," he declares, "it might do quite nicely."

And just like that, all the distresses in the ring's surface acquire a meaning.

"A *teething* ring," I say.

"Worth a fair sum, too," says Vidocq, rolling it across the plain of his palm.

The Baroness's blond brows form high tight arches. "It's pure gold, if that's what you mean. However, its value derives largely from its original owner."

"A baby?" he asks.

"He was a baby then."

"And did you know him?"

"I met him once or twice. I knew his mother slightly."

"She must have been well-off if she could give her son a hunk of gold to chew on."

The Baroness pauses. And when she resumes, a new quality has crept into her tone: a sense of words beneath words.

"She *was* well-off, as you say. For a time. The ring, though, was a gift from the child's grandmother."

And now an even longer pause—a full half minute—before she breaks it herself by reaching into the drawer of a curio cabinet and extracting a pair of opera glasses, of ancient provenance.

"Here," she says, proffering them to Vidocq. "The grandmother's emblem has been engraved in miniature. You may see for yourself."

The glasses, being too small for his ox-head, give him the look of a harassed chemist as he lowers his face toward the table. For several long seconds, he gazes. A crevasse appears between his brows.

"You should be able to discern a double eagle," says the Baroness. "Quite different from Signore Buonaparté's emblem. Do you recognize it now, Monsieur?"

Closing his fingers round the ring, Vidocq gives a dazed nod.

"You have spent some time there, perhaps?" she asks.

"A few weeks. Fighting with the cuirassiers of Kinski. I got to know their insignias quite well."

"Kinski?" I stammer. "But that's Austria."

"Of course," says the Baroness, sweetly. "We are looking at the heraldic emblem of the Empress Maria Theresa."

"See for yourself," says Vidocq.

I press the opera glasses against the bridge of my nose, and the miniature universe of the ring comes rushing toward me. The two-headed eagle . . . the Teutonic cross . . .

"And the child's name," says the Baroness. "You can just make it out."

Sure enough, a line of letters appears on the ring's inside rim. Some of them are gnawed away, but enough remain to make out what was once there. . . .

LO IS CHA L S

"Louis-Charles," I whisper, and the words seem to pool on the table beneath me, reflecting the name back to me. "The dauphin."

From behind me comes the Baroness's voice, edged with irony.

"I believe, after all these years, the word *king* may now be in order."

And, as if it were answering a cue, the ring slides from view. When I next look up, it's resting in Vidocq's palm; in the next second, it's being flung against the nearest section of wall. With it goes the last reserve of Vidocq's decorum, for the word that now emerges from his mouth is something that should never be uttered in the same room as a blue satin stool.

"*Shit!*"

"In a manner of speaking," says the Baroness. "Yes."

CHAPTER 11

The Lost Dauphin

IF THE BARONESS has chosen to excuse Vidocq's vernacular, she is simply being true to her times.

You see, these early days of the Restoration are meant to be a great forgetting. We are meant to forget that a world was overturned, that a king and queen were carried to the Avenger, that the Place de la Révolution ran red with blood, that the rich man and the bishop quaked before the artisan and the peasant.

We are meant to forget that, from the ashes of this conflagration, emerged an upstart who overran half a continent and made monarchs tremble before his name and cost France nearly a million of its men.

We are meant to forget—all of it—everything that happened between 1789 and 1815, between the Bastille and Waterloo. No hard feelings. Let the Restoration begin.

And here's the interesting part: Forgetting can be quite easy. In just the last two years, without a backward glance, we have thrown out our monogrammed Bonaparte dinner plates, our eagle pictures. We've torn down the emperor's statues, stripped every *N* from the Louvre walls, painted *royal* over every *imperial*. We have cheered our new king as loudly as we once execrated our old one.

It has been, in part, a blessing to do this, for living in historic times is no life at all. Better to pretend it never happened.

Only we *can't*, hard as we try. In the end (and by now, you've figured this out) there *is* no forgetting. History lies low but always rises up.

And so, when we least look for it, we are visited by the specter of a boy. A boy whom, more than anyone else, we would like to forget.

His name was Louis-Charles, Duc de Normandie. He was a prince from storybooks: lovely and flaxen, bright of eye, rudely healthy. He was baptized in Notre-Dame. He had armies of servants: chamber-women, ushers, porters, room boys, servants to dress his hair and clean his silver and do his laundry—his own personal cradle rocker. He gamboled through groves of orange trees, he had eight black ponies at his call. He rode in carriages, and palaces were his playrooms.

He never asked for any of it, he was merely born into it, but the revolutionaries, in their wisdom, found him guilty nonetheless. Guilty of living in luxury while so many thousands of France's children suffered. What better punishment than to make him suffer, too?

They sent him to a fortress called the Temple. Night and day they set a guard over him. They stripped him of his title and dignity, they beat and starved him. They didn't dare execute him, as they had his parents. (The world was still watching.) They merely created the conditions in which he would die—and then they watched him die. Slowly, in agony and squalor, cut off from those who might have given comfort.

And when they had sucked the last breath from him, they tossed him in an unmarked grave, to mingle with strangers' bones. No tomb, no marker. No prayer. *Equal* to the end. He was ten years old.

As a nation, we've worked hard to forget this boy. You can understand, then, why someone like Vidocq, who has ridden each new wave of history without losing his footing, should resent being called back, like an inn guest who hasn't paid his bill. A modern man, he wishes to speak of the future. Which, I don't need to tell you, is the past.

———————

"A COUPLE OF EAGLES," he mutters.

He's repented enough of his outburst to retrieve the ring from the floor. His fingers close round it now.

"And a fancy cross," he adds, more loudly. "And I'm supposed to believe a boy's risen from the dead."

"I can only tell you that Leblanc believed it," says the Baroness. "To his great cost."

And as though she's already dismissed us, she lowers herself onto the bench that sits unmoored in the center of the room. She squares herself toward the wall and extends her arms, and in a flash, it becomes clear what used to be there.

A pianoforte.

"I remember when the rumors first reached us in Warsaw," she says. "All these high-pitched whispers. *The prince is alive!* Everyone had it on the highest authority, and everyone's story was the same. A little cabal of royalists had managed to switch the prince with another boy and spirit him to safety. We were told it was only a matter of time before our monarch returned to claim his throne."

She rests her hands on her invisible keyboard. The fingers begin to flutter.

"Well," she says, "it all sounded very mystical to me. And, of course, as the years went by, no dauphin ever emerged, which did nothing to diminish the faith of certain individuals. There was a duchess, I remember, who would declare at all her soirées that our boy-king was due back the following week. *Next week, I tell you!* After many months of this, I said, 'My dear, if he insists on taking so long, I fear Jesus Christ will get here before he does.' She never did invite me back."

Her fingers flutter into stillness. She gathers them into her lap.

"For my part, I always assumed the rumors were propaganda to pick up our spirits. God knows we needed it."

Vidocq is standing by the window now, rubbing the water vapor from each casement. You can hear the friction of his knuckles against the glass.

"Madame," he says, "do you know how many dauphin pretenders have come out of the wormholes already? I've had the pleasure of meeting a few myself. One was a tailor's son, one belonged to a clockmaker. There was a boy who claimed to have the pope's mark on his leg, but it was a scar from poaching rabbits. Mathurin Bruneau, maybe you've heard of him? A *shoemaker's* son. Very celebrated trial down in Rouen. You will find him now holding court in the dungeon of Mont-Saint-Michel." Sneering, he raps his fist against his chest. "If you've got another lost king to peddle, Madame, you'll have to knock on someone else's door."

"I am peddling nothing," she answers, the first touch of frost crisping her voice. "It was Leblanc who believed, not I. And if he was wrong," she says, rising and fronting him, "may I ask why he is dead?"

She waits, with great courtesy, for his answer. Then, tilting her head in deference, she adds: "Surely, there would have been no need to kill a man who was laboring under a delusion."

Vidocq's arms are locked across the spur of his belly. A long stream of breath issues from his nostrils.

"Tell me this," he says. "How would Leblanc know anything about Louis the Seventeenth? You said he wasn't an aristo."

It's the first time I've seen her flinch. That old epithet of the Revolution—*aristo*—strikes her like a clod of dirt. She pauses to gather herself. Then, in the coolest possible voice, she replies:

"Leblanc would be only too glad to tell you, I'm sure. If he could."

"And the only proof he had was this damned ring? He might have stumbled over that anywhere. I've seen Marie-Antoinette's old plates turning up in the beet market at Les Halles."

"He swore to me he had other tokens. When I asked him to show them to me, he told me it would have to wait. He was too occupied in finding someone."

"Who?"

"The man who could conclusively identify this missing king."

"And who was this man?"

A touch of exasperation abrades her voice now.

"Dr. Hector Carpentier, of course."

Until this moment, I believe they've even forgotten I'm in the room. And as they give me the full gift of their attention, I feel the air around me warming and cooling at once.

"It's absurd," I mutter.

But the air won't stop roiling, and my voice climbs once more into that register of guilt.

"He had the wrong man, I tell you. I was—I was *three* when Louis the Seventeenth died. I never—how could I possibly speak of someone I've never met?"

"No," muses the Baroness. "You couldn't be expected to do that."

She turns toward her looking glass now. Briefly tousles her strawberry-blond curls, stretches the skin across her cheekbones. Fingers away every last corruption of city air. And still she neglects to arrange her mouth, which is slightly askew as she turns back to me.

"And now, Doctor, at the risk of being trite, may I ask: What did *your* father do during the Revolution?"

CHAPTER 12

The Reeducation of a Parrot

GROWING UP IN a quiet house on a quiet street, I became, through no choice of my own, a connoisseur of silence. From the earliest age, I could distinguish early-morning from late-evening silence. A husband's silence from a wife's. Hope versus despair . . . if you listen long enough, everything gives off its own timbre of quiet.

But I've never known anything quite like Vidocq's silence, which lasts from the time we leave the Baroness's apartment to the time we turn up the Rue Soufflot. A silence of *containment,* with all manner of emotions vying against it. Imagine a pig's bladder, noiselessly expanding before your eyes. *This* silence grows quite terrible, and there is, if anything, a profound relief when it breaks.

"Why didn't you tell me your father had the same first name?"

Still in his old-man garb is Vidocq, but there's nothing old about this voice, which rattles off the market stalls, knocks the melting pot from a street tinker's charcoal fire . . . *claws* through the shawl of fog that still hovers round the Panthéon's dome.

"Why didn't you *tell* me there was another Dr. Carpentier in the world? You didn't—you didn't think I might want to *know* such a thing?"

"But he *wasn't* a doctor."

"What's that supposed to mean?"

"It means—it means he gave up medicine when I was still quite young. He ground *glass* for a living. For as long as I knew him, no one ever called him *Doctor* Carpentier."

AND HERE I MUST interject and call myself . . . a liar.

Because, every once in a while, about as often as the sun aligns with the moon, someone not too deeply ingrained in my family's circle—a mason, a mendicant, a functionary with the Ministry of Justice, someone concatenated to him in ways too obscure for me to fathom—would slip and call my father "Dr. Carpentier." To his face.

I always studied him closely in those moments, and yet I find it hard even now to describe his reaction. He never corrected the mistake, he simply let it hang there in a perfect suspension. At first you might have thought him insulted; only later would you realize he was *embarrassed*, as if an old nanny had reemerged and called him back, with a single name, to the days of chasing pigeons.

What I mean to say is it *cowed* him, this name.

You will understand, then, why I learned never to associate my father with the word *doctor*. And why, when I made it my life's goal simply to break through the carapace that surrounded him, I could think of no more effectual mallet than to declare myself . . . a doctor.

"Hm."

That was my father's first response when I told him I was enrolling in the École de Médecine. The second was this:

"Hm."

I will confess that his usual veil of abstraction did lift for a few moments. His eyes were pinked with alarm, as though I had coughed up sputum. And then he could no longer look at me.

He would have been less concerned, maybe, if he'd known how long it would take me to become a physician. Indeed, in these early days of the Restoration, it seems unlikely I ever will.

So when a dead stranger, a certain Monsieur Leblanc, chooses to grant you a title before you've earned it, you may be excused, I hope, for accepting the promotion. Yes, I've quite enjoyed being Dr. Carpentier, if only for a few days. I like to think I've been enjoying it for both of us.

And if I never worried overmuch about that *other* Dr. Carpentier . . . well, grant me this. Even my father wanted nothing to do with him.

"When did he flop?"

That's Vidocq's voice, black and guttural, pulling me back to the here and now. I stare at him, uncomprehending.

"Die," he explains. "This papa of yours, when did he die? How long has he been eating dandelions by the roots?"

If you want death broached from an oblique angle, Vidocq is not your man.

"A year," I tell him. "A year and a half."

"What a fine empirical mind you've got. *A year. A year and a—*"

"Eighteen *months,* will that do? And twenty-one days and—eleven hours . . ."

Frowning softly, he fingers his Saint-Louis cross.

"Not much fuss, I expect, with the funeral," he says.

"He didn't want any. At least Mother didn't. We had a little service, it was five minutes, no more."

"Who was there?"

"No one. Mother and me and—and Charlotte, that's all."

And someone else. A *fourth* figure, stirring now from memory's vault. Shrouded and comma shaped, leaning over the open coffin and breathing in that peculiar odor of wool and paraffin . . .

"Father Time."

"Ohh," snarls Vidocq. "It's to be *allegory,* is it, Doctor?"

"No, he's—Father Time's a friend of the family, that's all. He has a *real* name. . . ."

"Which is?"

"Umm, Professor Racine, I think. No, wait, it's *Corneille.* . . ."

And then another thought comes hard on, surprising me with its force.

I wish my father were here.

"There were no notices in the newspapers?" asks Vidocq, in a quieter tone. "No memorial services?"

I shake my head.

"So . . ." He removes his shako, glances heavenward. "Word must have been slow to reach the—the *lamented* Monsieur Leblanc. He went to his death looking for a man who was already dead. The angels weep."

And now another voice enters the picture. Not the voice of angels.

"Good afternoon, Monsieur Hector."

Nankeen stands before us in a cloud of swallowtail, framed almost perfectly by the Panthéon's portico. Gold buttons and a lace jabot and a trailing indolence—he must have just slept through a lecture on torts.

"You're not going to introduce me?" Smiling, he angles his spectacled nose toward Vidocq. "May I ask whom I have the honor of addressing?"

"You'll have the honor of my foot up your ass if you don't move along."

It's important to point out he hasn't raised his voice a fraction, but his intent is clear enough to mottle Nankeen's pale brow. Who would have expected this from a veteran of Louis XV's army—who, by the looks of things, is eighty if he's a day?

"See here." A bitter smile crawls across Nankeen's face. "I don't believe there's any call for that."

Vidocq seizes him by the lapels of his swallowtail coat and hoists him straight up in the air. Nankeen's boots, suspended a foot above the ground, execute a pas seul. His eyes twitch, the very threads of his clothing recoil . . . but the smile never quite unfixes itself, even through the gale of Vidocq's roar.

"Was I unclear? *Was I unclear?*"

One good thrust, and Nankeen falls to earth a good body's length from where he started.

"Mind your elders!" cries Vidocq. "Move along!"

With clinical attentiveness, he watches Nankeen reach for his toppled hat and, without a backward look, trot round the corner.

"This papa of yours," he says, peering off in the direction of the Val de Grâce. "He never mentioned any dauphins, I don't suppose?"

"Never. He was—he was the son of a notary. Mother came from potato merchants. We weren't the type to mix with royalty."

"Ah, but you know the old saying, I'm sure. Strange times, strange bedfellows? And if there was ever a strange time, it was the Revolution."

He does something quite unexpected then: loops his hand round my elbow and, with a gentle pressure, pulls me along. We're *strolling* now through these narrow, gently decanting streets: gentlemen of leisure, fresh from the Théâtre des Italiens.

"I was in Arras," says Vidocq, "when all the wheels were coming off. We had a woman there, I'll never forget her, Citizeness Lebon. Used to be a nun in the abbey at Vivier until the Jacobins forced her to marry the curé of Neuville. A real love match, as it turned out. *She* decided who the Republic's enemies were, *he* made sure they died for their sins. I was there the day they executed Monsieur de Vieux Pont on account of his parrot.

"Seems Citizeness Lebon had overheard said parrot crying, '*Vive le Roi!*' Before the week was out, the parrot's owner had been divorced from his head. The bird himself was pardoned and handed over to the citeness for reeducation. She was still working on him, probably, when they came for *her*."

Half smiling, he tilts his head toward mine.

"You can see how things worked in those days," he says. "A woman of the cloth becomes a woman of the people and spends her waking hours with a royalist parrot. *Three* estates, rubbing shoulders under one Republic."

Without my realizing it, the Rue Neuve-Sainte-Geneviève has stolen up on us. Once more we stand on the corner. Once more I stare at the crackling plaster housefronts, the old well, the mud-blackened gutters . . . the street itself, falling away at such a pitch that horses rarely venture down it. Everything looms more *real*, somehow, through the departing fog-floes.

"So you think my father might have rubbed shoulders with a Bourbon or two," I say.

"It's possible," he answers, shrugging. "The only problem—*Doctor*—is that everyone who can sort it out for us is dead. And unless you can figure out a way to make the dead speak, I'm afraid I must classify you as an official waste of my time."

And with that, he loosens his grip on my arm. He nods curtly, bids me good afternoon, and becomes once more that veteran of forgotten wars, marching down the Vieille Estrapade de Fourcy. Only two details mar the illusion: the right foot, dragging ever so slightly after him, more afterthought than wound—and the skewed smile that wrinkles his face as it turns back to me.

"Now might be a good time to get reacquainted with your father. Don't you think, Hector?"

28 THERMIDOR YEAR II

Must speak w/ Barras & commissaries re restrictions. Am permitted to see Charles for only 1 hr in early A.M. Guard must be present
at all times—confidences of any kind btw patient & me impossible. If I wish to stay longer, I must petition Committee 3 days in
advance.

For rest of time, Charles remains utterly alone in cell. No fire, no
candle. Only sounds he hears are <u>bolts</u>; sliding of earthenware plate
thru wicket; voices commanding him to go to bed; voices waking
him up, periodically, thruout night.

Before incarceration, boy was, by all reports, outgoing, good-
natured. 6 mos. of confinement have left him almost entirely w/o
affect: eyes languid, expression fixed & disinterested.

Food <u>extremely</u> poor. 2 daily portions of soup, watery, flavorless.
Morsels of beef. Loaf of black bread. Pitcher of water. Have explained to Barras that poor diet & long confinement have substan-
tially weakened patient. Have expressed desire to personally escort
Charles out of cell for limited exercise. Must await decision of Committee of General Security.

This A.M., Charles asked why I was taking care of him. Because it is
my duty, I said. But I thought you didn't like me, he said. Quite the
contrary, I said.

It's clear he experiences far greater alarm at kindness than at ill
usage. <u>Must learn more</u> about prior treatment.

3 FRUCTIDOR

<u>Progress</u>. Charles able to walk for greater distances w/o support. Still experiences great pain in knees, ankles.

Have just received word from Committee: Exercise request has been granted. Patient may leave cell for 10 minutes, no more. Must be escorted at all times by me + 2 guards.

Upon further consid, have made addit petition. Given patient's extreme sensitivity to light, wd like to schedule exercise for twilight. Am awaiting Committee's decision.

6 FRUCTIDOR

Request granted. We are now required to have <u>3</u> addit escorts.

7 FRUCTIDOR

Prospect of leaving cell did not appear to gladden Charles. Expressed serious <u>doubt</u> at idea. Agreed to join me only after I promised he might return as soon as he liked.

As precaution, I tied linen bandage round eyes. Led him carefully out of cell. Guards followed at 10 ft. We approached stairs—<u>1st</u> stairs patient has undertaken in 1 1 years. He leaned heavily on my arm. Climbing v. hard for him—legs gave way more than once—was breathing v. hard when we reached top of Tower. I sat him down until such time as he cd stand again.

Platform here = <u>gallery</u>, offering views of Temple courtyard + streets outside. We stood there for some time bf Charles, w/o asking leave, removed bandage from eyes in single motion. Stood blinking in dusk. Able to keep eyes open for 5–10 seconds, no more.

Patient's attention gradually shifted toward sounds. Asked me what bird that was singing? I informed him it was nightingale. Yes, he said. That's right. One by one, he asked me to identify sounds: water carriers, crossing sweepers, hacks, stagecoaches, fruit carts, etc. One sound in particular. What's that? he asked. <u>Whistling</u>, I said. He begged to know who was doing whistling? Grp of children, coming down Blvd du Temple. Describe what they were doing? Chasing each other, somersaulting, laughing, rude noises, buying cakes at corner, etc.

Intelligence appeared to satisfy him. However, I observed alteration in demeanor. Asked if something was wrong. He shook head. Later, tho, as we descended stairs, he asked (in a whisper) if the children were coming to kill him.

17 FRUCTIDOR

Have made repeated requests for assistant. 1 hr/day of care not sufficient. Guards refuse to carry out instructions. Lacking anyone to administer physics, salve & dress lesions, exercise limbs, etc., patient unlikely to recover. Have been told that Committee has it under consid.

20 FRUCTIDOR

No word.

22 FRUCTIDOR

Still no word. Delays v. <u>frustrating</u>.

23 FRUCTIDOR

Word reached me late A.M.: Committee has granted request. Assistant to begin work next week.

Have been told little about him. Trade: upholstering. Repub credentials: impeccable. Modest experience in nursing. Name: Chrétien Leblanc.

CHAPTER 13

An Ancient Relic Rediscovered

HERE'S A WONDER. At dinner, Nankeen breathes not a word of our recent encounter. Whenever I catch his eye, *he's* the one looking away, and as soon as dinner's over, he excuses himself and retires upstairs to his studies.

He's ashamed, is that it? Or else, in those few moments when Vidocq held him by the shirtfront, he caught scent of a different world—where civilization and nankeen trousers availeth a man not. Or maybe I'm only saying that because it's the way I feel.

At any rate, the disappointed Rosbif and Lapin retire without bloodying any of their fellow eaters; Charlotte takes away the dishes; and the only ones left in the dining room are Mother and me. Not that she notices. This being Friday night, she is polishing her silver.

The silver was part of her bridal trousseau, and to the best of my knowledge, it has never actually been used. (All the lodgers of Maison Carpentier make do with pewter.) In no way does this discourage her weekly ablutions. She wraps one of Charlotte's aprons round her black tulle dress, sheathes her sleeves in muslin, and bears *down*, with a surgeon's fixity. Before five minutes have passed, her arms are coated in a viscous, pearly lather, as though she had plunged them into a whale.

"Mother."

She doesn't look up or greet me or do anything that would loosen her mind's grip. She says only:

"The newel post is still loose."

"I know."

"You said you'd get to it."

"I will."

"You said that yesterday. The day before, too, if I—"

"Mother, please. I need to ask you about something."

My temples are pulsing, and as I pass my hand over my face, a slick of sweat comes free.

"Not something," I correct myself. "Some*one*."

"Who?"

"Father."

And here she does, in fact, pause in her labors. For one second.

"What could I possibly tell you," she says, taking up her chamois once more, "that you don't already know? You grew up in this house, you saw him every day of your life. That *was* you living here all those years, wasn't it?"

"That was me."

"Well, what a relief. I thought perhaps you were . . . a changeling or . . . something like that. . . ."

For the next half minute, the only sound is the friction of cloth against teaspoon.

"Of course," I say, "just because you live with someone doesn't mean you won't have questions about them."

The cloth halts for a fraction of a second, then hurries on.

"People are what they are, Hector. There's no point in . . . there it is."

"He was a doctor once."

"Who?"

"Father."

Her eyes now are flat and gray, and orbiting, as though she's mislaid something.

"That was many years ago, Hector."

"Why did he stop?"

"Ohh."

She wipes her forehead with her sleeve. The gray froth clusters over her eyes like a third brow.

"He had his reasons," she says. "I'm sure he did."

"What were they?"

"Oh, how ridiculous you sound, Hector! *What were they?* As though I could even—when it was so long ago." She shakes out the cloth. "Over and done with. Not worth another thought."

There you are: a perfect specimen of Restoration thinking. My mother does exactly what her nation asks of her. For many years, she hung a tricolor from her window; now it's a white flag with three golden fleurs-de-lis at the center. The eagles and bees that once graced her porcelain cups have given way to the royal arms. The only thing she has that even hints of the past is a bud vase with a single gilt *N*. She keeps it in a secret niche in the drawing room and never puts flowers in it.

"When Father was a physician," I say, keeping my voice light, "what sorts of people did he treat?"

"Oh, all sorts, I expect."

"He wouldn't have—I was only wondering if he might have had occasion to—to treat an aristocrat. Someone like that."

The silence bears down.

"Perhaps even a member of the royal family," I suggest.

She snatches up a butter knife. "Hector," she says, "I can't say I like your line of questions. Whoever your father knew or didn't know—a quarter of a century ago—can be of no concern of yours."

"It *is* a concern."

A statement of fact, that's all I intend, but something startles her eyes back toward mine. The scrubbing subsides, and in a dark brown tone, she says:

"That horrible convict."

"No."

"*He's* put you up to this."

"Mother."

"Badgering you about your poor father."

"It's *me* asking, Mother. No one else."

She turns away from me now. As far as she can manage without actually leaving.

"Shame on you, then, Hector."

"Shame," I repeat in a low voice. "Why *shame*? If Father led such a quiet, such an *unimpeachable* life, what shame could there be in knowing more about him?"

A long silence before she coils herself back round.

"Your father was a good man. That's all you need to know."

She's holding my eye now—the better to gauge her missile. On it comes, low and deadly.

"He certainly never squandered his family's assets on a common whore."

The strange part? Instead of cowing me, it frees me. Something in my head turns lambent and still, and I draw out a chair, and I sit in it, and I look at her, and because all the niceties have been burned away, I can *stay* looking at her, I can stare her out of all countenance.

And when I speak, how gently my voice ripples.

"It's true what you said before, Mother. I've lived here all my life. And I've never really known the first thing about Father. Or you. Of course, I never worried so much about *him* because no one else seemed to know him either. You least of all. I guess I just assumed he didn't *want* to be known."

With great deliberation, she strips the muslin sheaths from her arms.

"And now? Now I think I was wrong, Mother. I think there was something in him that didn't want to be known. Something *happened* to him. A long time ago. And he couldn't square it away, and he couldn't forget it. Of course, I don't have any proof. But I think *you* might, Mother. I think you know exactly what happened."

There is a kind of woman who will throw tears in your way when you draw too near. Eulalie was one of those; Mother, to her credit, has never been. To intruders, she has only one answer: rage.

And this is its truest expression. A raucous, fast-descending cry, like a crow rustled from a tree.

"I have nothing more to say to you on this subject!"

And as I walk out the door, she sends a last cry after me, and this one carries, to my ear, a note of ragged hope—as if it could erase an entire conversation.

"Your father was a good man!"

TEN MINUTES LATER, I'm standing in the foyer. In my coat and hat, my hand resting on the doorknob. Ready for my evening walk, you see—and *not* ready. Beneath those counterpulses, the knob actually trembles.

And then I hear a cough. *Cough* doesn't quite cover it. A barking, heaving, chest-splitting sound.

It's Father Time. Leaning against our grandfather clock.

The coughing at least gives me leisure to study him, more closely than I ever have before. That patriarchal beard—that's the beard Moses came down from the mountain with, isn't it? That tall, tottering frame: a Doric column ever on the verge of toppling. Whatever was straight in him is now bent. He's all *angles,* like an attic.

"Are you all right, Monsieur?"

He puts out a hand to allay my concern. With the other, he pounds his chest until the air begins once more to stream.

"Nothing to . . ." One last cough. "Nothing to *worry* about, just a bit of—salivation, I think, going down the—the wrong *aqueduct*."

"Can I help you with anything?"

"Me? Oh, no no no. You see, I couldn't help but—*hear* you. You and your mother, I mean. . . ."

He does something *startling* then. He touches me. A scaly, *salty* hand, pressed against my shoulder.

"See here, my boy, you really ought to look kindly on her. It's been a hard road, hasn't it? Ah, but if it's your *father* you're wanting to hear about, there are plenty of *other* people to ask."

This look he's giving me . . . it's the same look he gave me the other night over the dining table. That helpless complicity, oddly soothing when it first came my way. Here, after all, was Father Time. Old friend of my *father's*.

Attendant at my father's funeral.

"Of course," I hear myself say. "Of *course*." I peer into the slow-opening crypt of his face. "You mean I could just—ask you questions about my father? His *past*, I mean?"

"Oh my, yes," he says, smiling. "It's one thing we're good for, old vanes like me. You can always get us to point *back*, eh? The further back the better. Why, if you asked me what we had for dinner tonight, I'm afraid I couldn't tell you. Whiting, perhaps."

"Chicken."

"Ah, you see? Gone. Utterly. Now ask me how I dined the day Mirabeau died, I can tell you. Down to the last drop of cassis, yes."

His eyes go rheumy with memory. His hand clenches and un-clenches.

"I know it's getting late," I say. "But would you mind terribly if we . . . ?"

"Mind?" His features swarm with confusion. "Ah, you'd like to—you mean *now*, is that it? Well, I suppose that might work. Yes, we could—we could even retire up*stairs* to my quarters if you . . . do you know, I might have some cocoa first. Things flow better, don't they, with a little chocolate?"

"Monsieur," I say, raising a hand. "Before we say another word, I must beg you to tell me. Did my father ever have cause to meet a prince?"

"Why, yes," he answers. "Yes, of course. *Everyone* was a prince in those days."

CHAPTER 14

Treasures of a Reliquary

"YOU MUST EXCUSE the . . . so seldom get *visitors* up here . . . not much in the way of a *chair* . . ."

Father Time, my new friend, sputters his apologies as he prods open the balky door.

And it's true, when a man ceases to pay his rent, no one comes any longer to sweep his floors. The dust that adheres as a matter of course to Father Time's belongings has become, over the past few months, a damp, brownish rime that leaves translucent slicks on the floorboards and on the patches of plaster that show wherever the flower-speckled wallpaper has pulled away.

The curtains are gone. There's an old rosewood dresser with twisted-copper drawer handles. An old washstand with a wooden top. No trace of a fire in the fireplace—how he must have shivered—and scant trace of the room this used to be. For when I was a child, it was my father's workshop, and every bit as forbiddingly private as he was.

Standing now amid the old detritus, I'm stabbed by the memory of him: stooped over his lathe, grinding out lenses for spectacles, telescopes, microscopes. I remember the smell of the turpentine and the melted pitch and the copper nitrate. I remember stepping on the old cartridge shells he used for cutting glass—they lay in the hallway like sprung traps.

My mother used to reprove him for the mess he left behind—the mounts, the brass tubes and spindles, centrifugally whirled in every direction. Beneath all her complaints lay the suggestion that a physician might have found a more suitable second career. To which he had but one reply:

"It was good enough for Spinoza."

All of that's gone now, even the smell. All except for Father's desk, still squeezed into the same lightless corner. One of the legs has gone missing, and the current tenant has taken the unorthodox step of replacing it with a molasses barrel, which turns out to have a door, carved rather artfully along the barrel's own grains, releasing with a single pulse.

"Here we are," murmurs Father Time.

Not even pausing for a candle, he plunges his hands into that dark cavity. And draws out . . .

We will call them history's tendons.

A Chinese fan, that's the first item in the inventory. It unfurls to reveal Liberty's rouged face. Then comes a tricolor snuffbox. Inkwells made from the rubble of *barrières*. Tickets (unused) to a Beaumarchais farce. A pewter mug of the Bastille, straddled by an enormous rooster.

Father Time is rich, it turns out, in precisely the sorts of relics that France no longer has use for. Ceramic renderings of the Tennis Court Oath. Saucers of patriotic children declaring their allegiance to the Convention. Sheet music for . . .

"*Ça Ira!*" cries Father Time. "That was quite the rouser, wasn't it? 'All the aristocrats will *hang* la-la. . . .'"

Even the wrappings prove to be relics: old issues of *Annales Patriotiques*, *Feuille Villageoise*, *L'Orateur du Peuple*. . . .

"*Le Courrier Universel!* Why, do you know I used to *write* for them? Very—very *febrile* essays under the pseudonym of Junius. And here's, oh my, Lequinio's Patriotic Prayer, wasn't *that* on everyone's lips for a . . . for a . . . now *here*. . . ." He drags out a mass of icicle blue yarn. "I am pleased to tell you this is an old mitten of Rousseau's. He left it behind on a hike. Usual great-man reverie, I expect. Hand must have been quite *chapped* by day's end."

"Monsieur, please." I give him a propitiatory smile. "You were going to tell me about my father."

"Yes . . ." He peers into the barrel's vault as though his old friend's face might come blazing forth from the darkness. "So I was. . . ."

"Maybe you could tell me how you met him."

"Ah!" His face brightens instantly. "The Collège d'*Arcourt,* that's where. I was a professor, of course; he was a student. Not one of *my* students, no. I was all about *botany* in those days. I was very busy refuting Reynier's findings on the—the amputation of sexual organs in hollyhocks. Work which was *quite* favorably mentioned, I don't mind saying, in—in Jussieu's *Genera Plantarum*. . . ."

"What was he like?" I ask, more loudly. "My *father.*"

"Well, he was—he was *quiet,* yes. Not so quiet as he became later, but he had—I would call it a natural *gravity.* A way of being *still,* I mean. He was unfailingly polite, he was—very *dogged,* as if he mistrusted his own gifts. I used to give him advice about, oh, courses to take, professors to avoid, that sort of thing. *Unsolicited* advice, goes without—he rarely *took* it, but I think he appreciated someone giving it. He'd never had much of that.

"Well, one thing and another, we began meeting for coffee. Thursday mornings at the Wise Athenian. I *paid,* of course, at the beginning, he didn't have the means. And do you know, for years, we never missed a single one of those coffees? Not even when he was in the worst throes of medical school. Not even when the world was falling apart. We used to—we used to *joke* about it. Because we were much more regular about the Athenian than mass."

"What did you talk about?"

"Oh, *girls,* of course," says Father Time, raking his beard. "Your father was always—ha!—more *marriage*-minded than I. I remember the day he told me about your mother. Yes, he was—he was blushing almost as much as you are right now."

Something unexpectedly cunning in his eye. If I weren't blushing before, I am now.

"And, of course, we talked politics. That's what people *did* then."

"Was Father a true republican? A believer?"

"Weellll . . . depends on how you define *believer.* He wasn't your sans-culotte type. Didn't wear the clogs, didn't carry the *pike*—kept his hair powdered—but he believed, yes, in his own way. What I mean is there was always, how to put this, a *core* of skepticism behind everything he affirmed. If I was the Rousseau man, he was *Voltaire* through and through. And of course, he never aligned himself with the Girondins or the Montagnards. Never had to. He was too busy—ha!—patching them up. Doctors had more work than they could handle in those days."

I jam my hands in my pockets. I flex the toe of my boots.

"So . . . my father had a practice?"

"He was a *surgeon,* my child. At the Hôpital d'Humanité. But his skills made him quite coveted among a—among a certain *set.* Oh, yes, rumor had it even—even *Marat,* who was a doctor himself, even *he* asked for your father. Ha! Might've saved the old sod's life—second opinion, eh? *Out of that grimy water, you dishrag!*"

"Did he ever . . . ?"

That's as far as I get until I am stopped by . . . my father himself.

THE MEMORY OF HIM, I mean.

Alone, as usual. Coveted by no one. Having his late-afternoon tea. (An English custom, who knows how he came by it?) The tea he always drank quickly, down to its last leaves, and then he set to buttering his toast, with every bit as much fixity as he brought to lens grinding. It took him a good minute, usually, to drag that butter across every last square of blackened bread—to scrape it down until nothing of the original solid remained. *Diligent*, yes, and at the same time, furtive, like an anchorite prying an old piece of chocolate from a crevice.

The idea that this man—*this man*—could be the coveted Dr. Carpentier...

"NEVER MIND," I say.

"Oh, but you were going to ask me something."

"It's nothing. I was just—I was going to ask if my father ever met Louis the Seventeenth."

And as soon as it's out, I'm trying to call it back in.

"I don't really have any *reason* to—"

"But of *course* he met Louis the Seventeenth. He was the boy's doctor."

CHAPTER 15

The Black Tower

ONLY LATER, WHEN I am shaking the webs from my brain, will I have the space to recall the look in Father Time's eye. The coolness that lingers there, a dry clarity—neither gentle nor cruel.

"You mean he never told you? Well, isn't that funny?"

Though he doesn't look amused. Particularly.

Without knowing it, I've plopped myself down on his bed. I'm smoothing out the rag that passes for his coverlet. A whirring cloud of dust is trailing after me.

"When?" I ask. "When did he ever have cause to meet that boy?"

"Oh my, it was summer of '94. Just a few weeks past the height of the Terror. I was *there*, you know, the day they took Robespierre. Horrible business. He was *bellowing* the whole way. Well, *you* might have complained, too, if—if you were missing half your *face*—"

"Please, Monsieur, I didn't ask about—"

"Oh, but the point *is* with Robespierre gone, people could afford to be a bit less *abstract*, couldn't they? The fever broke—the fever of

Theory, yes—and everyone sat up in bed and looked about. Asked after friends and relations. So it was only natural someone would ask about that boy. Because nobody had seen him in—well, it felt like forever. . . ."

IN FACT, IT HAD been two years.

I will look up the dates later, and I will find that the last time the public at large had glimpsed the dauphin, Louis-Charles, was on the thirteenth of August, 1792. On this occasion, the royal family was being driven from the Tuileries to their new prison in the Temple—escorted by what looked to be the entire population of the Parisian faubourgs. All of them shaking fists, waving pikes, raining down oaths. *Pointing* to every toppled marble monarch. *Do you see the fate that awaits you?*

A good two hours it took to travel a relatively short distance. At last a low drone of pent rage escaped the mob as the *berline* pulled into the courtyard and the thick iron gates of the Temple swung closed after them.

For the royal family, the respite was short-lived. Five months later, the boy's father would be dragged to the Place de la Révolution. (His neck a little too thick for the occasion: the blade had to fight its way through.) Fourteen months later, the mother would follow. Seven months more, the boy's beloved aunt, gentle Princess Élizabeth, would climb the scaffold.

But *he* stayed where he was, that boy with the brook blue eyes and the strawberry-blond ringlets hanging to his shoulders. Immured in a great tower. Behind walls of stone, nine feet thick.

I was a boy myself when I first saw it. Late summer, and Mother and I had been walking for hours, as we often did in pleasant weather, and we'd just stopped at a chemist's shop on the Rue du Meslay (Father needed copper nitrate), and on a whim, I suppose, I veered down the Boulevard du Temple.

Mother hesitated, I can see this now. But the day was lovely, and we were in no hurry to be home, and so she followed. *Still* hesitating, for she remained a step or two behind me the whole way.

We speak of buildings rising up before us, as if they somehow unfurled, brick by brick. The tower that met my eyes now had unfurled many centuries ago. It was emphatically past tense—and still very much present. Silly to say you were discovering it. If anything, it was finding you.

Other towers, other turrets protruded from the medieval château they called the Temple (deceptively religious name!), but this tower was different. Larger—easily sixty feet in height—and *black*, like the inside of a chimney, and lord of all its secrets. Only after staring at it for some time could I discern the flaws in its masonry: the tiny pinpricks of windows scattered around its skin. Too small, surely, to admit much in the way of light. Or air. Whatever was in there stayed there.

I knew nothing then of the tower's history, but I do remember, yes, *picturing* someone, of no distinct character or color, on the other side of those walls. Looking down at me. Calling out, even, it would make no difference because—this was what unnerved me—I would never be able to see or hear. Whoever it was might just as well have been erased from this earth.

And the notion that a human being could be erased like that, so easily, so entirely, this was somehow worse than the tower itself. Or perhaps the same thing.

I felt a prickle in the back of my shoulders, and in the same moment, I saw Mother clasp her arms tightly round her chest.

"Come, Hector."

Down the street she drew me and round the corner. Neither of us looked back.

By then, the tower had already fallen into disuse, and before I was twenty-one, it had been torn down, on Napoleon's orders. It rears up again, though, at the mere mention of that name.

The Temple.

———

"HE WENT THERE every single morning," says Father Time. "Took a cab, though he hated spending the money. Always a *different* cab, too—different route—never knew if someone might be following you, eh? The Temple commissaries gave him a special pass—he showed it to me once—and then, of course, if you had to see one of the prisoners, why, you needed a *visa*, too. 'For the Tower' it said, or something like that.

"And that's right, he could stay no more than an hour. *Same* hour every day. Any *more*, he'd have to—what?—oh, petition the commissaries or else—ugh!—that awful Committee of Public Security. And everything was in *utmost* secrecy. Not a word."

"Why did they choose my father?" I ask.

"Mm." He weaves his fingers through his beard, as though he were carding wool. "Bit of a fluke, really. Your father had once treated General Barras' sister. For a *goiter*. Mightily impressed she was. Didn't hurt, I expect, that he was—such a handsome cur in his youth. *Barras* certainly wasn't above noticing such things, if you—if you take my meaning. Well then, once Barras was put in charge of what was *left* of the royal family, he realized the boy would need a doctor. Forthwith!"

Father Time shrugs now. The briefest of motions, and yet the fabric of his old coat actually retains its new shape even as the shoulders return to their former position.

"Naturally," he says, "the job was advertised as a—a *high* sort of duty. Requiring a doctor of pure republican credentials. Rare skill. I doubt your father had ever been *courted* so fiercely before."

I close my eyes. I try to imagine—me—surrounded by good citizens, hearing words like *honor* and *calling*. *Patrie*.

"How long did he attend the dauphin?"

"Right up to the *end*, nearly."

"But—why did he never tell me?"

"Oh, well, at the *time*, you see, you were a little sprig. No more than three, eh? You wouldn't have known a dauphin from a—from a *dolphin*."

"But, Mother . . ."

"She didn't know, either. He went out, mm, an hour *earlier* every morning, that was the only difference. Told her he was needed at the hospital. Yes, and always came home for lunch. *Punctual* sort, your papa. No one . . ." He reaches over suddenly, brushes a speck of dirt from my vest. "No one would have guessed anything was amiss."

"He couldn't even tell his own wife?"

"Oh, he didn't *dare*. It might have been her death warrant. Don't you see, your father was taking an enormous risk. In those days, assisting the royal family—helping the children of Louis the Sixteenth in *any* way—why, you could pay for that with your life. Hundreds already had. *Thousands*."

"But Barras asked him to. The Committee asked him to—"

"Ah, that's just it! Today, the Committee's on board. *Tomorrow*, it changes its mind. Day *after* tomorrow, a whole *new* Committee! And whoever did the bidding of the last one . . . giving up his head to Old Growler before sundown."

Without thinking, he sketches a line across his throat. A *firm* hand, not a tremor. He might have made a fine surgeon himself.

"Monsieur," I say. "You must forgive me, I still don't understand. How could anyone blame my father for trying to save a young boy's life?"

"Oh." His eyes swirl out of focus. "That's—that's not what they—wanted him to . . ."

"What, then?"

Squinting, he crouches and scans the full perimeter of the room—as though the train of his thought were even now scurrying toward the floorboards.

"Yes," he says, folding his lips down. "I asked him that myself once. We were at our usual table—the Wise Athenian, I've told you about the Wise Ath—I have?—the weekly coffee, yes, it was your *father's* turn to pay—he would *insist* on that, he would—where was I? Oh, yes, he was going on about these dreadful commissaries and committees. Ha! Death by *bureaucracy*, he called it. Nicely turned, eh? Well, I suppose I must have become a little irritated on his behalf because I said, 'Well, now, why would they hire such a—such a *sublime* physician as yourself if they weren't going to *listen* to him?'"

"And what did he say?"

"Nothing at first. That was his way, of course, he was—ten parts *thought* to one part speech. And at last—it was just as we were getting up from the table, we were—ha!—brushing the macaroon crumbs from our coat sleeves—well, that's when he said—and I'll never forget it—he said, *They don't want me to heal that boy. They want me to make sure he dies.*"

CHAPTER 16

A Fatal Disease Is Diagnosed— at the Very Precipice of Death

LIKE A TALLOW CANDLE, Father Time's brain gutters and crackles and throws off a good greasy light, but its span is brief and its end conclusive. Speech fails, then consciousness, and before another five minutes have passed, he has fallen across his straw pallet—at a cumbersome tangent, like a dropped ceiling beam. All that's left to do is to remove his boots before bidding him good night.

Over the next two days, I do all I can to resume our conversation. Outwardly he is all eagerness. *Inside,* something balks, and no manner of private hints—the Temple, the Wise Athenian—will quite uncork him. The best I can secure is a promise, vaguely worded, to take me to "the archives" someday.

Where these archives are, what they contain . . . none of this can be determined, hard as I ply him. Through all of Saturday and Sunday, I wait for the clouds to pass. Monday comes round with nothing more to show for my labors. Only the old routine, waiting to be shouldered. I leave the house at the same time: nine-fifteen. I am bound for the same place: the École de Médecine. The one difference is this. When I'm twenty or so paces from my door, a fiacre rolls up. A gendarme leans out of it.

"Dr. Carpentier?"

"Yes?"

"You're wanted."

He's under no charge to say *who* wants me. There's no need. I climb in, and the gendarme calls up to the driver.

"Number Six, Rue Sainte-Anne."

My initiation into the Sûreté (Number Six, as it's known to intimates) comes via the rear courtyard. My escort leads me into a marble-floored entry and presses casually against a leather wall panel, which swings in to reveal a spiral staircase. On the first floor, another panel swings open on a long corridor, illuminated almost entirely by skylights.

Down this hallway the gendarme leads me, and as I peer into the open offices, a clammy fear takes hold of me. Who *are* these men, with their red hands and their coarse blue trousers and the patches sewed on with twine? Where are the police?

A good half minute passes before I realize . . . and you will have to imagine the sudden lift in my stomach . . . these *are* the police.

Unbidden, the words of Nankeen circle back. *Impossible anymore to tell the law enforcers from the lawbreakers.*

Well, it *is* hard for Parisians, in these early days of the Restoration, to twine themselves round the idea—Vidocq's idea—that catching criminals might require men who *look* like them, think and act like them. The officers of the Brigade de Sûreté may lack for uniforms but not for pasts.

Take Aubé. The fellow in the yellow cap. Renowned forger in his day, specializing in royal writs and church encyclicals. Never met a signature he couldn't make his own. And that bull in the woman's blouse? Fouché. Went to prison at age sixteen for armed robbery. The only one who looks he's on the right side of the law is Ronquetti—still lounging in last night's evening clothes—a confidence artist who set himself up for a time as the Duke of Modena, with an Italian mistress and a blackamoor servant.

And behind the unmarked pair of doors at the end of the hall: Coco-Lacour. Grew up in a brothel. Did most of his schooling in prison. Likes to ply whores with trinkets he's fished out of the Seine. He's now Vidocq's personal secretary.

"Dr. Carpentier, is it?" A good third of Coco-Lacour's teeth are missing, but he smiles as if he had garnets in his gums. "The chief will be with you soon. May I fetch you some coffee, perhaps?"

"Send him in already!"

The voice comes roaring from the adjoining room. Coco-Lacour leans into it without blanching.

"Won't you please follow me, Doctor?"

The elegance of the office takes me aback. Bookshelves, framed etchings, a black marble fireplace with an ormolu clock on the mantel-piece, white cotton gloves on a mahogany table. And, seated in a black leather armchair behind a massive fruitwood desk: Vidocq, every bit as massive, every bit as elegant, in a black suit with yellow tulips tucked in the lapel. Today's issue of the *Indépendent* lies before him, turned open to the theater page.

"Sit down, Hector."

And if some small part of me has been toying with the notion of withholding my news, that part gives way utterly in this moment. For in the act of planting me so squarely in his official circumference, Vidocq has enrolled me in the same freemasonry that binds Ronquetti, Aubé, Fouché, and Coco-Lacour. I'm one of *his* now.

It's the most natural thing in the world, then, to tell him everything I've learned from Father Time—and for him to take it in like a confessor, threading his hands under his chin, grunting occasionally over some detail. When I'm finished, he tips his head back, as if he were pouring the whole tale straight into his skull.

"Well, that's very interesting, Hector. I bet you never dreamed you had such an illustrious papa. Mine was a baker. *Bastard,* that was his real trade. Used to thrash me every chance he got. In all fairness," he adds, "I stole from his till every chance I got. On the scales of justice, we'll have to call it a draw."

A wizard's cackle flies from his chest. His gray eyes brighten into a noonday blue.

"Shall I tell you what I've been up to, Hector?"

"If you like," I answer, faintly.

"Ah, you're too kind." Cocking his shoulders, he turns toward the window, where Sainte-Chapelle lies framed: sun-sanded and immaculate. "You recall, I hope, the dying words of Monsieur Leblanc."

"He's here."

"Exactly. *He's . . . here.* The *he* part, well, we've at least got our mitts on that one, but what about that *here* business, eh? Such a simple word, and look how it wriggles when you try to grasp it. Does it mean *here* on the very street where Leblanc died? Not very likely. Does it mean Paris itself? I confess I thought it did. If you're some kind of idiot impostor king and you want to keep yourself hidden, you could do much worse than Paris. *Here,* you can make yourself scarce for years on end, and don't I know it?

"Ah, but then I started looking at it from the perspective of the—the *deeply* loyal Monsieur Leblanc. And the damned word started shifting on me again! Because to someone like Leblanc—someone who's been waiting his whole life for Louis the Seventeenth to come back—that word *here* could mean simply"—he extends his arms—"*France.* The native land. Crying out for its savior. Are you with me so far?"

"Of course."

"Well, now, if *here* extends as far as the nation's boundaries, we're in for quite a search, I'm afraid. But it must be because we're such good Christians, Hector, because God throws us a bone. Whoever was communicating with the lamented Monsieur Leblanc"—a lewd wink—"doesn't know he's dead."

"The newspapers reported it, surely."

"Ah, well, I called in some favors. A few free-market exchanges, and *voilà*! Nothing in the 'Local Notices' column. No memorial services, either. The body's still where you and I left it. Other than the Baroness, the only people who know he's dead are his creditors, and they're not likely to squawk. Bad for their reputations." Smiling, he folds his hock-arms against his belly. "Maybe you can guess why I've denied Monsieur Leblanc's corpse the customary Christian rites."

"To see if the parties in question attempted to contact him again?"

"Score one for you!" he bellows. "Oh, but Hector! You are *not* looking well, my friend."

"I don't—I don't feel—"

"No, don't argue with me. There's only one possible treatment for what you have. A change of *air*."

"Change of—"

"*Climate*, too, you're absolutely right. A day or two, you'll be back in the oats."

"Please, I don't—I haven't a clue what you're saying."

Grinning, he flings up his hands like a symphony conductor.

"We're going on a trip, Hector!"

CHAPTER 17

The Case of the Headless Woman

I'D RESOLVED NEVER to ask Vidocq where we're going. And because I'm a man of my word, more or less, all I can ask him on this occasion is:

"How do you *know* where to go?"

HE WALKS ME back then to a point early in his investigation. Chrétien Leblanc has been dead only three days. The dead man's apartment has been searched, crevice by crevice, for correspondence with unknown parties. The only items that have turned up are a saucer, a shuttlecock, a single yellow glove, and a program from the Jardin des Plantes, all encased in years of dust. Day after day, officers of the Sûreté sift through Leblanc's incoming post for telltale envelopes—nothing but tradesmen's bills, still waiting to be paid.

Did Leblanc choose some *other* means of corresponding? The old man was a cautious fish, after all. He might have had a trusted confederate, who could keep the messages close at hand and yield them up when needed. But who?

Not, if her testimony is to be credited, the Baroness. Conversations with the dead man's neighbors turn up little in the way of close friends or even regular acquaintances. Leblanc was, by habit and nature, a solitary man: light with drink, frugal with talk. Somehow, through all of his years of living, he contrived to leave the smallest possible indentation in Paris's envelope.

Undaunted, Vidocq makes the rounds of the dead man's neighborhood—cafés, wineshops, barbershops, tailors' shops—asking if anyone is keeping mail for a certain gentleman answering to this description. Again and again, he comes away empty.

Then, one afternoon, he is refreshing himself with wine and cutlets at an outdoor table of the Trois Frères when his eye is arrested by something on the far side of the street.

A mannequin, nothing more. Headless and voluptuous, holding court from the damask vacancy of a shop window.

In this instant, the mind of Chrétien Leblanc opens before Vidocq, like a book of spells. Here is the one place that no one would ever connect to an elderly and unattached man.

MADAME SOPHIE'S
Gowns and Frocks à la Mode for Paris's Most Beautiful Ladies

Boldly he sallies through the half-open door. Madame Sophie is away on errands, but a milliner named Émilie rises from behind the counter. A brunette, of round and comely figure, with long eyelashes that suggest a heart easily inflamed. When Vidocq announces he has come to pick up a package for his uncle Chrétien, these same eyelashes jerk up like awnings.

Oh, she doesn't think she can help, she says, folding down her lip. She wasn't to mention them to anyone.

"Ah, but don't you see, Mademoiselle? He *sent* me here, didn't he? How else should I have known to come?"

Mm . . . well, if he puts it like *that*. Oh, but she hasn't received any packages in—dear me, it's been two weeks.

"Well, no matter. Uncle's off taking the waters at Bad Em, and he asked me if I might look in. You—you're a good friend of my uncle's?"

Oh, no, Monsieur! Why, she never laid eyes on him until three months ago. He simply came in one morning and asked if he could engage her to keep packages for him, as he was on the road so often. He told her she need only hide them behind the counter, where they won't get in anyone's way and where Madame Sophie won't notice. He said he'd pay her two hundred sous on each package.

"Ah yes. That sounds like Uncle Chrétien, all right. Such a strange, secretive old turtle. Ha! My sister and I think he must be receiving billets-doux from a young mistress. His step is so light these days. . . ."

But how silly! interrupts Émilie. These aren't letters!

Instantly conscious of her transgression, she hastens with burning cheeks to assure Monsieur that she would *never* betray his uncle's confidences by opening the packages. It happened *once*, no more, and only because a burlap corner came loose and she was in the act of resealing it when the thing actually fell out! What could she do? She had to *look* at it.

"Of course, my pet. Was this by any chance the most recent package?"

Yes.

"Oho! I know exactly what it was, then. A gold ring, eh? So wide?"

Indeed it was, Monsieur! (The final battlement of her resistance falls.) And the strangest sort of ring, too, with all manner of scratches and marks. Why, you'd be lucky to get three francs for it at Les Halles. And if it belongs to your uncle's love, she must have fingers as big as knockwurst!

"Is it this?"

As luck would have it, the article in question is sitting in his watch pocket.

That's it! cries Émilie. Oh, it's frightful, isn't it?

"Yes, indeed," he agrees. "Why, even Uncle Chrétien wants no more of it. Do you know, just as he was leaving town, he asked if I might return it to its original owner? Which I'm only too happy to do, but damn me, I've lost the address. What a wretch I am!"

Well, ventures Émilie, if it's the same person who's been sending him those packages, then it must be from . . .

And out comes the name of a place. A city no more than an hour's coach ride from Paris.

"Why, of course!" he answers, rapping himself on the temple. "I *knew* it had something holy in it. Now then, if I can just recall the good lady's last name, I won't even need the street number."

And from the eternally charming Émilie, a name flies forth.

HOURS AND HOURS of searching, Vidocq will think afterward. And all the while, the answers were waiting on this young woman's fruited lips.

In a fit of ardor—or through the coolest possible calculation—he applies to these lips the unguent of his own. She omits the customary ritual of slapping him, which raises her even further in his estimation. He asks if Madame is due back within the next hour. She says no. He asks if he might turn the CLOSED sign on the window. She says yes. He asks if he might lower the blinds.

No, she says, taking him aback with her self-possession. *I'll do that.*

THAT VERY AFTERNOON, one of Vidocq's men travels to the jurisdiction identified by Émilie and returns with an address to attach to the name. The game has begun. Aubé, after studying a few samples of Leblanc's penmanship, scratches out the following note:

Awaiting further instructions

The note is dispatched by courier to the party in question. Two days later, as Émilie is only too happy to report, another of Uncle Chrétien's packages arrives. A simple note, reading only:

Your bundle is ready

"Arrived yesterday by special post," Vidocq tells me now, striding round his office. "We're closing in now, Hector."

"But when are we to go there?" I ask.

"*When?* Why, this very minute."

"I'll need to pack . . ."

"Screw that. I've got clothes ready for you."

"I'll need to—"

Tell Mother.

"I've already sent word to her," says Vidocq, smiling dryly.

"What did you say?"

"Oh." He gives a bored wave of his hand. "Ask Coco, that's his specialty. Symposium on ergot fever, probably. Outbreak of leprosy in the Loire valley. Something no one would dream of asking you about." Laughing, he grabs me by the collar. "Listen to me, my friend. If all goes well, you'll be back at Mama Carpentier's tomorrow night. With the air—the mystique, yes!—of a man who's *seen* something. How they'll envy you, my friend, how their little piggy eyes will start from their—say now, you don't have a pistol, do you? Never mind. Oh, but the thing is, you really *are* looking pale, Hector. You want a nip of arrack before we go?"

8 Brumaire Year III

Leblanc has proven true godsend. Extr kind, conscientious, willing. Surprisingly gd conversationalist. Ive now passed several happy hrs in his company.

Like me, he is v. concerned about Charles, esp. as nature of child's mental/emotional afflictions becomes increasingly <u>clear</u>. Before being incarcerated in cell, Charles experienced egregious abuse at hands of one Simon—<u>shoemaker</u>—hired, for unknown reasons, to be boy's "tutor." Fm Leblanc, I have learnt full details. Simon was charged by superiors w/ effacing "stigma of royalty" fm child. He forced boy to wear red cap, drink large amts of liquor, sing obscene & anti-royalist songs in full hearing of royal family. Boy became Simon's slave, serving him at table, shining Mme Simon's shoes. <u>Regularly</u> terrorized, beaten for smallest infractions. (Often, in middle of night, Simon wd shake child awake, only to kick him down again.) <u>Strong</u> suggestions of abuse of highly intimate nature.

Boy ultimately coerced into manufacturing appalling lies re family—most esp. re former queen. Thruout, he was utterly cut off fm comfort. Small wonder he remains in mortal terror of adults, esp. men.

Leblanc told me that if he ever met Citizen Simon, he wd happily repay him for his "tutelage." France has seen to that, I answered, for Simon perished w/ his master Robespierre on 10th Thermidor. Leblanc expressed opinion that Simon "got off easy."

10 Brumaire

This A.M., took Charles to tower platform. Vision has improved. Even in sunny conditions, boy able to keep eyes open for 1–2 minutes at time, see objects at distance of 100+ yds. <u>Most promising</u>.

Curious event: artillery regiment happened to pass by. Sound of drums initially disturbing to boy—he gripped my arm v tightly, cast eyes down. Drums left off near Ste. Élizabeth. Boy able to listen to remaining music w/ some pleasure. Said he had not heard music in v long time. (At least 2 yrs, by my estimation.) Band, whether fm calculation or accident, began to play "Marseillaise." How pretty, Charles was heard to say.

1 other thing. W/ permission of keepers, boy was suffered to collect some few blades of grass from tower platform + 1 dandelion, which had grown amid cracks in stones. These he attempted to fashion into primitive bouquet. Stalks too small and slight to oblige. Boy's mood consequently depressed as we returned him to his cell.

18 Brumaire

Leblanc has shown notable patience, persistence in drawing boy out. Also has been able to effect modest improvements in boy's quarters. Lamp may now be lit at twilight, thus allaying fear of dark. Knowing of Charles' aversion to loud noises, Leblanc has taken steps to muffle sounds of bolts on cell door. Addresses boy always w/ marked respect & kindness.

Boy's condition continues to improve. Modest weight gain, most visible in face. Some color in cheeks. Expression in eyes & mouth remains languid, affectless. Speech still difficult.

Rations have improved, too. Breakfast = plate of vegetables. Dinner = broth, boiled meat + 1 other dish. For supper, he receives at least 2 dishes. Food plain but relvly abundant.

On more than 1 occasion, he has asked to see his sister, who resides on floor below. Commissioners will not permit. "Tyrant's children" to be kept apart. I have argued that they shd not be punished for sins of fathers, etc. (Me, quoting Scripture.) Wolf cubs grow up to be wolves, they say.

6 FRIMAIRE

Summoned for meeting w/ Citizen Mathieu, Comm for Pub Safety, who asked if I'd read article in yesterday's Courrier Universel. Article expressed opinion that "a human being ought not to be degraded below the level of humanity, because he happens to be born the son of a king." Commissioners shd "take care that he be not, as in former times, deprived of the necessaries of life."

Mathieu asked me point-blank if I was behind "calumnious & royalist" trash. I answered that I was doctor, not journalist. Mathieu pointed out I have friends in 4th estate—one in particular, he believed? I reiterated my oath of secrecy.

Mathieu not satisfied. Warned against "exciting perfidious pity" for "last remains of our tyrant's race." (Spoke as if addressing Convention.) Said son of Capet shd be treated no better than any other child.

Cd not forbear fm answering that, in my opinion, he was being treated far worse.

Mathieu: "There are many more children worth much more than he who are worse in health. There are many who die that are more necessary to the world."

Meeting <u>distinctly</u> unpleasant. Followed soon after by meeting w/ Commissioner Ducaze, who felt obliged to remind me that royalist plots being fomented on ev side . . . France's enemies wd reinstall boy as king if they cd . . . gd citizens of the Repub must take all precautions to repel "missions of mercy," whether they come fm w/in or w/out.

I pointed out: Temple guarded by 194 members of Natl Guard, 14 artillery members, 4–5 gendarmes. <u>More than 200 men to safeguard two children.</u> Surely no further precautions necessary?

Was admonished to take better charge of my tongue.

10 FRIMAIRE

This A.M., Leblanc and I surprised Charles in cell w/ 4 pots of flowers. (Chrysanthemums, v fresh.)

I believe you used to have your own garden, said Leblanc, smiling.

Boy's response gratifying. At 1st he doubted evidence of senses. Hovered <u>over</u> pots, scarcely daring to touch. Spent some consid time <u>smelling</u>, then began, with great care, to examine them. Examination consumed 10–15 minutes.

Thank you, he said.

CHAPTER 18

In Which a Great Man Is Threatened with Extreme Violence

IF YOU'RE GOING to build yourself a château, you could find far worse places than the town of Saint-Cloud. A mere six miles from Paris's madness, lofting up from the Seine and bearing the clouds with it. A view fit for kings, yes, and before the kings, there were dukes and Florentine bankers, and after the kings, there was a certain emperor, who turned the Salon de Vénus into his personal throne room. And now the royals are back in Saint-Cloud, as eager as ever to flee Paris. And the tourists, equally eager, are following close behind.

I would have been no more than seven the first time I came here, and the only thing I can summon back now is water. Great sluices of emerald water, pouring through the aghast mouths of gargoyles. And a fox terrier, charging out of the woods—rising up on its hind legs and cocking its chin like a pugilist. I've been afraid of dogs ever since.

We must have come in a coach like this one, under towering steeples of trunks and valises, mire flying from the iron wheels and a great cape of dust trailing afterward. Wouldn't Mother be shocked, though, to see the change in my costume? Coarse gray woolen socks . . . wide cotton-velvet trousers . . . an old violet waistcoat, torn at every fold . . . and no shirt! Vidocq was particularly keen on keeping my neck and arms bare—never mind the chill—and before we left, he took great pleasure in drawing a faux tattoo on me. A dromedary, toiling across my right biceps.

"Why?" I asked him.

"Because tattoos make a bastard look *bigger*. And if anyone could use some size, it's—Jesus, Hector, where'd you get these?"

"What?"

"The scratchy things all down your arm. Been crawling through nettles, have you?"

"Little accident in the laboratory, that's all."

"Well, it does give you a breath of danger. Oh, but Christ, you're still pale as an empress."

From his desk drawer, he fished out a tortoiseshell compact.

"What's that?"

"Bit of rouge," he answered breezily. "A dab here, a dab there, you'll look like you've actually met the sun once or twice in your life. Oh, but the hands are still too soft. Here, rub 'em with sandpaper. We can't have you looking like a Parisian, can we?"

What with the last-minute toilette and a final fusillade of orders to "the boys," it's three-thirty by the time we leave and a little after five in the afternoon when the coach lumbers across the stone bridge into Saint-Cloud. On the far side of the Seine, chestnuts and hornbeam trees droop down in grapelike clusters. At ragged intervals, the gable of a *folie* noses through the foliage.

"We're day laborers," Vidocq is telling me. "Hoping to get in nice with the tourists. Oh, don't bother with an accent, Hector, you're the quiet one. A little *simple*, if you get my drift. You can manage *simple*, can't you?"

The inn goes by the name of the Golden Fleece. Five years ago, it was called the Golden Eagle, but all signs of eagles—or of the emperor who inspired them—have long since been expunged (except for the faint impress of an *N* on the street door). The proprietress is Madame Prunaud, a freely swearing widow with great patches of aggrieved scalp showing through scruffs of beige hair and a single brown tooth, flopped over her lower lip like a loose shingle.

"You'll get no beds from me," she growls.

"We're not particular, Madame. The attic or stable would do just fine."

Vidocq's pains have not been unavailing, for her eyes shimmer with contempt as she studies our rags.

"You don't set a paw inside 'til I get forty sous. In advance."

Supper is a slice of mutton and a bottle of Romanée served before one of those tavern fires that can neither be killed nor coaxed into full roar. Vidocq takes advantage of the cold to introduce himself to a group of cartmen and wagon drivers, who by their absence of bundles, give sign of being regular drinkers at the Prunaud tavern. To better commend himself to them, Vidocq steals two bottles of gin from Madame's cellar and serves them up in pewter mugs. Someone else brings out the cigars. A musical tribute to the pudenda is drawn out through ten choruses, the mottled tin lamp shakes to the stamp of clogs, and things are far enough along that Vidocq can say, in the very instant the tobacco smoke forks from his nostrils:

"Anyone here know a bugger by the name of Tepac?"

"What's he to you?" comes the general reply.

"Me and my pal," answers Vidocq. "We heard he had some coins to spread around."

"Tepac?" cries a tinware peddler, who is perhaps not really a tinware peddler. "I've never gotten a sou off him."

"Lucky you," says a wagoner. "I've never gotten a *word*. Tip your hat, he looks right *over* you, doesn't he? Lord of all creation or some such shit."

"I know the type," Vidocq says, winking. "Farts roses, does he?"

"That don't even—you'd think he was the pope's snot, he carries hisself so high."

"Fuck." Vidocq hangs his head low. "No chance of squeezing him for work, then. He's bound to have loads of servants."

Ah, but this same Tepac, we learn, has only two servants: a cook and a man of all work. He arrived in Saint-Cloud three months ago, in the thick of winter. A certain altitude to his personality led many to think he was affiliated with the royal family, but no one has ever seen him visit the court. He seldom eats out, has no known source of income, and has never been witnessed in the midst of labor. No one has seen him do *anything* except stroll the streets, twice a day, with a knobbed oaken staff that discourages even the hardiest thief.

"Well, that's it, then," says Vidocq, throwing up his hands. "We'll have to find us another fish."

"Hold a bit!"

The oldest of the cartmen has just finished baptizing the fire with a day's fund of urine, and as he tucks himself back in his trousers, he snarls:

"What you nosing round Saint-Cloud for? A lot more fish in Paris, ain't there?"

Vidocq gives his gin a stir with his index finger and mutters:

"We got our walking papers handed to us."

"Yeah, and who gave 'em to you?"

"Vidocq."

The response is pure gratification as, one by one, the onlookers ply us for more—*more*. Is it true Vidocq's got eyes in the back of his head? Me, I heard he can sniff a lie from ten miles. What *I* heard? He's in league with the devil, and once a month, he's got to burn some poor hardworking thief *alive*. No, it's only 'cause he's got fire coming out his eyes. Honest to God, I saw him burn someone's hat just by looking at it funny. . . .

The only one who refuses to traffic in the general mythography is the cartman, who announces, in a voice loud enough for all Saint-Cloud to hear:

"I ain't afraid of no Vidocq. If he was sitting there—right where you are, brother—I'd give him what for, believe it. Tear his brains out and shit in his skull, that's what I'd do. Hey!" From his pyre of rage, he glares down at me. "What're *you* smiling at?"

"I told you already," interjects Vidocq, catching me in the temple. "He's a bit of a simple, that's all."

"Don't no one come on our turf and laugh at us," says the cartman, giving his waistband a belligerent hitch. "Ain't polite, is it?"

Before anything can escalate, the high, squiggling birdcall of Madame Prunaud comes sailing through:

"I'll tell *you* what ain't polite!"

An avenging vision in her nightgown, already reaching for the cowhide strap on the chimney corner.

"I ain't wasting a good fire on the likes of you! Out with you all!"

At first, she means to include Vidocq and me in the diaspora. It takes another ten sous and a measure of sweet talk to propitiate her.

"To the attic with you, then."

No bed, of course, but there is a mattress. Oozing straw.

"*You* take it," says Vidocq. "I'm not tired yet."

For about the twentieth time today, I mourn my absent shirt as the air congeals round us and the cobwebs, one by one, leave veins of ice across my bare arms. Shivering there in the dark, I watch the broad outline of Vidocq sidewinding through the dust. Round and round he goes—until at last, he says, in a not-ungentle tone:

"Good night, Hector."

MANY HOURS LATER, I awake with a great inrush of air—utterly persuaded I'm drowning.

My hands claw the air for half a minute before the sensation of water begins to ebb. And even then, even after I've tested the floor and the wall and the mattress and found everything still solid, I can't shake the feeling that the ocean is roaring over me.

As the minutes pass, this sensation funnels down into a sound, and this sound draws me away from the relative warmth of my mattress and sends me crawling across the attic floor.

There, in a splash of starlight, sprawls Vidocq in all his mass. A single horsehair blanket cushions him against the ground. He lies uncovered, utterly still . . . except for the tidal pulse of muscle along his jawline.

Who would have imagined that the mere grinding of a man's teeth could produce this sound? Like water, yes, storming into a boulder's cranny—and clamoring to be let out again.

Vidocq is legendary, among police and criminals alike, for scorning sleep. And in future weeks, when I think back to this moment, I will wonder if it's because sleep hauls him back to the galleys—the iron collar, the chained ankle. For they are *raging*, these teeth, toward liberty.

He's awake before dawn.

CHAPTER 19

The Sad Fate of a Seagull

BREAKFAST IS BOILED chestnuts. Punishment enough, but Madame Prunaud, out of some torturer's instinct, has set a marmot, a goose, and a partridge crackling over the kitchen fire. My head, of its own volition, keeps swerving toward the spit, but Vidocq gnaws with a quiet grace, even makes a point of complimenting Madame on her seasoning. And when she declares it's time for us to go, he tenders her a small bow, picks up his knapsack, and bids me follow.

Only when we've left the inn far behind does Vidocq, with a grunt of satisfaction, reach into his knapsack and pull out three strips of grayish bacon, a hard roll, and a slab of white cheese.

"Stole 'em right off her plate," he crows.

We eat on the go, wiping our mouths with our hands, and for the first time, I feel the freedom that a disguise can bring. To be no longer myself! The sun drizzles down my neck. A river breeze ambles through, bearing scent-threads of clover, yarrow, wild oats. In the jasmine, the first drowsings of bees.

And from Vidocq's great frog-throat, a swelling of song. The same Mozart motif we heard in the morgue.

"Tepac," I say, half to myself. "That's a curious sort of name."

"Oh, for the love of—spell it *backward*, will you, Hector? *C-a-p* . . ."

". . . *e-t.*"

Capet.

The name of a long-ago landowner who begat a great line of kings. The name that Temple guards hurled at the dauphin as though it were the most loathsome of epithets.

"Do you know," says Vidocq, "I'm very near to being insulted by that name. What a vulgar touch! *Tepac.*" He bats at a low-hanging alder branch. "That's what I get, dealing with amateurs. Give me professionals anytime. You always know where you are with them."

After five more minutes of walking, we come to a pile of oak logs, fashioned in a pyramid, standing sentrylike atop a long, steeply pitched hill. Vidocq slows his gait—to get his bearings, I assume, until I see him make a quick scan of the horizon and lean over the woodpile.

On the other side is a long, lank, swaddled customer with a lush growth of whiskers and a pair of close-set mole-eyes, gray from exhaustion.

"Ah, Goury!" says Vidocq. "Such a pleasure."

Drawing back his eyelids, Goury takes my measure.

"Who's this?"

"My good friend Dr. Carpentier. Makes very little fuss, you won't even notice him. Tell me, has anyone come and gone since yesterday?"

"Not a soul."

Leaning round the woodpile, I peer down the hill and I see—we'll say *two* houses. The first is a four-room, foursquare cottage with a steeply cut hipped roof and flat slate tiles. The kind of door-mad house that looks unabashedly outward and grows grapevines like hair and relishes every ray of sun on its plaster skin and harbors an eternally kindled hearth.

Slowly, though, the morning mist superimposes a second house over the first. From nowhere, I see blackened slashes of wall, fissured with cracks. I see two broken windows, stuffed with bales of straw. And nailed to the front door, a seagull, stretching its wings wide in taxidermic rapture. It could be the hideout of an Ostend smuggler.

"And other than that," says Goury, "he's your basic hearth-and-home stiff. Honestly, boss, I don't know what you want with this one. Never stops for a drink. Never bats an eye at the girls. Don't think he's got a single vice."

"I hear he likes to go for strolls."

"Twice a day, yeah. Nine-forty in the morning, four-forty in the afternoon."

"Creature of habit, is he?"

"You could track the sun and stars by this one."

"Well, let's see, that gives us—twelve minutes till the next orbit. Just enough time for refueling, eh?"

From an inner recess of the knapsack comes a small canteen, which Vidocq, after a swig, passes round. Goury downs his portion in half a second; I spit mine out at the first sign of trouble.

"My own recipe," explains Vidocq. "Brandy and stout and a sniff of absinthe. Takes the rust off, don't it? Careful, though. You drink too much, you'll sleep through whole *eras*, it's true. Hang on now," he says, screwing the cap back on. "I think this is our boy."

We *hear* him first: a squeaking of hinge, a laboring of door. Then comes a single boot, extending past the plane of the doorframe, in the manner of an Opéra-Comique dancer preparing her entrance. In the next second, he's standing there in his entirety: Monsieur Tepac of Saint-Cloud, surveying the planet.

At this remove, nothing remotely dynastic clings to him, unless you count his burgher's air of entitlement. His build is squarish, portly. His hair is the color of late-summer wheat. His feet join at the heels and turn outward at the toes.

"Well, now," murmurs Vidocq, pressing a pair of binoculars to his eyes. "They got the age right, anyway. Thirty, thirty-two. Coloring's close enough. Not that it's any *hardship*, mind you, finding a blue-eyed Frenchman. But what a spectacle he makes of himself! Look for yourself, Hector."

The first thing I see is the high-crowned hat. Moving downward: a dandyish, outsize collar, an even larger necktie. *Three* waistcoats, worn one over the other, each a different shade of olive. A short-waisted fishtail coat and a double row of silver buttons marching straight up a rather prosperous belly.

"Eats well," says Vidocq, sourly. "Hold on. Who's that behind him, Hector?"

An apron with a dusty-rose border billows into the doorframe, pursued by a single chapped hand.

"It's the cook, I think."

Tepac turns his head back, lifts his hand in farewell. Then, from the interior of the house, comes another figure: the man-of-all-work, striding past with a kettle full of wood chips. He angles his chin toward Tepac and disappears round the side of the house.

The briefest of tableaus, yes, but enough to give me a sense of . . . easy terms, I suppose . . . domestic covenants, lightly shouldered. This fellow may take airs with his townsmen, but in his own castle, he wears the master's robes lightly.

Giving his oaken staff a rapier twirl, Monsieur Tepac sets off down the road, in the general direction of the river.

"After you," whispers Vidocq. "After you, my highliness."

CHAPTER 20

In Which Tourism Is Shown
to Be Hazardous

QUICKLY VIDOCQ LAYS out the parameters. Two of us will follow Tepac; the third will circle round and rejoin the party after five minutes; the first man will then peel off, and the rotation will continue.

Always we stay in conversation with one another. Under no circumstance do we make eye contact with the quarry. Periodically, we step aside to make small changes in our appearance: adding a scarf, dropping a tie, turning a vest inside out. Vidocq, during one changeover, slaps on a pair of leather gaiters, and a short while later, Goury appears in a red Phrygian bonnet that was last seen on the Bastille ramparts.

What would Monsieur Tepac think, I wonder, if he knew how much effort was being expended on his behalf? But he never looks back, never even moves his head as he keeps his course through Saint-

Cloud's half-deserted streets. To the people who pass—a tinman, an umbrella peddler, an old woman cadging for change—he pays not the slightest heed.

"Even Bonaparte would have given 'em a fucking nod," grumbles Vidocq.

We follow him over a brook, through a copse of sycamores, over blankets of moss and a sward of Henry the Fourth's ruff. For entire intervals, Monsieur Tepac's stout figure disappears entirely from view, only to reappear in some unexpected place, like the cleft in a linden.

A half hour more, and he is veering south. No curlicues this time. He walks with greater purpose, as if a destination has suddenly occurred to him. And as the Seine breaks once more onto our eye, and the stone bridge rears up on our left, I realize, with a sting of something like hilarity, where he's heading.

"Oh, the bastard!" says Vidocq.

THE KING OF FRANCE's park is still a grand place to visit in these early days of the Restoration. Most people make a point of going in the summer, when, on any given Sunday, twenty-four jets of water come blazing into life. There's always a watercolorist with an easel propped under an old chestnut, and there's always a band playing, and complete strangers dance together in the high damp grass.

On a Tuesday in April, however . . . well, the château is closed, and there are maybe a dozen and a half people strolling through the grass and bindweed—most of them English missionary ladies in black fender-bonnets. The waterworks are on hold. Le Nôtre's great *parterres de broderie* are no more than boxwood skeletons.

The birds are here, though, threshing the lawns. And the *air*, that's here, too. Even Monsieur Tepac pauses alongside the carp basin to take his fill of it.

———

Is it now that I remember? That it was the same air beloved of Marie-Antoinette?

She tasted it, yes, and resolved that the air of Saint-Cloud was fit for royal children to breathe. And so, at her behest, the King bought the château from his cousin, and this became the royal family's haven from the Parisians who stared daggers at them through the long days and nights.

It was Saint-Cloud they were trying to reach before everything fell apart. April 18, 1791: The royal *berline* came thundering out of the Tuileries courtyard, bound on the usual route . . . but this time the way was blocked by a mob of sans-culottes so unappeasable that even General Lafayette couldn't disperse them. For more than an hour, they surrounded that carriage, lobbing volleys of spit, every species of Parisian invective—baying for the head of the Austrian bitch and her cuckold. And through it all sat the King and Queen of France, trapped by their own subjects . . . knowing in their heart of hearts they would never again see Saint-Cloud.

But maybe, during that long hour, they allowed themselves a hope. That one day, not too far distant, their *son* would breathe that air once more.

And once more I gaze at this plump bourgeois gentleman with his steel-tipped bluchers and his three waistcoats, strolling down from the Terrasse des Orangers, moving with inerrant straightness, as if a silk train were unfurling behind him.

Is this why you came here? To finish their journey for them?

And then Vidocq's voice comes jabbing in.

"Jesus, quit *staring* at him, Hector!"

———

THE KING OF FRANCE'S park boasts a shrub, lately arrived from the Indies. A tangle of branches, fine as hair, powdered with millions of tiny white blossoms. Its positioning near the Fontaine du Gros Bouillon gives it a certain status so that, if you're anywhere in its vicinity, you feel obliged to pay respects. The missionary ladies stop for a bit. Also a gitano in an embroidered blue turban, and in the same crowd: an abbé with a torn cassock; a pair of mariners, somewhat the worse for last night, locking arms round each other to keep themselves erect; and a pride of Russian soldiers, tilting their shakos at the exact angle of defiance they sported when they were occupying Paris three years ago.

Even Monsieur Tepac joins the throng. Through Vidocq's binoculars, I see him fold his hands into his waistcoats and bend ever so slightly forward. A fluttering of eyelid, a quickening of nostril.

One minute, that's all he grants this particular plant. Then, gripping his staff like a scepter, he continues in the same stately fashion toward the Grand Cascade, where even now, the emerald water I remember from childhood is pouring through those gargoyle mouths.

He hasn't said a word to anybody in the crowd, but his leaving somehow loosens the social fabric. The missionaries disperse, and the Russian soldiers make toward the nearest restaurant, and those two sailors unlock arms and go careening northward, in widening parabolas.

"Those sailor boys will . . ."

This is what I'm about to say. *Those sailor boys are going to kill someone if they're not careful.*

And I look over at Vidocq, and I see, stamped on his face, the same thought—carried to a different conclusion.

"Goury," he says. "It's time to break up this party."

HOW DID HE KNOW? Curiously enough, it's the thing he was at such pains to correct in me.

Their skin.

Not the sun-cured crust that Vidocq remembered well from his own brief career at sea but the lymphatic whiteness so exclusive to Paris.

And once that discordance has registered, every pretense of being a bystander vanishes, and Vidocq is calling back to Goury and *driving* forward, like a baggage wagon breaking free of its harness, powering toward the Grand Cascade. . . .

And already he's too late.

The two sailors have shaken off their drunken fog, and in the same breath, they reach into their pockets and *converge* on Monsieur Tepac, moving in the straightest possible line with the least expense of energy.

Oh, it's evil.

The staff is knocked from Tepac's hand. The first blade catches him in his left side. A foot-deep thrust that freezes him in place for the second blow, a long slash across the neck.

An instant, that's all it takes, and the sailors have flung the blades away and peeled off in opposite directions, and Vidocq, his face a furious purple, is barking orders at Goury and sprinting down the château terrace, and Goury is heading straight for the woods, and Monsieur Tepac is still, against all possibility, standing.

And then, in the next second, he's crumbling like old mortar. Tipping into the Grand Cascade's waiting basin with a muffled splash.

I hear a woman shout. I see a blur of wool and steel as the missionaries gallop toward the river and the Russians circle in confused alarum. And then, from nowhere, the waterworks come screaming into life—weeks ahead of schedule. Great plumes of sun-dazzled water, hooping and spiraling round us—and weaving a cocoon round the whirling figure of Monsieur Tepac.

Later, I won't be able to recall jumping into the water. My memory will click in at the precise moment that my hands close round Tepac's shoulders. The weight of him! Which is the weight of the water, too, soaking through all those waistcoats—and the weight of that *face*. Pale and trembling. Coughing up columns of water.

"Is there a . . ."

Doctor . . . That's the word that hovers on my lips.

And what a shock! To realize I'm calling for myself.

With a mighty heave, I drag his body out of the basin, tip him by degrees over the balustrade, and drag him toward the grass. I look round. The grounds are utterly deserted, and his breath is still coming, in long straggling rasps, but the only symptoms I can read in this moment are my own. The magnetic crackling of the hair on my arms. My heart slamming off my breastbone . . .

And in the seconds that follow, a span of three years drops away, and I am standing in the dissecting laboratory of the École de Médecine, and Dr. Duméril is bidding me to . . .

"Slow down, Monsieur. Take it, symptom by symptom, if you please."

Contusion on forehead . . .

That's it.

. . . likely related to fall. Does not appear serious.

Continue.

Throat wound: relatively superficial. Carotid artery . . .

Yes . . . ?

. . . and jugular vein still intact. Patient still able to breathe, w/ difficulty.

Continue.

Side wound . . .

And here . . . here the act of enumerating for Dr. Duméril gives way before the act of touching—*feeling*—that raw flap of skin.

Possible . . . possible rupture of spleen . . .

But it's not the spleen I'm conscious of, no, it's his eyes. He looks somehow as if it were happening to someone else.

I at once applied pressure to wound.

Except all I have to apply is my own hand, and how inadequate it is. The blood runs through the crevices of my fingers, and the skin round his mouth grows whiter and whiter, and . . .

"You'll be all right," I whisper.

A coldness, quite different from the chill of the water, is stealing over him as the blood draws back to his heart and the orphaned extremities quiver.

"No," I say. "No. *Look*."

Extending my index finger, I lower it toward his half-seeing eyes. I draw it back. I lower it once more.

"Watch the finger. That's all you have to do."

Something sparks in the depths of his irises. The pupils slowly narrow to a point.

"That's it," I say. "Don't think of anything else. Just the finger."

And gradually, as he draws me into focus, the trembling begins to ebb, and a vein of color reveals itself in his cheeks, and even the blood—or do I imagine this?—even this begins to abate.

With a stifled cry, I look up to find Vidocq—cast in such a deep shadow by the sun that, at first, I think he's flung a satchel over his shoulder. But then the satchel reconfigures itself into a man. In a mariner's suit.

The man is conscious, yes, but utterly still in the grip of a larger will. Vidocq flings him onto the grass as if he were a bag of feed. Places one knee on the man's back, draws out a pair of handcuffs, and binds the wrists together in a single practiced stroke.

"Move a fraction," he growls. "Move a *fiber*."

Panting, he kneels beside me. His eyes lock onto mine.

"How is he?"

"I can't—he's too—"

With a dark wonder, I hold my hand up to the light, and it's someone *else's* hand: palsied from effort, painted with blood. Vidocq is already stepping round me . . . leaning over the dying man . . . purring raspily into his ear.

"Help's on the way. You'll be just fine, your—your *king*ship. . . ."

I'll never know exactly how he means that title. I can only testify to the change it produces in the dying man. A violent bucking rhythm that takes him from his bluchers to his shoulder blades but concentrates itself most intensely in the head, which swivels from side to side, like a clock pendulum—*repelling* the title Vidocq has granted him.

And this denial, finally, is what costs Monsieur Tepac his last drop of force. The eyes, having lodged their objections, scroll up. The head falls still. The lower lip rolls down.

"The game's done," says Vidocq.

CHAPTER 21

A Garden Grows in Saint-Cloud

GOURY COMES BACK alone. Nothing to tender but apologies.

"Sorry, Chief, he was a fast one for being so tall . . . made straight for the woods . . . I kept *at* him. . . ."

But Vidocq is locked in a silent colloquy with the dead man.

"Well, now," he says, to no one in particular. "Bastards learned their lesson, eh? Didn't want any dying speeches, like the late Monsieur Leblanc. So they took out his throat. Ah yes," he says, nodding. "But they couldn't keep him from talking, could they, Hector?"

"He was saying . . ."

"He was saying *no*. He was saying you've got the wrong man, brother."

Frowning, he kneels once more by the dead man. Circles his finger round a small pond of sepia by the temples.

"Iodine?" I guess.

Vidocq shakes his head. Thrusts his hand deep into the dead man's locks. A single brute swipe, and then the fingers reemerge in the morning light, with a phantasmal coat of gold.

"Hair dye," whispers Goury.

"Mm," grunts Vidocq. "Bit young to be coloring his roots, isn't he?" He wipes his hand on his trousers. "*Someone's* been made an ass of. Damned if I know who."

For the first time, the sound, the spectacle of the waterworks impose themselves on his senses. His nostrils twitch like a salamander's. His eyelids quiver down.

"Goury?"

"Yes, Chief."

"Keep a watch on our little prisoner over there. Hector?"

"Yes."

"I wonder if you'd join me for a bit of exercise. . . ."

WHEN CHATEAUBRIAND WAS first presented at court in 1785, he was favored with a smile from his queen, Marie-Antoinette. It must have captivated him because, twenty years later, he could still pick it out from the bones exhumed from the mass grave near La Madeleine. One sight of those enameled tiers, blazing forth from a skull, and he could say in perfect faith: *That was her.*

As for me . . . well, no queens have ever smiled on me. How, then, should I know a Hapsburg lip when I see it? Maybe I stumbled across it in a textbook. (*Pathology: mandibular prognathism.*) Maybe I glimpsed it at the Louvre. But when I see Vidocq sprinting away from the dead man, I don't have to ask where he's going. My mind is already traveling back there.

To the strange cottage we left just an hour ago, where a young man—a man-of-all-work, or so we thought him—came striding through a doorway with an armload of wooden chips and thrust his chin toward Monsieur Tepac.

A chin that was already thrust forward.

As it has been thrusting, more or less, through generations of Hapsburgs. The Empress Maria Theresa passed it on to her daughter Marie-

Antoinette, who married a king of France and gave birth to a boy, and this boy met the world in the same way as his ancestors: the upper jaw retiring, the lower jaw crawling out like a cantilever—producing a drooping lip that looks either pugnacious or dim or shy, depending on the context, and resembles no other lip in the world.

THE COTTAGE IS glazed and serene when we reach it. Woodsmoke crawls from the chimney. In the near distance, a cow and a horse woo each other. . . .

We find him at the rear of the house, kneeling in the damp spring soil, sweating freely through his blouse.

He doesn't know we're there. Vidocq has to insert his massive frame between the sun and the earth—*drown* the fellow in shadow, like Alexander towering over Diogenes. Only then does the young man pause in his labor and look up.

"Good day," he says.

The hair is dirty blond, unkempt, straggling halfway down the neck. The eyes are blue. The skin is freckled and creased by long exposure to the sun.

The *hands* . . . scratched, calloused, caked in dirt. The hands of a laborer.

And what have they wrought! My eyes can't even take it in. The austere boxwood patterns of Le Nôtre—wheels and spirals and paisleys—but crawling with life. Pansies and tulips, crocuses and lungworts, the beginnings of roses and tuberoses and jasmine and pinks. All of it somehow crammed into a twelve-by-fifteen plot.

"What's your name?" I ask him.

The sketch of a smile emerges from that prominent lower jaw . . . then withdraws. He extends one of his loam-coated hands and, like a child reading from a primer, says:

"My name is Charles."

PART II

Saint-Denis

7 Pluviôse Year III

Weather last night exceedingly stormy. Wind swept down thru chimneys, filling Charles' room w/ smoke. Leblanc asked permission to put out fire in child's room, lest child suffocate. Commissioner Leroux so agreeable to request that Leblanc asked if boy cd eat w/ them in council-room. Leroux, being warm w/ wine, had no objection.

Thus, for 1st time since being shut away, Charles ate in room <u>other</u> than his cell. Behaved, says Leblanc, w/ great poise & civility. This occasioned much bafflement in Commissioner Leroux, who said: Dr C informed me this boy was v. ill. He dont look like hes dying to me.

Leblanc: Hes most certainly not well, Citizen. Knees & wrists v. swollen. Still underweight & in consid pain from walking.

Leroux: Hes well enough. Kindly inform Dr C to stop exaggerating.

Charles' depression returned forthwith. Refused to eat cake. Nibbled on crust of bread.

Look at him sulking, said Leroux. We shd have left him to suffocate.

5 VENTÔSE

Charles has managed to make his chrysanthemums last thru winter. Remarkable achievement, given lack of air & sunlight in his cell. Today I asked him his secret. He said he learned long ago—in Tuileries gardens—one must <u>talk</u> to one's flowers.

You dont think me mad? he said.

On the contrary, I said, I consider you ingenious. But do flowers like to play piquet?

With that, I presented him pack of cards. (Had been saving it for this moment.) His eyes grew quite large & he began to rub at them w/ fists. At 1st I supposed him to be angry, but I recalled that's how he looks when he is trying not to cry. I have yet to see a tear from him.

You know how to play? I asked. He nodded. But for sevrl mins, he was unable even to touch cards. As w/ flowers, he seemed to doubt evidence of senses.

If you dont mind, he said, Id like just to hold them a bit.

7 VENTÔSE

Yesterday afternoon, Leblanc & Charles were stopped in act of playing piquet by Commissioner Leroux, who informed them they were engaged in <u>unlawful acts</u>.

Unlawful? said Leblanc. Just a little game, Citizen.

Little game! cried Leroux, snatching up cards. <u>Queen</u> of hearts! <u>King</u> of clubs! Hast thou not heard, Citizen? France has rid herself of hereditary monarchy.

Leblanc reiterated it was "all in good fun." Commissioner refused to relent. Said boy cd only play cards if he referred to "queen" as "citizeness" and to "king" as "tyrant." At which Charles pushed away his cards, wanting nothing more to do w/ them. Cards have now been confiscated by state. <u>Confiscated by state</u>.

Upon hearing this, I told Leblanc that tomorrow I shall bring Charles 2 new packs of cards. If Citizen Leroux wishes to confiscate these, he will 1st have to confiscate <u>me</u>, which he cannot do w/o express consent of Genl Barras.

8 VENTÔSE

On way to Charles' cell this A.M., I was pulled aside by Commissioner Leroux, who asked if I was guilty of restoring card-playing privileges to Prisoner. I confessed I was. Leroux told me he does not like my "presumptions," which he hastened to call "aristocratic." I told him I do not like his manners, which are not greatly improved by his drinking. I believe he was ready to strike me. I am glad he did not, for I wd not have been answerable for my own conduct.

12 VENTÔSE

Charles asked if he could go to top of tower again. He was quite concerned re condition of his ornamental cabbages & was relieved to find them still flourishing. In course of "conversing" w/ plants, he asked if I had not incurred a great deal of wrath on his account?

I assured him it was not on his account but on mine. I have never cared for bullies, regardless of what office they hold.

For some time, he persisted in tending to plants, occasionally humming to them. He then asked if I might point out my house to him.

From here? I said. Oh, you cannot see it. Notre-Dame gets in the way. We live on other side of Ile de la Cité. In the Latin Quarter.

We, he said, rather shyly. You have a wife?

Yes.

A child, too, perhaps?

A boy named Hector.

And is he my age?

No, he is but 3. Although (I cdnt help but add) he knows at least 200 words.

I shd like. . . .

Here Charles stopped.

To meet him? I conjectured. Someday you will.

No, he said, I shd like to take <u>care</u> of him. As you have me. If you took me home w/ you, we cd be brothers, he and I, and I'd keep very close watch on him, youd never have a moment's worry.

God willing, I said, you shall enjoy far greater comforts than my humble home cd offer.

No, he said. Yrs wd do very well.

CHAPTER 22

The Fox and the Rabbit

THE INTERROGATION OF Tepac's assassin takes place in the dead man's scullery. I am not invited in, and so, like a child straining to hear his parents, I press my ear to the door. This is what I hear.

NOTHING.

NO, THAT'S NOT quite right. A series of tiny soft implosions, the sort a kettle might make on a wet hob. The door opens then to find our counterfeit sailor bound by the feet to an old spindleback chair. Vidocq, his cravat loosened, stands over him; off to the side leans Goury, whose hands, for reasons mysterious, are coated in flour. On the assassin, no obvious signs of violence, except for the droop of his head, just outside the normal axis, and a roiling afterecho, as though the air itself had been singed.

Later I will learn just how Vidocq did it.

Remembering the man's name was the easy part. Just a quick rummage through his inner archives, and out it pops.

"Monsieur Noël, isn't it?"

A twitch is all the confirmation he needs. From there, he reconstructs Noël's dossier card, line by line.

"Stole twenty-three streetlamps in the Rue Fontaine-au-Roi. . . . Fifty-eight pieces of calico from Trouflat's Novelties . . . Oh, that's right, you've got a mother. Distinguished artiste, with a charming apartment on the Rue Saint-Claude. Gives piano lessons, doesn't she? Ooh, I'd hate to see her lose her livelihood."

Amazing. You take out one brick, the whole wall falls. In the very next second, Noël has coughed up the other assassin's name.

"Herbaux, eh? That's funny, I thought he was still counting cockroaches in La Force."

Turns out this same Herbaux managed to stroll out of prison two months ago, dressed in his sister's petticoats. ("*That* old trick," mutters Vidocq.) A few weeks after that, he approached Noël about a job in Saint-Cloud.

"And who was the brain behind it?" asks Vidocq.

Don't know.

"Who was the bank?"

God's truth, he doesn't know. The only one who ever talked to Monsieur was Herbaux.

"*Monsieur?*"

That's what they were told to call him. No first name, no surname. Just a title.

"Did Herbaux ever describe him?"

Couldn't. Monsieur was just a voice, that was all.

"Herbaux never saw him?"

He only ever met the man at Saint-Sulpice. Monsieur sat in a confessional booth the whole time with the curtain closed.

"He's a *priest?*"

No idea.

"Old voice? Young voice?"

Herbaux never said.

"How much did this Monsieur promise you?"

A hundred francs up front. Two hundred on completion.

"Ha! Knowing Herbaux, it was probably double that. This Monsieur . . . he never gave a reason for wanting Tepac gone?"

Not that he knew of. A fellow learns not to be curious about such things.

"When'd you get the go-ahead, then?"

Yesterday.

"Yesterday?"

Herbaux came by Noël's lodgings in the afternoon. Said the plan was a go. They were to reach Saint-Cloud that night and wait for Tepac in the King of France's park. As soon as they had a clean line on him, they were to bring him down.

"And so you did. Were you in charge of the throat or the gut, Noël?"

The throat. Doesn't make such a squooshy sound.

NOËL IS DEPOSITED with the local constabulary. Attention then turns to Monsieur Tepac's maid, an Alsatian named Agatha, built along the lines of a dwarf pine, and dry down to the roots. Not a tear does she shed on behalf of her late employer . . . but then she hasn't cried, she tells us, since she was three. All the same, he was a good sort, Monsieur Tepac. Wages on time. Never dragged a lot of people home, never quibbled about afternoons off. You don't find many situations so nice.

"Did Tepac tell you where he came from?"

From his accent, she took him for Swiss.

"Did he tell you what business he had in Saint-Cloud?"

No. Wasn't her place to ask.

"What about the young man, then? This Charles fellow."

Why, Charles just came with the house.

"Was he a servant?"

Oh, no, indeed. Her very first day here, Tepac told her she was to treat Monsieur Charles as a gentleman. Even if he didn't quite dress like one.

"And what did he tell you about this Charles?"

She figured him for some relation of Tepac's, but he never said one way or another, and it wasn't. . . .

"Your place to ask. I know."

Oh, but the boy's a joy to have around. Truly. Always willing to lend a hand with the dishes, loves to clip laundry to the line. Eats anything you give him. Really, the only bother is the shoes.

"The shoes . . ."

Well, he can't tie his own laces, can he? Strangest thing.

"Did you ever ask why?"

Guess he never learned. And, you know, he *is* a bit simple, so you can't expect too much.

His bedroom is no different from a peasant's. A cracked pitcher, a worm-riddled stool, a looking glass the size of a slipper. And a bed . . . which is, in all its essentials, a coffin, scarcely three feet wide, set on two half-barrels.

That's where we find him, perched on the straw mattress, his hands squeezed between his thighs. A cloud of sweat-musk rising off him.

From the start, I notice Vidocq taking a different tack: several feet of distance, a minimum of eye contact. And an entirely new tone: not gentle, exactly, but conversational, as if they had come across each other playing chess.

"Charles, is it?"

"Yes."

"This is Dr. Carpentier. And I'm Vidocq. Inspector Vidocq."

If he expects the name to make an impression . . . well, I don't think he does. He's already gliding forward.

"Do you have a last name, Charles?"

"Yes."

"Maybe you could tell us."

"Rapskeller."

His head is bowed. Not from grief, as I initially think, but to better follow the shuttlecock that he's passing between his feet.

"Do you have a mother, Charles Rapskeller? A father?"

"In heaven," he says simply.

"Any other family? Living or—anywhere?"

"You know . . ." He tucks one of his boots under the shuttlecock, flips it into the air. "I think I must have family somewhere. But I've never met them."

Still careful to keep his distance, Vidocq eases himself onto the mattress, so warily that the straw barely stirs.

"Charles," he says. "Do you know why Monsieur Tepac brought you here?"

"Oh, because I've never been."

"Do you understand that Monsieur Tepac is dead?"

A small furrow in the young man's brow.

"Oh, I see. He's going to meet Mama and Papa."

And with that, the furrow vanishes, and the shuttlecock continues its progress, back and forth.

"Charles . . ."

Whether it's to reassure him or to lay claim to him, I'll never know, but Vidocq chooses this moment to extend his hand. It is traveling toward the vicinity of Charles' shoulder, but it never gets there. In a single galvanic pulse, the young man jerks upward. Backs away two steps and takes three long breaths. A kind of ritualized quality to the entire sequence, as though he had just concluded a sacrament.

"I don't really like that. Being touched. Out of the blue like that."

"I'm sorry."

"No, it's all right. You didn't know."

Vidocq tucks his hands under his thighs. Lets the silence build up again.

"Now, then, Charles. There's something I want to ask you if you don't mind. Are you the King of France?"

The young man stares at him for a short space—then begins to giggle.

"Don't be silly!" he says. "We've already got a king. Although they tell me he's very fat, and has trouble walking. Poor king."

Vidocq laces his hands behind his neck. "Have you ever been to Paris, Charles?"

"Sometimes. I'm fairly sure I was dreaming, though."

"Why do you think that?"

"Because I flew there."

"Ahh." The tiniest chuckle shakes itself from Vidocq's throat. "Well, now, Charles, Dr. Carpentier and I would like to take you back to Paris with us. As our guest."

"When?"

"Now."

His mouth twists down. "I'll need my coat."

"Of course."

"And also . . ."

"Yes?"

"Do you think Agatha would mind looking after the flowers?"

"We'll ask her, shall we?"

"The bulbs need tying down, you know. After the first flower."

"Is there anything else?"

He spends a few more seconds tracking the shuttlecock. Then he raises his head, and once more, that jaw angles toward us.

"Do you suppose we might visit the Luxembourg?"

"The palace? We could try to arrange something, yes."

"No, I'm sorry. I mean the Luxembourg Gardens."

"Well, as a matter of fact, Dr. Carpentier and I were strolling in the gardens just the other day. Weren't we, Hector?"

"Why, yes."

It's the first time I've spoken since entering the room—and the first time Charles has really drawn me into his ken. As if to atone for the oversight, he spends the next half minute absorbing me. In all my particulars.

"You were there?" he asks. "Were the chestnuts in bloom?"

"The chestnuts . . ."

How to tell him this? *I don't know.* On every side of me lay a bank of fog.

"Yes," I say. "They were in bloom."

He studies me a while longer.

"Doctor, you look like a rabbit I used to have."

"A rabbit?"

"He was very loyal, but something ate him. A fox, perhaps."

CHAPTER 23

A Scene of Great Carnage
Involving Pistachios

WE LEAVE FOR Paris late that afternoon. Not in a stage, as we came, but in a cariole personally hired by Vidocq. As punishment, he puts Goury on the driver's box, but the only protest we hear on the way back to town is from the vehicle itself, arthritic through the rims, spitting up stones and rotten pears—even, at one crossing, a turtle, pitched on its back, waving farewell as we turn the corner.

Next to me Charles Rapskeller slumbers. In a dead man's clothes. The carefully brushed round hat, the old-fashioned waistcoat, the black trousers and black wool socks . . . these came straight from Tepac's wardrobe. The only articles that are unmistakably Charles' are the copper-buckled shoes and the coat, which is, providentially, the same shade of yellow as the mud. Into this coat he climbs and, as soon as the carriage is in motion, falls straight to sleep. The only sign that something lives inside that yellow carapace is his protruding face, soft and sun-reddened.

"Is he really sleeping?" growls Vidocq.

"I think so."

"Maybe you'd be so kind as to check."

Gingerly, I pry open an eyelid.

"Asleep. Yes."

"Then maybe you can tell me. How'd we get ourselves in such a fucking mess?"

In our short acquaintance, I've never seen him this glum. Two men dead. A killer still at liberty. Murderers queuing up for instructions at confessional booths . . .

"And don't forget," Vidocq says, as if he were divining my inventory. "A so-called king. Who doesn't know he's supposed to be a king. What the hell am I supposed to do with *him*?"

"I don't know. . . ."

"Ahh." Vidocq tips his head in mock deference. "Dr. Hector's got something on his mind."

"No, it's just that . . ."

"What?"

"He *fits*."

"How do you mean he *fits*?"

"What I mean is if Louis the Seventeenth really *was* rescued—spirited away, as the old story says—then we would expect to find in him a certain amount of damage. Even today."

I'm waiting for him to stop me. But for once he's all ears.

"Think," I say, "of all that boy suffered during his years in the Temple. Think of the abuse to his mind and body. He was beaten, he was shut away for months in confinement. He suffered a painful and wasting illness. He was separated from his sister. He saw his own father dragged away, he was forced to testify against his mother. Even if he'd survived it all, the trauma might have forced some—some rearrangement. . . ."

"*Rearrangement?*"

"Well, consider the medical literature. Bidaut-Mauger has found that children, regularly beaten, can manifest all the signs of brain damage even when the cerebellum and cerebral cortex are intact. The slowness, the inattention, all those *symptoms* we associate with idiocy might simply be a way of—detaching from hostile surroundings."

"Detaching," he says, reaching into his pocket for a handful of pistachios. "So much so they forget what happened to them?"

"Hypothetically."

"So you're saying Louis the Seventeenth would have developed amnesia."

"I'm saying he could have survived only by *excluding* certain parts of his past from his consciousness. Parts of his identity, even."

Chewing, half smiling, Vidocq shakes his head.

"Christ in heaven."

"What?"

"You *believe*, Hector."

"No . . ."

"I can see it on your face. You think he's the real article, don't you?"

The faintest twitching then in Charles' hand, as if he were going to protest the turn of our conversation.

"I don't know what he is," I say.

And once again, I'm filled with a surprising longing for my father. I want him to be, yes, in this very carriage, telling us everything that happened behind the Temple's thick stone walls. . . .

Vidocq pries apart another pistachio shell, pops it into his mouth.

"Something you haven't yet considered," he says. "What if our boy here is making up his symptoms?"

"I think that would require more sophistication than he has."

"Ha! If you'd ever been conned, you'd know how complicated simple people can be. This *Monsieur* fellow, for instance. Is he a genius or an idiot?" He folds out his hands in an agnostic attitude. "A public assassination. That's an awfully good way of calling attention to yourself, isn't it?"

"Well . . ." I stifle a yawn. "Maybe *you* forced his hand."

"Oh, yes? And how'd he know old Vidocq was making for Saint-Cloud? Did *you* tell?"

"I didn't know I was coming myself."

The air is fragrant with pistachio and mud and spores—and Vidocq's own scent, unmistakable, hastening the decay of everything round it.

"Well," he says, "we've got one advantage on our side. Monsieur killed the wrong man. What's more, he doesn't *know* he killed the wrong man. And that gives us time."

"To do what?"

"Find our other assassin, Herbaux. That's *my* job. *Your* job is to figure out what that father of yours knew. Damn him for being dead," he adds, in an undertone.

"What about . . ."

I nudge my head toward that sleeping figure.

"Monsieur Charles? You're right, he *will* need somewhere to stay. And I've just the place for him."

"An apartment, you mean?"

He nods. "In a very fine establishment in the Latin Quarter. The Maison Carpentier."

CHAPTER 24

A Vicomte Expires Unexpectedly

TEN MINUTES BEFORE the cariole reaches the Barrière du Maine, Charles crawls from the chrysalis of his coat. Stretches his arms, rubs his eyes.

"Are we there?"

"Nearly."

On either side of us, there's nothing but fallow wheat fields and abandoned tracts. Through the long scraggly stretches of close-clipped grass, some wild poppies are stirring, and in the distance, you can make out a gypsum quarry and a mill, turning in violent hitches.

"I don't see any," he says.

"What?"

"Buildings. Paris has such tall ones."

"Oh, but we're still outside the city walls. Once we're in, you'll have all the buildings you could desire. Why, look, even from here, you can make out the Hôtel des Invalides."

"I don't like churches so much," he says. "They make me sneeze and fart all at once."

He blows an oval of vapor onto the glass. Rubs it away with his finger.

"Oh!" he cries. "That must be Paris!"

Up ahead, a brownstone wall, three meters high and twenty-four kilometers round, cinching Paris like a chastity belt. Any other city, I think, would have built such a wall to keep the barbarians out. Paris built its wall to keep the money in.

"What do they want?" asks Charles. "Those men."

"They're customs officers. They have to inspect us."

"Why?"

"To make sure we're paying our duties."

"What's a duty?"

"That's the—that's the money you pay the city. Whenever you bring something in."

"How funny," says Charles, hooking his thumb westward. "You pay for something back *there*—and then you pay all over again *here*."

"And keep paying," grumbles Vidocq, just as the flat-crowned, broad-brimmed black hat glides into the window frame.

"Goods to declare?"

"Nothing," Vidocq assures him. "Not so much as a scrap of hay."

"Well, then," he says, scratching his earlobe. "Maybe you'd be so kind as to show me your passports."

Through the mirror of his eyes, I'm recalled to the spectacle we present: Vidocq and I, bare-armed, in our old waistcoats, patched trousers.

"Monsieur," says the *douanier*, bearing down on Charles. "I believe I asked for your passport."

Charles keeps staring out the window.

"Monsieur," says the *douanier*, more pointedly.

"I'm afraid he doesn't have one," says Vidocq. "This gentleman has been apprehended on police business."

"That so?"

"I'd be happy to show you my identification. I'm—"

"You'll kindly keep your hands in plain view."

Grimacing, the customs officer bends his head over our papers. Then he steps back a pace. From nowhere, a stupefied grin snaps his face open.

"It *is* you! I knew it!"

Snatching the black hat off his own head, he presses it to his heart.

"Monsieur Vidocq . . . what an *honor*!"

"You're too kind, my friend."

"Oh, my! Oh, this is—see here, Monsieur, I've got this brother. Been having a spot of wife trouble."

"Gone missing, has she?"

"*Catting,* more like. Was thinking one of your boys could follow her round, catch her mid-*thrust*, know what I'm saying. . . ."

"Mm." Vidocq gives the matter a juridical pause. "I'll tell you what. Have him come round next week. Mind he asks for me in person, eh?"

"Oh, Monsieur, my whole family is in your debt. Eternally." Grinning, he claps his hands to his cheeks. "I can't wait to tell my wife! The great Vidocq!"

The glow of his regard follows us all the way through the city gates, and it leaves Vidocq looking not so much flushed as *chaffed,* like a bull swiping its tail at a fly. For a full minute, he refuses to meet our eyes.

"Well," he says at last. "I saved myself thirty sous in bribes."

Then, rapping absently on the ceiling, he calls up to Goury.

"Headquarters!" Followed by this scarcely audible afterthought: "Please."

THE BLOOD *DOES* come off my hand, thanks to a toothbrush (supplied by Coco-Lacour) and a liberal application of Windsor soap. Monsieur Tepac won't scrub off so easily. The memory, I mean, of his skin, flapping like a mouth—the pulse of his blood through the crevices of my fingers. Another man's life, yes, passing through mine. . . .

"Listen, Hector."

With a quiet cuff to the jaw, Vidocq jars me back.

"We're going to send you back home in a cab, all right? But before you go, I need to give you Charles' new identity. I'm going to give it to you *once*, and I need you to plaster it right in that noggin of yours, can you do that?"

In an instant, the old narrative—Tepac, Agatha, Saint-Cloud— gives way to the new. Charles Rapskeller is now the natural son of the Vicomte de Saint-Amand de Faral (by way of a chambermaid whose skirt caught fire one afternoon within the Vicomte's reach). The old hedgehog has at last succumbed to a heart inflammation, and in the absence of legitimate heirs, his estate (if not his title) passes to Charles, who curtails his religious instruction in Strasbourg to hasten toward Paris. On the westward-bound stage, he encounters—me—returning in glory from my . . .

"Scrofula symposium," says Vidocq. "In Reims."

Charles confesses he has nowhere to stay, and I urge him to take a room at my mother's, where the rent is low but the tone high.

"But if he's coming into money," I say, "shouldn't he be staying somewhere . . ."

"Nicer? Yes, but the money hasn't quite *landed*, has it? Last-minute wrinkles, a long-lost nephew in the Massif Central, nothing serious. Lawyers will have it smoothed out in a matter of weeks."

Clicking his tongue, he counts five twenty-franc pieces into my palm.

"Living expenses, Hector. Courtesy of the Prefecture. Use 'em well and keep a good ledger, will you? I don't want those damned book-keepers up my ass."

"But what about Charles?"

"What about him?"

"Somebody's bound to ask him questions. . . ."

"Well," says Vidocq, with a thin smile, "that would only be a prob-lem if he had a fucking brain. As it is, the only thing I've ever heard him confess to is his own name. He'll be fine. And if folks get curious, tell 'em he was dropped by the midwife."

IN MY MOTHER'S case, the only thing I have to mention is the entirely fictional name of the Vicomte de Saint-Amand de Faral. This produces at first a flinching and then a ripening. By the time Charles has tendered her a bow and dropped three gold pieces in her hand— gaily, as if they were marbles—she is extending her hand in her best chatelaine fashion.

"Any friend of Hector's, Monsieur Rapskeller, is doubly welcome in this home. And how fortunate! You've arrived just in time for supper. Charlotte, my dear! A setting for our new guest, please. And perhaps some ices for dessert. . . ."

No one gives a rap where I've been. Even Charlotte, who normally peppers me with questions if I'm gone so much as an hour, has something else on her mind when she beckons me toward her just before dinner.

"Oh, Monsieur Hector! What a love he is!"

"Who?"

"Your friend! He came in just now, the dear, and asked if he could help set table. When he doesn't even know where a fork goes! Or a spoon. Oh, he was quite hopeless, but still he tried, didn't he?" She gives me a nod of boundless sagacity. "You can *always* tell a gentleman, Monsieur Hector. Blood will *out*."

CHAPTER 25

Mama Carpentier Stands Firm

BLOOD, IN FACT, is very much on my mind when I watch the three law students align themselves round the dinner table. Father Time is not here to deflect them, and there's something quite chilling in how they inspect the new guest for weaknesses. Any other man could be warned. Charles can only be watched, helplessly, from the other side of the table. As great a distance as the moon to the sun, or so it seems to me when Lapin, blotting the claret from his lips, sallies forth.

"Monsieur Charles, I believe our hostess has been too modest in her claims on your behalf. She speaks only of your coming into a fortune, when you appear already to have carved out a formidable military career."

And when Lapin receives (as he expected) a look of puzzlement from his prey, he says, as dryly as he dares:

"Those *are* spurs I see on your boots?"

Lifting his leg, Charles surveys his feet with unfeigned surprise (for these are not his boots).

"Spurs! You're right!"

"I expect you are likely a cuirassier," says Lapin. "Perhaps you will regale us some day with stories of battles won."

Smiling as though in perfect concord, Charles answers:

"I had a pony once."

A slight pause. Then Rosbif comes gliding forward.

"Are you sure it was a pony, Monsieur? Your vest looks to be made entirely of goatskin."

"So it is," says Charles, newly astonished.

"I wonder, Monsieur, did you dress yourself in the dark?"

Far from resenting the question, he *absorbs* it, like an oyster wrapping itself round a piece of grit.

"Dress in the dark," he says, wonderingly. "What fun! Tomorrow, we shall all dress in the dark!"

And as I watch a scowl flit across Rosbif's face, I realize a wonder has come to light. The same qualities that leave Charles unprotected leave him unprovokable. The students succumb to a vexed silence, which is broken only after several minutes—by Nankeen, their chief.

"Do you know, Monsieur, I find your *jaw* of great interest."

The sharp intake of air—that's mine. But as fate would have it, I've overestimated Nankeen's powers of discernment. For in the next breath, he says:

"I saw a jaw just like it in the Bicêtre asylum. Lovely lady. No longer able to wash or dress herself, but the jaw was quite useful for catching her drool."

Charles' brow creases for a second. Then, tilting his mouth down, he says:

"I had a dog that was shot in the jaw once. His name was Troilus."

Nankeen sets down his fork—the surest sign he is girding for another charge—and just as I'm moving to interpose my own body, someone beats me to it.

My mother.

Setting down her napkin, she announces:

"*All* guests in my home will kindly be respected."

The shock of her own pronouncement causes her cheeks to puff out, like a goddess of wind. Her head sinks over her plate, and amid the questions that weave silently across the table, mine is the one that registers most strongly in my inner ear:

Why has she never done that for me?

THE PREVIOUS TENANT of Charles' room was a general's widow who, in her haste to abscond, left behind a bed with a rather fine canopy of antique damask, as well as a silver vanity case and droppings of talcum. These last lie scattered about the room like plaster dust and emit a scent so sharply feminine that I fight the urge to bow whenever I enter the room.

"The room's a bit—sorry—Charlotte will get to it—tomorrow at the latest. . . ."

I set his carpetbag on the bed, and because he makes no move toward it, I unpack for him. Blouses, trousers, striped linen underdrawers, and a large morocco cap, the kind a six-year-old boy might wear to go sledding. No more than three days' worth of clothing, all in all, and not a single keepsake. Not even the hint of an estate.

"Well, now," I say, after I put the clothes in the dresser. "That should do it."

"Are there scorpions?" he asks.

"Are there . . . you mean *here*? Not that I've seen."

"Then I'm sure I shall enjoy it."

Sitting on the edge of the bed, he gives the mattress a pair of speculative bounces.

"Where do *you* sleep, Hector?"

It's the first time he's addressed me by name.

"Upstairs. In the garret."

"Well, that's fine, then. Am I to go to bed now?"

"You may do as you like. We don't have any rules about sleeping."

"Oh, I see," he says, smiling shyly. "Well, then, Hector, you should know I never go to bed without someone sitting nearby. Now please believe me when I tell you it's very easy. You needn't say a word. In fact, it's better if you don't. And please don't read to me because that tends to make me fidget. All you need do, really, is sit there, and I go right out."

It never occurs to me to remonstrate with him. My hand, indeed, is already drawing the chair over.

"Monsieur Tepac," I say. "Did he sit with you?"

"Why, yes. Agatha, too, sometimes, but her bones would creak, and one can't ask a bone to be quiet, it can't be done."

"I don't suppose it can."

"But you're still young," he says, agreeably. "I don't imagine you creak at all."

"No," I say, lowering myself with terrific care into the chair. "I'll try not to."

We sit for a few moments, regarding each other.

"Perhaps you'd care to get ready for bed," I say.

"Oh!" He stares down at his dead man's clothes. "You're quite right. Let's see now. . . ."

He gives the boots a gentle tug. Tugs again and then relapses into confusion. And when I think back on this moment, what will most amaze me is the absence of hesitation on my part. I am already moving toward him, you see. With the express purpose of kneeling before him and prying his boots loose. The only thing that stops me is the cracked tremolo issuing from the doorway.

"There you are!" cries Father Time.

Not on his way to bed, no, but dressed for going out. And brimming with the prospect. Even his ragged necktie and old square coat look as if they were bracing for new possibilities.

There are two additions to his customary wardrobe. A lantern, still unlit. And a spade.

"I wonder if you'd care to join me," he says. "I'm off to the Bois de Boulogne."

"Professor, it's . . . nighttime. . . ."

"Yes, I know. But I just remembered where the archive was."

"The archive."

"The one you were asking me about! Concerning your *father*, I mean. When he was taking care of You-Know-Who at the You-Know-Where. Oh, good evening!" he says, suddenly drawing Charles into his ken. "How rude of me. Would you like to tag along, Monsieur?"

CHAPTER 26

In Which a Corpus Is Exhumed

"Burying someone, are we?"

We're standing at the corner of the Rue d'Ulm and the Rue des Postes, and from the height of his box, a cabdriver scowls down at the spectacle of Father Time, who is caressing his spade like a bound lamb.

"Why, no," answers the old man. "We're all very much in the pink, I think. Although with *me*, one never knows. Now if you'd just take us to the Bois de Boulogne, we'd be your eternally devoted *vassals*."

"Don't need vassals," the driver says. "Remuneration'd be nice."

Stunned by this demand, Father Time turns slowly round to face me. "I say, my boy, do you—"

And before I can equivocate, Charles chimes in: "Oh, yes! That smelly man gave him a whole *pile* of gold coins."

One of these coins is now prized from my purse and dropped in the cabman's rein-calloused palm. He gives it his closest attention, then drops it down his trousers—straight into some waiting receptacle, from which the faintest clank emerges, like a far-off tocsin.

"Well, gentlemen," he says. "At these rates, you can bury ten bodies."

————

SPRING HAS SET up house in the Bois de Boulogne. Just a few strokes
shy of midnight, and life thrums on all sides. Linnets, sparrows . . . a
single butterfly, the color of young cheese . . . and *lovers,* discarding
things in their haste—a pair of clogs, a canezou jacket, a lace stocking.
Through the shrubbery, we can hear them, rustling and moaning, as
we follow Father Time from the city wall to Lac Inférieur.

Some three hundred yards east of the Parc de Bagatelle, he stops
abruptly. Wrinkles his nose and gazes round.

"Do you gentlemen know what a *linden* looks like?"

"Tilia cordata," answers Charles, with a trace of outrage.

"Oh, dear me! A fellow Linnaean! Very well, my young worthy,
tell Hector what he should be looking for."

"Well, lindens don't drop flowers till June. But I've always thought
they have an April smell. You must imagine a *toad,* Hector. Lying in
hay for several days altogether, not a care in the world. That's what
it smells like. You'll also find very distinct bore holes in the linden's
bark, courtesy of *Chrysoclista linneella.* I could trace them out for you,
if it—"

"Please," I say, putting out my hand. "I know what lindens look
like. But there are hundreds in this vicinity alone. Which one are we to
look for, Monsieur?"

"Oh." Father Time's mouth unhinges, then quickly snaps to. "Why,
the one with the *X* on it, of course."

We walk now in slowly contracting circles, and the light from Father Time's lantern walks ahead of us, startling the buds from the trees.
For the first time tonight, I notice the cold. Waves of wind, rolling in
from the east. At last one gust catches Father Time by the arm and
nudges the lantern from his grip. The taper gutters out, the shadows
dissolve . . . and moonlight rains down.

A *full* moon. It's taken me this long to notice.

Father Time reaches into his pockets for a sulfur match and strikes

it against the nearest tree. Instinctively, I turn to look for Charles . . .
and find him ten yards off, standing before a linden tree. Slowly tracing a long cross.

The initial wound of that *X* has been healed over so many times that
I might have walked by it a hundred times and noticed nothing out of
order. But it's there all the same.

From Father Time's limp mouth, a yellow smile buds forth. "You've
done it!" he shouts. "All we need do now is look *up*. Find Jupiter. Ah,
there he is! And now . . . walk *north*. . . ."

He takes one pace . . . two . . . three. With his boot, he gouges a
circle in the ground.

"Shall we begin?" he asks.

"Begin *what*, Monsieur?"

"The digging!"

I strip off my coat. Grab the spade and drive it straight down. The
soil, still compacted from a long winter, answers with a dreary clink.

"How far do we need to go?"

"Oh, no more than four or five feet," says Father Time, easily. "Do
get a move on, my boy. It's a bit nippy."

On its first sally, the spade claws out no more than a few thimble-
fuls of dirt. It's several minutes more before the surface layer is cleared
away. From there, the soil grows more yielding but only for a short
time—until I reach the stratum of clay.

And now the sweat blossoms right out of me . . . the breath comes
in gasps . . . I hear:

"May *I* try, Hector?"

If anyone else had asked me, I should have answered yes immediately. What makes me hesitate with him?

"Please," says Charles. "I'm very good at this sort of thing."

In fact, he's a natural wonder. Exerting half as much effort as I, he
works at three times the pace. Every so often, he pauses to finger a lock
of hair from his eyes, but mostly he digs, with a fixity of purpose that
breaks down the earth's last reserve.

I watch, dazzled, as the chunks of soil fly past me. The only thing that stops him finally is a sound—can you hear it?—a muffled concussion like . . .

Fwook.

"Uh-oh," says Charles.

"What is it?" cries Father Time. "What's happened?"

"We've struck something," I answer. "A stone. A root, possibly."

"No root," says Charles.

Fwook, cries the spade once more. At last Charles bends down and extracts his prize.

A simple wooden school box. The kind that, as a boy, I might have used for storing my pencils and quills.

"What's *in* it?" asks Charles.

"Why, it's the archive!" answers Father Time.

I gaze at that strange box, with its carved swan, its flaking green and gold foliage, its painted tulips popping out of a rust red field. *An archive.*

"But why did you bury it?" I ask.

"Oho! You'd have left it in the house, is that it? For the Committee to find? Dear me, I'd forgotten about the lock. Hector, can you . . . ?"

I grab the spade and swing it down. Three blows, and the lid springs open, like a mouth gulping for air. And there lies a tiny sketchbook, bound in green calf's leather and girt with a linen cord.

I open its thick, calcified pages. I read:

13 THERMIDOR YEAR II

1st meeting with Prisoner: shortly after 1 A.M. Prisoner alone in cell. Dinner had not been eaten. Nor breakfast.

"But whose is this?" I ask.

"Come now," says Father Time, bending his mantis-frame toward me. "You must recognize the hand. It's your father's!"

CHAPTER 27

A Boy Named Hector

WITH A SHOW of reluctance, Vidocq takes up the green calf's-leather sketchbook from his desk. Gives the spine a stroke, inspects the residue on his finger. Then inspects the even grubbier prospect of Father Time, surely as unlikely a visitor as his office has seen in some time.

"Professor Corneille, is it?"

The old man has been studying an etching of François Villon so intently that the sound of Vidocq's voice makes him jump like a puppet.

"Oh, my! Yes. That's the name."

"I want to be sure I have this right. Twenty-three years ago, you and Hector's father decided to—bury this journal in the middle of the woods."

"Indeed."

"Now maybe you can tell me *why*."

"*Why?* Because we didn't want the authorities to find it! If any of the Jacobins had known the—the full *extent* of Dr. Carpentier's sympathies for the royal family, he might have been arrested. At the very least! Not to mention Monsieur Leblanc, who was *every* bit as complicit."

"Then why didn't you just destroy the damned thing?"

The old man's eyes graze over the journal now. How small it looks in the expanse of Vidocq's desk.

"I believe Dr. Carpentier wanted people to *know* what happened in that tower. When they were ready to hear it."

Vidocq turns completely away now. Fills the window frame with his bulk and takes the sunlight with him.

"And he never told anyone else? His wife? His son? Seems odd he should leave such a valuable addition to History in the safekeeping of . . ."

A doddering old man. My thought, not Vidocq's. But a note of apology does seep into his voice now, as if the same idea had crossed his mind.

"You must admit," he says, "it wasn't a very rational thing to do."

"They were hardly rational times, Monsieur."

"Strange days," I say, echoing Vidocq's own words back to him.

He cocks his chin at me. Cocks it back toward Father Time.

"I assume, Professor, that you're familiar with the journal's contents."

"Dear me, yes."

"Do you have anything to add to what's been writ down in this book?"

"I don't believe so." His hands come together at stiff angles like a Gothic saint. "Of course, it was so very *long* ago. But if anything pops to mind, I shall—I shall certainly come and *tell* you, Monsieur . . . oh, I'm sorry, I've quite lost the name."

"Never mind. If something occurs to you, just tell Hector, there's a good fellow. In the meantime, we do thank you for your assistance. Shall I have one of my men drive you home?"

"Oh, no, I'm quite capable of walking, thank you." A strain of milky hope shines from his eyes. "Unless you have someone exceptionally pretty on the premises? No? Well, I'll be off, then. I shall look for you back at the family manse, Hector!"

Vidocq closes the door gently after him. Lets out a soft whistle.

"Well, what do you know?" he says, dropping heavily into his seat. "Your father's own words. Crawling out of the earth just when we need them. Quite a coincidence."

"Not at all," I remind him. "I'd already—I'd raised the subject with the old man, remember? Before we even went to Saint-Cloud. It just took him time to—snap the pieces together."

"And you think because some pruny bugger dredges some pages from the Bois de Boulogne, our king is going to hand over his crown to a Swiss *gardener?*"

Strange to say, the words have a physical effect on me. They fold me in on myself, leave me saying my piece to the floor.

"Charles hasn't declared himself to be . . . *anyone*."

"Not yet he hasn't."

Once more, he sets to stroking the journal's binding.

"You're sure this is your father's hand?" he asks.

"I know it as well as I know my own."

Very slowly, he begins to leaf through those age-thickened pages.

"How long do the entries go on for?"

"More than a year. I'm still translating from the old Revolutionary calendar, but as best I can tell, the last entry was written on the first of June, 1795."

One of his eyebrows kicks up. "That was a week before the prince died."

"Yes."

His voice stays calm, but his hands lose themselves in the act of riffling through those pages. Coming at last to the final entry, he reads:

"Enough for now." He looks up. "What's that supposed to mean?"

"I don't know," I answer. "I've only had the journal a few hours. I've scarcely read a word of it. . . ."

———

IN FACT, I BEGAN reading from the moment it fell into my hands. At first I was only dimly aware of the words. I was too lost in retracing my father's handwriting. How it had fascinated me as a child. I would copy those vowels and consonants again and again until they began to creep into my own writing—so that my mother, glancing casually into my copybook one day, was shocked to find her husband's own signature staring back at her.

And indeed, as I sat in bed last night, the act of retracing those old letters by candlelight did seem to call him up in some fashion. Hungrily, I combed those journal entries for some mention not of kings but of—*me*. And when I found it, it was almost more than I could bear.

A boy named Hector.

Father's own words staring back at me.

—And is he my age?
—No, he is but 3. Although (I cdnt help but add) he knows at least 200 words. . . .

The book fell shut, and for perhaps another hour, I sat there, burning with wonder that my father had once—in a moment beyond my recalling—been proud of me.

Well, all this goes unsaid in the confines of Number Six. Or else it's all said without my volunteering a word.

"Wouldn't you know?" says Vidocq, dancing his fingers across Father's journal. "The week I want to know about is that *last* week, which is the only one that's not here. And from the looks of things, the only two people who can tell us about it are in the grave." He shoves the journal toward me. "All right, Hector, I want you to give this diary your full attention, do you understand me? Shake out every last line for evidence."

"Evidence of what?"

"*Anything*. A conspiracy, a plot. Find out who your father talked to, what he saw. Look at the text itself. Are there certain *words* that keep cropping up? Anything that might indicate a code?"

"A code . . ."

"Yes, damnit! If somebody was trying to spring the dauphin from his cell, I want to know about it."

I gather the book into my arms. And just as I'm reaching for my gloves, Vidocq says:

"One other thing. I want you to take your new friend Charles round the city. He's a *tourist*, isn't he? Show him the sights, for pity's sake. See what tumbles out."

"You think he'll remember who he is?"

Vidocq's face is so close now I can taste the herring on his breath.

"Hector, as far as the rest of the world, there's nothing to remember. Louis the Seventeenth is dead. Which means our Charles has to be someone else. The only question is who. Now I want you to take him round the city until he tips his hand—or has it tipped for him."

I look at him. Then I look down.

"So you can arrest him for fraud," I say. "Is that it? Throw him in La Force with all your precious thieves and murderers? He'd have a better chance in the Bois de Boulogne, I think."

Vidocq's voice wafts down to me.

"That's not my decision to make, Hector. Or yours."

And then his voice shifts into a sharper register.

"Of course, if you don't have the *stomach* for this work . . ."

"I have the stomach," I answer, lifting my face toward his. "It so happens I have a heart, too."

"Oh, yes," he says, breezily. "I've got one of those myself. I keep it in a box somewhere."

CHAPTER 28

A Disappearance Solved

THE LAST THING Vidocq says to me is this:

"Never let Charles out of your sight, do you follow? Even if you have to crawl up his asshole and stay through next Easter."

Well, you can imagine my feelings on returning home and finding Charles nowhere.

I run from garret to cellar. I squint under beds, peer into closets and pantries. I jerk open casement windows. I rattle through that empty house like a bird in a chimney.

He's lost.

I won't say it, I can't, and at some point, it ceases to matter, for another sound has stolen forth from the back of the house.

Why did it never occur to me to inspect the rear courtyard? I can say only that it's been so many months since I wandered there—Mother reserves it for wealthier lodgers—that it has long since dropped off my map of the place. But Charles is there, all right. In the very position in which I first met him: on his hands and knees, plunging his hands into the earth.

Standing over him is my mother. Her tulle cap has been traded for a blue calico bonnet. She is holding a parasol with a Chinese ivory handle—I'd no idea she owned such a thing—and someone (Charles?) has woven a tendril of honeysuckle round her ear. She has kicked off her slippers and left her feet to wander bare and white, like fallen clouds.

And this, too: There is a smile on her face. Which cannot be diminished even by the sight of me.

"Hallo, Hector! At the laboratory, were we?"

"That's right," I say, haltingly.

"Oh, what a shame you couldn't join us! We've been having the loveliest morning, haven't we, Monsieur Rapskeller? Dear me, what your friend knows about gardens, Hector! You remember my poor plantain lilies, don't you?"

"Mmm . . ."

"Every summer, they get more and more charred—and they're always in shade! Monsieur Rapskeller found they were getting sunlight by *refraction*. Bouncing right off the kitchen window, do you see? As for the *crocuses* . . . well, the squirrels got them, as usual, but your friend knows a sauce from—where again, Monsieur?"

"Martinique."

"It's got peppers in it and garlic and I don't know what else. You soak the bulbs *before* you plant them, and the little beasties want nothing more to do with them."

The shock of finding my mother in this condition gives way to a larger dazzlement. The sun, the air. The garden itself: hawthorn fruits; carnations sprawling across the mossy brick wall; a scouting party of leaves in the plane trees.

"And do you know what else I learned?" says Mother. "Azaleas dote on coffee! Who would have guessed? You know, I can't help thinking, Monsieur, that when you come into the Vicomte's fortune, you'll have a whole retinue of gardeners to do this for you."

Charles knows nothing of any vicomte, but he answers without a moment's hesitation.

"Oh no, Madame. I shan't have anyone do it but me. The plants always *know* you, don't they? They know your touch, your *voice*, too, I believe that. If anyone else talked to them, they mightn't behave so well."

"Plants with eardrums!" shrieks my mother. "Ha-ha!"

Yes, it's true. She laughs.

Which is to say her teeth, brown with hiding, surge toward the light, shivering apart the lips that had thought to contain them. No one is more stunned than my mother. She drops her parasol and slaps a hand to each side of her head, as though to assure herself that she's still in one piece.

And as quickly as that laugh stole over her, a new mood sweeps down. She beholds her bare feet, she feels the tickle of the honeysuckle vine round her ear. Her eyes blacken, and in the next second, she's half striding, half running toward the house.

"I'm afraid I'm . . . you'll excuse me . . . errands. . . ."

I have an errand of my own. For the rest of the afternoon, I stretch out in the window seat overlooking the courtyard and I read my father's journal. And whenever I tire of that, I need only glance through the glazed panes to find Charles. Spreading mulch. Scattering pomegranate seeds. Planting an oleander in a blue porcelain pot. Digging, weeding, watering, pruning.

As the afternoon wears on, his neck grows pinker, and great ellipses of sweat bleed across his blouse, and still he works on, and still he colors everything I read.

This A.M., Leblanc and I surprised Charles in cell w/ 4 pots of flowers. . . .

He said he learned long ago—in Tuileries gardens—one must talk to one's flowers. . . .

The aversion to being touched. The fear of going to sleep in the dark. Line by line, the congruences yield themselves up.

When evening comes, Charles is too exhausted for dinner. He makes straight for his room, and after I've helped to take his boots off, he drops straight into his bed.

"I don't think I shall change tonight. . . ."

"Well, that's all right," I tell him. "You've had a long day."

"Yes. . . ."

"Tomorrow, I'll take you to see the city, would you like that?"

"Mm." He stares at the ceiling. "I'm going to sleep now."

I draw the chair to the doorway. I breathe in the talcum powder of the general's widow. I listen to the fretting of the grandfather clock downstairs.

"You should probably wait ten minutes," says Charles, faintly. "Just to be sure I'm *really* asleep."

"Would you mind if I read a little? To myself?"

"Not at all." Yawning, he lifts his head to squint me into his sights. "Is that the book? It looks old."

"It is, yes."

His head hovers there for two seconds longer, then drops onto the pillow.

"Good night, Hector."

"Good night."

THE PAGE I OPEN to is the same one that consumed me last night. That scene (for so I conceive of them: scenes) where a young king first hears about his doctor's son.

If you took me home w/ you, we cd be brothers, he and I, and I'd keep very close watch on him, youd never have a moment's worry.

I read it once more now, and my thoughts run straight to that slumbering figure in the bed. My new *friend,* who likes me to sit watch over him every night and who may, in the same breath, be watching over me.

An hour later, I'm back in my garret, bending over the taper, when my attention is snagged by something on the street below.

For several minutes more, I stare down at the familiar outcroppings, trying to recapture what it was. A flash of scarlet, like a cock's crest. No face, no body to connect to it . . . and yet this part is somehow larger than any whole.

Monsieur killed the wrong man, said Vidocq. *What's more, he doesn't know he killed the wrong man. And that gives us time.*

But if that's true, then who is out there watching us? And when will the time for watching end?

CHAPTER 29

The King of France Is Held Hostage

THE SÛRETÉ HAS a closet of costumes that would do credit to the Opéra-Comique, but Vidocq has decided that, if Charles and I are to wander Paris unnoticed, we need something a little more "breathed upon." There is on the Rue Beautrellis a Jewish merchant known as "the Changer," who makes it his business to transform rascals into honest men, for the bargain price of thirty sous a day.

"Monsieur Jules!" he intones, falling back on one of Vidocq's old aliases.

"And a good morning to you. Here are the two rogues I told you about."

"Mm," says the Changer. "Never know it to look at 'em, would you? All mother's milk."

"*Curdled,*" answers Vidocq.

"Well, let me see now." He worms his arm through the stacks of garments. "We've got a magistrate, just been washed . . . curé . . . Russian soldier, *most* popular these days . . . English not so much. . . . *That* one's a poet. Got ink on the jabot, see? Doubles for beggar . . . And over here, I think you'll find a *very* plausible leper. Sores cost a bit more."

"I was inclining toward statesman," says Vidocq.

"Now if *that's* your line, you're in luck, my friend. Got a matching pair, just came back yesterday. Black cloth coats, see? Trousers are *double*-milled cassimere. Silk waistcoat. And since you're so beloved in these here precincts, Monsieur Jules, I'll even throw in boots."

With a haggling scowl, Vidocq holds one of the black coats next to me.

"What's it supposed to be? Ambassador?"

"*Emeritus,* you might say."

"Come with accessories?"

"Wigs, very recently deloused. Green spectacles, with optional silk shades. Watch fobs, plus trinkets for hanging from same." His lips melt slowly away from his gums. "You can keep the trinkets. My gift to *you,* Monsieur."

"Well, then," says Vidocq. "What are you waiting for, boys? Try 'em on, for Christ's sake."

"The usual weekly rate, Monsieur?"

"Put us down for *two* weeks. No more."

"Very good. And please to remember it's double the fee for every day they're late. And no eating of garlic. Gets in the fibers."

We test our new identities that very afternoon—on the wide sandy paths of the Luxembourg Gardens. My boots pinch much more than they did in the shop, and my wig is home to something small and mobile and latently hostile, and every worn seam, every dangling thread seems to cry: "Impostor!"

But then a pretty young girl walks past us, her smile spilling over us like water. A slumbering Scotch terrier snores itself awake. One of the swans scrapes its rump on the stone. Vidocq guessed right. Ridiculous as Charles and I look, we've been absorbed, with no discernible struggle, into the warp and weave of Paris. (Where everyone is an impostor.)

"Hector!"

With a trembling voice, Charles takes me by the arm.

"What is it?"

"The chestnuts," he whispers, pointing to a long branch with gaudy white feather-blossoms. "You were right. They're in bloom."

It's what he's been waiting for all along. The thing he was promised back in Saint-Cloud.

And now it seems perfectly natural to demand something in return. To look into those pacific blue eyes and say . . .

"Tell me about your parents."

He doesn't actively resist my queries, he simply huddles round them. When that fails, he bounces them back. We spend far more time talking about *my* parents than his, and whenever I try to return the conversation back to him, his eyes skim over, as though he were trying to remember an old poem. All he can say definitively is that his parents died.

"When I was very young," he adds.

"Do you remember anything about them?"

"They loved me."

"Did they leave you anything to live on?"

"I suppose they must have. I've always had people taking care of me."

"Like Monsieur Tepac."

"Yes."

"Was there someone before him?"

"Ohhh . . ."

A yawn palsies his jaw, sets his wig to jiggling.

"What's that?" he asks, pointing.

"The Luxembourg Palace."

"Where the king lives?"

"No, the Chamber of Peers sits there."

"And who are they?"

Old men. Chateaubriand's words rise to mind: *The dried-up débris of the Old Monarchy, the Revolution, and the Empire. . . .*

"They're gentlemen," I say cautiously. "Who've been given titles. Marquises and barons and so on. They gather at the palace, and they sit around and talk."

"Imagine," says Charles. "Doing nothing all day but talking."

And, as if chastened, our own conversation tapers down. We leave the garden behind, we stroll north on the Rue de Seine, gathering speed as we go, and we're nearly to the Pont des Arts when we are stopped by a backward swell of bodies. The Parisian people, quite oblivious to most vehicles, are making an exception for one. A golden coach of ridiculous proportions, surrounded by silver-trimmed, saber-wielding bodyguards.

"Oh, look," says Charles. "It's got lilies painted on it. Come along, Hector!"

In later years, I confess, I won't be able to trust my account of this moment. Surely it couldn't have happened as easily as all that? On our very first day abroad?

And yet the King's carriage is a common enough sight in these early days of the Restoration. Invalided by gout and obesity, Louis the Eighteenth compensates by setting his carriage loose through the streets of Paris at ever-greater speeds. More than one of his subjects has known the sensation of narrowly escaping the royal cavalcade's progress—and being rewarded with the cool, incurious stare of His Majesty as the carriage shoots past.

Today, however, that journey is foiled by an advance party of pigs, fording the street and cinching the royal carriage into stillness.

"Is that the King?" whispers Charles.

Who else? I want to answer. Who else would be sitting in a posture of such erect indolence? With a litter of white satin cushions to buffer him from any collision?

Across from the King sits the captain of the guard, and next to him, leaning into the window's frame and registering, in the curve of his mouth, a twining of pique and amusement. . . .

There sits Vidocq.

No. THE FIGURE slowly reconfigures itself. *No, not Vidocq.* Vidocq as he might look in twenty years. The reserves of flesh melted away by respectability, the expression of animal absorption refined down into large, encompassing eyes.

"That man must be very good friends with the King," says Charles, "to be sitting so close."

"Not friends at all. They're merely related."

"Related how?"

"Well, that man is the Comte d'Artois. The King's younger brother."

"How funny." Charles reaches under his wig, gives his scalp a good long scratch. "I never think of kings having brothers or sisters, but I suppose they must. Are there any others?"

"Brothers, you mean? There was an older one."

An unfortunate gentleman, thickly built, thickly walled. Handed the keys to the manor just as the serfs were bashing down the door. He married an Austrian princess, and they had a boy who was thrown into a great black tower and never came out alive.

We all know that. We know what's possible, and this is not possible: that this same boy could still be alive, a grown man, pressed into a throng of Parisians, watching his two uncles drive past without even recognizing them. Such things don't happen.

But when I look up and feel the eyes of the Comte d'Artois on me, it's as if the space between us has contracted. I hear a voice behind me say:

"Marie! He's looking this way."

And another voice:

"Ooh, such a handsome figure of a man. Regular cavalier. Everyone says Monsieur has the finest manners in the world."

MONSIEUR.

————

IT'S IMPORTANT TO say that there's nothing strange in that address. *Monsieur* is simply the honorary title bestowed on a king's younger brother. But the Monsieur I'm pondering in this moment is that *other* fellow, the mastermind first mentioned by Tepac's assassin. The Monsieur who revealed himself as only a voice and a title. Who sat behind a confessional screen and sent Herbaux on that deadly errand to Saint-Cloud. Sent him to kill a king.

And why has it taken me so long to see? That there is, in all of Paris, one *particular* Monsieur who would loathe the prospect of long-lost kings laying claims to the crown that will one day be his.

"Charles," I whisper. "Turn away."

"What?"

"Turn away."

And as I fasten onto his arm and drag him away, a new fact, stark and plain, leaps out at me.

We've just presented ourselves to him.

CHAPTER 30

Vidocq Takes an Overdue Interest in Art

"LET ME MAKE sure I've got this right, Hector."

I'm back in Vidocq's office, and he's reclining once more in his black leather armchair, wedging his shoes against the rim of his mahogany desk.

"The King's brother," he says, "the Comte d'Artois, has decided that a certain young man named Charles Rapskeller is really the long-lost Louis the Seventeenth. Rather than let this young fellow claim his rightful throne, he hires a pair of assassins. Scoundrels from the Parisian underworld who manage, in the way of scoundrels, to get the wrong man. Artois doesn't know it, though, until yesterday afternoon when he just happens to drive by and see this same Charles Rapskeller staring out at him from beneath an ambassador's wig. . . ."

This is what's changed between us. I no longer quail before his skepticism.

"Whether or not Charles is the king," I say, "*someone* believes he is. *Someone* had Leblanc and Tepac killed. And if that's the case, who would lose the most if Louis the Seventeenth came back to life?"

"Start with Louis the *Eighteenth*."

"No." I give my head a robust shake. "The King is old, he's ill, he has no children of his own, he's ready for his reward. It's the Comte d'Artois who has the most at stake here. If *another* king were to rise up, a king capable of having children of his own, then Artois' line is disinherited in a trice. And if Artois doesn't go quietly, then France will be forced to choose between *two* monarchs. What's to keep things from escalating into civil war? Which almost certainly would finish what the Revolution started. An end to monarchy, now and forever. I ask you . . ." And here I raise my eyes to his. "Is the Comte d'Artois the sort of man to take kindly to that prospect?"

Vidocq says nothing at first. He only cups his hands round his empty bowl of coffee, twirls it in quarter turns.

"Serious charges, Hector."

"I know."

In the next second, he's pushing away the coffee bowl and slamming his hands down on the desk.

"I *like* it, Hector!"

"You mean you agree?"

"No, you're brimful of shit, but who cares? You're thinking like a policeman. When I remember what a timid little sod you were just a couple of weeks back, scared of your own *voice*, and now look at you, with your grand, beautiful theories! I couldn't be prouder if—well, enough praise. Tell me where you left Monsieur Charles."

"In bed."

"Ohh, sleeps well, does he? Well, let him know from me, it's early to rise tomorrow. The first test is at hand."

I'M CAREFUL NOT to use the word *test* with Charles. Later, though, I won't remember what I call it. *Outing*, maybe. *Lark . . . adventure . . .*

Well, at any rate, that's the spirit in which he enters into things. It's no trouble at all to shepherd him into the office of Vidocq's secretary,

Coco-Lacour, and to leave him there with nothing more than a deck of cards and a red ball for entertainment. I slip into Vidocq's adjoining office, where the etching of François Villon has been removed to reveal a peephole, carved in the shape of an eye.

This particular orifice is scaled to Vidocq's height, which means that the Baroness de Préval requires a footstool to reach the peephole, and even then, to see through it, she must rise an inch or two more on her slippered toes.

"Well, Madame?" says Vidocq, leading her back to earth.

She crosses slowly to the window, stares out at Sainte-Chapelle, ivory with sun. At last:

"What would you have me say, Monsieur?"

"No more than you care to say."

Her shoulders give a delicate shrug. "I am loath to disappoint you," she says, "but you must understand. A quarter of a century has passed since I laid eyes on the dauphin, and he was a mere boy at the time. Surely someone of your *indefatigable* nature, Monsieur, could find someone more suited to this task than I."

"Ah, Madame, you do yourself a disservice. Were you not a bosom companion to the Princesse de Lamballe?"

She turns on him with a flash of fan. "I hadn't supposed you to be a student of ancient history."

Grinning, he claps his hands to his breast. "We brutes do require civilizing influences, Madame. Toward that end, I've begun acquiring art."

"The police trade is more lucrative than I realized."

"Loyalty has its rewards, yes. As it happens, my most recent acquisition came from the Galerie Barrault. Would you care to see?"

Stooping under his desk, he draws out a canvas, loosely wrapped in burlap, and lays it across his desk.

A trio of young women, captured in the very ripeness of their beauty. Their bodies are sheathed in cotton lawn. Their necks and shoulders burn moth-white. Violets lie strewn about their straw hats with bohemian dishabille.

"You can see the artist's name right there," says Vidocq. "Madame Vigée-Lebrun. Not the original oil, of course—Barrault would have charged a great deal more for that—but not without a certain interest, either. The figure in front, of course, is the Princesse de Lamballe. Lovely, wasn't she? But perhaps, like me, you're *most* struck by the woman positioned over the Princess's left shoulder. As you can see, the artist has done her the distinct favor of portraying each iris in its true color. One blue, one brown."

The Baroness's hand trembles, yes, but the closer it comes to the canvas, the steadier it grows. Until it comes to rest, finally, not on her own long-ago reflection but on the seated figure of the Princesse de Lamballe.

"Paintings never did her justice," says the Baroness.

Her hand draws slowly away.

"You are correct, Monsieur. She was my dear friend. She stayed on in Paris when all the rest of us left, for no other reason than that the Queen needed her. You may recall how her loyalty was rewarded."

Vidocq bows his head, mumbles into the carpet. "It was a terrible episode. . . ."

"Yes, the mob was unusually thorough in her case. They ravished her first. Then they set to tearing her apart, piece by piece. Her *head*— her beautiful head—was cut off and set on a pike. *Paraded* beneath the Queen's window at the Temple."

"Such a tragedy," says Vidocq, letting a moment of silence unfold before once again picking up the thread. "I believe—am I correct in saying the Princess was superintendent of the royal household?"

"She was."

"In which capacity she would have seen much of the royal children."

"Of course."

"And *you*, in your capacity as the Princess's intimate . . ."

". . . would have enjoyed no more entrée to the dauphin than any other member of court." Frowning, she pulls her shawl round her neck.

"Really, Monsieur, if you expect me to tell you that Louis the Seventeenth is standing in your antechamber, I'm afraid I cannot oblige you."

"Perhaps," says Vidocq, "you might oblige the memory of Monsieur Leblanc."

Her eyes narrow ever so slightly. She crooks a finger round her mouth, then slowly releases it.

"There *is* something," she allows. "Your young man—I noticed he has a habit of *passing* things. Between his feet. Balls and the like."

"Yes," says Vidocq. "What of it?"

"I mention it because it was an old habit of the dauphin's. His mother used to admonish him. *If you keep that up, Charles, you'll go cross-eyed!* No doubt she believed it, too. The Queen was always a credulous soul." She pauses, startled to find herself smiling. "Well, it's not an *uncommon* habit. Any boy might have picked up something like it."

There is a note of genuine apology in her voice as she adds:

"I'm afraid I have nothing more I can tell you."

She rearranges her shawl, her gloves, the line of her skirt. She nods to us. She makes straight for the door.

That, at least, is her intent, but then her petticoats shudder round her, and she begins to topple, like an elegant poplar.

We move as one, Vidocq and I, catching her on either side and walking her gently to the nearest armchair.

"Shall I fetch some vinegar, Madame?"

"No. Thank you."

She looks down and finds her fan, still miraculously prized between her fingers.

"I'm sorry," she whispers. "It all came flooding back. Talking of the Queen, I mean. The Princess. All those dead times." A tiny groove of sweat wells up on her powdered forehead. "The women all in white and the men in their—their Florentine taffeta. Marvelous marble fountains. Perfumed water. Every night, a *concert spirituel*. Gluck, Piccinni. . . ."

Just as she did in her shabby apartment on the Rue Férou, the Baroness extends her arms, begins to play an invisible keyboard.

"I wish I could tell you," she says. "How beautiful it all was."

"Not for everyone," answers Vidocq, in the mildest of tones.

Her fingers fall gradually still. She says:

"I regret I cannot be of further use to you, Monsieur."

"Your cooperation has been greatly appreciated, Madame. The Prefect will be duly apprised of it."

"Ahh."

A small laugh escapes her as she grips the arms of the chair and rises in a dry rustle.

"Monsieur," she says. "Do you really wish to know who that young man is?"

"Of course."

"Then there is but one person alive who can tell you."

"Just so," he answers, lowering his head the barest half inch. "The Duchesse d'Angoulême, the dauphin's sister. Shall I convey her your respects, Madame?"

Etched on the Baroness's face now is an uncanny echo of the smile preserved on that canvas, not six feet away. How many men must have crumbled before it.

"I must beg you to leave me to my obscurity," she says.

She hesitates one last time, just as she reaches the office door.

"I'm sorry, Monsieur. Would you mind showing out the young man first? I fear one more encounter with my past will be the death of me."

CHAPTER 31

Dead Bones

CHARLES IS LURED to an adjoining room, the Baronne de Préval is hustled out back in a soft squall of wool, I'm tasked with replacing the Villon etching over the peephole, and Vidocq . . . well, he props his feet on the lip of the desk and bends his shoulders back and says:

"The problem, Hector, the real *problem* is there's no body."

"What do you mean?"

"Marie-Antoinette's remains, those were found. Same with the King's. But they've never found Louis-Charles' body. And without a *body* . . ." He squints his eyes down. "Without a body, we can't say for sure the dauphin died all those years ago. We can't say anything for sure."

He swivels round in his chair and contemplates the pink penumbra around Sainte-Chapelle.

"The Baroness is right," he says at last. "The Duchess is the one woman who can tell us if our boy is the real article. And she's the last one I'd dare approach."

For another minute he sits there, weighing all the considerations. Then, with a slow-mounting growl, he says:

"Tell Charles he's going on another trip tomorrow. *Northward* this time."

"May I tell him where?"

"The abbey of Saint-Denis. See if that sets his balls aquiver."

CHARLES I CAN'T speak for, but something in *me* certainly vibrates. How could it not? The town of Saint-Denis is the final resting place of France's rulers. Charles Martel, Henry the Second, Louis the Fourteenth . . . one by one, the mummified husks of our kings have been deposited in these dripping crypts.

For a time, it's true, the revolutionaries turned the basilica into a Temple to Reason, then a town hall, then a military hospital. Wheat was threshed on its floors. But a Gothic church can never entirely escape its origins, and the Bourbons have had the good sense to make it once more the mausoleum it so devoutly wants to be.

Saint-Denis is only six miles from Paris, but the trip, in its early stages, is all hills. Vidocq's horse isn't used to them. It groans in its harness, lurches and slides, swallows down oceans of water. Some two hundred yards short of the Montmartre buttes, we have to get out of the carriage and walk. But the road decants as we pass through the Porte Saint-Denis, and the buildings fall away, and Charles is able at last to doze off—with the same unconditional surrender he showed on the trip from Saint-Cloud.

"Christ," says Vidocq. "Does he do anything but sleep?"

At a little after ten, the Seine crooks west, and before us spreads a plain, swirling round a walled town. From inside the walls come vendor cries, the stinging sound of a whip, the inquiries of cows. And then, when you least expect it, the abbey bells: shivering everything else into nothing.

"Time to get to work," says Vidocq.

Reaching under his seat, he draws out a cardboard tube, from which he extracts a map, marked at intervals with charcoal.

"The necropolis is *there,*" he says, spreading the map between us. "You can't go straight in, you have to come at it through the abbey. Now this *particular* crypt has a gate leading out of the Lady Chapel . . . *there,* you see? The gate is locked, usually, but today the verger has orders to leave it open, from eleven to twelve."

"Why don't they just open it when she comes?"

"She hates calling attention to herself. It's why she dresses so drably, she wants to slip past with no one the wiser. Now listen to me. Under no circumstances are you to follow her. Your job is just to hang around till she comes out again."

"And then what?"

"You fasten Charles onto your arm, you take a little stroll. Right in front of her, the quickest of passes. Say 'Good day, Madame' if you like, but don't mention her name *or* her title. Bow—smile—walk on. Is that clear?"

Through the morning musk, the town wall sharpens into view. Like something scissored out of an old codex.

"What if something goes wrong?" I ask.

"I'll be there in the nave with you. Something happens you can't handle, give me a signal."

"What signal?"

"How the fuck should I know? Pat your head, pinch your *ass,* will that do, Monsieur Give-Me-a-Signal?"

"There has to be an easier way," I murmur.

Frowning, he scrolls up the map, pushes it back into its tube.

"If she recognizes him, Hector, our job is going to be a lot easier. And if she *doesn't* recognize him—well, we'll come to that in due course."

THE FIRST CREATURE to greet us inside the town walls is an Ile-de-France ewe that clambers up the side of our carriage, giving a bleat of such unvarnished welcome that it jars Charles straight awake.

"Where are we?" he cries.

"In the graveyard of kings," Vidocq says. "You'll love it, I promise."

Ten minutes later, Charles is tugging on my sleeve.

"Can we go now?"

Because there's nothing to see, really. Thanks to the carnage of the Revolution, the niches are empty, the floors are scarred, flagstones are missing from the choir. There's no altar or organ or screen. I think that must be why I like the place. You can see it fresh.

"Well, we can't go just yet," I say. "There's a lady I want you to see."

"That old one, you mean? Saying all those Agnus Deis?"

"*Another* lady. She hasn't got here yet."

"Then how do you know she's coming?"

Under normal circumstances, I'd defer to Vidocq, but he's already separated himself from us. And at this remove, he looks exactly the German banker he's pretending to be. Strawberry blond hair, a box-wood shrub of a mustache . . . he's even given himself a new walk. The only sign that it's Vidocq under that cambric shirt and white piqué vest is the right foot, dragging slightly after the left.

"She promised to come at the dot of eleven," I say. "That's just ten minutes away."

To make the time pass, I tell him of the great men who were once buried here. I speak of Charles Martel and Hugh Capet . . . Henri the Second and Louis the Fourteenth. They might as well be census figures.

"Is it eleven yet?" he asks.

"Soon."

"But when?"

I can hear the testiness in my voice now. "Did you behave like this with Monsieur Tepac? I'm sure *he* took you places."

"Not *cathedrals*," answers Charles, sulkily. "We went fishing once, but that was nearly as dull. I believe the *fish* were bored, too. I think they swallowed the hooks just to—hold on! Is that her?"

WHAT WILL AMAZE me afterward is how he knew it was a woman. The five personages processing down the side aisle are notable for their plain and shapeless dress, and the small bent figure in the center is virtually hidden under a black mantilla. Vidocq was right on this point, anyway: She travels light.

"Yes," I say. "That's her."

"Well, then, what are we waiting for?"

He's all set to race after them, but I catch him by the arm.

"Not just yet. She has to pay respects to her parents first."

"And where are *they*?"

"Down below."

He stares at me, uncomprehending.

"They're *buried* there," I explain.

"And how long does it take to pay respects?"

"Depends," I say. "On how respectful you're feeling."

As the mourning party files into the Lady Chapel, the rear guard glances back, and I switch my eyes toward the immense rose windows overlooking the transept. I make a show of studying them, but really, I'm just ticking off the seconds: one . . . two . . . three. . . .

I don't even reach ten, because it suddenly occurs to me I've forgotten something.

Charles.

I take a step toward the west door. He's not there. Another step toward the triforium. Not there.

I scan the pews and aisles, I peer down the apse . . . and then I turn to the one place I've been avoiding. Which is exactly where I find him: scurrying into the Lady Chapel.

It won't do to sprint. Long strides are the most I can allow myself, and as I move toward the high altar, I'm waving my arms at Vidocq, but he's contemplating the clerestory, and I see Charles draw open the iron gate and disappear into the darkness, and I nearly cry out, but all I can do is keep moving.

The gate is still ajar when I get there. Breathing out mold and damp—and the same suggestion of rot that washed over me in my first carriage ride with Vidocq. I take a single step forward. The darkness surges round me.

"Charles," I whisper.

How I wish I'd stopped for a candle! There's not a single torch in the place. I move one step at a time, and even so, I nearly come to a bad end when, out of nowhere, a descending staircase appears. Grabbing for the wall, I haul myself erect. A pool of cold, piquant air billows up from below, *seals* me on that top step, as if it were marbling me round.

"Charles . . ."

Out of the murk, ghostly shapes bleed free, and it is with a deeper chill that I realize what they are. Sepulchers. Bearing France's illustrious dead.

It was here the revolutionaries came, fifteen years ago, tearing open tombs, hammering effigies into crumbs, emptying royal hearts and entrails from lead buckets, throwing bone after bone into great open pits. Erasing more than a thousand years of history in thirteen days.

Why, then, do I feel like the one being erased? I could hammer this darkness, and it would simply absorb me, cell by cell.

"Hector?"

He speaks only once, but I fasten onto that sound and haul myself toward it, stone by stone. The scrape of my boots has a liquid resonance, so that, as I descend, I have the sense of being a cataract, spilling ever downward, waiting for a receptacle.

Which is nothing more than a trembling hand. And a trembling voice.

"It's so dark here. I hate it."

"I know. Let me see if . . ."

Rummaging through my pockets, my fingers close round a sulfur match. I swipe it—twice—against the stone wall, and the light carves away the darkness, and I find myself staring up at an inscription: "Here lie the mortal remains of . . ."

In the next instant, I'm swinging the light away, but it's not Charles who pops out at me but a stranger. Discernible only as an oval of white, with a mouth-chasm.

I *see* the scream before I hear it. The uvula vibrating, the soft palate receding.

From behind us come confused shouts. A pair of rough hands flings me to the ground; another pair flattens Charles. I feel the press of cold stone and a blade against my neck and, above me, a voice of unusual cultivation.

"Move another inch, and you *will* die."

CHAPTER 32

Germany to the Rescue

So BEGINS MY first audience with the Duchesse d'Angoulême.

Although, if I'm to be strictly accurate, my *first* audience took place four years earlier—on the third of May, 1814.

For a steep sum, my mother and I rented a window seat in a pothouse overlooking the Rue Saint-Denis, where we proposed to join a few million of our fellow citizens in welcoming King Louis the Eighteenth.

Happiest of days. The Corsican had been sent off to Elba, the Bourbon exile was done. Let the forgetting begin! From every window there fluttered a white flag or white flowers . . . white curtains, carpets, bed linens. As if the homes in Paris were disemboweling themselves for joy.

At precisely ten o'clock the King's carriage came through the triumphal arch of the Porte Saint-Denis, drawn by eight white horses. *Long live the King!* came the roar. *Long live the Bourbons!*

Our eyes then turned, by common consent, to the small thin

woman in the King's carriage. The last time she'd met this many Parisians, they were dragging her to the Temple. Now they were throwing open their arms. She had outlived the Directorate and the Consulate and the Empire. She was our Antigone, our Clio, our *new* Marianne.

And yet, as she passed down the Rue Saint-Denis—clutching her white parasol, averting her head—she left in her wake only an itchy muttering. My mother, in the end, had one thing to say on the subject of the Duchesse d'Angoulême. . . .

"Such a bonnet!"

Well, having spent the previous eight years in Buckinghamshire, the Duchess was sporting the small headwear favored by the English. No one had told her that Parisian women preferred bonnets the size of funerary urns.

The bonnet, of course, would have mattered nothing at all if there had lain beneath it the face of our imaginings. This was what we saw instead: a stern, grief-parched woman, still in her thirties but already closed to light. Madame Royale (as she was known from birth) may have quit the Temple; the Temple had never quit her.

Her marriage to her cousin, the Comte d'Artois' son, was barren in every respect, and since her return to France, the Duchess has abstained from virtually all social functions, preferring to devote herself to acts of charity. She visits hospitals and workhouses, she prays for souls, and twice a month, she makes the pilgrimage from the Tuileries to Saint-Denis—always with the smallest possible retinue—to pay respects to her parents.

On this particular day, however, her devotions are interrupted by the arrival of two men, unknown to her, who are repaid for their presumption by being thrown to the ground.

"Please," I stutter. "Apologies. No harm meant."

But my voice scarcely registers amid the cloud of sound and is trumped finally by the man who stands directly over me—the man who has just threatened our lives.

"Who are you?" he demands to know.

No gainsaying the authority in that timbre. *The voice of French civilization,* I think.

"How do you come here?" he asks.

From out of the darkness comes an answer:

"My name is Charles Rapskeller."

How near he sounds! Squinting, I can just make out his head, squeezed against the musty stone.

"And this is Hector," he says. "You mustn't be cross with him, he was only trying to help. I have a way of getting lost sometimes, I can't seem to help it."

"Getting lost is one thing," says the voice of civilization. "Coming down a flight of steps in complete darkness smacks of *purpose.*"

In the end, we are saved by another voice, calling after us.

"There you are!"

A high, brittle sound, suffused with Rhine water. Such a perfect simulacrum of German banker that it's not until Vidocq is actually standing over me that I know who it is.

"Ha! I turn my back for a moment, and you run off like a pair of highwaymen! Just wait till your mama hears about this."

"And you are?" inquires the voice of French civilization.

"Alois Herrhausen. Of the Schaaffenhausen bank."

"And these are your sons?"

"My God, no! *Nephews,* Monsieur. My dear sister, upon learning I had business in Paris, begged me to take them to Saint-Denis, so that a prayer might be offered for their recovery."

"And what are they recovering from, Monsieur?"

"Oh, it's—it's a bit . . ." A pall of embarrassed silence, punctured by a stage whisper. "Dropped on their *heads,* the both of them. By the same midwife. And with the same result."

"They seem entirely rational to me."

"That's the tragedy of it, Monsieur. On the surface, all's well. Down *below* . . ." A soft whistle. "Nobody home but the bats."

And now another voice emerges. Female and tentative and, at the same time, harsh. Like a crow calling after her young.

"I'm sure no harm has been done."

IT's ONE OF the least-remarked perils of reading. You meet people often enough in print, you believe you really know them. So it is with me and Madame Royale. I feel as if I've blundered into her life, the way one stumbles into a water closet, mistaking it for a parlor.

And so, when the guard releases his grip and suffers me to rise— when the Duchess's pale, swaddled face swims toward me once more—I find myself casting my eyes down, for fear of what she will find there.

"Truly," she says, "there was no need for me to shout in such a manner. I was merely taken aback."

"And who could blame you, Madame?" Vidocq gives a mighty click of his heels. "In such a place as this, one expects only ghosts and goblins, not a pair of bungling *taugenichts*. I do apologize. They meant no harm."

And now, for the first time, the voice of French civilization becomes flesh and blood. Which is to say a man of perhaps fifty years steps into the light. Dark-complected and full-lipped. The torso pulls slightly back, as if to deny the violence promised by the right leg, which is thrust forward. He's *taut*, in a way one no longer expects aristocrats to be, with just enough curl in his hair to hint of *sauciers* and tailors.

"I would entreat you," he says, "to keep closer watch on your nephews in the future."

"Never fear, Monsieur. Tomorrow morning, they'll be packed on the first mail coach for Strasbourg, and they will never trouble you again, I swear on God. Do you hear me, rogues? Now come along, we've just enough time to make the stage. . . ."

———

No stage awaits us, but Vidocq's carriage is stationed just where we left it, and from there, we beat a straight path to the city gates. It isn't until we're five minutes outside of Saint-Denis that Vidocq raps on the roof of the carriage and orders the driver to stop.

"Charles. Go play."

And so he does. Plunges into the surrounding meadow with the air of a medical student excused from his last examination.

"Well," says Vidocq, watching him grimly. "Our boy is a bit more complicated than he looks."

"Why do you say that?"

"Because unlike *you*, I was watching him. And I'm telling you he spied his moment. I'm telling you he waited till your head was turned, and he made a beeline for the Duchess."

"He was restless to leave, that's all. I told him we couldn't go until we'd seen her. He was—he was shortening the process."

"Oh, is that it?"

For another minute, we watch him crawling through rye, querying each wildflower.

"He didn't seem to recognize her," I venture.

"True."

"Nor she him."

"That's also true. The only face that really consumed her was *yours*, Hector."

Stooping, he plucks a clover blossom, twirls it between his index and middle fingers.

"Your father *met* Madame Royale, didn't he?"

I nod.

"And how closely do you resemble him, Hector?"

"Well . . . quite a . . . quite a bit, I'm told."

"Very good. Now maybe you can explain why the sight of your father should bring a tear to the Duchess's eyes."

3 Germinal Year III

Charles has repeatedly asked after his sister. Ive explained that Mme Royale's welfare is not w/in my sphere of responsibility, but of late, his inquiries have grown mr urgent. It occurs to me that happy tidings fm his sister cd be of <u>great</u> use in improving his spirits & <u>health</u>.

Asked Leblanc this A.M. if we might obtain audience w/ princess. Impossible, he said, w/o express consent of Comm for Public Safety. Perhaps I might petition them directly? My previous experiences with Comm (esp. Citizen Mathieu) being unpleasant, I resolved to take matter directly to Genrl Barras, who has often looked favorably on my petitions.

This very day, I visited him at his quarters. Was surprised to be granted immediate audience—and to find Genrl <u>well disposed</u> toward my request. He asked if I might like to join him for supper at his private apts—tomorrow eve—for purposes of discussing matter further. I readily consented.

5 Germinal

Have now some cause to regret Barras' invitation. Details of our encounter too vulgar to recount. Suffice it to say his protestations excited no small disgust in me. For holding my peace, however, I now have letter, personally signed, allowing me to visit Mme Royale on reg basis.

At what cost to scruple! It is true what my friend Junius says: We live in flexible times.

6 GERMINAL

1st interview w/ princess took place immediately after visit w/ Charles. She lives on 3rd floor of tower—apts prev shared w/ mother & aunt. Leblanc & I found her seated on sofa alongside window, embroidering. This, I'm told, is one pastime permitted her.

Mme. Royale is now 16, by our calculations—still very much a maiden. Her hair is worn w/o powder, tied in knot. Headdress = handkerchief, tied in rosette. She has but one dress, of puce silk. She is permitted no hat.

In good health, genrlly, but her expression is <u>extrmly grave</u>. Upon seeing us, she made no sign or word of welcome. To our repeated questions, gave no reply.

As Leblanc reminded me, princess has been imprisoned for more than 2 yrs, w/o fire or light . . . daily diet of verbal abuse from guards . . . thrice-daily searches, often in middle of night . . . no comforts. Cards, even <u>books</u> are withheld, for fear she will engage in coded communications, absorb royalist propaganda, etc.

These reflections moved me twrd deg of pity. Upon withdrawing fm her room, I made pt of bowing low. Leblanc, w/o hesitation, followed my lead. This, I cd see, astonished her. It has been <u>many months</u> since anyone did her this honor.

7 GERMINAL

2nd interview w/ princess likewise wordless. By certain movements of her eyes, however, I concluded her silence has proximate cause: She fears being overheard by guards (who are under orders to listen in on all conversations). I therefore took advantage of our departure to whisper in her ear:

Perhaps you cd tell us if you require anything?

From my pockets, I withdrew paper & pencil. She regarded these articles for some time. Then, taking them from me, she hastily scribbled. . . .

<u>Some chemises, & some books</u>.

9 Germinal

Commissioners will not disburse funds for new clothes. Ive accordingly borrowed 2 chemises fm my wife, Béatrice. Princess seemed pleased enough w/ them. Some <u>awkwardness</u> over book. Voltaire's Micromégas: partic favorite of mine & in keeping w/ current pol climate. W/ manifest regret, she shook her head & handed it back (politely).

I apologized for my thoughtlessness, vowed to bring more suitable vol tomorrow. (Will ask Junius for suggestions.)

11 Germinal

At close of todays interview, Mme Royale spoke her 1st words to us:

<u>How is my brother?</u>

19 GERMINAL

Leblanc (excellent fellow!) has made signal discovery. NE quad of princess's cell, due to some concatenation of furniture & wall, is acoustically "null"—i.e., we may speak there, in low tones, w/o being overheard by guards. This has had most beneficial effect on our conversations. Princess now speaks openly. Is most grateful for audience.

Leblanc & I remain seriously constrained in what we can tell her. No details of Charles' condition. No news of outside world. We cannot even tell her that her mother & aunt are dead!

This A.M., Mme Royale told me she wished to nurse her brother. I said Id be too happy to oblige, but was expressly forbidden to reunite them. Commissioners do not even allow them to see each other when they are taken outside for walks.

Princess was insistent. Her mother, her aunt Élizabeth begged her to look af Charles, she said.

They cd not expect you to burrow thru stone walls, cd they?

She made no reply. However, was <u>in no way</u> deterred fm her course.

28 GERMINAL

This A.M., Mme Royale drew me into our usual corner. W/o any preliminaries or greetings, she whispered: We must get Charles out of here.

Endeavoring to be calm, I explained to her why such a thing cd nv happen. Hundreds of soldiers, certain death for anyone who assists royal family, etc. I expressed hope that negotiations w/ foreign govts might yet secure his release if cert conditions can be . . .

W/ no small brusquerie, she cut me off. We don't have time for negotiations, she said. He's very ill, Doctor. No, don't deny it, your eyes tell me everything. If we don't get him out of this hellish place, he'll die. Tell me, then. <u>What are we to do?</u>

A good question, alas. What are we to do?

We can no longer depend on authorities to do right thing. It is up to us to arrive at course of conduct. This I have <u>resolved</u>, & Leblanc has seconded me. God help us all.

CHAPTER 33

A Lilac Grows in the Tuileries Gardens

THE NEXT MORNING, Charles and I take up what has become our daily routine. We wake at eight. We eat a concise breakfast. We go out through the rear courtyard and put on our costumes and start walking.

Passing down the Quai des Augustins that first morning, we are set upon by a seagull, roaring in from the river and, with a cry of pure obscenity, snatching the powdered locks straight from Charles' head. Stunned, Charles watches his wig disappear over the Pont Neuf. Puts a hand to his naked locks.

"Do you know I think I like it better without?"

"So do I."

Off comes *my* wig. Off go *his* eyeshades. At the very next clothes dealer, we splurge our Ministry of Justice funds on new boots. And now, for the first time, a note of larkishness clings to our enterprise. We walk more quickly, we laugh more readily. We nod our heads to the ladies and we compliment old gentlemen on their three-cornered hats and we lose any sense of having to be anywhere in any order at any time.

The Tuileries, the Louvre, the Conciergerie . . . these provoke not a whisper of recognition in him, so I very soon abandon any itinerary, and we simply walk. From the Hôtel de Ville to the Faubourg Saint-Honoré, from the Barrière du Maine to the Quartier Saint-Antoine, from the Place Louis XV to the Place Vendôme. Day after day, miles and miles in every direction, steeping our cassimere coats in coal dust, plastering our new boots in mud and night soil—and moving always according to the most contrary of compasses. North on the Pont Notre-Dame . . . south on the Pont-au-Change . . . north again on the Pont d'Iéna . . .

Paris shrinks before us, and Charles takes it in like a man sent to wander through the moon's lost realms. He regards the silk-stockinged *vicomte* in the same fashion as he does the chemical-factory worker with the blackened face. He surveys Napoleon's half-finished arch on the Champs-Élysées and decides that it should be left "just like that." He declares that he's never seen anything quite so lovely as the rotting, rat-infested plaster elephant in the Place de la Bastille.

"But whose idea was it?" he asks.

"Just some fellow. Who's not here anymore."

"You mean Monsieur Bonaparte," he says, unexpectedly.

"The very one."

"I saw him once."

"Did you?"

"On a five-franc ecu. He was turned sideways."

In the next instant, I am myself turning sideways and seeing a flash of scarlet, disappearing round the Rue de Charenton. No more sub-stantial than it was the other night, when I glimpsed it from my garret window, but more vivid somehow for being so fleeting.

"Come on," I say.

"But where are we going?"

"To the boulevards."

———

It's the safest place I can think of. On the boulevards, the line between pursuer and pursued collapses because nothing stays in place. The turbaned girl playing the hurdy-gurdy becomes, in the next step, a sword swallower. The pantomimist becomes a ballad singer or a Racine tragedian or a woman spinning silently in a vat of water—or just a milliner, strolling by with a bandbox.

From the Madeleine to the Bastille we stroll, Charles and I, past a million coffeehouses, past baths, restaurants and *pâtisseries*, past theaters and billiard rooms, keeping a steady pulse against all those counterpulses, stopping only to refresh ourselves or duck out of a passing shower.

And if, now and then, a familiar flash of scarlet registers on the edge of my retina, I just take Charles by the arm and disappear into a crowd of vendors.

Apples, monsieur! . . . Ah, messieurs, buy my potatoes! . . . Old clothes! . . . Rabbit skins! . . . Petits pains au lait! Hot! Hot!

One afternoon, we are stopped on the Boulevard de la Madeleine by a cortège of great solemnity. The street itself falls silent before the spectacle. Seven wagons. And in each wagon, twenty-four men, sitting back-to-back, their feet in wooden shoes, their necks secured by iron collars, their arms bound, like vertebrae, by a single chain.

As they pass, we hear a gourdlike rattle and the crack of lashes, and the men themselves, shivering in the sun, give off a hum like plainchant, in which you can hear fragments of obscene tavern songs.

"Who are they?" Charles whispers.

"Convicts."

"Where are they going?"

"To the galleys."

The lucky ones, I might add. The others . . .

Well, one need only scan the men lying in that final wagon: baled like hay, glossy with fever. *They* won't last another day. More than half their company will die, too, before the journey is done; those that survive will wish they hadn't. Chained at the ankles from dawn to dusk . . . set to toil in pestilential heat . . . flogged, spat upon, beaten, sodomized. And their reward at the end of the day? A wooden plank to set their shaved heads on—and the ever-receding prospect of freedom.

"Hector!"

Charles' nostrils recoil, as if an invisible hand were pressing against them.

"That smell," he says. "It's just like your friend."

And he's right.

Amazing to think a smell could adhere to a man fifteen years after he left the galleys. My gaze, untethered, wanders from wagon to wagon until it lights on a haggard, toothless, string-thin fellow, bobbing in and out of sleep—and at last giving way altogether so that, in the very next second, he's tumbling straight out of the wagon and taking with him the rest of his comrades in chains. One by one, they topple onto the cobbles, like sparrows falling from chimneys.

At once, the marshals and guards spring on them with cudgels and horsewhips and the flats of swords. With great effort, the bound convicts stagger to their feet and totter back to the wagon—shuffling as they go, for though their ankles have been left free for the journey, the sheer *memory* of those shackles causes each man to drag his right foot after him.

Just like Vidocq, I think, dazzled.

And now, by common impulse, Charles and I take flight. We leave the convicts, we leave the boulevards, and we dash away, in no particular direction, simply following the city's own declivity. Around us, the air begins to seethe and crackle, but we keep walking, and it's the river that stops us finally.

We look round in a stupor and find ourselves under a dark mass of chestnuts, peering down a long promenade.

The Tuileries gardens.

A hard northwest wind is thrashing the orange trees, bending back the topiary globes, scooping the water straight from the fountains. To the south, the Seine is churning like surf, and to the east, candles are winking on at every window, as the palace bundles down for the coming blow.

All the promenaders have long since left—their rented chairs lie tipped over, their abandoned newspapers kick up like sails—but Charles refuses to move. And as the first heavy drops of rain strike his bare head, he blinks twice and says:

"Wait."

He walks, very slowly, toward a lilac bush.

He kneels down. He fumbles through the bush's lower branches, gropes all the way to the root. Then, after several seconds of concentrated effort, he draws out his trophy. Holds it out to me in his palm.

A ribbon. Of Bourbon white.

Dirty and torn and half-unraveled—and still luminous, as though the rain were washing away the years. And washing Charles into— someone else. Someone I've never met before.

I kneel alongside him. I talk straight into his ear.

"Did you know this ribbon was there?"

After several seconds, he nods, very slowly.

"Did you put it there yourself?"

Another pause. Another nod.

"Did it happen a long time ago?"

Only a foot separates us, but I have to raise my voice, simply to be heard above the wind and rain.

"Were you a *boy* when it happened?"

To this he makes no reply, except to close his hands once more over the ribbon, as though he could squeeze the memory from it.

"*Why* did you hide it, Charles?"

"So they wouldn't find it," he answers, his own voice rising.

"Who?"

"The bad men."

The rain is rivering down his face now.

"They . . ." He wipes his mouth with his forearm. "They took away my garden. They said I couldn't keep any of my flowers. So I took my lilac and I planted it *here* and I put the ribbon where they . . . where they . . ."

He puts a hand to his face.

"No," he says. "That was a dream."

Very gently, I put one hand under his jaw. He doesn't recoil. I put the other hand alongside his temple. By degrees, I tilt his head toward the west side of the Tuileries palace—the one angle I never thought to afford him—the one angle that Louis the Seventeenth would have seen every day, coming back from his outings. The one he would have remembered best. If he were still alive.

For what seems like an eternity, Charles studies those pavilion roofs, and I study—*him*. Which means I am watching in the exact moment when he opens.

Yes, that's the best word, I think. A world of light rushes into him. The lilac bush . . . the ribbon . . . the cornices and columns of that ugly palace . . . they all gather into meaning. With such force that he's literally thrown onto his back.

"I have this dream sometimes," he moans. "I dream I was . . ."

"You were," I say, surprised at the assurance in my own voice. "You *are*."

His eyes glow white amid the rain and mist. His mouth opens. . . .

"What?" I say. "I can't hear you."

"Is it too late?"

"Too late for what?"

"To go back?"

———

NOW IT MIGHT be he simply wants to get out of the rain. But when I look back on this moment, I will see our fates twining themselves more tightly round us, as a vine hugs a trellis. Why else would I answer as quickly as I do, without a thought for any other answer?

"IT'S TOO LATE."

CHAPTER 34

Not Since Waterloo

THE STORM PASSES quickly enough, but we're too wet to do anything but go home. There we find clothes and a fire already blazing and a baguette and two cups of hot, bitter coffee and even a good-humored reproof from my mother.

"Goodness' sakes. Gentlemen should always carry umbrellas."

By now, Charles' customary good nature has been chaffed into something heavy and inward. Every question invokes only silence, and Charlotte, in the act of spooning cabbage onto his plate, feels compelled to ask after his health.

"You seem a bit quiet is all," she adds.

"Perhaps the Vicomte's estate has uncovered new heirs," suggests Nankeen.

Charles, knowing nothing of vicomtes or estates, fails to rise to the bait. His movements, his expressions grow steadily more listless, until at last he sets down his knife and fork entirely.

"It is a great puzzle," says Rosbif. "Thank the good Lord we have in our midst an esteemed *physician*. Your diagnosis, Monsieur Hector?"

For several long seconds, I study my plate. Then, in a voice of new-found authority:

"Monsieur Charles needs only to shake off his cares. I propose to help him."

"How?"

"By taking him to the Palais-Royal," I announce. "We shall leave in two hours."

LATE AT NIGHT, the former palace of the Duc d'Orléans glows like a pyre. Floods of light, streaming up from the foundations, sweep over an army of Parisians, captured in the act of choosing sins. Will they go down to the cellar for the dancing dogs and the blind ballad singer? Or will they stride along the ground-floor arcades, sampling snuffboxes and alabaster clock-cases and obscene etchings of milk-maids?

Or will they go still higher, to the glittering realm of the dining rooms? Thirty years ago, it's said, Camille Desmoulins leapt onto one of the café tables here and declared revolution. These days, you'll seldom find anyone leaving his chair. Wives sit inches away from prostitutes; tradesmen buy drinks for adventurers; rogues and swindlers twine their arms like lovers.

And the wine flows, though the intoxication here is something more general. Something to do with being alive, I think.

And in the Café des Milles Colonnes, the champagne flows.

"Mm," says Charles, drawing in the fumes. "It tickles and burns at the same time. . . ."

I call back the waiter and order another magnum and, for good measure, *pâté de foie aux pruneaux* and cold *boulettes* and two apple tarts and . . . I forget what else. We eat and drink in the gleam of all those glassed columns, watching romances bloom and die—until we are accosted by two women in low-cut silk ball dresses, who look at us as though we're every bit as interesting as what we're watching.

"We were thinking you gentlemen might care for company."

"By all means," mumbles Charles, half rising from his seat and then crashing back down.

My appointed companion is perhaps twenty-two, with rough freckled hands and brown eyes shining over a thin, pickled mouth.

"Virginie," she tells me.

"I was just going to guess that."

The woman who claims Charles is named Berthe. She has a granite head and an air of interrupted industry, as though she's left a pile of dirty laundry in the coffee room.

"No thanks," she says, pushing away her glass. "Champagne makes me burp."

If a human being has ever said anything funnier than that . . . well, Charles has yet to hear it.

"Burp," he gasps. *"Burp."*

Virginie's fingers scuttle up my arm.

"My, aren't you handsome?"

"Ladies," I say, rising unsteadily to my feet. "Shall we scatter?"

I fully expect us to head upstairs to one of the houses of tolerance, but Virginie takes us straight down to the garden and out the gate.

"Aren't we . . . ?"

"Bit of a problem with our licenses," she answers. "Never mind, we've got lovely rooms not four blocks off."

To my right, I see Charles listing east to west, with only Berthe's stout arm to keep him vertical. By the time we reach the corner of the Rue Droit-Mur, he is leaning almost all of his weight into her, and a song is pouring out of his throat, high and raucous:

> *"There's a chérie I know*
> *And her boat I shall row*
> *Frontward, backward*
> *Any way she'll go—"*

"No more," I whisper in his ear.

"And it's in . . . out . . .
Lord, how she shouts!
In . . . out . . ."

"Shut up!" hisses Berthe. "You'll get the gendarmes on our tail!"

"You remind me of a goat I used to have," he says.

"Thanks very much, I'm sure."

"Do you have playing cards where you live?"

"I should think so," she answers vaguely.

"Ninepins?"

"Oh, ninepins."

We turn down the Petite Rue Picpus and come to a crackled white plaster housefront, wreathed in ivy, with a single night lamp burning in the window.

"Just three floors to climb," says Virginie.

With Charles lurching and stumbling, it seems to take nearly half a day. As soon as he's shown his room, he falls onto the cot bedstead with the weight of a hundred men and goes directly to sleep.

"Not much of a drinker, is he?" says Berthe.

Shrugging, she draws over a chair to the room's single candle and takes up a square of embroidery, blue and puckered.

"Look here," I say. "He'll be all right, won't he?"

"What, you think I'm going to *wake* him? This is the first break I've had all day."

"But he doesn't like being left alone. He likes having company when he sleeps."

"Dearie, he's fine," murmurs Virginie, tugging on my arm.

VIDOCQ ONCE THEORIZED that I hadn't been fucked since Waterloo. In fact, I've had enough recent experience with prostitutes to recognize the advantages of Virginie. She has, to begin with, teeth. Her face doesn't resolve into harsh grooves the moment you touch her. Through it all, she retains the same air of benign encouragement she had when she sat down at our café table.

One thing I *have* forgotten: how stirring a woman's humidity can be. A whole continent waiting to be claimed, yes, and I can only be grateful that my little explorer shakes off the slumber that has seized the rest of me. In the exhaustion that follows there's a seam of satisfaction, as if I've been clearing away brush.

"How much do I——?"

"Oh, no hurry about that," says Virginie.

At some point, I realize I am embracing not her but the sheets where she lay. As these are every bit as pliant, I drop straight to sleep. And in no time, I'm hustled back to Saint-Cloud. Once more the Grand Cascade has kicked into life, and Monsieur Tepac lies pale and heavy before me, blood flowing freely from his side.

Gathered round us, in a loose triptych, are more watchers: Vidocq, in his best finery, and Charles, wearing a lopsided crown, and Tepac's assassin, Herbaux. There is about all of them a sort of hesitation—they'd like to help but don't know how—and blood flows through the flap of Tepac's skin and jets from the Grand Cascade and falls from the sky.

I wake, with shreds of Saint-Cloud trailing after me. I reach for the candle by the bed, thrust it into the darkness. In the doorway, a tall shadowy figure stands framed.

The man raises his own candle, and in the pool of our joined light, I behold him. No dream, after all. Herbaux, flesh and blood.

CHAPTER 35

In Which the Vulnerability of the Hamstring Is Clearly Demonstrated

THE THING IS, if you'd asked me *before* what Herbaux looked like, I doubt I could have told you. Somehow, without my knowing it, those features imprinted themselves on me. The hero's jaw, tapering into a cleft chin. The boxer's nose (broken at least twice in its career), and the satyr eyes, too wideset for comfort, coming at you from every possible angle.

One thing I didn't recall from Saint-Cloud: the *scale* of him. The very doorframe peels back to accommodate him.

"Get up," he says.

This is harder to do than I would have guessed. Champagne has rotted my head from the inside out.

"May I—put my clothes on?"

"Your trousers," he says. "That's all you'll need."

I move slowly, not from any strategy but simply to slow my heart.

For several seconds, my gaze lingers on the window—until I hear Herbaux's measured tone:

"I wouldn't. It's a four-story drop. Now let's go wake your friend, shall we?"

"But I came alone."

"'Course you did."

He grabs me by the back of my neck and, with very little effort, flings me down the hallway. I land about three feet short of Charles' door.

"Go fetch," says Herbaux.

Nothing about what happens next is planned. With one hand, I'm turning the knob. With the other . . . I'm grabbing Herbaux's candle and driving it toward his face. A grunt of pain, and then the candle clatters to the ground and Herbaux staggers back. I plant a foot in his midsection and send him sprawling onto his back. Then I fling the door open and slam it after me.

"Charles!"

My eyes, adapting slowly to the darkness, find him exactly where I left him—on the cot, breathing in long slow drafts.

By now Herbaux has recovered himself enough to hurl his bulk against the door. Again and again he comes, and as I press myself against the door, it seems to shrivel between us, as though it were aging before our eyes.

"Charles! For God's sake, wake up!"

My feet, scrambling for a purchase, knock against a white porcelain pitcher. With a single swing of my arm, I send its contents flying toward him. At once, the room is filled with an acrid stench, and Charles bolts upright in bed.

"Did I piss myself?" he cries.

"It's all right. Listen, now. . . ." How calm I sound to myself! "I need you to do something for me, all right? I need you to get up right now and bring that dresser *here*. Can you do that?"

His faculties are even muddier than mine, but after several seconds of groaning, he manages to drag the dresser across the wooden floor. And with his help, I'm able to wedge it against the door.

"Now I need you to *push*. Can you do that?"

"Like this?" he asks.

"Harder. As *hard* as you can."

He leans into the door—and is stunned to feel it buck back.

"Someone's out there," he says.

"Yes, that's right. We're playing a *game*. If we can keep the man on the other side from coming *in*, he'll"—a second or two of wild groping—"he'll make us breakfast."

Clouds of nausea pass over Charles' face. "Bit early for that, isn't it?"

"Just keep pushing."

And he does. Even after the door begins to splinter beneath Herbaux's weight, he doggedly applies the counterforce. I can hear the sounds of his exertion as I sprint to the window and call down into the darkness below. . . .

"Help!"

No answering call, just the echo of my own voice, bouncing off the gutters and rubbish heaps and grease drains.

Then I see, espaliered on the building face below me, a network of lead waste pipes, branching out in a hundred elbows, like an old grapevine.

"I think . . . we're going to lose," gasps Charles.

"Just a few more seconds!"

Scrambling now, I drag the cot away from the wall, wedge it against the dresser.

"All right," I tell him. "On the count of three, we're going to run to the window. One . . . two . . ."

The dresser gives way at once, but the cot holds fast. For now.

"This is the most fun part of all," I say. "We're going to climb down."

"Down?"

"Yes, it's all part of the game. First one to the ground gets a special prize."

"I'm not sure. . . ."

Behind us, another section of the door panel splinters apart.

"I'll go first," I say. "Then you can follow. . . ."

"Oh no, you don't!"

Without a second's more hesitation now, he sets his foot on the first length of pipe and, finding it secure, lowers himself to the next level. Three seconds later, he's vanished.

I follow close behind. There's no more than a sliver of moon to light the way, and my legs are heavy and my hands numb. My eye sockets feel as if someone is pressing a thumb against them. And looking up, I can see Herbaux's candle, lit once more, weaving circles in the night.

I take a long breath. I lower my leg, and another elbow of pipe is miraculously waiting to greet it.

By now, I've lost all sense of where Charles is. I could almost imagine I'm alone in the world—until my bare foot wiggles into a strange niche, not part of the original architecture. There is an answering squeal, then a chivvying at my toes. And then they're all over me.

An ocean of rats, red-eyed with outrage. They scuttle through my hair and shrill in my ear and fasten on my limbs. Groaning, I shake them off, but more come from every quadrant: silken fur, rasping teeth. And as I slide down the building face, swinging from pipe to pipe, they follow like a thousand reprimands.

It may be that I leap that final distance, but it feels more as if I'm *riding* those rats, as one might ride a wave. We breach together in the alley below, and we lie there for a while, stunned and spent.

I get to my feet. From behind me comes a light, high mewling.

"Ohh," says Charles, pressing his knees to his chin. "Oh, God, rats . . . God . . ."

"Never mind," I tell him. "They're gone."

Not a sound in the alleyway, not even a breath of wind. Dimly, I register a brindled dog . . . a skein of fish bones . . . a heap of fermenting rubbish, exhaling vapor . . . and somewhere in the distance, a tassel of amber light.

And then, from nowhere, a figure comes between us and the light.

"Pardon, Monsieur!" calls Charles. "Do you think you might—"

"There you are," says Herbaux.

Not an ounce of civility in his voice now.

"Listen," I say. "We can *pay* you. Between us, we've got quite a lot of money."

"I'm paid well enough."

"Then let my friend go," I say. "He's done nothing."

"Oh, that's the hell of it, Doctor. He *has*."

And then, from the folds of his peacoat, Herbaux withdraws a pistol.

"Is this part of the game, too?" asks Charles as I shove him behind me.

"Doesn't matter to me which of you goes first," calls Herbaux. "All cats are gray at night."

Very slowly, very carefully, he points the muzzle straight at my heart. He cocks the pistol. He squeezes one eye shut. . . .

And then, confoundingly, one of his knees buckles.

And the other.

With a great roar, he topples to his side.

Something stirs now in the shadows behind him. A crouched figure: shapeless, except for a luminous length of razor. This figure rises now, swallowing the space so lately vacated by Herbaux.

"Who are you?" I call out.

Calmly, the figure sheathes the blade and steps round the fallen man's writhing body.

"I demand to know who you are!"

"What?" comes the dry reply. "No *thank-you*?"

A woman's voice. That's enough in itself to stun me into silence. Charles, though, finds only encouragement. He peers down at Herbaux's crumpled form and inquires:

"What did you do to him?"

"The hamstring," she answers, shrugging. "Saw it done to a race-horse once."

"Bitch," hisses Herbaux, attempting to rise.

She kicks him back down. "Quiet! Or I'll tell your friends you got brought down by a girl."

"He's only mad because he lost," Charles explains. "He has to make us breakfast now."

Half laughing, the woman whips off her cloak and, in a startling gesture, offers it to me. For the first time, I'm conscious of my naked torso, speckled with cuts and bruises and bites. I'm conscious of something else, too: the lining of her cloak. A bright scarlet. The color of a cock's comb.

"*You,*" I say, dully. "You've been following us round town. Following us for days."

"What if I have? You didn't really think he'd let you go running across Paris all by yourselves?"

No need to ask who *he* is. Vidocq, like God, requires no antecedent.

"He's no fool, after all," says the woman. "Whatever else he is. But I don't believe you recognize me, Doctor."

Numbly, I shake my head.

"I'm Jeanne-Victoire. Arnaud Poulain's girl."

Quickly, the coordinates reassemble themselves. The thief who robbed Leblanc. That terrible apartment in the Marais. Rags everywhere and stolen shoes and broken boards . . . and there, resting on a chafing dish. . . .

"A *baby,*" I blurt.

It's too dark to see her eyes, but the slight recoil of her head . . . that much I see.

"She's with my brother now. In Issy. She likes it there."

From under her scarlet cloak, she draws a silver whistle and puts it to her lips. Straightaway, we hear the rumble of answering boots.

"The gendarmes'll be here in a minute," she says. "Go with them to the guardhouse, Doctor, and maybe they'll fetch you some new clothes, eh? As for *me*, I'm going to catch some winks. You boys are enough exercise for one day."

She's halfway down the alley before I think to call after her.

"Wait! Mademoiselle! What should we tell. . . ."

She coils herself back round.

"Tell your master that Jeanne-Victoire has held up her end. Now it's *his* turn."

CHAPTER 36

Vidocq's Confessional Booth

"She said *that*?" Vidocq asks.

I nod.

"Oh, the little polecat," he murmurs. "But wait a bit, did Herbaux really call you *Doctor*?"

"He knew who I was, I tell you. He knew who Charles was, too."

"Hm."

Fissures darken his forehead, and he says nothing for a good long time. Then, sounding almost insanely cheerful, he says:

"Let's go shake some fruit off Herbaux's tree, shall we? You know, it isn't many civilians get to see an interrogation. I should charge you admission, Hector."

And so I learn just what it means to be a suspect. Vidocq walks me through the cellar of Number Six and into an antechamber, where I find, scattered across a table, the tools of the torturer's trade—leg irons, leather whips, iron manacles—and, hanging on the walls, a painting of a cadaver swinging from a gibbet, another of a guillotine slicing through a neck. By the time we enter the interrogation room, I'm ready to confess every sin I've ever committed and some I haven't.

Herbaux, by contrast, seems to have resigned himself to death. His head is bowed from the moment we come in, and to all queries he makes no reply—until, jerking his head up, he bares his teeth at us.

"I'm going to hang anyway. What do I get by talking to you?"

Vidocq rests his hands lightly on Herbaux's ox shoulders.

"You've got a *friend*, don't you?"

The smallest tightening in the prisoner's jaw.

"I think you met him in La Force. Oh, what's the boy's name? *Wettu*, that's it. *Pretty* thing. What I hear, he only made it out alive because he had a nice big rooster looking out for him. Now if for some reason he should find his way *back* there—without *you* to protect him—oh, I shudder, Herbaux, I really do."

Vidocq walks his fingers up the back of the prisoner's neck. His voice grows petal light.

"Such soft skin Wettu has. Such a white throat."

The manacles round Herbaux's feet rattle like a box of coins. He starts to rise, but Vidocq presses him back down.

"Although I suppose he could always find himself *another* rooster. . . ."

And now Herbaux sags in his chair, as if he'd been cudgeled a thousand times over.

"What do you want to know?" he says.

Vidocq settles back in his chair. "Tell me about this *Monsieur*," he says.

IT BEGAN, SAYS Herbaux, not two days after he escaped from La Force. He was holed up in Wettu's apartment in the Rue Jacquelet when a porter arrived with a note, addressed to him.

"A porter? Did you know him?"

No.

"You weren't suspicious?"

Sure he was. But it couldn't hurt to have Wettu read it.

"What did it say?"

Meet me at three-thirty, in the confessional booth at Saint-Sulpice, the one nearest the baptistry. You'll get two louis for showing up—a great deal more after. Signed, Monsieur.

"Don't suppose you kept the note, did you?"

Burned it.

"So you showed up as you were told?"

'Course he did. You think anyone else was offering employment to escaped convicts?

"And the money was waiting for you."

It was. Genuine, too, don't think Herbaux didn't give those gold coins a good bite.

"Can you describe this Monsieur?"

Never saw him. Met him every day—same place and time—but the curtain was always closed. Only saw the hands, and they were gloved.

"Describe his voice, then."

Strange. Whispery. He was probably disguising his real voice.

"Old? Young?"

Somewhere between.

"Educated-sounding?"

Oh, yeah, *real* cultured.

"And what did this Monsieur ask you to do?"

Leblanc was the first job. Herbaux and his friend Desfosseux tailed him from his apartment and brought him to earth.

"Brought him to earth? That was all?"

They were supposed to ask him a question. *Where is he?*

"Where is *who?*"

Monsieur never said. Said Leblanc would know who they were talking about.

"And Leblanc never told you?"

No, the bastard. Took a load of punishment, too. But at least they found a letter in his pocket. It was from Saint-Cloud.

"How did you know, if you can't read?"

Monsieur told him.

"And that led to your next job?"

Sure. Except, by then, Desfosseux had gotten picked up on a forgery count, so Herbaux asked Noël to come along.

"And Monsieur told you exactly what to do?"

Supplied everything: Tepac's description, his address, his walking habits. Had it all scouted out and planned.

"So you did your job, you made it back to Paris. And you kept seeing Monsieur every day at Saint-Sulpice? Even though you knew the police were after you?"

Figured it was safe, seeing as how no one expected to find the likes of *him* in a church. And Monsieur was true to his word. Paid him in full each time.

"And after a few weeks, he said—what?—he had one more job for you."

Yes.

"And that job was to follow Dr. Carpentier and his friend?"

That's right. Monsieur gave Herbaux the doctor's address, so he would know what the two men looked like. Herbaux was to follow them wherever they went and wait till they were alone. Well, that very night, he tailed them to the Palais-Royal, and off they went with the two tarts, and Herbaux followed right behind. Waited a bit, then went straight up. Told the tarts if they knew what was good for them, they'd leave now.

"So it was going to be just another quick kill, was that it?"

Oh, no. Monsieur was in a merciful mood. He said if Charles agreed to leave town on the next diligence, his life could be spared. Herbaux was just to scare 'em a bit.

"Come, you expect us to believe that? You were aiming your pistol at the good doctor here. You had it cocked."

Well, they made him mad, that was all. Resisting like that. Wasn't gentlemanly.

"So your instructions were to *scare* them?"

And put 'em on the next carriage, and then he'd be done. And then that bitch came along and ruined everything. Two more days, and Herbaux and Wettu would've been clear of town and another fifty francs richer. You can do a lot with fifty francs.

"You certainly can."

At last Vidocq rises. Tucks his chair under the table and beckons me to follow. His hand is almost to the doorknob when he wheels round.

"Oh, I almost forgot! Tell me about the fingernails, Herbaux."

The what?

"Monsieur Leblanc. You separated him from his fingernails, remember? I'm just wondering where you got the idea."

Herbaux shrugs. He saw it done to a squealer once in Toulon. You never heard such a hollering.

FIFTEEN MINUTES LATER, Vidocq and I are standing in the rear courtyard of Number Six, watching the staff carriage trundle toward us across the cobbles.

"You're to go right home, do you hear?" he says. "And you're to *stay* there. Neither you nor Charles is to set a single foot outside until I tell you. Is that clear?"

Waving away the coachman, Vidocq opens the door himself.

"Meantime, we'll try to find a little bit more about our Monsieur. If he knew where to find Herbaux, chances are good he's made other inquiries in the neighborhood. I wouldn't be surprised if—oh, for Christ's sake, Hector! If you've got something on your mind, then out with it."

Here's the funny part. I nearly *do* tell him. The words have been piled up for so long that, with just the slightest pressure, they could come tumbling out. . . .

Charles knows *now. He knows who he is.*

But I know something, too. If I seek to persuade Vidocq, I will have to do better than epiphanies in the Tuileries gardens.

"I just remembered," I say. "I never gave Jeanne-Victoire her cloak back."

CHAPTER 37

The Proper Disposal of Worms

THAT NIGHT, I'M SITTING in the chair by Charles' door, watching him arrange his pillows . . . and before I even realize it, I've nodded off, and I'm back in that alleyway, and Herbaux is leveling the pistol at me, and my heart actually stops in anticipation of the end to come, and then I hear . . .

"*Hector?*"

Charles is sitting up in bed.

"May I ask you something?" he says.

"'Course," I mumble, rubbing myself awake.

"Last night—when that man was chasing us—it wasn't really a game, was it?"

"No. No, it wasn't."

"So you were protecting me."

"Well, yes."

"Because you didn't want me to be frightened."

"Something like that."

Frowning, he traces a half-moon on his bedspread.

"It was very kind of you, Hector, but I don't think you should do that. I can't be treated like a child anymore. If I'm to be *that*, I mean . . ."

Which is as far as he can go to naming the thing that hovers over us. And bless me, I can't go much further.

"Well," I say, "if you're to be *that*—then you can be whatever you want to be. And everyone else will just have to accommodate *you*."

He doesn't sound persuaded. And for that matter, neither am I. Nothing about his future is persuasive, least of all his own place in it. Once more the question comes rising up:

Is this man ready *to be king of France?*

And not for the last time do I answer:

No.

"Hector?"

"Yes."

"I was just wondering—when all this is over—do you think I could stay with you?"

"You can stay as long as you like. And even if you have to go away, we can still be friends."

He gives this some thought.

"I'll need a physician, won't I?"

"Why, yes."

"Well, that's splendid. You can be my doctor, and that way, you can still put me to bed every night. Unless I get married, of course. D'you think anyone would care to marry me, Hector?"

"Oh, yes."

A few more seconds of thought.

"Then you can put us *both* to bed," he says. "Won't that be a lark? I hope she doesn't snore. . . ."

IT'S ANOTHER TWENTY minutes before he's asleep, and by that time, I'm so completely awake that my own bed holds no charm for me.

I wander downstairs with an idea of dipping into the cognac—only to be stopped by the sight of Mother, hunched over the dining room table.

Here is one function of my wanderings with Charles: They've broken down my sense of time. At any given moment, I have no idea what day it is. It takes the image of Mother in her muslin-sheathed sleeves, polishing the life out of her silver, to remind me. . . .

It's Friday.

Except that *this* has never happened on any previous Friday. My mother has never before called after me.

"Hector!"

"Yes, Mother?"

"Is everything all right?" she asks.

Is everything . . . is everything . . .

I take two long steps back until I'm standing in the doorway.

"Everything's fine," I say.

She nods. Picks up a dessertspoon and bears down on it.

"Would you—perhaps you'd care to sit down?"

I draw out a chair. A good minute passes before she speaks again.

"Hector . . ." She addresses herself directly to the spoon. "I hope you don't mind my asking you something. If you'd rather not answer, I'll understand."

"I don't mind."

"Do you still miss her?" she asks.

"Mmm." I realign my chair. "Miss *who*, exactly?"

"That woman. That dancer of yours."

"Oh. You mean . . ."

She means Eulalie. The architect of my downfall. The companion of my every waking thought.

"I don't miss her," I say, surprised to find it true. "Not so much. What I mean is I'm—I'm sorry I made so many mistakes. On her account. I regret making you suffer. . . ."

Each word thrown up like a cloud of incense. My mother puts out her hand and, in a low tight voice, says:

"No, Hector. Don't apologize. It's my turn."

And then she does something I've never seen her do before on any of her Fridays. She pushes away her silver.

"I know you'll find this hard to believe," she says, wiping the remnants of froth from the muslin over her sleeves. "But the one hope I used to cherish about this place was that some marriageable young girl might come to lodge here, and the two of you might get along and—well, there you are." She turns away. "Something *good* might come from all this."

And there, at the very cusp of sentiment, she explodes into laughter—so robust it fairly stops my heart.

"Silly of me," she says. "The only female lodgers we ever get are well past marrying age. *Old* women, yes. And young men."

She plucks a rag from the table, dabs the merriment from her eyes.

"Do you remember the other morning in the garden?" she asks, quietly. "With Charles?"

"You left in a hurry. I remember that."

"I don't know if I can explain it. There I was, watching Charles and thinking, Oh, what a *child* he is, really. And then I . . ." She draws in a long breath, which catches at the very end. "I remembered I used to stand in that very same place when *you* were a boy. Watching you do the very same thing. Except you were digging for worms. Do you remember?"

"Of course."

"And I would stand over you, and every time you found a worm, I'd say, 'Ooh, that's a *juicy* one!' And you'd always laugh. And you'd *always* put the worms back. I'd say, 'Don't you want to put them in a jar or take them fishing with you?' But no, you always wanted them to—go *home*, you called it."

This much is clear. Each of the tears welling now from my mother's eyes is extracted at enormous cost.

"Amazing," she says. "To have all that come sweeping back. So sweet and so *terrible*. The laugh in your voice . . . the look you had. You *trusted* us, Hector, and we . . ." She gives her eyes a smear. "Well, we didn't make a very happy life for you, did we?"

"You tried your best."

"Our *best*," she echoes.

A new scent in her voice now: scalding, bitter. And behind it a gathering purpose.

"Not too long ago," she says, "you asked me about your father. About when he was a physician. I don't know why I was so unkind. You only wanted to know, and who could blame you? I suppose . . . oh, Hector, whenever I look back on that time, all I see is . . . everything *ending*, that's what I see. Because your father was never the same after."

"After what?"

"After that boy died," she says. "The boy in the tower."

CHAPTER 38

A Case of Domestic Espionage

"WELL, WHY SHOULDN'T I have known?" says Mother, smiling darkly. "You think I don't have a brain in my head?"

"But I thought Father was under strict orders. . . ."

"When you get married, Hector, you'll understand. A man may be following orders, but no one will ever read him better than his wife. Every hesitation, every little withholding, she hears it. Of course, she always imagines the *worst*. Then she finds—she finds she didn't imagine the worst after all.

"Oh, Hector," she whispers. "There's so much to tell."

May 22, 1795. The day after my third birthday, and in its beginnings, a day like any other. Clothilde (our former maid) scraping grease off the stove; me, building a tower of old eggshells; Mother, tweezing the dead blossoms from the geraniums.

"Duty calls," says Father, gulping down the last of his coffee. Reaching for his greatcoat and bag, he kisses her in the usual manner: three quick collisions of lip.

"Off to the hospital," he adds.

And with that tiny superfluity, he once again betrays himself. Why would a man announce he's going to the place he goes every morning? Unless he's not really going there?

"Good-bye," she hears herself say.

She's about to turn away when she notices he hasn't quite closed the door after him. She puts her hand to the knob—and to her surprise, finds that her hand won't budge. For several long seconds, she interrogates it. Then she calls out to Clothilde:

"I've just remembered. Monsieur Beaucaire wants me to pick up that brooch. My mother's old brooch? The one that had to be recast? It's only a few blocks, I should be back within the half hour. No *more* than an hour . . ."

It pains her to admit that she's every bit as bad at lying as her husband. She kisses me on the forehead. She announces (again!) that she'll be back within the hour. On her way out, she reaches for a shawl. Not because the morning is cool but because she has already begun to see the wisdom of concealing herself.

And as she follows that familiar greatcoated figure down the Rue Neuve-Sainte-Geneviève, she finds herself, without any prompting from Vidocq, observing the principles of surveillance: keeping a safe distance from the quarry, avoiding direct eye contact, rearranging her appearance. So many precautions, and none of them needed. After many months, Dr. Carpentier has ceased to care if anyone is following.

She tracks him up the Vieille Estrapade, down the Rue d'Ulm, right on the Rue des Ursulines . . . and then, at the corner of the Rue Saint-Jacques, she watches in dismay as he hails a passing cab. Before she can plan her next course, he has bundled himself inside and closed the door after him. Whirling, she finds, like a fairy-tale contrivance, *another* cab—smaller, seedier—the driver slouched on his box, scoring his cuticle with an apple knife. Reaching into her apron, she draws out three silver coins: the money she has set aside for the wine merchant.

"Where do you care to go, Madame?"

Madame. She stares at the wedding ring on her finger.

"I was—"

In the end, she can only point at the carriage that is now speeding northward on the Rue Saint-Jacques. The driver requires no further instruction. He cracks his whip three times and sets the horse at a gallop. A block later, he's calling down to her:

"Got 'em!"

He, too, understands the principles of chase. Never let the other fellow know he's being followed. At times, he slows the horse to such a leisurely canter she feels compelled to question him.

"Do you see it? Is it still there?"

And he calls down, easy as water:

"Still there, Madame."

She is glad, after all, that she doesn't have to look at him. If she puts her mind to it, she might imagine herself on a simple excursion, with no destination and no end, except the pleasure of being driven. The vehicle crosses the Pont Notre-Dame, turns right on the Rue Saint-Antoine, and she tries to crowd her mind with the prospect of shops and cafés—all those foresworn pleasures.

Five minutes later, without warning, the carriage jolts to a standstill.

"What's wrong?" she calls up.

"They've stopped, Madame."

At first, she sees only a massive stone wall, through whose gate her husband is even now being ushered. The gate closes after him, and her eyes, rising, take in the spectacle of that ugly black square tower, erected all those centuries ago by the Knights Templar . . . the crosses resting atop the turrets like ships' masts . . . an ambience of ancient quarrel.

The Temple.

The implications of her act suddenly radiate outward. She has been spying on her husband, who is, by all appearances, an agent of the Di-

rectory. Which makes her guilty of treason. For which, in these otherwise confused times, there is but one punishment.

"I'm sorry," she tells the driver. "I made a mistake. It must have
been another carriage."

She asks him to take her back. At once. Not to her house, no, to the corner where she engaged him. Once there, she hands over all her coins and
hurries home—harassed the whole way by the memory of the fortress.
How, she wonders, can anyone enter such a place and come out alive?

But he does. Strides through the front door at his usual time, a half
hour before noon, looking the same as when he left. She can scarcely
trust her senses.

"Oh, you're trembling," he says, taking her hand in that efficient
grip of his. "Have you caught cold?"

The tremor passes after a few minutes ... only to overtake her again
four years later, when her young son, on a late-summer whim, veers
down the Boulevard du Temple. Chasing after him, she finds herself
stopped once more by the sight of that charred tower. Feels once more
the chill, climbing rib by rib.

"Come, Hector."

She drags him down the street and around the corner, refusing to
look back.

TRAVEL FORWARD ANOTHER eighteen years. The boy is grown,
the mother has reached a certain age, and the shudder is still there,
guttering the tallow candle that stands between them on this Friday
evening, agitating the moth inside the ivory lampshade.

"But you only saw him go inside," I say. "How did you know what
he was doing there?"

"It couldn't be anything else. Everyone knew the dauphin lived
there. Everyone knew how sick he was. *Someone* had to look after him.
Who better than your father?"

"And you never told him."

She gives her head a slow shake. "It would have been a betrayal, I suppose. Or so it seemed to me. *Now*, of course—well, now I wonder if things might have been different if I had told him."

From the hallway, the clock is tolling the tenth hour. Around us, the candlelight is the color of cognac. Upstairs, everyone else is asleep: Charlotte and Father Time and the law students. And Charles, turned as usual on his left side, dead to the world.

"May the twenty-second," I say.

"Yes," she says, raising her eyes suddenly toward mine. "Eighteen days before that boy died. There's some wine, Hector. On the buffet."

A bottle of Beaune, still breathing. The act of setting it before her carries me back to my first encounter with Vidocq. He was seated in this very chair, sloshing down wine and raw potato and, for all his filthy manners, making the room seem shabbier than him.

"The night before that boy died," says Mother, "your father came to me. It was just after supper. He was very plain, very brief. He told me he had business to take care of that very evening. Very *important* business, he said, the nature of which he couldn't divulge except to say—how did he put it?—*it was not without danger*. Oh, and there was a good possibility he might not return, and if he didn't come back by morning, then I was to take you and leave at once for my uncle's in Grenoble. *Don't even stay to pack*, he said. *Leave at once*."

She raises the glass to her lip, rests it there a few seconds.

"He even gave me money for the trip: a bag of silver! And then he kissed me good-bye. And he left. I suspect he didn't want to draw things out any longer than he needed to. In case his resolve failed.

"Well, I ask you, how was I to sleep after *that* performance? And to make matters worse, that very night, you came down with a fever. *Roasting* with it, you didn't even have the strength to cry. So I held you and . . ." Her eyes widen at the memory. "I rocked you asleep. Yes, and I set you in your crib, and I didn't want to leave you, so I—I lay down on the floor next to you. And I think I must have fallen asleep myself because I didn't hear him come back.

"He was standing in the doorway. It must have been around three in the morning. I saw him, I—I couldn't do anything. I couldn't even get off the floor. And then he spoke, it was only three words. *All is well*, he said. He looked down at you, asleep in your crib. He touched you on the brow. And then he went to bed.

"As for *me*, well, I never even got off the floor. I lay there till morning."

She runs her finger round the rim of her wineglass.

"Well," she says, "two days passed, and the papers were full of the dauphin's death. I read the news to your father over breakfast, and of course, the whole time I was *watching* him to see how he reacted. But he never flinched. Never said a word. And still—I don't know how, exactly—but I could *feel* it, the change in him. The change in *everything*.

"He'd staked so much, you see, on keeping that boy alive. And when he couldn't—oh, nothing seemed to matter to him anymore. He began by dropping his patients, one by one. The wealthiest first. Before the year was out, he'd resigned his hospital post. At which time he told me he desired to be a *glass grinder*."

She shakes her head, as if the news were a minute old.

"*Unusual* sort of career. Well, I knew then what my own career was to be. I was to become one of those helpless, *sad* women. I used to notice them when I was young. It seemed to me their lives had slipped away when they weren't looking, and the only thing they could do was"—she contemplates her silverware, strewn across the tabletop—"*polish*."

She picks up a pierced serving spoon. Watches her image dance in and out of the light.

"You should know something, Hector. When your father came to me—the night before that boy died—he left me a letter."

Well, here's how it is. The things people tell you are fragile in direct relation to their being vital. So it is now. As soon as I hear of this letter, I don't dare say another word. Anything but silence could kill it.

For another minute, Mother is silent, too, swirling her wine.

"He said I was to open it only if he didn't return. Otherwise, I was to burn it unread."

"Did you?"

"Of course. I did exactly as he asked. Tossed it straight in the kitchen fire."

You have to be leaning toward the candle to catch the glimmer in her iris.

"The *envelope* I tossed," she says. "The letter . . ."

AND WHAT A WONDER is this. The thing that everything's been building to has been lying on the table the entire time, not two inches from a pile of teaspoons. A rectangle of grease-stained parchment: it might have been an old menu or a handbill.

"Take it, Hector. What do I want with it anymore?"

And still I can't touch it. Any more than I can look away from it.

"He gave up everything," she says. "Everything we'd ever worked for, and he never . . ."

Her hand flies to her mouth. Stays there a good half minute before she trusts herself to speak again.

"So I gave up, too. I gave up trying to please him. Trying to *know* him."

Gazing at that paper one last time, she plucks it from the table surface and drops it in my hand. Closes my fingers round it.

"I'm hoping you'll have better luck than I did," she says.

The candle by her elbow has burned down to a stub. Neither of us moves to replace it, and gradually, the light contracts into a hard corona, and the air round it thrums like a heart.

"I never thought I would end up like this," says Mother. "No, I definitely had something else in mind. I just can't remember what it was."

Very slowly I rise from my chair. I stand there for some time, deciding whether or not to kiss her good night. This is the course I take: resting my hand on her shoulder for the barest second before retracting it again.

Her voice follows me out of the room. The *old* voice, briefly reasserting itself.

"Hector, I've been after you for weeks about that newel post. It's not going to fix itself. I don't know why you can't . . ."

And then, as I walk back up the stairs, I hear:

"Never mind."

CHAPTER 39

The Dire Fate of Charlotte's Chickens

I DON'T READ it right away. I settle myself in bed first, I place the candle just so on my nightstand. For several long minutes, I hold the letter in my hands, unopened. At last, a little shy of midnight, I unfold the paper and find . . .

My dear Béatrice,

If you are reading this, I have failed in my task.

The precise nature of that task I will not divulge, for fear of incriminating you further. I will say only this. There was a creature who needed my help.

If it were our own dear son in peril, I could only hope that someone else's father would do as I am doing. And when Hector is himself a man, I trust and believe he will stand ready to do the same.

Much will be imputed to me, Béatrice. I will be called a devil, a royalist agent, an enemy to the people, etc. I am none of these things. I am a physician, whose highest calling (or so I have always believed) is to heal—to comfort—not to sit by and watch a Life be extinguished.

The thought of placing you and little Hector in danger on my account pains me beyond measure. How I wish I could have spared you! Please know—please believe—if I could have found another course, I should have taken it.

Know this, too, my dear wife. I love you, more than is healthy for anyone. You will be a good mother to our son, and if he should ever ask about me, tell him that until the very last second of my life, I was thinking of him.

Farewell,
Hector

I read it a good dozen times—maybe more—struggling to reconcile the man I knew with the largeness of this letter, the rashness of this act. To smuggle a young boy out of a fortress guarded by two hundred men! What combination of principle and courage and sheer insanity would that require?

And did he succeed?

All is well, he told my mother. Did that mean he had carried off his improbable feat? That even now the dauphin was being spirited to Switzerland? And what of the death notices? Were the Temple commissaries simply trying to cover up the boy's disappearance? Was anyone *really* buried that night in the Madeleine churchyard?

Questions, a blizzard of questions. And gathering beneath them a mission. I can see now there's a reason Charles was dropped into my world. There's a reason this letter was spared from the fire. For the first time in my life, my father is speaking directly to me.

And when Hector is himself a man, I trust and believe he will stand ready to do the same. . . .

Again and again I read that line. And in my heart, I say: *I am ready.* To finish the work you began.

No surprise: I dream of my father that night. Except that Charles Rapskeller's voice is coming out of him. He's playing quoits with Chrétien Leblanc, and no one can agree about what to call the King, and as they argue, they begin to melt round the edges—until a voice from the waking world breaks through.

"Doctor!"

I peel my eyes apart.

"You must wake up!"

The image of Jeanne-Victoire. Panting and purposeful. Shaking me by the collar.

"What are you—"

"Watching over you," she snaps. "As usual. Come, we haven't a moment to lose!"

She grabs my arm and guides me down the steps like a nurse leading a convalescent.

"Charles," I mutter.

"The old man's got him. Come along!"

But why? I want to ask. *Why do I have to come along?*

And then I reach the ground floor and I know why.

Fire.

I feel it first as a blast of heat emanating from the rear courtyard, transforming the air into something both solid and liquid. Timbers crackle and shriek above our heads. The remains of the kitchen ceiling gust toward us in a shower of confetti, and the air is choked with a strange and savory aroma.

Chickens, I realize as Jeanne-Victoire drags me out the door. The chickens that Charlotte keeps in the rear courtyard. Roasting alive.

Charlotte herself is the first to greet me. Her face even more chaffed than usual, her eyes black and fathomless.

"Monsieur Hector," she exclaims in broken accents.

Quickly, I make a mental inventory of our party. There's Father

Time, wrapped in his own coverlet. The law students, all three of them, and in their enclosure, a young woman in a blanket, with bare shoulders and beautiful auburn hair. Tonight's conquest, although it's not clear which student has conquered her.

From that loosely knit crowd, a small disheveled figure emerges. Mother: her tulle cap discarded, her curls lopsided.

"Oh," she says.

Her bird bones quiver as she folds herself round me.

"You're alive," she says.

"Of course."

"Well, then." She releases me with a nod. "That's fine."

Over her shoulder, I catch a sudden glimpse of Charles. So lost in rapture that he doesn't see me approach. I have to wave my hand in front of him.

"You're all right?" I ask.

"Oh, yes. But what a grand fire it is!"

The flames are no longer contenting themselves with the rear of the building. Tongues of yellow and orange snarl the curtains. The floor joists crackle and heave. Smoke churns through the cracks in the walls and doors—as if the building's deepest rages were being released. Yes, it's a grand fire.

"Oh!" cries Charles. "You forgot your book."

Father's journal slides once more into my hand. I stare down at the green calf's leather.

"Did you—"

Did you read it? That's what I want to ask him. But all I can manage is . . .

"Thank you."

Night after night, the occupants of Maison Carpentier have waged war across the dinner table. In extremis we find a fraternity. Neighbors swirl round us—Monsieur Sénard the moneylender, Madame Fleuriais and her elderly aunt and their Pomeranian—full of questions and commiserations. We turn our backs to them. This is *our* calamity.

And when the front window cracks open and a jet of white flame shoots out, bisecting the air around us, we shout in unison. Another window splinters. The building's bass rumble rises to a baritone, and just then I hear Charlotte say:

"Where's Madame?"

It's in the firelight that I find her: a swaddled figure stealing toward the house like a burglar.

"Mother!"

Charlotte and Father Time both try to restrain me, but I'm too fast for them. I'm too fast for all of Paris, I'm racing the entire populace toward that front door, but the fire wants only me, for the heat that greets me as I step over the threshold seems cut to my exact form. I sink into it, and everything goes black for a second, and then I find myself crawling across the remains of our dining room, I feel the crunch of glass, I smell the contents of Charlotte's pantry: burnt flour, caramelizing sugar. My throat seizes up, my lungs squeeze down. And my brain turns to fog, which is why it takes me several seconds to recognize the obstruction in front of me as my mother.

I wrap my arms round her, and I try to lift, but the sheer mass of her defeats me. Rolling her over, I find, pressed against her bosom, her box of silver.

In vain do I try to pry it from her. I have to hoist her *and* the box and carry them both to the door, the fire roaring after us. Within seconds, the rectangular fruitwood table and the convict-made china and the ivory lampshade have been submerged in flame. And as I race out the front door, I can feel the fire skipping after me, stinging my heels, pulling my hair.

It's only when I reach the street that I realize my nightshirt is on fire. Jeanne-Victoire is the one who pulls it off me, stamps the flames into silence. I almost laugh, finding myself half-naked again in her presence, but there's no air to laugh with, and I drop to my knees and bend over Mother's half-conscious form.

Her skin has turned a faint blue, and her mouth is smeared black, and the spasms in her vocal cords make a strange music, high and thin, like a recorder.

"Don't worry," I whisper. "You're safe."

The sound stops. The tarred fingers of her right hand reach for mine, and the heat of the house seems to weld us together. By degrees, though, the heat evaporates, and her fingers grow cold, from the tips down to the root. Then the palm turns cold. Then the arm.

I reach for the other arm, still folded round that box of silver. It's every bit as cold. Every bit as still.

No one says a word to me at first. Then Charles steps forward. His arms form a kind of fidgeting square around me. Later I will realize he is trying to touch me.

"I know how it is, Hector. I lost my mother, too."

PART III

Place de Grève

17 Floréal Year III

<u>Is my mother alive?</u>

Charles posed that question to me today. I reminded him it was not my position to say. Am forbidden to speak of outside events, on pain of . . . etc., etc.

Very well, he said. You neednt say a word. If my mother lives, then simply nod, how shall that be?

After sm time, he said: You're not nodding.

19 Floréal

This A.M., on tower platform, Charles made a point of collecting flowers & laying them outside door of his mother's cell.

26 Floréal

Charles' symptoms have become most <u>alarming</u>. Tumors have proliferated in right knee & left wrist. Fainting fits increasingly common. Weakness <u>excessive</u>. Feet too tender to permit of much walking. This A.M., I was obliged to carry him up final steps to platform.

Spirits have also taken decided plunge. Even sight of "his sparrows" did nothing to gladden him. Ive entreated him to be of gd cheer. All not lost. His sister in gd health, has asked af him daily. Many people, myself included, long to see him better—

You dont understand, he cut me off. My mother is dead because of me.

Cit Simon, he said, had forced him to say terrible things about his mother & aunt. How they had touched him in private places & done unspeakable things to him, & he knew it to be lies, but Simon kept at him & wdnt let him sleep, and finally he came to believe it was true, and thats what he signed his name to, he scarcely knew what he was doing. And then they used those lies against his mother, and thats why shes dead, and how cd he ever forgive himself?

No argument wd dissuade him. Again & again he berated himself. Said he feared death all the more now because he was sure God wd judge him most harshly.

I replied that, on contrary, God wd frown on men who so cruelly used a child to serve their bloodlust.

He was not used to my speaking so frankly. How angry you sound, he said.

1 Prairial

Charles experiencing prolonged & extreme episodes of sore throat & fever, w/ accompanying delirium. Leblanc reports child has claimed to hear his mother's voice. Insists she is in "next tower."

6 Prairial

This A.M., Mme Royale once more asked me about her brother. I said his condition was not improving as rapidly as Id like.

She saw thru my evasions at once. He's dying, she said.

Then something unaccountable. My self-mastery gave way. I turned to one side, explaining I had piece of grit in my mouth.

Youve done your best, Doctor, she said.

7 Prairial

Genl Barras has left orders he does not wish to see me. His attaché informed me if I have any questions relating to my official duties, Im to take them up w/ Comm for Genl Security.

I swallowed my pride & approached Cit Mathieu. Apologized for my intemperate remarks in earlier meeting. Said I had come to speak w/ him on matter of utmost urgency.

Yes? he said. (Looking v. weary.)

Louis-Charles, I said, must be removed fm Temple. Poisonous air of cell laying waste to his powers. In healthy mountain climate—Switzerland, e.g.—he might recover his strength, reverse progression of disease. Leaving him where he is wd be <u>death sentence</u>. Surely a civilized society cd not desire that? Surely Charles is worth more to them alive than dead?

I assured Mathieu I wd be only too glad to accompany child, w/ as many armed guards as Comm saw fit. Said I wd agree to any restrictions—work w/o compensation—if Comm wd just agree to remove him fm his cell.

He frowned & was silent for gd while.

I dont understand, he said. Why are you bothering so much about this child?

Because he cd be my own son, I said. And if he were, then I shd wish someone to care—as I do.

I hf expected him to laugh. Instead, he said, in a tone almost kindly: Doctor, that boy cannot leave. You & I both know it. If you can make his final days easier, so be it. If not, you have done what you can. The Republic can ask no more of you.

I believe he expected that to be a comfort.

10 PRAIRIAL

Charles able to eat only a little soup + a few cherries. Time running out.

11 PRAIRIAL

Junius will know what to do.

13 PRAIRIAL

Enough for now.

CHAPTER 40

The Rebirth of Junius

MY MOTHER IS BURIED next to my father under an old yew. The Vaugirard Cemetery is mildewy and unfashionable, and the mourners are few: Charlotte, Charles, myself, and Vidocq, in a black-banded hat. Vidocq himself tips the pallbearers and the gravedigger and the priest and, after paying for Charlotte's cab and dispatching Charles to Sûreté headquarters, he treats me to a bottle of Argenteuil at the Good Quince. I drain two glasses in quick succession.

"How are you holding up?" he asks me.

I query myself as if I were my own doctor. Pulse: regular. Breathing: regular. Hand: steady.

"I seem to be fine."

"You're not," he says. "I think you should rest a few days, Hector."

The black suit I'm wearing is one of Vidocq's castoffs, far too large in the legs and shoulders and forcibly cinched to my waist. The wine has stirred a dull sputter in my head, and the tavern air is thick with mouse droppings, and over Vidocq's massive shoulder, I can see the sun, relatively puny, setting over the dome of the Invalides.

"Three people are dead," I say. "I might have been one of them. That's reason enough to stay awake, don't you think?"

Staring into my glass, I find my own thumbprint glowing back at me. I try to remember what Vidocq used to say about fingerprints . . . no one's the same as anyone else's. . . .

And then I'm remembering something else. The last glass of wine I had with Mother. The way the light folded round us.

"Have you learned anything?" I ask.

"As best we can tell, the fire started in the grease drain between the woodshed and the kitchen window. Seems to have spread from there to the meat cage. As to what *started* it, we didn't find any incendiary devices, but we did find the remains of a phosphoric bottle."

The news filters slowly down through my skull.

"Arson," I say, nodding.

"Likely, yes. Of course, we don't yet know if it's connected to Charles."

And for the first time in memory, he can't hold my gaze. Makes a point of brushing the crown of his hat.

"Do you remember what Monsieur told Herbaux?" I ask, pushing my chair back from the table. " 'Don't kill them,' he said. 'Just scare them away.' "

"I remember."

"Then why would he try to burn us all alive? A houseful of people to get to one man . . ."

Vidocq shrugs. "Just because you start a carriage rolling doesn't mean you can stop it."

"And what does that mean?"

"It means Monsieur may no longer be master of himself. Or his schemes."

Vidocq empties the rest of the bottle into my glass. Watches with an air of regret as the last drop rolls out.

"Where do you and Charles propose to stay, Hector?"

It's a good question. Father Time is staying with friends in the Rue Gracieuse. Charlotte is ensconced with her sister's large brood in the Marché Lenoir. Until now, it's never once occurred to me I need shelter myself.

"There must be someplace," I say.

"There is," says Vidocq.

TEN SPITS FROM Notre-Dame, a mere block from the river, just around the corner from the Place Saint-Michel . . . and yet chances are good you'll walk right past the Rue de l'Hirondelle without knowing it. Which is exactly how Vidocq likes it. Few people come to this narrow cobbled street, not even Vidocq's own staff, so it is with some sense of my own unworthiness that I pause before the imposingly high front of number 111.

Charles has no such inhibitions. He's already charging up the marble steps.

"Look! They've got salamanders carved over the door."

"Now listen," growls Vidocq. "When you get inside, take your boots off. That's an Aubusson rug, do you hear?"

It is, indeed. And an Empire console table and a marble staircase. And high ceilings and burnished parquet floors and *two* maids. The boy from Arras has done well.

Without leaving Arras behind. It is still very much present in the round person of Vidocq's mother: peasant earth in the midst of beribboned sleeves and lilac powder.

"My boys!" she cries, drawing us toward her. "What you've been through! Never mind, you'll sleep safe under *our* roof, I promise you. And you're to stay as long as you need to, aren't they, François?"

"Whatever you say," answers Vidocq, throwing up his hands in surrender.

"Now you can wear François' clothes until you find some of your own. They're a bit large—yes, I do see that, Doctor—but Catherine will take them down for you, she's a wonder with the needle. I'm told you're to share a room, but don't worry, the bed's big enough for an army. Louis the Sixteenth, you know the style. By all means, sleep as late as you want. No one here will *ever* rouse you before you're ready. . . ."

On an impulse, she cups her hand round my ear and whispers:

"She's at peace, you know. Just like my dear husband. The Lord has seen to them both."

That night, for reasons I don't examine too closely, I choose to sleep on the floor, with rolled-up bedding for a mattress. Charles, for equally unexamined reasons, lets me do it. For a good hour, I lie there, and it's as if last night's fire is still raging. I can smell the smoke on my hands, I can feel the blisters on my back. I can *see* the black bundle of Mother on the dining room floor.

Just after dawn, I wake to Charles' long, riverlike breaths. Putting on Vidocq's black suit, I tiptoe down the marble stairs. Turn the lock on the front door, step onto the doorstep.

"Dr. Carpentier?"

From the street below, a gendarme regards me fixedly.

"Just going for a walk," I explain.

"Then you must bring me along. Chief's orders."

It's not, after all, a very long stroll to the Rue Neuve-Sainte-Geneviève. The smoke can still be smelled from a block away, and in the early-morning light, Maison Carpentier has the look of someone in a tavern brawl. Black-eyed windows, missing door-teeth . . . cauterized innards and shreds of curtain dangling like torn-off hair. Through the holes in the roof a half-dozen rooks wheel and dive. Colonizing the only home I've ever known.

"Hector!"

Father Time is coming down the hill toward me, wearing the same shabby clothes he took with him out of this house. In the light of dawn, he has the look of someone roused from the dead.

"So glad I could—oh, I *say*," he exclaims to the gendarme blocking his path. "Is this a friend of yours, Hector?"

"It's all right!" I call. "Professor Corneille comes in peace."

The gendarme grudgingly steps aside. Clutching his coat, Father Time minces toward me, a smile teasing his gray lips apart.

"Thousand apologies for missing the funeral, my boy. Such a—such a *dreadful* business. I always assumed your parents would be burying *me*, you know, not the other way. . . ."

He's stopped by the sight of that building, hollow and savage.

"So . . . so very . . ."

And for several minutes, we say nothing at all. We watch the rooks, we smell the fumes. And then, in a low and elegiac voice, Father Time says:

"How I wish you could have known your mother, my boy. When she was young, I mean. What fire she had! Truly, a *remarkable* orator."

"Orator?"

"Oh, yes! She was a *leading* light in the—the Fraternal Society for Patriots of Both Sexes. I remember the first time I heard her speak. 'Toward the *Next* Enlightenment,' that was her theme. Men and women, side by side, striding toward paradise. Rip-roaring stuff. I was ready to throw out civilization and start from scratch."

"But why didn't she . . ."

"Oh, well, *you* came along, didn't you? Wouldn't do to drag babies to midnight meetings, like some fishwife. No, in the end, she was the good *bourgeoise*. Stayed home with her baby."

And became . . . how did my mother put it? One of those helpless, *sad* women. Whose final act was to reclaim her dowry. The chest of silver that even now lies buried with her.

"Are you all right, my boy?"

I don't answer at first. I just keep rubbing my face until the only thing I can feel is the friction in my skin.

"I'm fine," I say at last. "But what about *you*, Monsieur? Where will you go?"

"Oh, as to *that*." A flush of purple in his slackened cheeks. "You know the expression, desperate times call for—what I mean to say is I've contacted an *old* friend of mine—owns a charming cottage in Vernon and—well, not to put too fine a point on it, I've asked for her hand in marriage."

"And she—consented?"

"Oh, my, yes. She's been after me for years, you know. But I *would* insist on my bachelor ways."

His chuckle seems to separate his jaw from the rest of his skull.

"Ah, well, it can't be helped," he says. "No more orchid volumes to sell."

He stares down at his miserable boots, with their lacquer of egg yolk, and I feel a sharp pang thinking of what *he* lost to the fire. That barrelful of Revolutionary artifacts. Tricolor snuffboxes and Rousseau's mitten. Reams and reams of old . . .

Old journals . . .

"You're Junius," I say.

I voice it in the very moment I think it. And the sound of that name jars open Father Time's mouth, sends his hand beetling across his chest.

"Well, yes. In another life, that was—"

"Your *pseudonym*. When you wrote for the *Courrier Universel*. You're the one who told them about the dauphin's condition." I pause to let the words seep back in. "*Junius will know what to do.* That's what Father wrote in his journal. Just days before Louis the Seventeenth died. He was going to speak with you."

"Yes. As a matter of fact, he did."

"About what?"

"You know, it must have been about the escape."

I stare long and hard at him, and it's only then that he understands what he's divulged. Confusion ripples through the gray tarns of his eyes.

"Well, you see, it was—there was no use keeping the boy where he *was*. That awful place! We had to—we had to *spring* him, you see. There was no other choice."

"But why didn't you tell me you were part of that?"

I know what he's going to say, though. Before it's even out of his mouth.

"Your blessed father, of course! He swore me to utter secrecy. No one was to know—*no one*—and after all, I *am* a man of my word, Hector. Whatever *else* one might say of me . . ."

He stares once more into the ruined interior of the house. Follows the motions of the rooks until he can't follow them anymore.

"And now?" I venture.

"Now? Oh, there doesn't seem much point anymore, does there? Keeping secrets." He sighs so faintly I can scarcely hear it. "If there ever *was* a point."

CHAPTER 41

The Trojan Hobbyhorse

THEIR SCHEME HAD an author, and his name was Virgil.

Like so many French revolutionaries, Professor Corneille revered dead Romans, and when my father approached him, he was reading the second book of the *Aeneid:* "How They Took the City." The great wooden horse, hauled inside the walls of Troy with its cache of Greeks. The city overrun . . . battlements in flames . . . Hecuba wailing . . .

Why not the same trick on a smaller scale?

And so Professor Corneille bought a cedar hobbyhorse, four feet in height, five in length, and hollowed it out until it was large enough to hold a child. He put casters on it, used an awl to poke air holes, installed a panel with a secret catch over the cavity . . . and, after two days of work, declared the thing ready.

"Ready for what?" I ask.

"To be carried into the Temple. That very evening, your father took it in. The seventh of June it was."

The seventh of June. The very night he left that letter with my mother. *Important business . . . not without danger . . . might not return . . .*

And here was his business: driving to the Temple in a hired wagon with Professor Corneille and a hollowed-out hobbyhorse.

"Oh, they were surprised to see your father, I've no doubt. Even more surprised to see him rolling a wooden horse! But he explained the situation very calmly. Said he'd been deputized by the Committee to present this—what did we come up with?—yes, a *peace* offering. From Prussia."

"Why would they believe that?"

"Well, of course, we had to forge some papers."

And here Professor Corneille found in himself a previously unsuspected gift. Using Father's own entry visas as a model, and with nothing more than a scroll of parchment, a candle, and a pair of inkwells, he re-created the signature of Citizen Mathieu and the unique stamp of the Committee of General Security, right down to the rancid-butter shade of wax.

The papers were unimpeachable, and it was too late in the evening to verify the orders personally. So the horse was suffered to pass through.

"And what then?"

"Your father personally carried it up to Louis-Charles' cell."

"Why?"

"Isn't it obvious? To put the boy inside."

"But how were you to get the horse back down? Without attracting suspicion?"

That was the work of *another* document, which arrived three hours later. Likewise from "the Committee," likewise forged. Announcing that the hobbyhorse in question was now to be removed forthwith.

"After only three hours?"

"You have to understand, my boy, we had one very important thing on our side. The sheer *capriciousness* of the Committee. Everyone knew whatever they blessed at sunset could be illegal by sunrise. So it was with the hobbyhorse. 'Upon second consideration, the Committee has resolved that no son of a tyrant shall be granted idle amusement while

France's children cry for bread'—oh, I forget the exact language, but it sounded *distinctly* plausible.

"At any rate, it *worked*. They let your father in. They even assigned him a couple of guards to help him carry the thing back down."

"But wouldn't they have inspected the cell after Father left?" I ask. "He said the guards checked on Louis-Charles several times a night. And first thing in the morning."

"Of course they did," says Father Time, unflappable. "That's why we brought the *other* boy."

AND HERE LEBLANC reenters the picture.

Through discreet inquiries, he had managed to locate a woman—a laundress and former prostitute named Félicité Neveu—who had been in the Conciergerie during Marie-Antoinette's final days and who had become, at no small risk to her safety, one of the queen's most ardent defenders. *Idolized* the woman and didn't care who knew. No one else had been so kind to her, she'd say, so gracious, so (for want of a more acceptable word) *Christian*.

Félicité especially liked to tell of the day her own son had come to visit. The queen had made a special point of saying how charming the boy was. And how—you must imagine her, brushing a tear from her noble cheek—how *closely* he resembled her own Louis-Charles. Félicité had been so moved by the queen's grief that she had resolved, upon her release, to give up her criminal ways and dedicate her life to Marie-Antoinette's memory.

Leblanc courted her over a round of drinks at Thicoteau's—and then took the perilous step of telling her the plan he had in mind. Before the evening was done, she was on board.

"On board?"

"Why, yes," says Father Time, blinking mildly. "*Her* boy would go to the Tower, and Louis-Charles would go free."

"But what sort of mother would agree to such a thing?"

"A desperate one. Her boy was *dying*, you see. In great squalor, with no hope for recovery. She must have reasoned—well, at least in the *Temple*, her son would have Dr. Carpentier looking in every morning, Leblanc the rest of the day. Exercise, games. Fresh air on the tower platform. Oh, and a decent *burial*, that was most important. She couldn't afford to bury him herself, and she wanted him to have a *stone*. Even if it had the wrong name on it."

And being a royalist sympathizer, she couldn't have guessed that Louis-Charles would never receive a stone. That he would be thrown into an unmarked grave, covered in lime, left to rot. . . .

"So this *other* boy was in the hobbyhorse that Father wheeled up."

"Yes, indeed. Terribly *weak*, poor thing, but before we closed up the panel, he—he managed to tell us how comfy it was inside. Really *charming* manners."

Three hours later, Father went back to the Temple with his forged papers to reclaim the hobbyhorse. Professor Corneille bided his time two blocks away in the baggage wagon. The night was still and damp, the crickets chirring, the stones slumbered in the heat. . . .

But the professor never once drowsed. How could he? The time passed like an agony. One hour. *Two* hours. Still no sign of Father.

"I confess I despaired of him more than once. Something must have *happened*, that was the only explanation, and I didn't know what to do. All I could think of was having to break the news to your poor mother.

"And then—oh, it must have been well after one in the morning—he came! Wheeling that silly horse.

"Well, we set it down in the rear of the wagon, and we both climbed back in, and we drove—oh, it was a good long time, yes. Your father was guiding the whole way. *Turn right at the corner. . . . And now left. . . . Bear right again*. Me, of course, I hadn't a *clue* where we were going. I assumed they'd arranged—oh, some kind of *safe* house, I suppose, your father and Leblanc. I never would've guessed we'd end up where we did."

"And where was that?"

"At the apartment of Félicité Neveu."

"The washerwoman?"

"Oh, yes! I remember, she lived in the—yes, it was the Rue des Coutures-Saint-Gervais. Nowhere you'd want to be *alone* at night, I can tell you."

"What happened then?"

"Well, your father tripped the catch on the hobbyhorse. He took the boy out, very gently. And then he—he *carried* him upstairs to Mademoiselle Neveu."

"But which boy was it?" I can barely restrain myself now. "The dauphin or the changeling?"

"I've no idea!" cries the old man, shrugging toward the heavens. "I had to stay with the wagon, so I never did see the face. And, of course, the two boys *did* resemble each other. You'd have had to study them rather closely to—to distinguish them.

"Well, you may imagine—when your father returned, I was—oh, perfectly *exploding* with questions—but he cut me off. Quite brusque about it. *All is well*, he said."

The same words he used with my mother.

"Naturally, I—I asked him what he meant. He was quiet a good while, and then he just—he said it again. *All is well*. And nothing more."

"And he never spoke of that evening again?"

"Oh, no. And don't think I didn't try to draw him out, either."

I stare once more into the old man's face. The bleary smile, the bleary brain. To think of him carrying off such a grand and dangerous folly. And never speaking of it until this very minute.

And yet what has he told me, after all? The mystery hasn't so much been solved as funneled down: into that span of two hours between when Father went into the Temple and when he came back. Somewhere in that interstice lies the answer. To Louis-Charles' fate. To Father's fate. To everything.

And I'm no closer to knowing now than I was before . . . and Father Time is slipping deeper into his cloud. The mouth is folding down, the eyes skimming over . . . the time for questions is drawing to an end.

"What did you think," I ask, "when you heard that Louis-Charles had died that very day?"

"Well, I—I didn't know what to think. The boy in the tower—*he* might have died. But which boy was it?" He pauses to let the prospect play out before him. "All the same, I wouldn't be shocked to hear the dauphin was alive *today*. Though I—I suppose we would have *heard*, eh?

"Oh, but I just remembered something else your father told me. This was many months later. He'd already given up his practice by then, and we were having—yes, that's right—the usual coffee at the Wise Athenian. Awfully quiet he was. *Thunderously* gloomy—well, by then, he was *always* gloomy.

"*D'you know*, he said—he was staring into his cup, I remember—*there's one thing I can never really forgive myself for.* I asked him what that was, and he said: *I actually believed that one boy's life was worth more than another's*. And before we parted that morning, he said one more thing. He said, *It's true what you used to tell me, Junius. I am no republican*."

THE LIGHT FROM the streetlamp at the corner is slowly dissolving into morning light. The abandoned well where Bardou used to sit is empty but for a pair of pigeons, picking at wood lice. The first cries of the chimney sweeps can be heard in the distance, and a quarrier's wagon comes trundling over the cobbles.

This is the last conversation I will ever have with Father Time. This is the last time I will ever look at this house. And yet the subject that's most weighing on me is something else entirely.

"What happened to Félicité Neveu?" I ask.

"I've no idea. I made a point of looking in on her a few days later, but there was no sign of her. Or her child. The neighbors seemed to think she'd fled town to avoid being arrested. It wouldn't do, you know, being a royalist in those days."

"And her son. What was his name?"

"Name," says Father Time. "Name . . ."

The light drains from his eyes, the cheeks droop . . . then from nowhere, a spark bursts forth, and the old man cackles to the sky:

"Ha! *Virgil!* That's it! What better sign that he was heaven-sent? Oh now, Hector, before you go, I don't suppose I could touch you for a—a *coin* or two? For the diligence to Vernon? Oh, that's very kind of you. As to the wedding, well, I'm *desolate* I can't invite you, but she prefers a *small* affair, my fiancée. *Simple* girl. Hope you understand. . . ."

CHAPTER 42

The Birthmark

"No," says Vidocq. "It's too much to believe."

I come back just as he's sitting down to breakfast. Such a pacific scene. The Sèvres coffeepot, the Sèvres coffee bowl . . . the coil of steam . . . scents of lemon and orange pouring in through the French windows . . . Vidocq himself—sleep-softened, night-calmed—in an open dressing gown, a frieze shirt, and red trousers.

And here comes Hector. Rude and urgent, bristling with news. The reverie is over.

"A lookalike boy?" cries Vidocq. "Smuggled past two hundred guards? *In a hobbyhorse?*"

"That's what the professor said."

"And why the devil should we trust him?"

"Well, you've—you've *met* him. He doesn't have any reason to lie. And he's the last living eyewitness."

"Oh? And what did he witness, Hector? Did he ever actually *see* Louis-Charles? Of course not. If I'm going to take this matter to the minister of justice, I'll need more than the word of some gamy old partridge."

Vidocq stabs a brioche with a butter knife, swallows it in three bites. In the next instant, the bells of Saint-Séverin come shimmering out. Followed by a chain of answering bells, fording back and forth across the river.

Sunday.

Which may be why Vidocq chooses this moment to invoke the deity.

"Lord above! Is it too much to ask for a little *evidence?* Something that won't get me laughed on my ass?"

"I don't know what more you can ask of me," I say. "I've given you eyewitness testimony. . . ."

"Hearsay."

"I've given you my father's *personal* account. . . ."

"Which leaves us just where we started, damn him."

Something in my expression, maybe, softens him into silence. Then, with a low grumble, he says:

"Very well. Get me the journal."

Not a speck of care in his fingers now as he whips back and forth through those calcified pages.

"Here's what's bothering me, Hector. That final line. *Enough for now.* Doesn't that sound to you like there's more to come?"

"There isn't. I've looked."

"But it doesn't make sense. We know your father wasn't interrupted. We know he didn't need to bury the thing in any haste—no one even knew it existed. So why didn't he stay to make a proper accounting?"

In the breeze from the French windows, the pages billow before him, like a meadow. Vidocq is just about to close them when something snags at his eye.

"Stop a bit," he mutters.

He raises the book to the sunlight. In the inside back flap, a small crevice—a violation in the book's fabric—stands revealed.

"Christ," mutters Vidocq. "I can't believe I . . ."

His finger disappears into the opening . . . and reemerges seconds later with a tightly folded bundle. He lays it out before us on the breakfast table, next to the preserves and the honey.

To Whom It May Concern:

You may verify the merchandise via the following particular: a mole, black-brown, 1 half-inch in diameter, located between 4th and 5th toe, on right foot.

Yours,
Dr. Hector Carpentier

Vidocq's eyes are hard. His mouth is a thin black line.

"Is this your father's hand?" he asks.

"Yes."

"You can positively identify it?"

"Yes."

He slams his fists on the breakfast table. So hard that the book jumps toward the ceiling and the coffee spoons shriek and the maid comes running, starchy with terror.

"Where's Monsieur Charles?" he bellows at her.

"Still in bed."

"All the better."

HE'S JUST AS I left him. The head wafting on pillows, the breath rolling out. We yank open the curtains, and the inrushing light picks out faint deltas of saliva at the corners of his mouth.

"Sleeps like a fucking angel, doesn't he?" mutters Vidocq, snatching the covers away.

The bare feet twitch, as if stunned by the light, then fall still again.

Vidocq drops to one knee. With the same delicacy he showed Leblanc's corpse in the morgue, he pries apart the fourth and fifth toes.

"Hector," he whispers. "Bring the lamp."

But it's already visible in the morning light. A brown-and-black mole, of irregular proportions, roughly one-half inch in diameter.

The bedclothes rustle; the mattress creaks. From the mesa of his pillows, Charles Rapskeller gazes down at us through half-open lids—perfectly agreeable, as if this were how every day began.

For several seconds, Vidocq hovers on the brink of a choice. And in the end, he decides to remain on bended knee. And to angle his head toward the floor. The very image of subjection.

"I will not call you *Majesty,*" he says. "Not yet. But if all goes well, I hope you will have occasion to recall my humble service."

He raises his head now. All traces of subjection are gone.

"We've more in common than you know, Monsieur Charles. They locked me away, too. They tried to *extinguish* me, just as they tried with you. And they couldn't. And they won't."

How to describe this next moment? With great care and patience, he pulls the coverlet and sheets back over Charles, tucks them round so that only the sweat-tousled head is still visible. I have never seen Vidocq so tender—or so strategic.

"Tomorrow morning," he announces, "we shall call on the minister of justice. May heaven help us all."

CHAPTER 43

The Dead Moth

VIDOCQ IS TRUE to his word. Before twenty-four hours have passed, he has secured the promise of an audience with the Duchesse d'Angoulême. A day later, he has a time.

"Thursday afternoon," he announces. "One o'clock. At the *hôtel* of the Marquis de Monfort."

"Who?"

"You've already met him, Hector. In the crypt of Saint-Denis. He was the fellow threatening your life."

At once it comes back to me: the voice of civilization. *Move another inch, and you will die.*

"The Marquis is a bosom companion of the minister of justice," adds Vidocq. "And a ferocious defender of the Duchess. And just so you don't get your balls in a cinch, a bitter enemy of the Comte d'Artois. Oh, don't think I've forgotten your grand conspiracy theory. Now we'll need to find our boy Charles some nice clothes. Nothing too grand, we don't want him looking presumptuous. But we don't want him looking like a peasant, either. You might have a go at those nails of his. And for the love of God, Hector, get him to take a bath, will you?"

Prefecture funds are appropriated for Charles' new suit and polished boots and doeskin gloves. As for me . . . well, one of Vidocq's old black suits is speedily adapted to my frame, but without the original owner's heft to cling to, the fabric falls away in pouches of protest. I am deeply conscious of these pouches as the carriage pulls into the porte cochere of the Hôtel de Monfort. I am even more conscious of them when a servant in dove gray livery shows us into an interior apartment, walled round in Gobelin and Beauvais tapestries. A tapestried armchair, a velvet settee. Voluptuous curtains, folded as elegantly as women's gowns. By the fireplace, an epic screen with nine panels of Attic warfare.

"Is this a museum?" asks Charles.

"You might say," says Vidocq.

He turns in that instant to find the museum keeper himself, with a fresh vest of white piqué and two diamond pins on his frill. If the Marquis recognizes Vidocq from their previous meeting, there is no sign of it. No sign of anything, really, but distaste. Warring with duty.

"Before we begin, Monsieur," says the Marquis, "I must beg of you a word in private."

"You may speak freely before these gentlemen," Vidocq answers. "They are as concerned in the matter as I am."

No sign he remembers us, either. Or wishes to.

"If this matter had been left in my hands," he intones, "none of you should be standing here today. I have opened my home to you strictly as a personal favor to the minister. I would bid you remember that."

"Duly noted, Monsieur le Marquis. In turn, I would bid you recall that three people have been killed in order to prevent this meeting. Doesn't their sacrifice make it worth a little bit of your time? And the Duchess's?"

As it did in the crypt, the Marquis's right leg advances into the pose of a duellist. His voice, though, retreats by just a fraction.

"Monsieur Vidocq," he says, "you must understand. I have known the Duchess since she was a little girl. She has weathered three lifetimes of suffering. I wish only to spare her more."

"And I hope only to bring her joy, Monsieur."

A little flash of reckoning in the Marquis's brown eyes.

"Fifteen minutes," he says. "No more. And the Duchess retains the right to terminate the interview at any time. As do I."

"Agreed," says Vidocq.

Such an air of confidence in him. I wish I had a tenth as much, but I can't seem to find a happy ending to any of this. I see the Marquis, tawny and inviolable. I see Charles, passing something between his feet. (A tennis ball! Where did he get it?) And then, a minute later, sweeping in like a winter storm: the Duchesse d'Angoulême.

Niece to the current king, daughter-in-law to the Comte d'Artois. A more complete vision than she was in the crypts of Saint-Denis but smaller, too, and more crabbed. No white cashmere or scarlet velvet for her. It's corsets and black crepe, thank you, and how are you proposing to waste the next chunk of my life?

"Good afternoon, Madame. I am Chief Inspector Vidocq of the Brigade de Sûreté."

"I have heard report of you," she says, in a voice every bit as chilly as her extended hand.

"You flatter me beyond all reason. May I present to you the gentleman who has so graciously assisted me in these investigations?" A concerted pause, during which my trousers bunch out in ten places. "Dr. Hector *Carpentier*."

"Carpentier," she murmurs.

Not knowing what else to do, I stagger forward.

"It is a very great honor to address you, Madame. I believe you had occasion to meet my father. In less happy times."

"Yes," she says. Past and present wash over her, blurring her features. "I remember your father, of course, with great fondness. He was most kind to me and to my . . ." One of her gloved fingers tinkers with the gold cross round her neck. "Me and my—"

"Indeed," says Vidocq, cutting in. "You have graciously brought us round, Madame, to the theme of our inquiry. As I have informed the minister, recent events have raised the possibility—and I mean only the *possibility*—that the young man you see before you *might*—a word I cannot possibly overemphasize, Madame—*might*, I say, be someone not unknown to you."

"Is that what *he* would have you believe?"

"No, Madame. About his childhood he recalls precious little. He has never professed to be anyone but Charles Rapskeller. The claim has only been made in his behalf."

"And who has made it?"

"Unfortunately, the claimants have had the—the singular misfortune of dying, Madame. In rather untimely fashion. One of them was Monsieur Chrétien Leblanc, whom you may also remember."

Another name, whirling out of the past. She lowers her head, as if she could actually dodge it.

"As this young man appears to be in some danger himself, Madame, we thought it expedient to bring him before you. For no other reason than his own safety. If you could absolutely and categorically *deny* that he is Louis-Charles, Duc de Normandie . . . well then, you might do him the not inconsiderable service of saving his life."

Appealing to her well-known vein of charity. A canny move—except there is not a drop of charity in the Duchess's face now.

"It seems pointless, Monsieur, to deny something so self-evident. You may recall that my brother is dead."

"Well, yes," concedes Vidocq. "That is the generally accepted notion. However, in the absence of—of an actual body . . ."

The Marquis rises from his chair, his mouth shaping itself round in admonition. But the Duchess is well ahead of him.

"This insolence," she says in a slowly simmering voice, "is too much to be borne. You tell me my brother lives. I tell you he does not. As it seems impossible to unite on this point, Monsieur, I therefore propose we conclude our interview at once."

And here interposes the one person in the room whom no one has been paying much attention to.

"You have lovely hair," says Charles. "What I can see of it."

In the shock of the moment, the Duchess's hand flies toward her small English bonnet. Patches of purple bleed through her cheeks.

"My apologies," interjects Vidocq. "The young man is not always—his *mind* appears to be . . ."

"Vile," she croons. "Vile creature."

With a look of disdainful attraction, she advances on Charles.

"I have already turned away several like you," she hisses. "All claiming to be my dear brother. It shall be my great pleasure to turn you away, too."

"I hope you won't," says Charles. "We just got here, you see."

And by now it's no longer a question of whether he will win her over. It's a question of whether he will get out of this room alive.

"Tell me," she says, raising her voice to a crowlike register. "Tell me, Monsieur *Pretender*. What day was it that my father died?"

The question doesn't so much baffle as fly right over him. With a twist of a smile, he turns to me, then to Vidocq, then back to her.

"Ah, you have forgot, have you?" says the Duchess. "January the twenty-first. Any student of history might have told you that. But perhaps you remember the firing of the cannon that followed hard upon his death. Do you? Do you remember how you reacted? Do you remember what our aunt said?"

The Marquis places a hand on her elbow. "My child," he murmurs. "Please . . ."

"Do you remember what she and Mother did for you that night? Out of the ordinary?" Her face squeezes down into hard straight lines. "Perhaps you recall the day you gathered my correspondence for me. In what room did you leave it? In what manner?"

For the first time, there is a look of fear in Charles' eye. He puts out his hands, as though he were bracing for a foil thrust.

"Oh, and please tell me what you did to me on New Year's Day, 1793? *How* did you do it? In what *room* did you do it?"

A long, long silence, as the last embers of hope die out. The Duchess's face? Well, I can only describe it as ecstatically grim.

"It appears to me that Monsieur *Rapskeller's* silence is all the confirmation that anyone could require. My brother, if he were alive, would have had an answer to each of these questions."

Vidocq begins to scratch his scalp.

"He suffers—I don't believe I've mentioned, Madame—*amnesia*. Dr. Carpentier here could corroborate—"

"I must regretfully bid you good afternoon."

Flicking her black fan at us, she reaches for the bell to summon her maid. A deliberately slow and ponderous motion: She knows no one can stop her.

No one but Charles.

"It was a moth," he says.

She squints at him.

"What did you say?"

"I found a moth. A death's-head hawkmoth. So strange to find one in January. I put it in a jar."

It's the same dawning I witnessed in the Tuileries gardens. His face, his person are wrenched open; the light pours in.

"And when you were napping," he says, "I stole into your room— you were sleeping on Mother's bed because she had a Marseilles quilt—and I put the moth down your shift. And you woke up screaming. And the moth, yes, it fluttered round inside your clothes. It was dead by the time we got it out, poor devil. I remember it left some of its—its *wing* dust on your skin. And you said, 'Never mind, we'll bury it, and it will go straight to heaven.' And we buried it in the wood cellar."

Her lips moving silently, the Duchess drops onto a settee.

"And your letters," Charles says. "I wrapped them in a white ribbon, and I stuck a rose inside, and I wrote: *These Belong to Madame la Sérieuse*, because that's what Mother used to call you. *Open on Penalty of Death*, I wrote. And I left them for you on that little winding stair that used to go from the wardrobe to the attic. And I didn't think about the death business. I was just being funny.

"And when the cannons boomed that day, I . . ."

He waves his hand before his face.

"I started to laugh. I was *crying*, really, but it came out wrong. Aunt Élizabeth wasn't angry at all. She said, 'Yes, my child. Your father is laughing, too, for he's with the angels in heaven, where there is endless joy.' And when I thought of Father being with angels, I really *did* cry, I couldn't stop. And Mother and Aunt Élizabeth let me stay up later than usual, and they let me play at backgammon, though I hadn't the heart for it. And they made me a sleeping draught with wine and soda water, and Mother held me—in her arms—till I went to sleep.

"And when I woke up the next morning, you were there. Standing right over me. And you had a senna tree, I don't know where you found it. And you said, 'We must plant this together. For Father. So that every time we look at it, we may think of him.'"

The Duchesse d'Angoulême wraps her arms round her ears. Lowers her head to her lap.

Slowly, tenderly, unopposed by anyone else in the room, Charles Rapskeller kneels before her. Rests his forehead on top of her bonnet.

"Marie," he says. "I've come home. Just as I said I would. Remember? Our last night together?"

And then, with her fan, she strikes him in the face.

The second blow is on his shoulder. By the fourth blow, she has discarded her fan and is using only her gloved fist.

Such is her rank that no one makes a move to stop her. Charles, least of all. No longer averse to touch, he simply suffers the blows to rain down, one after the next. A blow for every year he has been absent.

At last he grabs her hand and presses it to his lips.

"The Lord is merciful," she murmurs, falling into his arms. "Gaze on His works. The Lord is merciful."

CHAPTER 44

A Rupture of Etiquette

SOMETHING I WILL always remember: the Duchess's face as it re-emerges from that initial embrace. Radiant with terror, not joy. Her fingers actually tremble as they cup Charles' face.

"It *is* you," she says.

And having reassured herself, the bottom drops out from inside, and she subsides into a torrent of weeping. Never before, I think, has Madame la Sérieuse mourned or rejoiced so freely.

"Pray excuse me," she stammers.

The Marquis lays his hand on her bowed head.

"No need, my child. I have prayed for this day, too."

Officially sanctioned now, her tears come hot and fast, forming a membrane between her and the world, transforming that pinched red face into some approximation of its youthful bloom. At last, dazed and drained, she wobbles to her feet. Takes the handkerchief proffered by Vidocq.

"Well," she says. "This does change things."

"It certainly does," agrees Vidocq.

"I must . . ." Her eyes scatter from tapestry to tapestry. "I must tell my uncles, mustn't I?"

"The *King*, yes," the Marquis answers. "I beg you to leave *me* the pleasure of informing the Comte d'Artois."

The meaning behind his icy smile is lost on her, for there is no irony in her world now. And no other object but this young man, crouching on the floor where she left him.

"Come," she says, extending her hand. "You must come with me now."

He takes her hand. Rises.

"If it's all the same to you, I'd like to stay with Hector."

Had he declared he was swimming to the moon, he might have met with the same bafflement. She doesn't even know at first whom he's referring to.

"Do you mean . . ." Her fingers waggle in my direction. "With *him*?"

"Just for tonight," Charles says. "Hector and I have been through quite a lot, you know. And he sits with me till I go to sleep and his bones never creak, and just for tonight, I think, that's where I belong. And then tomorrow . . . I'll belong to you."

"We've so much to talk about," she protests. "Years and *years* . . ."

"And many more years in which to do it," says the Marquis, advancing. "But, my dear, before we start assigning this young man a bed at the palace, we must first be sure of his welcome."

"His *welcome*? How could the rightful King of *France* not be welcome?"

"I fear not everyone will see it as you do, my child. No, indeed," he adds, with a meaningful look at us, "not everyone. For the time being, we must proceed with great caution. Now Monsieur Vidocq here and the good doctor have watched over Charles all these weeks. I think we may trust them to shelter him an additional night."

Vidocq quickly seconds the point, and to both their arguments, she has only her own will to oppose. Which proves not quite so formi-dable as her habit of obedience, even to social inferiors. (The Temple schooled her well.) It's almost breathtaking, the humility with which she finally addresses me.

"Do you think I might come to call tomorrow morning?"

"But, of course, Madame!" interjects Vidocq. "You may consider my home your personal pied-à-terre."

One condition she extracts before leaving: She must touch her brother one last time.

Her hands rove round his face, rehearsing the old features. To which Charles submits gladly.

"We have God to thank for this," she whispers. "There is noth-ing He cannot do. Till tomorrow," she says, releasing him under slow duress.

"Tomorrow," he answers.

And so the Duchesse d'Angoulême leaves the room a far different woman than when she entered. The Marquis escorts her to the car-riage, and as the door closes after him, Vidocq flings his hat straight to the ceiling. It never comes back. We look up to find it wrapped round the teardrop crystals of the Marquis's chandelier.

"We did it," he says.

A nice pronoun, that *we*. Except that for the next several minutes, he talks only of himself. The grand future that awaits him. Bounties and rewards, receptions at the Tuileries, invitations to Baron Pozzo's salon. Before long his own division. (Watch out, Inspector Yvrier!) And if he gets the title he fully expects, what's to stop him from laying claim to the Prefecture itself?

This destiny floats before him a few seconds longer. Then he makes for the door.

"Where are you going?" I ask.

"To celebrate, you damned fool. Just so happens I've got a young filly back home. Waiting to be broken in, you get my drift. Oh, she's got a field of clover you'd—"

"I love horses, too," says Charles.

"Yes," says Vidocq after a pause. "Fine animals. Now see if the Marquis will spot you to dinner and a couple bottles of wine. Least he can do. And don't leave the manse by yourselves. Send for some gendarmes, there's a station house not two blocks away. Drop my name, if you must. And meet me back at Maison Vidocq, all right? Before we retire tonight, we'll raise a toast to our triumph."

"Do you have champagne?" asks Charles hopefully.

"Do flies eat shit?" he calls back, hauling open the doors.

As usual, he takes with him a goodly portion of the room's oxygen. The air is definitely thinner, yes, and the walls themselves seem to close round us as Charles says, in a soft tone:

"I'm not ready."

"I know."

He drops onto the settee. Holds his head in his hands.

"I don't think I'll ever be ready."

"Well, I imagine every king feels that way. When he starts out. And then he finds his way, doesn't he?"

The contours of his new suit collapse, inch by inch.

"I sometimes wish . . ."

"What?"

"I wish you'd left me back in Saint-Cloud."

With more time, I might be able to dissect the pang that catches me midsection. I could even ask myself if he's right. But in the next instant, the massive salon doors are flung open, and four gendarmes rush in.

There must be some mistake, I want to say. *I haven't sent for you yet.*

"In the name of His Majesty Louis the Eighteenth, we hereby arrest *you*, Charles Rapskeller . . ."

Stunned, Charles rises from his settee.

". . . for the crime of conspiring against the life of our beloved monarch . . ."

"Beloved who?" he whispers.

"... and *you*, Hector Carpentier, as accomplice to aforementioned act."

They trip over the words, that's the first sign. And their uniforms don't fit them much better than Vidocq's suit fits me. Monsieur may have dressed up his lackeys, but they still smell unmistakably of the *barrières*.

"How dare you?" The voice of civilization comes at them from behind. "Leave at once!"

It takes but a single club to silence the Marquis. Down he goes on the silk runner, like a cartload of wood.

After that . . . well, it's doom, that's all. Struggle as I might, I'm pinned limb by limb. To my left, I see a boot catching Charles in the temple. I see him crumple and fall. A hand closes round my throat. . . .

The strange part is I never once call for aid. (Who, after all, would come?) But just as the canvas sack is placed over my head, I do manage to say:

"He'll know."

No antecedent, of course. They might as easily think I'm talking of God. In truth, they make no such mistake.

"Your Vidocq will be dead before the sun has set," they say.

And then, almost as an afterthought:

"So will you."

CHAPTER 45

The Fate of Parricides

AFTERWARD, WHAT WILL amaze me most is the speed of it all. One moment, we're bidding farewell to the Duchesse d'Angoulême; the next, we're saying hello to the Hôtel de Ville.

All the middle stages are skipped. No trial, no appeal. No cell in the Conciergerie. Two men named Cornevin and Husson are ushered out of a holding pen; Charles and I are ushered in; the lock clicks. Everything is carried off with a minimum of fuss.

In the end, I would guess, no more than a handful of officials needed to be bribed. The rest simply absorb us into their appointed rounds. At the strike of three in the afternoon, for instance, a guard comes to tell us:

"It's time."

"For what?" mumbles Charles, still drifting in and out of consciousness.

The man doesn't stay to answer. And when the next guard comes, he says only:

"This way."

A long drafty corridor . . . a flight of stairs . . . we stop in a dark vaulted chamber.

"Sit," says the guard.

The dawning comes in three stages. First: a sound of splashing, as if the Seine had overrushed its boundaries—broken at intervals by human laughter. A crowd is gathering. Outside. In the Place de Grève.

The second clue: the white-haired priest by the door. His name is Father Montès, and he's chaplain-in-chief to the Paris prisons.

And finally: that stout, doughy, agreeable-looking fellow in the frock coat and rumpled tricorn hat. *His* name is Charles-Henri Sanson, and he is public executioner of Paris. He's the man who held up the heads of Louis the Sixteenth and Marie-Antoinette to the baying mob. He's about to do the same to us.

"Good afternoon," he says, with a bashful smile.

Somebody strips me of my jacket. Somebody else ropes my wrists behind me and undoes my shirt. Cold metal grazes against my neck; locks of hair begin to fall on my shoulder.

"You've got the wrong men," I say.

"Oh, yes."

"We're not Cornevin and Husson. My name is Dr. Hector Carpentier . . ."

"I see."

". . . and this is Charles Rapskeller. Brother to the Duchesse d'Angoulême."

"Mm."

"The lost *dauphin*, do you hear? If you harm a hair on his head, you will be guilty of *regicide*. Do you know what that means?"

And for a second, the word actually seems to splinter his self-possession. His eyes startle open, and with a shrug of apology, he says:

"Honestly, where's my head? We've one thing to do before we go."

He gives a nod, and two of his assistants seize Charles, spread him across a stone platform.

"Wait," I say. "Wait."

They unroll the sleeve of his shirt. ("Nice fabric," I hear one of them mutter.) They pin down his right forearm. Unfurl his balled fingers.

"What are you doing?" I shout.

"Just a little formality," answers Sanson.

Like a child with his nose buried in a primer, he begins to recite in a singsongy voice.

"By order of Penal Code Provision 23-A, subsection 9 . . ."

"Please," I say. "You've got the wrong man."

". . . any person found truly guilty of conspiring against the King's life is, in the eyes of the state, guilty of parricide . . ."

His hand gropes toward a butcher's cleaver. Raises it toward the ceiling.

". . . and receives punishment commensurate with same."

For a second or two, the blade hovers there, jeweled in a prism of light. Then down it comes.

"No!"

In the same breath as my cry, the blade bisects the exact point where Charles' arm meets his hand.

A shriek . . . a squall of red . . . and Charles sinks to the floor, blood rolling out in tides.

With a businesslike motion, Sanson sweeps the severed hand into a potato sack, calmly ties it round. Then, catching sight of my face, he says:

"No worries, Monsieur. You get to keep yours."

"For God's sake," I gasp. "Can't you—can't you *wrap* the wound? Can't you . . ."

The words fly out before I see their absurdity.

"He'll bleed to death!"

"Give the fellow a blanket," instructs Sanson. "And don't worry so much about waking him up. Best for him if he doesn't."

All their attention turns to me now. The assistants bind my feet together. They throw a jacket over my back and knot the sleeves under my chin. A cold sweat breaks out across my brow. My brain is dashing against the walls of my skull.

"Come, my son," says Father Montès.

IT'S RAINING. SOMEHOW in the last hour, the sun went into hiding, and the clouds came, and none of it makes the slightest difference to the thousand spectators gathered in the Place de Grève. They've been here, many of them, since early this morning (before I even knew I was to be their entertainment), and now, as the four o'clock hour approaches, they lie piled atop one another with a geological force, like layers of shale. They jockey for views on the steps of the Palais de Justice, they dangle from alehouse balconies, they make the very bridges shudder beneath their force.

A group of gendarmes walks me toward the gatehouse threshold, dragging Charles close behind. At the sight of us, the roar comes down like a gale. I stagger back, but a hand keeps me erect. Another guides me toward the waiting cart.

Sanson heaves himself in first. Then comes Charles, still unconscious, still bundled in that blood-sodden towel. Then I come.

Around us, a single word is being chanted again and again, a million times over.

"*Two! Two! Two!*"

Guillotinings are rare enough in these early days of the Restoration, and to have the spectacle of *two* condemned men in the same afternoon is an unheard-of pleasure. *Just like the old days,* you can feel the crowd thinking. *Before the Old Growler got a bad flavor to it.*

An officer gives the order, and the cart gusts forward, as though propelled by the din of the spectators. Cobble by cobble we pass, the crowd parting only to close round us again—through the Quai aux Fleurs (a discombobulating smell of roses), over the Pont-au-Change, along the Quai de Gesvres.

Strange that, in this moment, all I can think of are *other* people's heads. Popping from doorways and windows. Peering out from behind lampposts and storefronts. Gazing down on us with a furious lust.

Next to me, Father Montès raises his crucifix and intones . . . something . . . it might be Latin, it might be Carpathian. The hubbub drowns out all the other sounds, and the only thing that breaks through to me, finally, is a jolt: Charles' head, jostled onto my shoulder.

I stare into his white, white face. A tiny flicker round the eyelids. A palpitation of the lower lip. Not much more.

He'll die, I think. *Before they even get round to killing him.*

And once more, I find myself wishing my father could be here. Or Vidocq. But the first of them is long dead, and the other soon will be. And in another ten minutes, I'll be joining them.

"Charles."

My legs and hands are bound. The only way to rouse him is with my voice.

"Charles, can you hear me?"

I feel it rather than hear it: the breath passing through his lips.

"I need you to *look* at me. Right into my eyes, can you do that?"

The lids widen, the pupils dance in their sockets.

"We're going on an outing," I tell him. "It'll be great fun."

"No," he murmurs. "Rain . . ."

Rain, yes, battening his lids back down, trickling down his chin like drool.

"Forget the rain," I say. "Forget *everything,* can you do that? Just look into my eyes. Charles, you must do this for me."

Several more seconds pass before his pupils lock into focus.

"Good. That's good. Now just keep looking. That's all you have to do."

The cart rolls on and on, past rows of shops, past walls of faces. Laughs and jeers . . . boots stamping in mud . . . children swinging from shop signs . . . we notice none of it. There is a dire intimacy to us now, as if we were soldiers in a surrounded redoubt.

At length, a measure of color returns to his face. The breath begins to stream at regular intervals. The back of his eye pulses with light.

And then the cart grinds to a stop.

"Bear it bravely," says Father Montès, shoving the crucifix toward me.

He's hoping I'll kiss it before I go, but I'm too caught up by the sight of Charles, being dragged down a stepladder. And the sight of this scaffold: iron, wood, and ropes. And looming above it, that familiar triangle of steel. Old Growler. The Widowmaker.

"Had it waxed just this morning," Sanson reassures us.

I glance toward the great clock face on the façade of the Hôtel de Ville. Two minutes till four o'clock, and every possible vantage has been seized. Tables and chairs have been rented for the occasion. Gamins hang from chimneys and window bars, calling down insults. Just below the platform, two men have stationed themselves with bowls for catching the blood.

This is what I've saved Charles for.

He has to be dragged up the steps, but once he's atop the scaffold, he's able somehow to walk the last few steps unaided—and with a serenity quite astonishing in the circumstances. The onlookers roar their approval.

"There's a man for you! Not a tremor!"

"Brave bugger, isn't he?"

One woman, quite young and fair, blows Charles kisses. Her face is contorted with weeping. *She'll write a novel about him,* I think. *A bad one.*

"Take me first!" I yell up to Sanson. "I want to go first!"

"Rules are rules."

Two gendarmes lay Charles down on the swinging plank, flat on his stomach. From the crowd, a low keening hum of pleasure begins to well, ascending in pitch and volume with each stage in the ritual: right leg bound, left leg bound. *Mmmm . . . Mmmmmmmm . . .*

"I've a statement to make!" I shout. "I've a confession! Please! I want to confess everything!"

"Then let me finish my business here," Sanson calls down, the first hint of aggrievement in his voice. "Then I can tend to you, Monsieur."

The last ropes are attached. The plank is swung outward, taking Charles directly into the path of the blade. All that Sanson need do now is pull the cord.

"A pardon is coming!" I cry. "Very soon! From the King himself!"

"Never heard that one before," says Sanson.

"There's a *pardon*, I tell you!"

But I just give the crowd new fodder. Before twenty seconds have passed, the word is echoing back to me from every corner of the Place de Grève.

"Pardon! Pardon! Pardon!"

Which is, in fact, the last thing they want. Indeed, nothing would disappoint them more than a last-minute reprieve.

And nothing seems less likely now. Charles is perfectly recumbent, perfectly still. Sanson is walking, with great purpose, toward the cord. All is lost.

And then, over the building hum of the crowd, comes a shrill corvine cry, so different in character and intent that it creates a wall of stillness round it.

"Stop!"

I gaze out into the human ocean. From nowhere, a small eddy has appeared. Two royal guardsmen, beating a path through the crowd with the flats of their swords, and following in their wake—dressed like an avenger—the Duchesse d'Angoulême.

"You must desist!" she shrieks. "These men are innocent!"

At this moment, I'd wager no one in the Place de Grève is more terrified than she. Here, on every side, is the mob of her deepest and most private terrors. Showing her not a hint of reverence.

"Get out with her!"

"We don't go and spoil *her* fun, do we?"

"Send her back to the palace!"

Undaunted, she makes straight for the scaffold, calling as she goes. "They are *innocent*, I tell you!"

A discontented murmur rises from the populace, and at the foot of the scaffold, Sanson stands in frowning colloquy with one of his assistants.

"Think we should get a move on. . . ."

"Behind schedule as it is. . . ."

"Rain's going to rust the apparatus. . . ."

But this exchange gives way before a much larger sound.

"You heard my daughter-in-law, Monsieur Sanson!"

On the parapets of the Palais de Justice stands a figure of unassailable dignity. Garlanded in ribbons and medals. Clothed in all the perquisites of dynasty.

The mere sight of him produces an altogether different sound in the crowd. For though many of them have never glimpsed the Duchesse d'Angoulême, *this* man they know.

And now, much to the surprise of everyone about me, I begin to laugh. For if I'd had to pick a personal savior, the Comte d'Artois would not have been my choice.

"These men are to go free!" he roars, unfurling a long document. *"By order of the King!"*

A moment of abeyance follows, during which Sanson can be seen actively weighing the claims of his two masters: mob and monarchy. It takes him a good half minute to come down on the side of the latter.

"Untie them, boys," he says, in a resigned tone.

And when the last rope is cut from my wrists, he tenders me his most gracious bow.

"No hard feelings, I hope, Monsieur."

By the time the Comte reaches our cart, the rain has already begun to dissolve his face into the familiar features of Eugène François Vidocq. The Duchess, sodden and panting, is grabbing me by the torn edge of my shirt and shouting:

"Can you save him?"

And just then Charles' whisper rises up to us:

"*Don't.*"

But Vidocq has already turned back toward the crowd, and in his most imperious voice, he's bellowing:

"Find me a tar pot!"

Such is his ability to remain in character that a good dozen people set off running in as many directions, crying "Yes, Monsieur!" as they go. The first to come back is a fish merchant, who has somehow discovered a roofer, who is bearing with him even now a pot of black sludge, oozing steam.

"Many thanks," says the counterfeit Comte d'Artois, using his own coat to take the pot. "Hector, give Charles your hand. He'll need something to squeeze."

The eyes of the lost dauphin are still glazed and opaque when Vidocq pulls the bloody towel from his arm and stares at those dangling fringes of vein and artery.

"Very sorry, Your Majesty," he says, making a quick genuflection. "It's how we used to do it at sea."

And then he plunges Charles' arm into the tar pot.

Even Sanson flinches before the confluence of flesh and heat. The sizzle can be heard twenty yards away, the smell much farther. As for the scream, well, the Duchess must stop her ears for a good three minutes before it dies out.

It's so consuming, Charles' pain, that only much later in the evening do I think to look at my own hand, where I find two fingers swollen and purple. Broken by the sheer force of his grip.

CHAPTER 46

Foiled Hopes

MUCH LATER THAT night—after Charles has at last been lulled to sleep, after the Duchess has left us with promises to return the next morning—only then do Vidocq and I feel at ease to tell each other our stories.

"*Four* men?" he shouts into his wineglass. "*That's* all it took to bring you down? Ha! They needed *eight* for me."

He was stepping onto the Marquis's portico when they came at him. With everything they had, he said. Saddler's awl. Poleax. Sheath knife. Cooper's adze.

He could tell right away they were trying to subdue, not kill, so he made it as hard for them as he could. Disarmed one with a well-timed kick. Clocked another with his elbow. Took out a kneecap or two, broke a windpipe. Might still be there if they hadn't come at him with a road mender's hammer.

"At least I *think* that's what it was. Too late to duck."

Taking advantage of his stupor, they trussed him like a horse in a rope and martingale, dragged him down the steps, and locked him in the Marquis's wine cellar.

"That was the cruelest stroke of all, Hector. Leaving me a foot away from all those vintages and no means to drink."

The wine, however, was his salvation. With his bound feet, he was able to pull one of the bottles from the racks and shatter it against the stone floor. The shards of glass he used to cut his ropes.

Before him and freedom stood only a locked door. A small barrier indeed, once he'd located a corkscrew. After reviving his spirits with a bottle of the Marquis de Monfort's best Burgundy, he proceeded to overpower the man assigned to guard him. Two more soon followed, at which point Vidocq seized the hammer and started swinging freely. Another three picked up their heels and ran.

"And then I turn round—and there stands our Monsieur, real as life. A pair of blackguards on either side of him. And in each of his hands, a fisticuff pistol, wrapped in a monogrammed handkerchief. Well, I was treed, I don't mind telling you. Calm as I could be, I said, 'You've gone to a great deal of trouble, Monsieur.'

"And he said, 'Oh, I'd hoped to avoid all this mess, but I can't have you taking someone else's rightful throne. It won't do, you know.'"

"What happened then?"

"Well, I figured my only chance was to prick the bugger's vanity. 'Come now,' I said. 'Shooting a man's not the way for you. Aren't you one of the premier swordsmen in the land? Why don't we settle this, just the two of us? Let's take the buttons off your foils and have at it.'"

"You challenged him to a duel?"

"Well, what I *failed* to mention is I'm a bit of an old hand with the foil myself. Learned when I was a kid, roistering with the soldier boys in Arras. First man I ever killed was a fencing instructor."

Never mind, Monsieur accepted the offer straightaway and set the time and place. Now. In the courtyard.

Strange sort of duel. Not pistols at dawn but blades in the middle of the afternoon. No seconds present, unless you count the two hired knaves cheering Monsieur on—even threatening to tilt the contest in his favor.

Vidocq had the advantage of being younger and larger. Monsieur, on his side, was spryer and, having fenced more recently, possessed the more dazzling technique. ("The footwork was a joy, Hector.") Round and round they went on the parterres, as evenly matched as combatants could be. Every parry led to its natural riposte. Counterparry followed counterriposte. The sound of the blades resounded against the white plaster walls, the rooks cawed from the roofline, Monsieur's knaves cheered and booed . . . and Vidocq soon realized he was running out of time.

"Oh, I was breathing hard, my friend. Then, out of nowhere, Monsieur comes out with the *rose couverte*. Wings me in the side, knocks me on the back. Next thing I know his foil's jabbing into my neck. You can see the scab right there."

"What did you do?"

"Well, the thing that saved me is this. I'm no gentleman. Many years ago, in the galleys, Goupil taught me a little savate move called the snapping turtle. Came back to me in a trice. And when I heard Monsieur's leg go, I suddenly remembered: '*That's* where the snapping part comes from.'

"So there he lies, poor devil. Leg broken clean. Groaning and gasping. 'You might as well kill me,' he says."

"And did you?"

"Didn't have to. One of his own men went and took a carving knife to his throat. There's loyalty for you. Bastard thought he'd get a reward out of it, too. I said the only reward you'll get is a free stay in an educational institution of *my* choice. Unless you tell me where they took my friends.

"Well, out came the whole plan. The ringleader of those mugs goes by the name of Cornevin. Oh, I know him well. When Monsieur came asking for his services, Cornevin told him, 'I'll do it for *free* if you can help my brother. He's set to meet Old Growler this very week.' Well, Monsieur saw his chance. If he could switch Charles with Cornevin— not too hard for a man of his connections—and then switch *you* with the other man . . . well, that would take care of all his problems in two strokes of the blade."

To the memory of that blade I shut my eyes. It's then I realize how dry my mouth is. I haven't been able to salivate since four o'clock this afternoon.

"*Changelings,*" I say, taking another swig of wine.

"I don't know if Monsieur quite grasped the symbolism, but yes. So there it was, Hector! Not much time, eh? I locked Cornevin and his pals in the wine cellar, and then who should come knocking but the Duchess? Had a special locket she wanted to give her brother—so he could put it under his pillow tonight. I said, 'Your brother won't be *needing* pillows unless you get to the Place de Grève as fast as you can.'"

"You didn't leave with her?"

"No, I already had another plan in mind. See, there was no way *I* could call off the execution, and frankly I had doubts whether anyone would listen to the Duchess—she doesn't fill a body with fear, does she?—but they'd have to listen to the King's younger brother. And it just so happens I look like the gentleman in question."

"I've noticed," I say, summoning back the image of Vidocq (or so I thought him) staring out from the King's carriage.

"Well, of course, I didn't have my usual clothes, so I had to make do with the Marquis's. Had to draft a fake writ. And being banged about, I had to clean myself up a bit. Oh, but you should have seen my coachman's face when I climbed in!"

"So you dressed up as Artois while the real Comte was lying dead in the courtyard?"

"The real . . . oh, Christ, Hector, are you still going on about that? Artois wasn't Monsieur."

"Who was, then?"

A moment of pure exasperation now, as though I've missed the whole point of an epic-length joke.

"Our host! The Duchess's dear friend. *The Marquis de Monfort.*"

THERE REALLY ARE advantages to being an intimate of the minister of justice. When you die under shameful circumstances, your friend makes sure that nothing is left to stain your memory. Vidocq is duly instructed to alter his report of the Marquis de Monfort's death; all known accomplices are banished to their cells; and the next day, Parisian newspapers bruit the shocking and unexplained murder of a peer of the realm by unknown assailants.

The palace declares itself saddened, and the Marquis is buried with all appropriate pomp. His eulogists praise his loyalty to the Bourbons during their long exile, and the Chamber of Peers votes to erect a tablet in his honor.

"They'll never give *me* a tablet," grouses Vidocq, tossing the newspaper in disgust.

We're sitting down to breakfast. It's been a long night for Charles—and a bleary morning for me. I'm on my third bowl of coffee, and I'm still waiting for the lint to burn from my brain.

"What I don't understand," I say, "is why the Marquis faked his own attack. I could have sworn I saw him knocked to the ground."

"It was all a ruse, Hector. If his plan fell through—if, by some chance, you escaped—he could pretend he wasn't behind it. It's why he didn't have me killed, probably. He figured I'd tell everyone about the big bad men who broke into his house."

"And he went to all this trouble to ensure Artois' succession? You told me they were mortal enemies."

"They were."

Vidocq covers his mouth, but there's no hiding that motile eyebrow.

"Oh, come," I say. "We can't have any more secrets after all this."

"Well, it seems yesterday morning, my boys were going through the Marquis's belongings, and they made an interesting find."

Behind a false panel, hidden by a round-bellied bureau in the Marquis's bedroom, the men of Number Six found a small shrine. Relic after relic, hoarded like ladies' fans. At first the object of devotion was unclear—until someone pulled out a tricolor flag. Then came a handful of bee napkins. Pamphlets and placards. Maps of Austerlitz and Jena.

And, in an inner recess, a whole host of effigies. Napoleon plates. Napoleon teacups. Napoleon busts. Coins, engravings, ivory cameos, rolled-up oil portraits. The totems of a savior, patiently awaited.

Further inquiries found that the Marquis had, in the past, voiced sentiments of a troubling and antiroyalist nature. More than one salon hostess had been startled to hear him say that Napoleon had schooled France to be great—and that the Bourbons were still truant. Waterloo was lost, the Marquis liked to say, because that peasant Lacoste didn't know about the sunken road to Ohain. With a better-informed guide, Napoleon would never have ordered the charge of Milhaud's cuirassiers . . . a third of Dubois' brigade would never have tumbled into the abyss . . . France would still be the envy of the world.

One of the Marquis's mistresses blushingly confessed that he had once secured a private audience with Bonaparte himself—and had come away with a silver signet, a small token of the emperor's affection that was affixed to a chain and worn round his neck. He wore it to his dying day and was, by his own charge, buried with it.

And now it seems to me that no amount of coffee will make me lucid.

"He went through all this—he killed all these people—just to keep the throne warm for Napoleon?"

"Well," says Vidocq, "look at it from his angle. Louis the *Seventeenth*, if he were to come back, would be a far harder fellow to topple than Louis the *Eighteenth*. No one cares about an old man in gaiters, but the orphan of the Temple? Raised to life again? We'd drown him in rosary beads. And never let go."

"And the Marquis honestly believed Napoleon would return? And France would welcome him back?"

"Pick your messiah," says Vidocq, shrugging. "There's never any accounting for people's faith. *Is* there, Hector?"

CHAPTER 47

In Which the Nature of
Hector's Research Is Revealed

THE ONE CONSPICUOUS absence at the Marquis's funeral is the Duchesse d'Angoulême. Word circulates among mourners that she is ill, but at the precise moment of her old friend's interment, she is actually sitting in a bedroom in the Rue de l'Hirondelle, tearing up Mother Vidocq's linen sheets for the purpose of making bandages.

Before her lies the man she calls brother. No longer plumped on pillows. Flat and still and pale.

"Has he awakened since last night?" she asks.

"No," I say. "But his pulse is steady, and his breathing is free. At present, we can only keep dressing the wound and making him as comfortable as we can."

She nods and carries on with the rending of sheets. Surprising strength in those white veiny fingers.

"If you have any pressing obligations, Madame, I should be glad to send word when his condition changes."

"Actually, I should prefer to stay. If you don't mind."

She stays the whole day. And nothing about Charles' wound or the dressing of it stirs the slightest revulsion in her. So quietly and methodically does she go about her work that I find myself more than once thinking she's missed her true vocation.

And then I recall that this was her objective all those months in the Temple: to nurse her brother. And now, at last, someone is letting her.

She has never once asked for a court physician.

AT FOUR IN the afternoon, Mother Vidocq arrives with a tray nearly as large as her.

"Here, Madame la Duchesse. I've brought you biscuits and a lovely pot of chrysanthemum tea. Just the thing to keep your strength up. Here's some water for our patient to sip when he wakes up. And for the doctor, a nice glass of cassis. Drink up, my dears. I've also brought more sheets. Tear them to shreds for all I care, a body doesn't need more than one at a time. . . ."

A few minutes later, Jeanne-Victoire wanders in, coolly nodding her respects.

"You ought to open his shirt," she says. "He'll breathe better."

Having so advised me, she leaves. Mindful, though, of the woman in black silk, she pauses in the doorway and abruptly drops into a curtsey.

It's not her awkwardness that makes me smile. It's the confluence: a duchess and a baker's wife and a thief's mistress gathering in the same room to tend to a lost king. You don't find *that* every day in Paris.

The next morning, the first signs of suppuration appear through the crust of Charles' wound. I do everything that comes to mind. Chlorinated lotions, nitrate of silver. Bleeding, leeches. The infection continues to spread.

Several days later, the Duchess, removing her brother's dressing, is sent reeling by the odor from his wound. Reaching for a handkerchief, she gazes down at freshly blackened skin, oozing humors.

"Gangrene," she says.

For half a second, I think of lying, but then she looks me in the eye and says:

"What do you propose to do?"

I don't know if I can convey it, the tone of her voice. No outrage, no altitude. She genuinely wants to know, and she thinks I'm the man to tell her. I don't even pause to ask what Father would have done.

"In my opinion, we should remove another length of bone."

"Another . . ."

She glances back to see if the patient has heard.

"The necrosis has spread too far," I explain. "By removing another two inches or so, I believe we can cut away the festering tissue and, with luck, save the rest of his arm."

"And *him*?" She holds my gaze. "Will you save *him*?"

"I think we can raise his chances to—roughly even."

She draws in a long breath and then, as she studies Charles' form thrashing beneath the blankets, expels the breath.

"As you wish," she says.

We operate that very afternoon. Jeanne-Victoire braces Charles' legs. Vidocq grips the torso, and his mother holds the lantern. The Duchess volunteers, against all attempts to dissuade her, to hold the tenaculum artery forceps.

I've dosed Charles liberally with laudanum, but once the bow saw gets to work and the dead flesh gives way to living bone, the drug's effects soon evaporate. His body begins to buck. Blood gorges his throat, his jaw drops open to reveal the full extent of his soft palate, and screams emerge in an unbroken sequence.

"Hector," mutters Vidocq, sweating from the effort of restraining him. "Will you hurry up?"

This time, at least, we dispense with the tar. A tourniquet slows the bleeding enough to allow ligatures to be applied, and Charles, with the help of another dose of laudanum, eventually falls into a vexed sleep.

Through the better part of two days, his fever builds, dropping only to rise again. More bleeding, more leeches. The Duchess tears up more sheets for lint, changes more dressings. Holds a damp towel to Charles' brow, meets his wildest ravings with a raspy coo. She doesn't even flinch when, late in the second day, he sings—three times—the ditty with which he favored our Palais-Royal prostitutes.

Mainly, though, his repertoire consists of groans and wails. One night, a particularly strenuous cry jars me from my cot, sends me flying toward his bed, where I'm astonished to find him, for once, in a deep sleep. A second later, an even louder cry rends the darkness.

Lighting a lamp, I creep into the hallway. The door to Vidocq's bedroom stands open about a foot, and in the aperture I see the satiated face of Jeanne-Victoire, sprawled naked across the bed. Driving into her from behind: the great Vidocq, mossy-chested and omnivorous, a deity in human form.

I'm too astonished to look away—or even conceal myself. In a voice decidedly suave, Vidocq drawls:

"Close the door, will you, old boy?"

The next morning, he comes down to find me picking at an omelette of chives and cheese. When he asks me how the patient is, I answer in two words, and I decline to meet his eye.

"Ohh," he says. "Sulking, are we? I didn't realize I needed your say-so to fuck a woman in my own bed."

"She's not just any woman."

"That's the truth," he answers, exploding into a grin.

I slide him a bowl of cream for his coffee. Toss him a napkin.

"Just promise me one thing," I say.

"Name it."

"You'll do right by her child."

"Child?"

"The *baby*. The one we found in Poulain's apartment."

He stares at me. "The baby died of smallpox, Hector. Not ten days after we saw her."

"But she—no, Jeanne-Victoire said the child was staying with her brother. In Issy."

"Well, yes, that's where they're both *buried*. I should know, I paid the expenses. Oh, come, don't look like that. Jeanne-Victoire's made of tougher stuff than either of us. She'll get through."

It flashes across my mind now: her face as I saw it that night in the alleyway, standing over Herbaux's crumpled form. Small white teeth shining in the moonlight. A feral prettiness. Still very much with the living.

"The question," says Vidocq, dropping his head into his hands, "is will *I* get through?"

THAT EVENING, INSTEAD of retiring to my cot, I fall asleep in my chair. A comprehensive sleep, dreamless, trackless. The next morning, Mama Vidocq has to shake me a good five minutes before she can wake me.

"Doctor," she says. "The fever's broken."

An hour later, when the Duchess arrives, Charles is, for the first time in his convalescence, sitting up in bed. A potted geranium rests in his lap. Orange pulp shines from the crevices of his teeth. His eyes are a Persian blue.

"Good morning, Marie."

She lowers herself onto his bed. Takes his palm and presses her forehead against it.

"I CAN SCARCELY believe it," she tells me later that morning. "He's his old self. . . ."

How strangely the phrase sounds on her lips. *His old self.* A man she's known but two weeks. A boy she last saw twenty-four years ago.

She and I are sitting in Vidocq's salon, taking coffee—which her state of mind has rendered her incapable of drinking. She raises the cup . . . lets it fall. Again and again, her very own Tantalus.

"Curious," she says. "My brother remembers virtually nothing of the scaffold or the guillotine, but he does recall what happened along the way. He said you made him—go to sleep somehow. Without actually going to sleep. Oh, he was very confused about it, but he was quite clear on one point."

"Yes?"

"You saved his life."

Fragments of self-deprecation form in my throat . . . but she frees me of the need to use them.

"Tell me what you did," she says.

I have held out all this time without discussing my research—with anyone. But now, under great caution, I raise the name of Mesmer. A Viennese physician who blew into Paris forty years ago on clouds of scandal, expounding a theory called "animal magnetism." Working with the most hopeless medical cases, Mesmer attached magnets to their bodies, waved a wand in front of them—and somehow effected remarkable cures.

Traditional physicians loathed him, and after the Faculty of Medicine declared him a fraud, Mesmer slouched home. The cures themselves were hard to overlook, and there arose a clique of Parisian scientists who believed that Mesmer's therapeutics might be detached from his dubious physics.

I was one of them. Having witnessed the effects of altered consciousness in a clinical setting, I came to believe that these same techniques could be used to reduce vascular flow. If so, then Mesmer's once-discredited practices might one day have revolutionary impacts on surgery and on the treatment of traumatic injuries.

The Duchess, I will give her this, listens to the whole business without a yawn or a drooping lid. Only when she's certain I'm done talking does she ask:

"How does one prove such a theory, Doctor? If there aren't any dying men at hand."

"Well, the *animal* studies were inconclusive." That's one word for it. "I could only conclude that the administrator—*me*, I mean—had to be able to instruct the subject. This, in turn, required a degree of trust between both parties. Something that can be difficult to realize with a mouse."

"Another human, then?"

"No. Not another."

And like a boy caught stealing blackberries, I roll up my sleeve and present the now-faint ladder of cuts, first remarked upon by Vidocq in Saint-Cloud.

"You tested the theory on yourself," she says.

"Five mornings a week. Staring into a mirror."

"You actually caused yourself to bleed?"

"Well, yes," I say, blushing as I turn the sleeve back down. "It never went on for too long."

Here is what I never tell her: that the act of drawing blood seemed an apt punishment for the waste I'd made of my life.

Here is what I am only now realizing: I don't want to do it anymore.

"Doctor," she says. "You're a very interesting man."

"Madame, I hope you will forgive me if I presume to ask *you* a question?"

"By all means."

"I'm sorry, but where does the palace think you are going every day?"

"I tell them I'm praying."

"And that satisfies them?"

An enervated smile plays across her lips. "They have long ceased to be curious about me. My husband, in particular."

"Well, then," I say. "That is his loss, Madame."

"I would agree with you."

———

LATER THAT AFTERNOON, I am passing by Charles' room when I hear him start from slumber. I am about to open the door when I hear his sister's voice calling out to him.

"Marie," he says. "Is that you?"

"Yes."

"May I tell you something?"

"Of course."

"I don't want to be king."

A long pause before her voice returns.

"I know."

CHAPTER 48

A Confession

WITH CHARLES ON the mend, I'm free to sleep as late as I like— and still I wake just past dawn every morning, and still Vidocq is at least ten minutes ahead of me. Always seated for breakfast when I descend, with his newspaper half swallowing the table, his bowl of coffee smudged all the way round the rim. He shoves over the coffeepot.

"Sleep well?" he asks, without expecting any answer.

Some mornings, Jeanne-Victoire is there, too, but the ritual remains the same, and in my drowsier moments, I could believe that he and I have been meeting like this for years. All the more surprising, then, when Vidocq breaks the accustomed silence one morning to announce:

"We have a guest."

I hear the scraping of boots on the marble steps outside. The rustle of a woman's skirt.

"Who is it?" I ask.

"Old friend."

And then the mighty door opens to reveal the Baronne de Préval.

Dressed very much as she was when I met her in the Rue Férou. A black damask dress, a well-mended fichu, yellowing doeskin gloves. But with this addition: a gauze of envy. Her eyes take in Vidocq's Aubusson rugs, the Empire console, the marble steps . . . all in the hands of a former convict. Oh, it's enough to draw her face into points.

"The gendarme told me you wish to see me, Monsieur."

"That's so. Might I interest you in some tea, Madame?"

"You are most kind. I should consider it a greater kindness, however, if you would come at once to your business."

"Very well." With a flourish, he blots his lips, flings the napkin down. "Before this morning is out, Madame, I am fully prepared to take you under arrest. As an accomplice in a capital crime."

Her head rocks back an inch. Her eyes flash with amusement.

"Accomplice?" she asks. "To whom?"

"The late Marquis de Monfort."

"For what crime?"

"Murder," Vidocq answers, easily. "To start with."

She knots her shawl round her. Glares him down.

"I can only conceive you are in jest, Monsieur."

"In these matters I never jest. Your friend the Marquis tried to kill Dr. Carpentier here. *And* Monsieur Charles, the young man you glimpsed in my office. Both of them managed to survive, but at least three other bodies may be laid at the Marquis's door." He waits. "One of them was your old friend Leblanc."

This takes the wind almost entirely out of her, as he must have guessed, for he is already guiding her toward the settee.

"Leblanc?" she whispers, sinking into the cushions.

"Oh, yes, Madame. We have all the confessions we need by now. To keep Monsieur Charles from claiming his crown, there was nothing the Marquis wouldn't do. But there's one thing he *couldn't* have done," Vidocq adds, in a quieter voice. "He couldn't have known about Charles in the first place unless someone told him."

She stares at him. "You believe that *I* was his informant?"

"You were the only one, Madame, who knew all the parties. The only one who stood at all the crossroads."

"But this is outrageous!"

"You deny it, then?"

Her face, credit her this, remains utterly impassive. It's her voice that begins to break down.

"I may have—*mentioned* certain things—in passing. . . ."

But she can't deceive herself for too long. As the memory of her actions washes over her, a look of fear steals in her eyes, and she cries out:

"But I meant no harm to anybody! You must *believe* me, Messieurs!"

"That will surely depend," says Vidocq, "on how believable you are. Perhaps you could start by telling us how you knew the Marquis."

She studies her gloves a long while. Then, in a voice decidedly smaller:

"If you must know, he was an old admirer of mine. Not long after returning to Paris—in rather a weak moment—I called on him at his *hôtel*."

"Why, Madame?"

"I confess I still clung to the—the entirely *absurd* hope, I know, that I might"—she gives her head a fierce shake—"might *reclaim* my former position. In what we call society. The Marquis seemed to me a useful champion in that cause."

"And how did he welcome you?"

"Coldly. I believe I may once have wounded his vanity. But he did call on me two days later, and he continued to call, on the order of once or twice a week. Naturally, he never promised me anything. No invitations were proffered, no introductions. But he was at pains never to dash my hopes, either."

"Of course not," says Vidocq. "He had use for you. When did you first tell him of the dauphin?"

"It was . . ." Her hands query the air. "I believe it was in the course of our very first conversation. Yes, we were discussing the royal family, and I let it drop that my dear friend Monsieur Leblanc had been—*approached* by someone—concerning Louis the Seventeenth. I can't remember what I said exactly, I—well, I considered it no more than an amusement."

"And was the Marquis amused?"

"As I recall, he showed scarcely any interest, even when I showed him the teething ring. But he did—yes, in subsequent conversations, he always contrived to return to the subject. Truthfully, he never appeared more than mildly curious. I had no reason to suspect him of anything."

And now, at last, the implications of her acts find their way home. In a tone of naked awe, she murmurs:

"I told him—"

"Everything," interjects Vidocq. "You told him of *me*. Of Dr. Carpentier here. You told him that Monsieur Charles was, contrary to his assumptions, alive and well in Paris. Yes, Madame, thanks to the information you supplied, we may now add the destruction of Dr. Carpentier's home to the Marquis's crimes."

Her head drops beneath the weight of each charge—until at last she is staring straight at the floor.

"I was only making conversation," she whispers.

"As Parisians do," says Vidocq.

Breathing heavily, she begins to knead her temples. For a second, I fully expect her to faint again.

"Oh, God," she whispers. "I sent Leblanc to his death."

"Not to mention Monsieur Tepac of Saint-Cloud," says Vidocq. "Not to mention Dr. Carpentier's mother."

There is something in his manner that forestalls any idea of clemency. Quite sensibly, then, she takes her petition to me.

"Doctor," she says. "Please believe me. I had no idea the Marquis would—he was the Duchess's dearest *friend*, how could I imagine he would—harm *anyone* who might be her brother. If I'd known, Monsieur, I should sooner have cut out my own tongue. . . ."

Well, I'm not ashamed to admit it. When a highborn woman lowers herself to pleading, it does tear a bit at your heart, no matter how democratic you think yourself. And all the same, I don't know what I'm going to say until I hear myself say it.

"I *do* believe you, Madame."

Whatever consolation that gives her, though, is dispelled by the sinister lightness of Vidocq's voice.

"Whether the *Duchess* will feel the same way," he says, "well, that's another matter. I can run and ask her, though, if you'd like."

The Baroness gazes at him wildly.

"The Duchess is here?" she asks.

"She has stayed the night at this very house. Tending to her *brother*."

The last bloom of understanding rises up in the Baroness's eyes.

"Brother," she echoes.

And here all attempts at self-control end. Her head falls into her hands, and the tears come in throngs.

"Oh, I am done for," she moans into her thrice-mended handkerchief. "I am done for."

Given her state of mind, the Baroness might easily assume that the figure now descending the steps has dropped straight from heaven, arrayed in judgment. And it's true the Duchess is strangely radiant for so early an hour. Of all of us, she's gotten the least sleep, and yet there is an effulgence to her that I'd wager her own husband has never seen.

With a compressed grace, she travels the remainder of those stairs, and in a quiet voice, she says:

"The Baronne de Préval, I believe?"

The disarray of the older woman's emotions, the condition of her clothes leave her almost incapable of speech. At last, bursting the bounds of propriety, she leaps to her feet and blurts:

"I *knew* you, Madame. When you were a child. I was dear friends with—"

"The Princesse de Lamballe, yes. I remember you very well. And with pleasure."

The spark of reassurance in the older woman's eyes fades as quickly as it rises.

"I fear that can no longer be the case," she says.

Very steadily the Duchess looks at her. Then, pressing the older woman's hands together, she draws her over to the settee.

"You must not be too hard on yourself," she says. "A great many of us were duped by the Marquis de Monfort. I am part of that sad sorority myself, and so it appears I require every bit as much forgiveness as you, if not more so." Leaning closer, she adds, in a low and clear voice: "You need fear no prosecution from me. Or from France."

Gently withdrawing her hands, the Baroness fingers away her tears. "Madame . . ." She takes a long, slow breath. "You have quite overwhelmed me. And you have given me the—the loveliest farewell gift I could imagine."

"Farewell?" I say.

"Yes," she answers, giving me a heavy nod. "It was a mistake, I fear, coming back to Paris. I did it to please Leblanc, and now that he's . . ." One last tear, fat and cumbersome, fingered away. "Well, in light of all that's passed, I believe I must cut my losses, as they say. Before I do any more harm."

"But where will you go?" asks the Duchess.

She laughs now, the Baroness. A strangely giddy sound, trailing from the long past.

"I've no idea," she says. "But women like me always manage. And with luck—with God's blessing—I might one day be able to forgive myself for what I've done. If such a thing can be conceived."

Concentrating her forces now, she rises in a single swift motion. Extends her hand to the Duchess.

"Permit me to *thank* you, Madame, for your abundant kindness. From the bottom of my heart, I thank you."

Under normal circumstances, such an affirmation would bring out all the Duchess's awkwardness. She is famously shy—suspicious of affection. The serenity that enfolds her now is the first sign that she has her own ideas about the future.

"No," she says. "It is *I* who ought to thank *you*, Madame. In advance. For I am about to ask of you a very great service. And I can think of no one better suited to carry it out."

CHAPTER 49

The Muslin Bag

LEAVE IT TO the Duchess to come up with America.

MANY YEARS AGO, at the height of the Terror, a noble family by the name of Lioncourt shipped out of Bordeaux, one step ahead of the men in red hats. Making their way across the Atlantic—first to Boston, then to the Hudson Valley—the Lioncourts were able, after many years of renting from a Dutch patroon, to acquire their own land. Forty-six acres of primeval glory.

Through all this, they remained faithful correspondents with the Duchess and, in their letters, are ever entreating her to visit. She has so far declined, but she has at last found someone to send in her stead.

"Oh, Doctor, can't you imagine how happy Charles would be in such a place? All that wilderness. Not a city for miles, and not a single French partisan. Never again will he have to concern himself with affairs of state. . . ."

"But what will he do there?" I protest. "How will he live?"

"The living you may leave to me. As to what he will *do* . . ." Her mouth lifts slightly at one corner. "Doesn't every manor require a gardener? Even in the New World?"

SO IT IS THAT, on a moonlit evening in late May, a curious party gathers at the Quai Malaquais. Three black-bundled men, of varying sizes, and two women in black lace. Nothing about this assembly would suggest that it includes two members of the royal family and the most famous policeman in the land. Or that something perfectly historic—the quietest of abdications—is in the process of unfolding.

Yes, in just a few minutes, an aged baroness and a man named Charles Rapskeller will step into a narrow flat-bottomed dory, manned by servants of the Duchesse d'Angoulême. They will be ferried downriver to Le Havre. From there, they will be placed on a three-masted barque to New York, with letters of introductions to all relevant figures.

For this journey, the Baroness has stripped herself down to essentials. A crop of thinning gray hair where her wig would otherwise be. A slack white face, unadorned with powder or rouge. And yet something of her old station clings to her even now. Mark the rigid spine she maintains as she walks down the steps to the landing. Note her smile, still dazzling, and the unaffected dignity with which she accepts the Duchess's hand.

"Madame," says the Baroness. "You may be certain I will watch over your brother. As if he were my own son."

"I know you will," answers the Duchess.

The Baroness is carefully handed down to the boatsmen . . . and now there's nothing to keep Charles from his new life. Nothing but Charles himself.

"Maybe I shouldn't go, Marie."

Stepping toward him now, she speaks in softly reasoning cadences, like a prioress.

"My dear, you wouldn't be safe here, you know that. If anyone were to learn who you are, you could never be happy or content again. And neither could I."

With a spasm of impatience now, she reaches into the folds of her cloak and draws out a bag of Indian muslin. About the size of a cabbage, lumpy and protuberant.

"There," she says, handing it to him with a grim satisfaction.

"But what is it?"

"Jewels."

Bracing the bag against his belly with his right arm, he uses his left hand to wheedle the drawstring apart. Even at nighttime, there is no mistaking the contents.

"But, Marie," he says, in a hush. "What am I to do with all these?"

"Sell them," she answers, simply. "Piece by piece, as needed."

With one stroke of her finger, she tightens the drawstring.

"There is enough here to keep you for life, Charles. As many gardens as you"—her eyes graze over the bandaged vacancy at the end of his arm—"as you wish."

Except for the slosh of the river against the landing, all is quiet, and all is dark—not even a single lighterman on the nearby barges. Which means that Charles' trembling registers as a vibration in our skin.

"I can't," he's saying. "I don't have a right to all this."

"Who has more right than you?" retorts the Duchess. "And what use do *I* have for jewelry? Ask anyone, I'm the least fashionable woman in France. Baubles are wasted on me. You will get far more use out of them than I ever should."

"But you could come with us!" he cries, springing up on his toes. "We could all cross the ocean together. We could even bring Hector. Wouldn't that be splendid?"

She studies him very hard. And this is the first (and last) time that I will append the predicate *laughs* to the subject *the Duchess*. Although even that requires a proviso, for it is the kind of laugh that drags sorrow behind it.

"Forgive me," she says. "I was just imagining how I would compose my note to the Duke. 'Very sorry. Bound for America. Please begin the whist without me. Oh, and tell the King I will send along his embroidered stockings next year.' No," she says, patting his cheek. "I'm afraid it won't do, my dear. You to your world, I to mine."

"And will you be happy in your world?"

"More so than in a very long time. More so knowing you are well and cared for."

Her poise has carried her this far. How surprised she must be to have it desert so abruptly.

"Marie," he says, fluttering his hands round her. "What's wrong?"

"Oh, it's—they said I was to take *care* of you. Mother and Aunt Élizabeth. Before they were taken away, they said—that was my *charge*—to . . ." She drives her fists toward her eyes.

"But you *have*," he says. "My whole life I owe to you."

Through red-rimmed corneas, she stares at him. No more than twenty seconds, I'd venture, but it feels much longer.

"And to think I must lose you twice over," she says.

"Not lost. Never that."

Wordlessly, she nods.

"I'll write you when we land," he says. "Would you like that?"

Another nod. Then she makes a quick sign of the cross on his forehead and seals it with a kiss, and in a hoarse whisper, she says:

"May God travel with you always."

Every fiber of her will is enlisted in the act of turning away. But once she does, she never turns back. Any more than she notices Vidocq bounding forward.

"Well, then, young man!" he says with a headmaster's chortle. "I don't mind saying I envy you. I've always wanted a go at America myself."

"Oh, then, you can come, too. You could disguise yourself as a seagull."

This is tendered in all seriousness, which is how Vidocq receives it.

"*Next* spring," he suggests. "I'll come as a swallow."

The evening is drawing on, the departure time has come, and the farewells are complete. Except for one.

"Hector . . ."

Charles searches for me in the darkness, but I make a point of staying where I am, arms crossed.

"Keep yourself bundled," I call out. "It's cold out there on the ocean, and we've all worked too hard to lose you to pneumonia."

By now, of course, he's used to being passed from owner to owner. He took the news of Monsieur Tepac's death the way one might learn of a detour in a road. And it is too much to say he is moved by this latest parting. Disarranged is more like it. A shifting of the inner plates, only faintly seismic.

"Good-bye," he says.

He takes his place next to the Baroness in the rocking dory. The muslin bag he drops into the space between his boots—passes it back and forth, twice, and then squeezes it into stillness. The boatman drives the oar-blade into the shore, the black water folds round the hull, the tide takes hold. And as the boat draws away, Charles' eyes, on impulse, flick back toward the landing. Where the only pair of eyes waiting to meet them is mine.

And in the instant that the boat disappears round the river's bend, I can feel Father standing alongside me. For the words that form in my mind are addressed directly to him.

We've done it. We've finished the job.

CHAPTER 50

The Making of a Forger

WELL, AT SOME POINT, a physician requires his own lodgings.

It's true, Mama Vidocq would let me stay as long as I wish, but I can no longer impose on her—and her son wouldn't allow it. Accordingly, he petitions the Ministry of Justice to grant me a reward for my services to the crown. The response is swift: two hundred francs, in a crisp envelope. Before another week is out, I am in possession of three rooms, two suits, a gold chain, and a new pair of calf-length boots. And—my proudest possession—yellow evening gloves.

The one thing I'm missing is a future. But the present, all in all, is agreeable. For several hours altogether, I wander my rooms, taking in every feature. Painted woodwork, gilded moldings. A worktable inlaid with pearl. In the dining room there's an old Persian rug, bought from Mother Gaucher's in the Rue du Figuier-Saint-Paul. I give up an entire morning to studying this—every arabesque and palmette—lingering with special relish on the Tyrian purple of the medallion.

At first I think it's the novelty of my belongings that attracts me.

Then I realize that their novelty is what troubles me. Couldn't they all vanish as quickly as they came?

One afternoon early in June, I'm admiring my Japanese-porcelain dressing table when I receive a surprise visit from Vidocq. He has put his own reward money to good use: a gray summer suit of lightweight English cloth; a silver-capped cane. Eau de cologne has kept his natural musk at bay. And there's something else about him: Call it belief. He carries himself like a man who *belongs* to these things.

With a tiny scowl, he tours my lodgings, poking the merchandise as heartlessly as a hog butcher.

"Not bad," he allows. "*Walls* are a bit bare. Never mind, I've got some art dealers I can fix you up with."

Smiling, I pass him a cordial of brandy.

"Why don't you just sell me the Baroness's portrait?" I ask him.

And to my surprise, I'm met not with an answering smile but a grimace.

"Not yet," he mutters. "I may still need it as evidence."

"Evidence?"

Seating himself at my new dining table, he takes a draft of brandy, holds it for a few seconds in his mouth, then swallows it down in a single gulp.

"I've been undertaking some inquiries, Hector."

"About the Baroness?"

"No, not exactly. Félicité Neveu."

I look at him. "The washerwoman?"

"With the sickly child, yes. *Virgil*, wasn't that his name? Well, I don't mind saying we've had the devil's own time tracking her. When she left Paris back in '95, she managed to drop off the map. The boy, too. But we *did* learn something rather interesting about her prior career. Seems that, before she was a washerwoman, she was employed as a lady's maid. With a very distinguished family. Care to guess who? No?" He gives me a quizzical smile. "The Baron and Baronne de Préval."

My first reaction is to laugh. The second is to weep.

"That's impossible," I say.

"So I would have thought. But there are old servants of the Prévals who remember Félicité quite well. *Pretty* thing. Of course, she left the Baroness's service after a short time. No one seems to recall the circumstances, but they do remember this. She was carrying a *baby* with her when she left."

Half smiling, he stares into his glass.

"Now who the *father* was, we'll never know that. Then again . . ." He shrugs. "We're not even sure who the mother was. No one remembers seeing Félicité in a family way."

Turning now, I stare out the window. The year's first heat wave has left a pall in the streets. Two apprentice bakers are hurling buckets of cold water against their storefront to cool the plaster, and an old man, his blouse streaked with sweat, is hawking fried potatoes with a crackling, famished cry.

"You can't believe it was the Baroness's child," I say.

"I don't know what to believe."

"Even if—even if one could *conceive* of such a thing—a woman of her station bearing a child out of wedlock . . ."

"It's happened before."

". . . one can't imagine her *abandoning* the child. Leaving him in direst poverty. That's the act of a monster."

"Ah, but you're presuming she had a choice. The Revolution came along, remember? She had to flee the country. Her lands were seized, her jewels were lost. She would've had no way to send money back, even if she'd wanted to."

"It's absurd," I say, shaking my head, unequivocally. "*Anybody* might have been the mother of that child. *Anybody* might have . . ."

And then I'm struck dumb by a memory. The Baroness's final words, just as she was being handed down into that boat.

I'll watch over him, she said. *As if he were my own son.*

As if he were . . .

"No," I say, in a low, hissing voice. "No, it's all just a bizarre coincidence. Nothing more."

Vidocq just clucks his tongue. Gives his brandy a swirl.

"Well, I'll say only this. I'd dearly love another crack at that Baroness of ours."

"And what would you ask her?"

"I'd start with this. How did your old friend Leblanc learn about Charles in the first place? Did *you* tell him? And if so, how did *you* know about Charles? And, come to think of it, why *did* you mention him to the Marquis? Just to pass the time? Or were you hoping to get him an audience with the Duchess? Was *that* the goal all along?"

Every emphasis in his voice has a sensual intensity now. How he desires her! It makes me shudder, imagining the Baroness in that windowless room in the basement of Number Six. No duchesses or doctors to save her. Just Vidocq, in all his savagery, bearing down.

And chasing a fantasy, I tell myself. Noblewomen don't hand over their own sons to washerwomen. And then try to plant them on the throne of France.

But then a voice rises up inside me: *Why is that any more a fantasy than your Swiss gardener?*

Yes, Vidocq could press the Baroness all he liked, but he would come, finally, to the question that no one—no one alive—can answer. Who *was* the boy my father carried out of the tower that night? And what happened to him?

I take a bottle of raw Burgundy from the armoire. I pour myself a tall glass. Behind me, I hear Vidocq's trailing sigh, and I turn to see him draw a pipe from his pocket.

"Got any matches, Hector?"

Such a painstaking quality to how he fills his pipe now. Measured and cool, like a sniper taking aim.

"The thing is," he says, "we can't lay *everything* at the Baroness's door, hard as we try. After all, the piece of evidence that *really* carried the day—well, she had nothing to do with that."

"What do you mean?"

"That little note of your father's! The one we found in the back of his journal. All that business of the birthmark—I mean, *that's* what got us to the Duchess, wasn't it? It's what set everything in motion."

"I suppose so."

By now the smoke has formed a nimbus over his head, and the fumes come rolling toward me, they crawl up the cavities of my head.

And then, out of nowhere, Vidocq sets down his pipe and reaches for a leather satchel. Snaps open a compartment and takes out that piece of aged stationery, still bearing its creases. Still bearing those familiar words . . .

To Whom It May Concern:
  You may verify the merchandise via the following particular: a mole, black-brown . . .

"Funny thing," says Vidocq, tracing the letters' outlines. "The stationer is Bromet's. I'm sure you know the shop, Hector. *Venerable* firm, very close to the medical school. But you see, when I showed Monsieur Bromet this particular example of his handiwork, he couldn't make heads or tails of it."

"Why not?"

"*Oh, dear me*, he said. *Such an old piece of paper, but that particular watermark—why, we've been making that one less than a year.* Oh yes, he was quite sure of it. He registered the watermark himself last September."

Vidocq rests his finger on the edge of the paper, gently pushes it away.

"Well, you could've blown me out to sea, Hector. Your father died—more than a year and a *half* ago, wasn't it? Now I may be missing something, but I believe that makes this document of ours—well, I hate to be crude, but most people would call it a *forgery*." He nods, very slowly. "Yes, indeed, someone has played us a pretty little trick, it seems. And, of course, being the sort of fellow I am, I had to ask: *Who?*"

He taps his pine stem against his nose. Once, twice.

"Well, last night," he says, "I couldn't sleep, no surprise. So, to pass the time, I started to sketch out a little profile in my head. I figured whoever our forger was, he had to be someone with—let's say, lots of *practice* writing like your father. *Years,* even. Someone who could do it in his sleep, practically. And whoever it was—I'm guessing he truly *believed* Charles was the lost dauphin and knew we needed just *one* more piece of evidence to nail the case shut.

"So this fellow, I imagine he sat down and asked himself: What's the one identifying mark on Charles Rapskeller? The birthmark between the toes, yes? I'm guessing he noticed it when he was"—a soft clearing of throat—"when he was helping Charles with his boots. So now he just had to plug that little detail into a fake document. Then sit back and let it do its work.

"And through it all—I'm convinced of this, Hector—the fellow was acting in perfect faith. With the very best of intentions, yes. He just wanted to see justice done."

I touch the small crust of sediment that's settled across the bottom of my glass. I put it to my mouth, and I feel my lips shrinking back.

"It's an interesting theory," I say.

"Yes, I'm chock-*full* of theories today. And none of them proven, more's the pity. Oh, Christ! I went and forgot why I came here in the first place."

Reaching once more into his satchel, he pulls out another document. Sets it on the table in front of me.

"What's that?" I ask.

"Just my little account of the whole affair. Everything that happened from—mm—Leblanc's death onward. Not for *public* consumption, you understand, strictly for *my* files. I figured since you were so much a part of everything, Hector, you could look it over for me, and if everything checks out, then just"—his gloved hand grazes along the bottom of the last page—"just sign your name *there,* would you?"

I pick up the first page and turn it over, but the words break down the moment I try to read them.

"This all looks much as I remember it," I say.

"Are you sure? I'd hate for you to sign your name to something that didn't happen."

You could put a hundred listeners in the room—no one would hear any other meaning in those words. No one but me.

"I'm certain," I tell him.

"Well, then, thanks very much. You don't have a quill about, do you?"

"On the desk."

"Ah! Here we are. Fresh inkwell, too! Everything's so *new* here."

He sets the implements in front of me and then—who knows why?—turns away. It could be he's feeling merciful, and yet his back is somehow a worse sight than his face. And as I move my hand across the paper, I still *feel* him—oh, yes—in every loop and slash.

"All done?" he sings out.

He stares at the signature with an unchanging expression. Then he sets Father's note alongside it. Studies both documents for a few moments longer. Then, nodding, he returns them to his satchel.

"That about does it," he says, quietly.

He's nearly to the door before I have the capacity to call after him.

"Chief!"

And that single word creates a kind of envelope around us. For it is the first time I've ever addressed him by that title.

"Why did you take me along?" I ask.

"Take you where?"

"To Saint-Cloud. You didn't need me there. I was only going to get in the way. Why did you bother bringing me in the first place?"

No way to parse the expression in his eyes now. If pressed, I might identify notes of regret, amusement, nostalgia. The barest hint of ire.

"Well, it's like any journey, Hector. It goes faster with a bit of company." He tips his hat forward. "I think the journey's over now, don't you?"

But still he lingers in that doorway. And in the seconds that follow, he is briefly erased by my earliest image of him: in Bardou's rags, bristling with suspicion. And then the Vidocq of the present comes sliding back, a far gentler being, and his eyes, against all expectations, ripen into merriment. He throws back his massive head and roars with laughter.

"Thank God you're not as innocent as you look!"

And then he's gone.

CHAPTER 51

Postlude

Two days after Vidocq leaves, I get a summons from the wife of Brigadier-General Beauséant. By now, I've become leery of invitations from society ladies, and I'm no more reassured when the lady in question, a dowager of two and sixty, complains at length about the condition of her hips. At the conclusion of which she wheels on me and, in a buzzing baritone, snarls:

"*Well?*"

"Well *what*, Madame?"

"It was my hope, dear Doctor, that you might favor me with your opinion on my rheumatism."

"Oh, yes . . ."

"What I *mean* is: Do you think you might fit me into your schedule?"

"Into my—"

"Please don't be coy, Doctor! The word is out. You effect the most remarkable cures in all of Paris."

Very carefully I set down my teacup.

"Forgive me, Madame, but who has told you this?"

"Why, the Duchesse d'Angoulême! Just the other night, she was singing your praises to anyone who would listen. . . ."

A WEEK LATER, an invitation to the Tuileries allows me to thank my benefactress in person—but the Duchess is in no mood. She wants only to know if I've had news of Charles or the Baroness. She received word from them in Le Havre that they'd been delayed and would take the next ship to America. Since then, no word.

"I'm very sorry," I tell her. "I've heard nothing."

When we part, she says, in a confidential murmur: "We needn't worry, Doctor. God has gone to great lengths to bring Charles back to us. God will not abandon him a second time."

IN THE END, Charles and the Baroness fail to keep their appointment with the Lioncourts of the Hudson Valley, and the Duchess, starved for news, receives none. She never, in fact, hears from Charles again.

But her belief in him, this remains steadfast, which is why she declines to meet any of the other "lost dauphins" who come to press their claims on her. And there are dozens. One, a German clockmaker by the name of Karl Naundorff, goes so far as to sue her for recovery of personal property. For his temerity, he is deported to England.

In 1824 comes the long-awaited death of gout-ridden old Louis the Eighteenth. The Comte d'Artois gets the crown he has long craved and, as Charles the Tenth, the chance to practice the absolutism he believes France needs. France disagrees. After six years, he is replaced by Louis-Philippe, a less objectionable cousin. Once more, the royal family is expelled; once more, the Duchess is obliged to leave her native land. This time for good.

Her wanderings take her from Edinburgh to Prague to Slovenia, but she is ever my most faithful correspondent. And if her letters rarely mention Charles, he is the figure that lurks behind every line—and, indeed, the wellspring of our intimacy, for what else do she and I have in common?

Other than my career. Within weeks of her public endorsement, I am besieged with inquiries from all over the Faubourg Saint-Germain. Women, exclusively: countesses and marquesses and ambassadors' wives and bankers' mothers, complaining of palpitations, insomnia, frigidity, avidity. Many of them believe they are dying; one is convinced she's a grouse. *All* of them have francs for the flinging, and before another year has passed, I have my own clinic in the Rue de Richelieu and a reputation as a man with rare (and, by some lights, indecent) powers of suggestion.

I'll let you in on a secret. Bring a certain kind of woman into a dark room, look her in the eye, and, where necessary, apply the simple physic of touch . . . you will find few ill humors that won't yield to that. And if this same woman should wish to cure *you,* who are you to say no?

After several years of this—and more than a few mistresses—I reach the conclusion that my specialty has wandered too far from the Hippocratic ideal. In a volte-face that startles even me, I dedicate myself to venereal disease. It's a specialty calculated to offend my previous constituency, and yet my very first patients are the noblewomen I used to treat for sluggish blood flow.

Soon, too, the men find their way to my door. Mariners, caulkers, deputy ministers, dukes . . . I make no distinctions, except that I charge according to capacity. One August morning, I am visited by a distinguished gentleman in a ruffled white silk shirt under a light summer jacket. He follows me into the consultation room, and when I ask him about his condition, he answers, in the most courtly of cadences:

"Got the wrong stuff coming out the dick."

I look up. A large gray-blue eye is winking back at me. Vidocq.

We haven't spoken in many years, but I've followed his progress through the newspapers. I know, for instance, that he married Jeanne-

Victoire—"held up his end," after all. Surely she would have held up hers, too, except that she died within four years. Mama Vidocq followed six weeks after, and according to scuttlebutt, the great policeman consoles himself now with the charms of a comely young cousin. That is, when he's not chasing actresses, artists' models, soubrettes . . . the wives of his own officers. . . .

He's stouter and grayer now, more polished in his manners, but every bit as easy with his body. As he spreads his half-naked frame across the examining table, conversation spills from him in a perfect cataract.

"Damn me, Hector, you've done well for yourself. Love the candelabra—porphyry, is it? With some malachite thrown in? Beautiful piece. The velvet hangings are a nice touch, too. Must have come from Lyon. Hey, are you married? No? Get on your knees and thank Christ. Here I am, one wife barely cold in the ground, and Fleuride-Albertine badgering me every day to take her to the Bureau of Registry. What's the point, I ask her? Ah well, there's a bright side to the clap after all. No one's going to drag you to the altar with a weeping cock. Not that it keeps me from doing the old heave-ho. Ha! I was *born* erect, it's the Lord's truth. . . ."

My proddings do nothing to stanch the words, but a new quality does steal into his voice: vulnerability, let's call it. I realize he's talking because he's nearly as uncomfortable as I am.

"What's that you're mixing?" he asks at last.

"Mercury and silver nitrate."

"Goes right up the old pee hole, does it?"

"Afraid so."

From his silence, I assume he's bracing for the syringe. Truth is, he's already drifting back to our common time.

"Strange business, wasn't it, Hector?"

"Yes, it was."

"The part I *really* regret," he says, "is we'll never know what happened in that tower all those years ago. And it's too damned bad."

<hr>

ONE NIGHT IN December, I come home to find an envelope addressed to me from the United States of America. It contains a brief news item from the *City Gazette and Daily Advertiser* of Charleston, South Carolina. My English is just adequate to making it out:

> Baroness Préval, the celebrated Lecturess, has arrived in the City, and is giving an Exhibition of her wonderful powers. Having had the pleasure of witnessing her in person, I cannot but give to this extraordinarily elegant and gracious French Gentlewoman the due praise which true talents are entitled to. Her theme is "Sufferings of a Peeress Under the Reign of Terror, At the Hands of Atheistic Jacobites." Particularly thrilling is the dramatic reenactment of the attempted guillotining of the Baroness's son, who, in actuality, barely escaped the event with the loss of his right hand. That part in the tableau is played by the gentleman himself, who also contributes a delightful talk on orchid varieties in Europe vis-à-vis the Americas. I sincerely trust that the Baroness and her collaborator will meet the encouragement such individuals deserve.
>
> —A CONNOISSEUR

I never show this to anyone—Vidocq, least of all—but I do take it out from time to time. Seeking clarity, I suppose, but finding only more muddle.

I ask myself: Has Charles simply attached himself to a new protector—squeezed himself into a new pair of shoes? Or is he really the Baroness's son? How, then, did he know all those intimate details of the royal family's imprisonment? The cannons . . . the death's-head hawkmoth in the princess's shift . . . the letters bound in white ribbon . . . how could anyone but Louis-Charles have known these things?

So here I sit, a man of middle years, no closer to certainty—and forced, finally, to make my own. Vidocq said there's never any accounting for people's faith, but there *is*. We make what we long for. Jesus was the son of a carpenter until a group of believers, contemplating him long after the fact, decided he was more. So, too, Charles, under the pressure of our hopes, became the man we yearned for. He's that man now. However imperfectly we come to believe something, the *belief* is its own perfection.

Which is to say: Against all evidence to the contrary, I believe that Charles Rapskeller is Louis the Seventeenth.

And even as I assert that, I dance away again. Maybe I've reached an age where not knowing is actually richer than knowing.

Or as Vidocq said on my clinic table, watching that syringe advance on him:

"We never solve a damned thing, really. We just make more questions. Now get my snake working, will you, Hector? There's a flower girl over in the Rue Saint-Claude. Ready for pollinating. . . ."

Acknowledgments

❧

My account of the dauphin's final months in the Temple is about equal parts history and invention. For the real deal, the reader is advised to consult Deborah Cadbury's excellent *The Lost King of France*.

Special thanks to Marjorie Braman, for breathing Vidocq's name in my ear, and to Vidocq himself, for giving me a reason to go back to Paris.

From there, the usual roll of debt: Christopher Schelling, Peggy Hageman, Sharyn Rosenblum, Abby Yochelson.

To these, add: Dan Mallory (whose talents now extend to book jacket design), Jean-Luc Piningre (French translator nonpareil), Paul Bayard (pro bono medical consultant), Denny Drabelle, Dan Stashower, Sheryl Kroen.

Top it all off with Don.

About the author

About the book

Read on

Insights,
Interviews
& More . . .

A Conversation with Louis Bayard

You have written many pieces for Salon, *among them "Why* Scarface *Is F—ing Great," "If McCain Wins, Should We All Move to Scandinavia?," "A Nation of Conspiracy Theorists Can't Be Wrong," "Why Ronald Reagan Didn't Completely Suck," and the exhilaratingly titled "Kiss My Ass." How do you approach these essays?*

Usually with the idea of pissing somebody off. It's part of the beauty of America—particularly now—that somebody is always ready to be pissed off about something. I think, in this respect, writers and readers have created a strange codependency.

How often do you publish pieces in Salon, *the* Washington Post, *and other venues?*

When I was a staff writer at *Salon*, I was reviewing books once a week. But then somebody there cottoned on to how financially unprofitable the whole bargain was. So now it's on the order of once or twice a month, which is honestly more manageable for a fiction guy.

Does your fiction writing benefit in any way from your program of essay-writing and book-reviewing?

I think one kind of writing feeds the other, honestly. When I look at my novels, they strike me as the kind of novels a reviewer would write. They're books that read other books.

66 When I look at my novels, they strike me as the kind of novels a reviewer would write. 99

The Paris Review once asked Truman Capote whether anyone had encouraged his talent as a child. He replied, "Good Lord! I'm afraid you've let yourself in for quite a saga. . . ." Does your own history include any such saga?

More an edda than a saga. Actually, I have no idea what an edda is, except it turns up in crosswords a lot.

You live in Washington, D.C. Were you on hand for the inauguration of President Barack Obama?

Shivering my ass off, yes. Miles from the actual event.

What's the strangest thing that has ever happened to you during a book tour?

I'm going to skip "strangest" and go straight to "most humiliating." I once showed up for a California book signing to find one human being in the entire store. And he was the drunk off the street.

Novelist James Jones, describing his approach to writing, said, "I smoke half a pack of cigarettes, drink six or seven cups of coffee, read over what I wrote the day before. Finally there's no further excuse. I go to the typewriter." How might your own ritual differ from or conform to this?

He calls that procrastinating? What a piker. Well, of course, he didn't have e-mail or Facebook or the blogosphere. Once I've got those out of the way, I do pretty much the same thing as Jones, without the cigarettes and maybe without so much ▶

Meet Louis Bayard

© Gina Eppolito

LOUIS BAYARD is the author of the national bestseller *The Pale Blue Eye* and *Mr. Timothy*, a *New York Times* Notable Book. Bayard has written articles and reviews for the *New York Times*, the *Washington Post*, Nerve.com, and *Preservation*, among other publications. He lives in Washington, D.C.

A Conversation with Louis Bayard
(continued)

angst. Writing is kind of fun for me, all in all, but then I'm not writing *From Here to Eternity.*

What are your ideal conditions for writing?

White noise. Black tea.

How much plotting goes into your novels?

More and more as I get older. Back in my youth, I sometimes flew by the seat of my pants, which is a good way to end up pantless. Or plotless. Or, on the other extreme, overplotted. I've learned that the more I block out the story in advance, the more work I save myself down the road. Then again, I don't want everything so preordained that I'm just dotting *i*'s and crossing *t*'s. I need to keep myself entertained, too.

Which of your books was the most difficult to write?

It's always the book I'm in the middle of writing. Once it's done, all the labor pains are erased from my memory, and the whole process becomes this gorgeous continuum. Which is why I leap with such absurd eagerness into the next book.

Name some of your earliest influences.

Oh, wow. Dickens? Mr. Magoo? Every time I try to stay on the high road, the low road comes a-calling. Um, the Hardy Boys . . . the Avengers . . . Lance Link, Secret Chimp. . . .

When will we read that you have moved to Paris?

Depends whether it needs to be true.

You went to Princeton. Was the town's Bayard Lane named after one of your ancestors?

We're a promiscuous tribe, so it's possible.

What are you working on now?

A book about the School of Night, a group of Elizabethan scholars who were rumored to dabble in dark arts.

And what are you reading?

Right now, George Pelecanos. George writes in a very different vein from me, but he gets at a part of my hometown, Washington, D.C., that nobody else does. His books have real heart, but they don't wear it on their sleeves. ◡

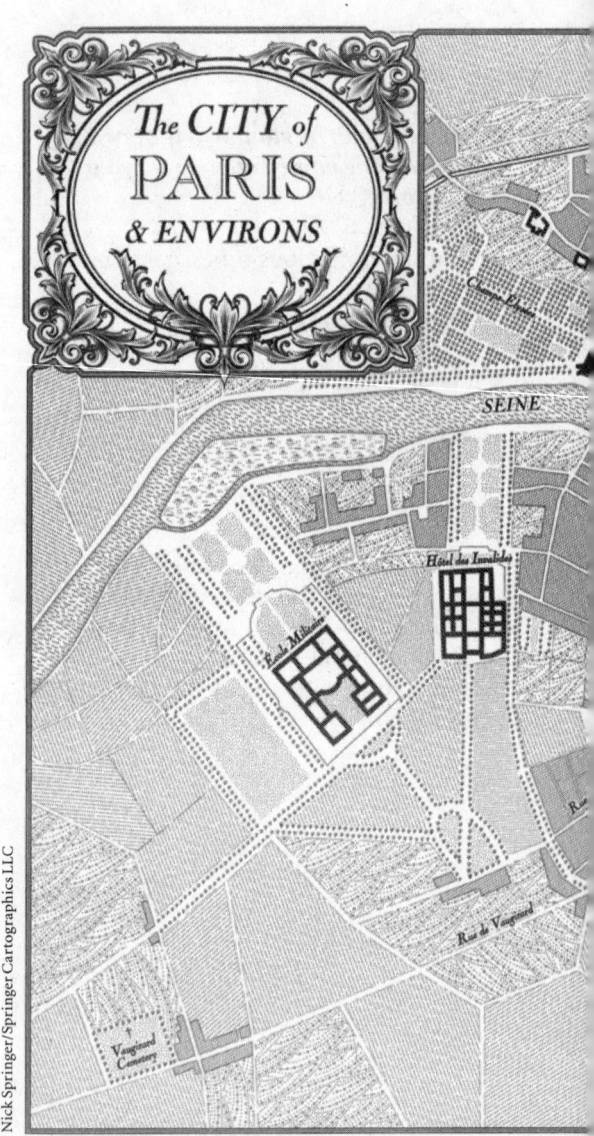

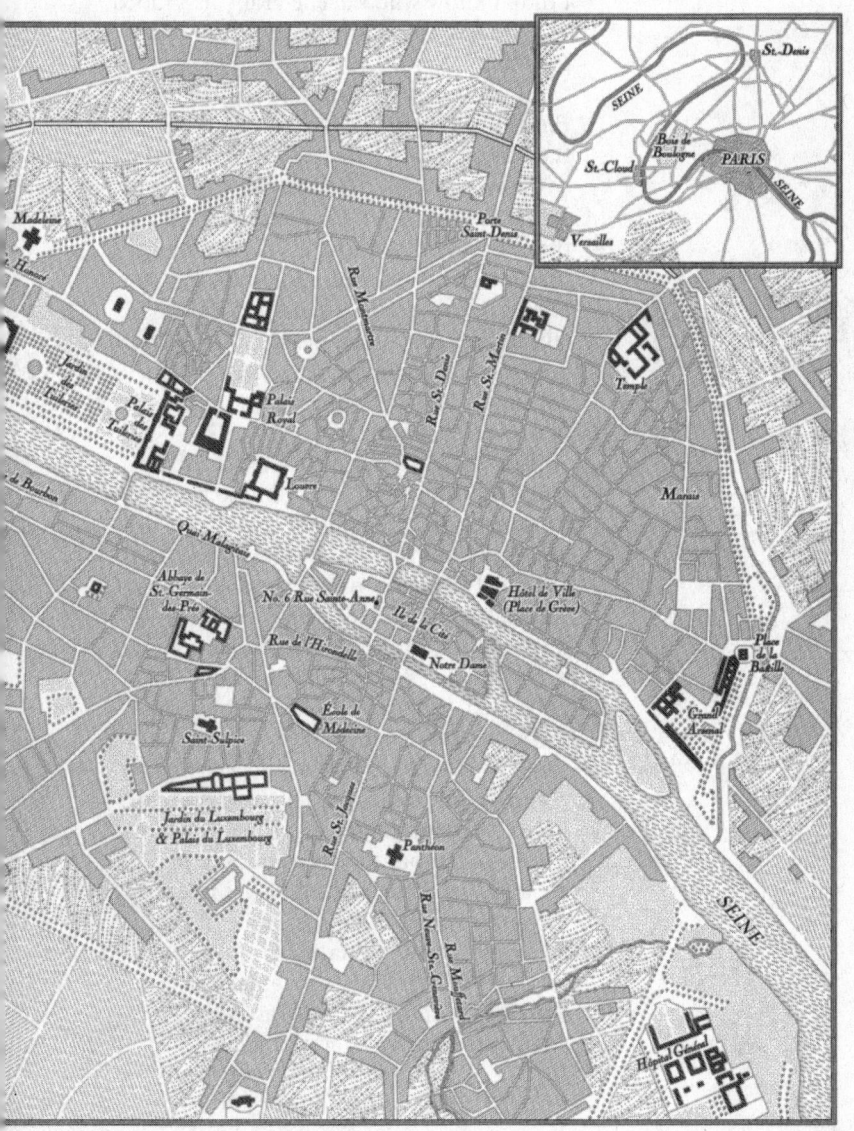

The Good Guesser

FIVE YEARS AGO, I'm embarrassed to say, I didn't know who Eugène François Vidocq was. It took Edgar Allan Poe to bring us together.

In the course of researching *The Pale Blue Eye*, I reread Poe's "The Murders in the Rue Morgue," which is widely regarded as the world's first detective story. But is it? Turns out that Poe's great sleuth, Dupin, in the course of describing his methodology, makes a glancing—and slighting—reference to a gentleman named Vidocq, whom he immediately dismisses as "a good guesser" lacking "educated thought" and constantly erring "by the very intensity of his investigations."

Two things struck me right off. First, Dupin considered it important to get a leg up on his predecessor (much as Sherlock Holmes would feel compelled to do with Dupin). And second, this particular predecessor needed no introduction to the general reader.

In fact, by 1841, when Poe's story was published, Vidocq was a household name on both sides of the Atlantic, a figure who could be cited by Dickens and Melville without any explanatory glossing. We can attribute Vidocq's fame in large part to his gift for self-promotion. Specifically, he was the author of four bestselling volumes of memoirs. These books were at least partly fictional; two were unauthorized; all were ghostwritten. But taken together they represent perhaps the first sustained detective narrative in any language, and Vidocq himself stands as our first modern detective. ▶

Before Vidocq, solving crime was an administrative matter; after Vidocq, it became a field of endeavor in which a man (or woman) could apply the full dint of his talent and intellect and call on the latest developments in both art and science. So it was that Vidocq was the first policeman to use ballistics evidence, the first to take plaster-of-Paris impressions of footprints, one of the very first to recognize the potential of fingerprints (decades before that potential would be realized). He was a master of disguise and surveillance, he held patents for invisible ink and unalterable bond paper, and when he left public service—under a cloud, as always—he founded the world's first private detective agency, the Bureau des Renseignements, which was the template for Allan Pinkerton's agency a quarter century later.

But to Vidocq's contemporaries—foes and allies alike—he was above all a convict. Initially imprisoned for a slight offense, Vidocq managed to escape from virtually all of France's penal institutions, each escape only adding more years to his next sentence. Eventually, he worked his way back to Paris, where, after being blackmailed by former confederates (one of them his ex-wife), he decided a change was in order. So he volunteered his services as a police spy.

In this capacity, he proved so invaluable to the Prefecture of Police that he was able to ascend the chain of command at a remarkable clip, and in 1812 he cofounded the Brigade de la Sûreté, one of the very first plainclothes police divisions. This was a controversial proposition in its day, especially because Vidocq insisted on staffing it with ex-convicts like himself,

66 He was a master of disguise and surveillance. 99

The Good Guesser (continued)

reasoning that they were the ones best suited to infiltrating criminal milieus.

And he was right. Thanks to the Sûreté's aggressive and creative policing, Paris's crime rate declined markedly, and Vidocq became a folk hero to the local populace. As comfortable as he was in working-class districts, he could play the other side of the street, too. He was an exotically menacing figure for the high-society hostesses of the Faubourg Saint-Germain, and his comrades included the likes of Balzac and Dumas.

If some of the outlines of Vidocq's life sound familiar, it's because they were appropriated by another author, Victor Hugo, for his masterwork *Les Misérables*. Hugo essentially split Vidocq in two, channeling the embattled convict years into Jean Valjean and transforming the fearsome servant of justice into Inspector Javert. I can't think of a better tribute to a man's significance than that he must be halved in order to be sufficiently understood.

Vidocq, I soon learned, was everything a novelist dotes on: robust, contrary, appetitive, and a good man to have in a brawl. If anybody could solve the mystery surrounding the Lost Dauphin, I knew it would be the baker's son from Arras. The life Vidocq contrived for himself was itself a kind of enduring fiction, and more than a hundred and fifty years after his death, he is still winking at us—and still shaping how we think and talk about crime and punishment. ∾

66 Vidocq, I soon learned, was everything a novelist dotes on: robust, contrary, appetitive, and a good man to have in a brawl. 99

An Excerpt from Louis Bayard's *The Pale Blue Eye*

Mid the groves of Circassian splendor,
  In a brook darkly dappled with sky
  In a moon-shattered brook raked with sky,
Athene's lissome maidens did render
  Obeisances lisping and shy.
There I found Leonore, lorn and tender
  In the clutch of a cloud-rending cry.
Hell-harrowed, I could only surrender
  To the maid with the pale blue eye
  To the ghoul with the pale blue eye.

LAST TESTAMENT OF GUS LANDOR

April 19, 1831

In two or three hours . . . well, it's hard to tell . . . in three hours, surely, or at the very outside, four hours . . . within four hours, let us say, I'll be dead.

    I mention it because it puts things in a certain context. My fingers, for instance, have become interesting to me of late. Also the lowermost slat in the Venetian blinds, a bit askew. And, outside the window, a wisteria shoot, snapped off the main stem, waggling like a gallows. I never noticed that before. Something else, too: at this moment, the past comes on with all the force of the present. All the people who've peopled me . . . don't they come thronging round . . . what keeps them from bumping heads, I wonder? There's a Hudson Park alderman by the hearth; next to him, my wife, in her apron, ladling ashes into the can, and who's watching her but my old Newfoundland retriever; and down the ▶

> 66 Within four hours, let us say, I'll be dead. 99

hall, my mother, who never set foot in this house, died before I reached twelve . . . well, she's ironing my Sunday suit. My father's somewhere out back, gathering kindling, or praying. None of them says a word to the others. Very strict etiquette in place, I can't work out the rules of it, no matter how long I look.

Not everyone, I should say, minds the rules. For the past hour, I've been having my ear bent—torn, nearly—by a man named Cadmus Foot. He was run in fifteen years ago for robbing the Rochester mail. A vast injustice: he had three witnesses to swear he was robbing the Baltimore mail at the time. He flew into a fine rage about it, skipped town on bail, came back six months later, crazy with cholera, and threw himself in front of a hackney cab. Talked all the way to death's door. Still talking now.

Oh, it's a crowd, I can tell you. Depending on my mood, depending on the angle of the sun through the parlor window, I can attend to it or not. There are times, I admit, when I wish I had more traffic with the living, but they are harder to come by these days. Patsy scarcely stops round anymore, the boys at Benny Haven's give me wider berth . . . Professor Quawquaw is off measuring heads in Havanna . . . as for *him*, well, what is there to call him back? I can only summon him in my mind, and the moment I do, all the old talks play out again. All those hours— hours and hours—trying to see if I had a soul. He was on the pro side of the question. It might have been amusing to hear him go on if he hadn't been in such terrible earnest. But then no one had ever pressed me so strongly on this point, not even my own father (traveling Presbyterian, too busy with the souls of the nearest flock to plant much of a boot on mine). Again and again, I said, "Well, well, you may be right." It only made him hotter. He'd tell me I was just putting off the question, pending empirical confirmation. And I would say that, lacking confirmation, what more could I say than "You may be right"? Round and round we went, until one day, he said, "Mr. Landor, there will come a time when your soul turns round and fronts you in the most empirical fashion possible. The very moment it quits you. You will clutch for it—ah, in vain! See it now, sprouting eagle wings, bound for the Asiatic eyries."

Well, he was fanciful that way. Gaudy, if you must know. Myself, I've always preferred facts to metaphysics. Good hard homely facts, a full day's pottage. It is facts that shall form the spine of this narrative, and where I stray from them, write it down as dotage, nothing more . . . a brain just this side of extinction.

"Extinction."

Oh, why wrap it in quotation marks when it lies so near at hand? When it was for so many years my *business*? Ceasing to be my business, it continued as habit. Foolish to expect anything else. One night, a full year into my retirement, my daughter heard me talking in my sleep—very distinct—welcoming a midnight caller, she thought. She came into my bedroom to find me questioning a suspect twenty years dead. *The corner won't square*, I kept saying. *You do see that, Mr. Pierce. . . .* This particular fellow had dismembered his wife's body and fed the pieces to a pack of watchdogs at a Battery warehouse. In the dream, his eyes looked pink and sad and half-flirty; he was sorry for taking up my time, such a gentleman as I was. I remember telling him: *If it hadn't been you, it would have been someone else.*

Foolish, as I said, to think the Pierces of the world will leave you in peace. To think you can slip away into the Hudson Highlands with your books and ciphers and your watercolors and your knobby-oak walking sticks . . . and leave extinction behind? It won't be left, I tell you. It will come and find you.

I might have run. A little farther into the wilderness, I might have done that. How I let myself be coaxed back I can't truly say. The best answer I can make is no answer at all but, God help me, metaphysical. I mean to say there are times I believe it happened— all of it happened—so we should find each other, he and I.

Even as I write that sentence, my hand jerks to a halt. . . . Reason catching me by the sleeve, that's what my young friend would call it. "What of the others?" Reason says. "Just tools, were they, for realizing your destiny?" I have no good reply to make her, I have only a theory: Destiny belongs to the survivors. Like history. And I am (for the moment) alive. It's my last qualification. Alive, with these memories and these other lives—oh, if you must, *souls*—to account for. And since those souls were, on many sides, close to me, I have made way where necessary for other speakers. My young friend most especially. He's the true spirit behind this poor history, and whenever I try to imagine who'll be first to read this manuscript, he's the one who presents himself. *His* fingers tracing the rows and columns, *his* eyes picking out my scratches. ▶

An Excerpt from Louis Bayard's
The Pale Blue Eye (continued)

It's not likely, I know that. Near impossible he will claim the authorship due him. Well. I suppose authors never know half of what they've written . . . any more than they can choose who will read them. We are the chosen ones. Nothing left, then, but to take comfort in the thought of this stranger—still unborn, for all I know—who will read these lines for the first time. To you, my beloved, dreaded stranger, I dedicate this narrative.

And so I become my own reader. For the last time. Another log in the fire, would you please, Alderman Hunt?

And so it begins again. ∾

Have You Read?
More by Louis Bayard

MR. TIMOTHY

Welcome to the world of a grown-up Timothy Cratchit, as created by the astonishing imagination of author Louis Bayard.

Mr. Timothy Cratchit has just buried his father. He's also struggling to bury his past as a cripple and shed his financial ties to his benevolent "Uncle" Ebenezer by losing himself in the thick of London's underbelly. He boards at a brothel in exchange for teaching the mistress how to read and spends his nights dredging the Thames for dead bodies and the treasures in their pockets.

Timothy's life takes a sharp turn when he discovers the bodies of two dead girls, each seared with the same cruel brand on the upper arm. The sight of their horror-struck faces compels Timothy to become the protector of another young girl, the enigmatic Philomela. Spurred on by the unwavering enthusiasm of a street-smart, fast-talking homeless boy who calls himself Colin the Melodious, Timothy soon finds that he's on the trail of something far worse—and far more dangerous—than an ordinary killer.

This breathless flight through the teeming markets, shadowy passageways, and rolling brown fog of 1860s London is wrought with remarkable depth and intelligence, complete with surprising twists and extraordinary heart.

Have You Read? *(continued)*

"Dazzling. . . . Soaring language, memorable characters, splendidly atmospheric settings"
　　　　—*People* (Top Ten Book of the Year)

"With its linguistic razzle-dazzle, *Mr. Timothy* is a mock-Victorian tour de force: a shilling shocker that touches the heart and makes it race."
　　　　—*Wall Street Journal*

"Clever . . . sly . . . wonderful."
　　　　—*Washington Post*

"Inventive and amusing."
　　　　—*New York Times Book Review*

"There isn't one throwaway sentence in this fabulous Victorian mystery. . . . A subtle character examination and a page-turning plot; one truly engaging book."
　　　　—*Entertainment Weekly* (Editor's Choice)

"This mix of thriller and literature is as rich as a Christmas cake. . . . A spirited adventure."
　　　　—*Atlanta Journal-Constitution*

"*Mr. Timothy* provides some poignant moments, making the always-valid point that families can be formed wherever there is trust, generosity, teamwork, and a little Christmas magic."
　　　　—*San Francisco Chronicle*